EDEN
AT THE
EDGE
OF
MIDNIGHT

BY
JOHN KERRY

EDEN AT THE EDGE OF MIDNIGHT

First published in Britain by EATEOM Publishing Ltd
Copyright © John Kerry 2012

Second Edition (a)
Copyright © John Kerry 2018

ISBN 13: 978-0-9572389-4-7

Cover illustration: Maxime Desmettre.
Titling and Design: The Designers Republic.
Editing services: Tanya Natalie & The Book Specialist.

Printed in Great Britain by Lightning Source UK Ltd.
Printed in the US by Lightning Source US Ltd.
Printed in Australia by Lightning Source AU Ltd.

www.eateom.com

For my girls

–ONE–
Followed

Few sixteen-year-olds had stalkers. They were typically reserved for celebrities, rock stars, maybe even reality TV contestants, due to their 'popularity'. An elusive quality not familiar to Sammy Ellis. Not that it bothered her. She was cool with it. But if the universe had to dump a stalker on her, did it really have to be a crusty old woman? As opposed to, say, a buff Sheffield University student?

In the margin of her maths book, she absent-mindedly doodled the terminator blasting an old woman in the face with a twelve-gauge autoloader. *Boom! Headshot!!!* she scrawled above it, underlining the words several times.

Rat-a-tat-tat. A fist rapped on the corner of her desk. It belonged to Miss Armatage.

"The square root of x does not equal death by machine gun," she said with a straight face. It was a bored, depressed face that had seen a thousand students come and go. An assembly line of kids that she regurgitated the same information to, before pushing them back out the door. She was a desiccated husk of a woman, probably in her fifties, but she could've easily been several centuries old.

"It's not a machine gun. It's ..."

"I don't care what it is, Miss Ellis. You're a tick in my register, a GCSE mathematics grade. A grade B is what I expect from you. And I'll be disappointed if I don't get it."

Sammy wondered if it were possible for Miss Armatage to look more disappointed than she already did. A bloodhound neutered on its birthday would look cheerier.

Miss Armatage drifted out of focus, replaced by the clock above the whiteboard. It displayed 3.15pm. Sammy raised her hand.

"I'm right here, Samantha."

"Can I be excused, Miss?"

"There's only half an hour before the bell. Can't you hold on?"

"Not really. I was dehydrated after PE, so I drank loads of water. Maybe I drank too much, but I was thirsty so I kept drinking—"

Miss Armatage held up her hand to stop her. "Look at my face."

"Do I have to?"

The teacher frowned. "Just go." She turned and walked back towards the whiteboard, then as Sammy reached the door, added, "Hurry back, my little statistic."

Sammy ran for the gates, zigzagging across the uneven tarmac outside the science block, dodging puddles, while clutching her backpack to the top of her head to protect it against icy rain.

She'd gone straight to the staff room after leaving class, as she had done every night so far this week. But this time, the room had been empty. So she'd snuck in, phoned the police and ditched the last fifteen minutes of school. Tonight she wouldn't be escaping across the football pitch and over the fence, tonight she'd be catching the predator.

She slowed as she approached the school gates.

A glimpse of powder blue shimmered through the grey sheets of rain. The old woman stood in front of the houses across the street, the same spot she stood every night, wearing the same pale blue headscarf and dressed in bedraggled brown clothes that resembled a heap of threadbare carpets. Her clothes were heavy, waterlogged and probably freezing. But there she waited, soaking up rainwater.

She'd clearly identified Sammy as a loner, probably due to the fact no one ever came to collect her. So, then, why hadn't she made her move yet? This had been going on for weeks and the old woman always stood outside, in plain view.

Dark eyes fixed on Sammy's. The woman smiled. Then her head snapped to the side and she tensed. It was Sammy's turn to smile this time. She couldn't see past the school wall, but she knew what was coming.

The woman raised her palms as two men in black trench coats came into view. The school gates framed a picture-perfect movie scene of two cops apprehending a criminal. One carried an umbrella above both their heads, the other held out a badge.

End of the line, old bag.

Voices clamoured behind Sammy. The lower school cloakrooms were emptying. A river of slate-grey bodies accented by flapping red ties swept towards her. She sidestepped, but not fast enough, and an errant satchel caught her in the face, knocking her down. She landed on all fours and pain spiked in her knees. She clenched her teeth, closed her eyes and waited while the other kids trampled past, kicking her satchel as they jostled to get to their parents' cars.

Sammy remained where she fell, facing the floor, the water streaming from her blonde hair.

No one stopped to help. No one had noticed her since she'd started at this new school, and no one noticed her now, even though they had to run around her to get out of the gate. Only the satchel that tugged at her arm as it got kicked around served as a reminder that she still existed in their world.

She waited until the traffic became lighter and flicked her sopping hair back from her face.

The two policemen and the old woman had gone.

She'd missed the action. And her knees were sore, and sleeves were saturated with puddle water. That was probably the most—maybe even the only—exciting thing that was going to happen this term, possibly all year. And it was over.

Miss Armatage stood at the corner of the science block, monitoring the stragglers. She peered at Sammy with an expression of exaggerated indifference and motioned for her to get up.

She should get up. Her tights were soaking up rainwater and the longer she stayed down, the heavier and colder they'd get. But then, if she got up, she'd have to start walking and suffer the damp, heavy fabric chafing back and forth across her skin.

As she considered her options, a hand grabbed her under the arm and jerked her to her feet bringing her face to face with a boy sporting a black eye and a tie knotted around his forehead like a Rambo headband. Wayne Grubby. They had maths and science together. A less unpleasant boy than most of the others in the year, but that wasn't saying much.

"You alright?" he asked.

Sammy examined the wet patches around her knees. "Yeah," she said.

"You should be careful," he said. "The playground is right lumpy. You new here?"

"I joined at the start of the year. So ... no, not really."

"Yeah? I guess we must have different classes.. See you around," he said and wandered off.

They had maths and science together. She sat between him and the whiteboard. How could he not know her? Maybe he should spend more time paying attention and less time setting his mates' books on fire with Bunsen burners. She didn't care anyway. He was a moron.

She watched him go. Cars crawled along the street outside the gates, their windows fogged with warm breath and smiling faces drawn in the condensation. Perhaps she'd stand where she was another minute. If she kept perfectly still with her legs spread and her arms out, then she could minimise the amount of wet cloth in contact with her body. Miss Armatage had gone, so there was no one left to shoo her away, and if she waited long enough the rain would stop and her body temperature would dry her clothes enough that they wouldn't chafe.

On the street, the last car pulled away. The rain wasn't going to let up and her clothes weren't going to get any drier. She should start on the long walk home.

She took a step towards the gates and froze.

The old woman stood there, barring the way. She wagged a finger disapprovingly and shook her head. Then she reached into a fold in her clothes and pulled out a leather wallet. She threw it to Sammy but it fell short, opening as it hit the floor and coming to rest in a puddle at her feet. Something in the wallet shimmered through the water.

When Sammy looked up, the woman had gone.

She reached down and picked up the wallet. Not a wallet, but a police badge with the name Peter Marshall CID underneath. The photo ID was of a middle-aged man with a tidy haircut, and protruding from the compartment behind the picture was a folded envelope. Sammy removed and smoothed it out in her hands.

Her name was on the front: *Samantha Ellis*.

For a moment it was all she could focus on.

She looked up, checked over her shoulder.

No one around. She took a deep breath, opened the envelope and pulled out a sodden note, careful not to tear it. The message on the paper had been written in pen and had run, but was still legible. *Meet me at the market.*

Sammy stared at the note until her heart rate returned to normal.

If it had been the woman's intention to kidnap her, she could've done it then. There'd been no one else around. But she hadn't, she'd kept a reasonable distance and had invited Sammy to the market, somewhere that was always busy. That meant the woman wasn't planning on harming her. But then again, she'd taken out two policemen, which meant she was a force to be reckoned with.

Whatever the old lady was up to, Sammy knew two things: one, she watched too many US crime shows; and two, more importantly, someone had noticed her.

She would go to the market and she'd find out what the old crone wanted.

Across the street, a figure got up from behind a garden wall. Sammy recognised him as the policeman whose badge she still held, Peter Marshall.

He leant on the wall, cradling his head. The second policeman got up beside him, stumbled and took hold of his colleague for support.

Then they saw Sammy.

Sammy dropped the badge and ran back through the playground.

One of the men yelled after her but by then she was already heading for the football pitch and the fence at the rear of the school.

–TWO–
The Dark

The sound of dripping water registered distantly. Behnam Baktash raised his head and agony propelled him screaming into full consciousness. Intense pressure compacted his skull, his eyes burned, and everything was black. He thrashed out, unleashing pins and needles in his limbs and bringing another wave of pain.

He needed to think, to calm down. He took a long, slow breath, tried to open his eyes, but couldn't; they were stuck together and felt like they were tearing when he tried. He winced. He wanted to put a hand to his face, to discover what had happened, but his arms were numb. He tugged at them and pain spiked in his joints.

A metallic clinking told him that his arms were shackled above. He rested his head to the side, against an arm. He wasn't going anywhere. What now?

There was a stone wall at his back and stone below where he sat. That's all he could feel.

He called out and his voice returned an echo. Stone walls all around and no furniture or fixings to absorb sound. A cell, or more likely a dungeon, because it was cold and damp.

An icy tendril of air slithered over his skin, chilling him and making his muscles tighten and his joints ache. He'd been left alone, propped against the wall. But for how long?

He needed to know how bad his injuries were. Then he could work out what his options were. Taking slow, controlled breaths, Behnam tried each of his limbs in turn, a small movement, one at a time. He was in bad shape. Nothing broken that he could tell, but his left leg was unresponsive.

He slumped. The room, the atmosphere, it all stank of hopelessness. He'd been left to rot, just as others had been before him. He knew this because he could smell them, or at least what was left of them.

He should never have come to the old city. It had been reckless, a suicide mission. What had he really expected to find there?

"Behnam?"

Behnam thrashed out, his joints spasming with pain. But he kept pulling. That voice. Deep, rasping—and if you heard it, you were moments away from dying in excruciating agony. He had to escape, somehow, anyhow. Saw his arms off. Rip them from their sockets. Saliva welled in his mouth, vomit rose in his throat. He was sucking in too much oxygen, hyperventilating. If he didn't slow his breathing, he'd pass out.

He held his breath.

An awful dread chewed at his stomach lining as rivulets of cold sweat ran down his face. Now he remembered how he'd been captured. But why was he still alive?

"I've been waiting for you to wake up," the voice rasped. "I was beginning to think you wouldn't." Each word was forced, like a corpse trying to extract speech from desiccated vocal chords.

"What do ...?" Behnam gritted his teeth.

"What do I want from you?" asked the voice. "I want information."

Behnam's mouth dried up, and he found himself unable to answer.

"I want to know everything the brotherhood knows about the event that's coming."

Behnam choked. "An event?"

"Come now, Behnam, you must know what's coming."

Behnam tried to think, but became distracted. Something pulled at his thoughts, his consciousness drifted out of focus. Memories and visions rushed through his head, appearing and then vanishing like the pages of a book flicked through at speed.

"Stop!" he cried out.

The sensation stopped. He dropped his head to his chest and gasped for breath. He was weak, but not yet weak enough to give up the contents of his mind.

"You really don't know anything," the voice said, sounding surprised. "I'll be back later. You'll know what I'm talking about then. And perhaps your opinion will be of more use to me."

"Why are you keeping me here?" Behnam asked. He took a deep breath and tried to slow his heart. "You know my kidnapping will bring unwanted attention to you. If my brothers find out I'm still alive, they'll come for me. You should have killed me already."

"They will come," replied the voice. "But I fear someone far more dangerous is on the horizon."

–THREE–
Footy, Anyone?

It was so much easier to get up when there was no school. Sammy kneaded her eyes, tucked her unruly hair behind her ears, and rolled out of bed. Downstairs in the kitchen, she fetched a bowl, emptied in a packet of porridge, added milk, stirred, then slammed it in the microwave. Load up on carbs for footy. Saturday was football in the park. And some other stuff that didn't really matter. Eat some meals, watch some telly, work on her Kill/Death ratio on the PlayStation. Padding. Not that she absolutely loved football. It was mostly about spending time with her dad. She'd rather be flicking through comic books or playing video games, but she could play football at the boys' level and it was the only thing her dad took notice of, making it the best way to get father-daughter time. She hadn't seen him in almost two weeks due to him going to an away game last weekend, but this weekend he'd be free. And she couldn't wait.

Sammy's mum swept into the kitchen. She twirled, flinging her immaculately straight, glossy hair out behind her, and suffusing the air with the scent of cocoa butter. She stopped to face Sammy.

"Morning, sweetie." She gave Sammy an air kiss so as not to imprint pink lip gloss on her.

"Hey," Sammy said. She couldn't help smiling. Mama was always happy and it was infectious. Her face was a little tired and her jeans squeezed her love handles up over her belt, but she was beautiful in all the ways that mattered.

"I bet you can't wait to trail around shop, after shop, after fabulous shop, behind me while I look for a new outfit."

The microwave pinged. Sammy took her porridge out and carried it to the table.

"I'm not going shopping," she said. She sat and began shovelling food into her mouth. "I'm meeting Dad at the park," she mumbled in between mouthfuls.

Her mum didn't reply.

Sammy waited, but her mum said nothing while gazing apologetically at her.

"You're kidding me."

"I'm sorry, sweetheart."

"Dad cancelled last weekend. He promised we'd practise keepy-ups."

"He texted this morning. Tracy's come down with a migraine. He's taking your stepbrother out so she can recover in peace."

"She hasn't really got a migraine."

"You don't know that."

"Where's he taking Ryan?"

"I didn't ask."

"They're going to the park, aren't they?"

"I really don't know. I'm sorry." Her mother turned away and began filling a bowl with bran flakes.

Cancelled again. Sammy used her spoon to scrape at a hard patch of porridge that had welded itself to the table.

"Will you come to Meadowhall with me instead?" her mum asked.

"I don't want to go shopping."

"I don't want to leave you alone."

"I'm sixteen. I think I'll be fine."

"Will you make sure to keep the door locked? A boy got stabbed two streets over the other week."

"Why can't you ask for maintenance from Dad? The other kids at school get it from theirs. If you asked him, he'd pay. Then we could move away from this crappy area and I could go back to St Josephine's ..."

Her mum visibly deflated. "I've tried hard to make this house our home. I earn enough to keep a roof over our heads and we have each other. That's all that matters. I don't need your father's money. I don't need anything from him."

Sammy stared into the bowl of half-eaten porridge.

"Things will get better. I promise. Let him have his new life with Tracy and Ryan."

"It'd be nice for me to be a part of his life, too."

Her mum went silent a moment, then brightened up. "I saw Chantelle's mum outside Roy's Fried Chicken the other day. She asked if you …"

"I'm not friends with Chantelle."

"What happened?"

"Relax, Mum. Nothing happened. We just don't have anything in common."

"You'll make friends, sweetheart. I know it's been difficult to adjust since we moved. Just keep smiling. Boys like girls that smile."

"You sound *so* old talking like that. And I'm not interested in *any* of the boys at Pitscrapes. Trust me."

"You may think so now—"

"Can we do something else today? Instead of shopping?"

"Sammy Ellis!" Her mother put the back of her hand to her forehead in a mock faint.

"We always go shopping." Sammy rested her head in her hands and stared into space. "I just thought …" She trailed off. She was looking at nothing in particular when her eyes came to rest on her coat hanging by the door. Still poking from the corner of her pocket was the crumpled envelope the old woman had slipped behind the policeman's badge.

"Mum?" she asked.

"You aren't going to ask me to play football again, are you? You know how my heels get stuck in the mud."

"How about the market?"

"The market?" Her mum frowned. "There isn't a lot of high-end fashion there. But I suppose we are on a budget." She sighed. "Fine. The market it is. Tomorrow we'll do something fun. Okay?"

Not exactly football with her dad, but at least they weren't going to the shopping centre. And perhaps the day would turn out to be an interesting one after all.

–FOUR–
OFF TO MARKET

The fortnightly market took place in the car park of an old steel mill, which had closed down decades ago. The building was an L-shape and the car park and market sat in the right angle of the L, closed in on two sides by corrugated iron.

Sammy stood at the edge of the market and watched her mum elbow her way into the crowd. She tightened her already tightly crossed arms and rocked back and forth on her heels. She should be smacking a ball around the park, not freezing her butt off at some lame market in the middle of nowhere. She'd got her own way, in that they'd gone to the market, but what did she actually expect to happen? Would the old woman even be here today? She let out a long, weary breath and wondered whether she should just wait on the street until her mum was done. She wanted to demonstrate how little interest she had for shopping, but the problem was that Mama loved having her around. Even when she was completely immersed in 'retail therapy'.

She couldn't upset her mum. Not after everything she'd been through with Dad.

Besides, the old woman might be in there somewhere, so there was no point dwelling on the missed kick-about. The mission was on and Sammy was ready. She'd tackle it like a 'Double O' agent. Constantly aware of her surroundings, treat every civilian as a potential threat. She should've arrived in the early hours of the morning to do a recce, but her mum wouldn't have gone for that. And it was too late now. The one ace she had up her sleeve was that the old woman wouldn't know what time she'd be coming. Perhaps she'd get the drop on the old girl.

The market stalls were of the old wooden variety with red-and-white or green-and-white striped canopies. They were piled high with goods and jumbled together in no particular configuration, with all the free space in between packed with people.

Sammy watched those people. A lot of them looked like they could handle themselves in a fight, but none took any notice of her, so she rated them as low threats.

A teenager in a baseball cap and hoody hurtled past, making her jump. He shouted something at a group of others behind him, but kept going. The others jeered without breaking stride and continued to patrol the outskirts of the market aggressively, perfecting their best gangster walks. Sammy walked quickly on without making eye contact. Not because she was scared. She had to remain inconspicuous for the mission. She could take them. Maybe.

It was mostly clothes on sale at the market. Novelty t-shirts, jeans, hats and coats. But also dotted about were stalls selling other items. The most unusual of which lurked in the dark, far corner, bordered on two sides by corrugated iron cliff faces and on the other two by heavily laden clothes stalls.

The stall was piled high with knick-knacks and old junk, and sat under a frayed canvas canopy covered in black mildew spots. And it appeared deserted.

Sammy shouldered her way through the clothes stalls and into the small clearing around the knick-knack stall.

She slowly turned 360 degrees to scope out her surroundings, waited a moment, then approached the table. Old door knobs, odd-shaped bottles and cheap-looking jewellery covered the surface. The items lacked any kind of arrangement and seemed to have been dumped where they lay. Yet beams of sunlight had found their way into the clearing, projecting directly onto individual items of junk, illuminating them like holy artefacts and

19

making them appear to possess value far in excess of their real worth.

"Come closer, child," encouraged a voice from the dark recesses behind the stall.

Sammy couldn't see her, but she knew who it was.

The old woman in the pale blue headscarf stepped into the light. Dark, piercing eyes scurried up and down over Sammy's flesh.

Sammy shivered but tried not to show any outward appearance of fear and folded her arms across her chest.

"Why have you been following me?"

"So we could meet each other," the old woman said. She had an unusual accent. The sort of accent you'd hear on a mysterious stranger in an adventure movie. It was nothing like Sammy had ever heard before and a million miles from the broad Northern accents of the other stall owners.

Sammy assessed the situation. She was trapped in a corner with nowhere to run if the woman attacked. But then, could the woman do anything in the middle of the market without someone seeing? Sammy reasoned that the woman probably wasn't going to attack. She would have done it yesterday after school when no one was around.

"Why do you want to meet me?" Sammy asked. "I don't know you."

"You don't know me yet, but I know you. I used to know your father."

"Who are you?"

"My name is Esther. You are Sammy."

"Yeah, I'm Sammy. What do you want? And how do you know my dad?"

"I want to show you something," Esther said. She gestured at the items on the stall. "It's on here. See if you can find it."

Sammy approached, but kept her eyes on the woman. What was her game? "This?" She picked up a golden sword hilt, inlaid with gemstones, and turned it over in her hands. The blade had broken off, leaving only a thin shard protruding from the end.

"That is an ancient dagger hilt. The blade snapped off in the black heart of a monster."

"A monster?" Yeah right. "What about this?" She was reaching for a teardrop-shaped bottle containing pink vapour when something special caught her eye. A golden bracelet adorned with a green gemstone the size of a fifty-pence piece in the centre. The gemstone was set into an ornate clasp that looked to be some kind of mechanical device. Clock-style hands pointed straight out, left and right on either side, as if displaying the time quarter to three, and engraved around the setting were strange, looping letters in an unusual script that Sammy had never seen before.

Esther watched Sammy, a smile on her lips. "I think you've found it."

"What is it?"

"The Midnight Emerald bracelet."

"The Midnight Emerald …" repeated Sammy, trying not to sound too interested.

"The Emeral Dial part found its way into Alexander the Great's possession several thousand years ago, but no one knows where it came from before that. He conquered most of the Middle East in his lifetime, so it could've come from anywhere; Egypt, Greece, Turkey, Armenia, Persia. All he ever said was that an old woman gave it to him and she told of a lock placed on it. One that could only be opened by the chosen."

Sammy wasn't even going to bother hiding her intrigue. "Was he the chosen?"

"I don't think so. He spent years trying to work the mechanism, but without luck. Finally he gave up and set the dial into a bracelet for his wife, Roxana. He died shortly after, struck down with stomach cramps after a banquet, never knowing the secret of the mysterious mechanism."

"Does that mean the Emerald Dial was never unlocked?"

"Maybe not, but something happened." Esther leant forward and lowered her voice to a whisper. "Alexander's wife, Roxana, was pregnant at the time of his death. Which meant a regent was chosen to govern the kingdom in the hope that Roxana would give birth to a boy who would later become heir."

"And did she?"

Esther nodded and smiled. "She did. Many regents ruled the kingdom while the boy was a child. But before he came of age, a new regent took over. His name was Cassander. He wanted to rule the kingdom for himself, so imprisoned the boy and mother, later giving orders for them to be killed."

"What happened?"

"Men came for them in the night. They entered the prison, where a great screaming and commotion followed. Soon after, the men ran from the place, saying that Roxana's bracelet had exploded, killing both boy and mother. But when the prison guards entered the cell, they found only the mother's body, along with the Midnight Emerald bracelet, on the floor. The boy had gone. Cassander acquired the bracelet and since then it has been passed down from regent, to dictator, to Shah. Here to there, backwards and forwards. And now it finds itself here on my stall."

Sammy stared at the bracelet, gripping the edge of the stall, her knuckles white. This must be how her mother feels when she finds a handbag she likes. She didn't like being so affected by an accessory.

"But how did you get it?"

Esther shrugged. "Better you don't know."

"You stole it?"

"Hush, child!" Esther glanced about, clearly on edge.

Sammy stretched her arm towards the emerald and her fingers tingled as they neared. She snatched her hand back.

"You feel something? Yes?" Esther smiled. "I thought you might."

"How?"

"You have a gift."

"A gift? What kind of gift?"

"I will get to that in good time, my dear. But there is more of the story I must tell. Now, it is well known that Alexander the Great spent many years tracking down the Vara of Yima, and I believe he thought this Emerald Dial held the key to finding it."

"What's the Vara of Yima?"

"It is what people of my origin call their Garden of Eden. You have heard of this Garden of Eden?"

"I've heard of it, yeah."

"When I was a girl, we were taught about a shepherd named Yima. The great god Ahura Mazda asked him to create a vara, and to fill this vara with the fittest of men and women, and two of each animal, bird and plant, because of a terrible natural disaster coming. You have heard this story? Or one similar?"

"Noah's Ark," Sammy said. "Noah took two of each animal into his ark to keep them safe when the Earth flooded. So was the vara a boat?"

"No. It was a vast enclosure, a great realm. Noah's Ark is the Christian variation of the story. But Noah is also in the Islamic Qur'an and in Jewish literature. In fact, there are also great floods in the mythology of the Greeks and in Indian texts. Many religions tell stories of people and animals rescued from floods and disasters. In my faith, Zoroastrianism, our great disaster is an ice age and our Noah is Yima. Yima created this vara with buildings, roads and cities, then sealed it from the rest of the world with a golden ring. People throughout history have searched for this place, believing it to be a perfect land, the real Garden of Eden." Esther sighed. "Which at one time it probably was, long before it became polluted by a great evil. Now it is time for the chosen to return and restore light to the lands of Perseopia."

"Have you tried unlocking it? The bracelet?"

"I have tried, but I don't have the gift." Esther took a long breath. "I've travelled the whole world to find someone who does. And I believe you do. That is why I followed you."

Sammy stared at the bracelet. She desperately wanted to believe she was special, that she was Neo, but it couldn't be true. "Let me get this straight," she said. "I'm the chosen one that can unlock the dial and travel to the Garden of Eden. And when I get there I will restore light to the lands of that-place-you-just-said? Do you also happen to have sweets and puppy dogs to help entice me into the back of your van? You know, just to seal the deal."

"You aren't the chosen one."

Sammy paused. "Wait. You said I have the gift."

"You have *a* gift. One that can unlock the dial. But you aren't the chosen one. I am."

"You're not doing a good job of selling me this stupid fantasy. I'm not climbing into the back of your van if I have to be Robin. I'm Batman. That's how these things work."

"I do not own a van," Esther said. "Would you like to know what the words around the clasp say?" She leant across the table and ran her finger over the text. "It is written in Avestan. Not many can read such a language."

Sammy shrugged. She didn't care as much now. She wasn't the chosen one so what was the point? "Let me guess. You can read it, because you're the chosen one?"

"It is the language of my youth. I have not spoken it in many years, but I can still read it." Esther traced the letters with her fingers.

"Raise your hands to the skies
"on the tone of midnight,
"and you will travel to the land
"of endless twilight."

Sammy repeated it back under her breath. It was a pretty cool rhyme.

"I have had this bracelet for many years and I've never been able to unlock it," Esther said. "Will you help me?"

Sammy wasn't the chosen one, but at least she had a gift. She shrugged. So, she'd be Chewbacca. That was better than nothing.

"I suppose," she said.

Esther didn't acknowledge the response. She stared off into the middle-distance, her eyes wide. "They've found me!"

She snatched up the bracelet, thrust it into a bin liner and dumped it under the table. Then she pulled the tablecloth corners over the contents of the stall and hoisted the bundle over her shoulder.

"The bracelet's in the bag under the table," she said. "Keep it safe. Don't tell anyone about it. Don't lose it. And, most importantly, don't try to work the dial yourself. I will find you again." Then she shoved her way out past the other stalls and was gone.

As Sammy gazed after Esther, a black shape entered the clearing behind her. She turned to face a finely cut black jacket stretched over a barrel chest. A large man with hair sprouting out over his shirt collar peered down at her from behind a pair of mirrored aviators.

"Who was that woman you were talking to?" he asked.

Sammy just stared. He was a very big man.

He bent down so that Sammy could see her oddly stretched face in his sunglasses. He gritted his teeth. "Is she a friend of yours?"

"I ... I've never met her before." Sammy's mouth became uncommonly dry. Was he threatening her? "I don't ..."

A mobile phone buzzed quietly inside the man's jacket pocket. He stood up straight, pulled it out, tapped the screen and held it to his ear.

"Gone," he said. "She'll try to go into hiding again. Yes, I've got someone on her." He watched Sammy while listening to the person on the other end of the line. "No one. Just a girl. She doesn't have it."

The man listened to the phone a while longer, then tapped the screen off and dropped it into his pocket.

"If the old woman contacts you again," he said, "call me." Then he handed Sammy a card and walked away.

Sammy turned the card over. It was blank except for a single mobile number printed in the centre. She climbed onto the table and watched the man go as she swung her legs back and forth like 'just a girl' would.

When she was sure he'd gone, she got down and crawled under the table to fetch the bin liner.

"Sammy!"

She leapt up, slamming her head into the underside of the table. Behind her a pair of tan leather boots and two floating carrier bags waited for her.

"What are you doing down there?" asked her mum. "And what's in that dirty bin bag? Give it here." She bent down and took it.

"Don't," Sammy said. "I need it." She crawled out from under the table.

Her mother removed the bracelet and her mouth dropped open.

"This is gorgeous," she said.

"Don't get it out! I'm looking after it for the woman."

"What woman?" Her mum lowered the bracelet. "Who does this belong to?"

"A friend. I'm looking after it ... for a friend."

"I thought you said a woman?"

"A friend's mum," Sammy said. "She's a woman, clearly. Please. It's important."

Her mum stared into her eyes. "This looks like a very expensive piece."

"I'm not a child. And I haven't nicked it. I'm looking after it."

Her mum squinted, peering deeply into her. "Okay honey, we'll take it home. But promise me you'll get your friend's mother to come over for it."

Sammy scanned the vicinity around them. She couldn't see Esther or the man in black.

"Fine," she said. "But can you put it back in the bag? Please?"

–FIVE–
No Place Like Home

Sammy's dad came in through the front door, shaking the rain from his umbrella onto the doormat. He closed the door behind him, put the umbrella in the stand, and hung up his coat. When he saw Sammy, he stopped.

Sammy smiled and got up off the sofa.

"What are you doing here?" he asked.

"Mum's going out tonight. I thought I could stay over, play with Ryan."

Ryan was on his belly on the sitting room rug, building a house for his dinosaurs out of plastic bricks.

"Oh," her dad said. "Where's Tracy?"

"Upstairs on the computer."

"What's for dinner?"

"Pasta with tomato soup and grated cheese. It's in the microwave."

Her dad groaned and rolled his eyes. "It's Saturday night and I've got pasta and tomato soup for tea. That lazy skank." He kneaded his eyes with his thumb and forefinger. "Can you get me a beer out? United are on in a minute. I'm going upstairs to get changed. Ryan, tell your useless mother to quit messaging her boyfriends and get you ready for bed. If you're quick you can watch the game with your old man."

At three nil down and with fifteen minutes to go, Sammy's dad clicked off the telly. He reached for the beer on top of the stack of Tracy's magazines, slugged back the remains, and crushed the can in his hand. Then he got up, collected the other empties from the floor, and carried them through to the kitchen.

"Bedtime, Ryan," he said, as he dropped the cans in the bin. He turned to Sammy. "You'll need to shift the washing off the futon. Just stick it on the floor." He switched off the kitchen light and walked down the hall. "You know where the sheets are."

"Dad," Sammy said, as she followed him, "I met an old woman today. She said she knew you."

Her dad's eyes narrowed. "I don't know any old women."

"She gave me a bracelet—"

"I don't know her. If you see her again, tell her to sod off." He nudged Ryan up the stairs in front of him and trudged up behind.

"Dad?"

He stopped, shoulders slumped. "Sam, I just want to go to bed."

"I was only going to say goodnight."

Her dad carried on up the stairs, taking Ryan to his bedroom and switching the hall light off as he went. "Goodnight," he said.

"Love you," Sammy called up.

The bedroom door clicked shut.

Sammy felt her way along the dark hall to the study. There were no curtains in the window and light poured in from the off licence next door. The desk was covered in paperwork and the futon against the back wall was covered in laundry. Sammy set about clearing the clothes and setting up her bed.

Two hours later, she was still awake, staring at the ceiling.

A group of students were hanging around in the carpark outside her window. They were passing around a cheap bottle of vodka, whooping loudly, and kept repeating the same joke. Sammy hadn't thought it was particularly funny the first time they told it, and it got even less funny with each retelling.

As she watched a spider slowly make its way across the ceiling, there was a smash outside.

Sammy sat up and peered over the sill. The bottle of vodka lay on the floor in pieces, and two of the students were drunkenly fighting. They grappled with each other, throwing lazy punches that didn't connect properly.

Sammy got out of bed and tidied away the futon. Five minutes later, she was dressed and quietly pulling the front door closed behind her.

−SIX−
LIGHTS IN THE NIGHT

Sammy let herself in through the front door. All the lights in the house were off. Did that mean her mum had returned from her night out? Hopefully she was in bed asleep already. She'd kill Sammy if she found out she'd walked home alone from her dad's.

At the top of the stairs, she took a right into her bedroom, ditched her rucksack, put on pyjamas, and pulled the duvet back to get into bed.

She'd check in on her mum first. After Dad left, Mama often needed a little extra care, a few more hugs. And she always appreciated the company.

Back on the landing, Sammy noticed a faint green glow flickering under the gap of her mum's door. The woman had passed out in front of the telly. Again.

Sammy put the hall light on, crept to the bedroom door and pushed it open.

Light from the hall threw a tapered rectangle into the room, coming to rest over her mum's sleeping figure. A zigzagging clothes trail ran from door to bed. Her mum's too-mini miniskirt laid closest to the door, then past that a sequined top, then underwear, stockings and high heels. Crossing the room in a straight line had been a struggle.

The red digits of the bedside clock displayed 11:54. Her mum was home early. She must've had a skinful and hadn't made it to the club this time. Sammy could jump up and down on the bed playing AC/DC and it wouldn't wake her now. That wasn't such a bad thing; her mum would often keep her awake wittering on about how things with her father were 'complicated' and about how much she loved Sammy. Which was fine, but then she'd get emotional and talk about being lonely, which wasn't so good. She preferred it when Mama didn't drink. If alcohol gave you enhanced abilities or access to some higher plane of reality, then she could understand. But all it did was make her dad angry and her mum depressed. Some of the girls in her old school had experimented with alcohol. Sammy hadn't felt the need to. She'd seen what it could do.

She pushed the door partially closed behind her. As the room grew dark, the green light returned.

An eerie dread permeated Sammy's flesh.

The TV wasn't on. The light was coming from under the bed, flickering. She needed to remain calm, think rationally. Early Christmas present? The light could be coming from the lightsaber replica she'd asked for. She actually wanted Obi-Wan's blue lightsaber, but she supposed she could live with a green one as long as it was Luke's from Return of the Jedi and not Yoda's from Attack of the Clones. Sammy's excitement faded. It was months before Christmas, and would her mum really have switched it on? She hated sci-fi, fantasy, anything like that, and she'd told Sammy numerous times that sixteen-year-olds shouldn't be playing with toys. Even though the lightsaber was a replica, and not a toy. Besides, there wasn't the buzzing hum that she would have expected to accompany the weapon.

She wanted to ignore the light and to go back to her own room, but that would be the sort of behaviour her dad would call cowardly.

A corner of the duvet hung over the edge of the bed, obscuring the mystery beneath. She knelt down by the bedside, rubbed her sweaty palms on her pyjamas. She was ready to whisk up the duvet, but stopped herself.

It might be an alien.

It wasn't an alien. She was making excuses. She glanced at the red display on the bedside clock again as the time flicked to 11:56.

Without thinking, she flung up the duvet.

And nothing. Nothing jumped out, anyway. The green light remained, silently flowing over her stomach in waves as she knelt there. She got down on her belly and crawled under the bed, commando style. Whatever was producing the light was behind a pile of clothes. With a swift breaststroke motion, she parted the blockage. The light dazzled her for a moment and she rubbed her eyes.

It was the Emerald Dial bracelet. Not an alien. The light was coming from the jewel on the front. She let out the breath she'd been holding and crawled closer. Something in the gemstone was creating the rippling wave effect. Wriggling shapes deep inside swaying back and forth like long reeds. It was strangely hypnotic to look at and time seemed to slip away as she watched.

She snapped out of her trance and shuffled back a little way to get a better look. The dial's hands were pointing straight out to the left and right, still set at a quarter to three, which was clearly the wrong time. It was closer to midnight now. For the briefest of moments, Sammy imagined the ancient text around the setting shimmering.

Raise your hands to the skies
on the tone of midnight.

On the bedside table, the time flicked to 11:59. If Sammy raised both clock hands to the top, the dial would display the correct time. Esther had told her not to work the mechanism herself, but it's not like she was going to break it. She'd be careful.

Sammy clutched the bracelet between her palms and used her thumbs to push the hands upward. They each shifted a little, but the mechanism was stiff and they stuck.

The reeds in the emerald swayed faster. Sammy pushed the hands again, but nothing happened. She shifted closer to the bracelet, until only her legs protruded from under the bed. Her face was now right up against the emerald and she had an elbow on the floor on either side of it. She took a deep breath and pushed. Both clock hands flew up with a snap. They locked together at the top and the emerald began humming, starting low but getting louder and higher.

Sammy scrabbled backwards, but too late. The emerald exploded in white-green light. Dazzling and brilliant, consuming everything around her, as the world melted to black.

–SEVEN–
LOST

Behnam was unwell. Worse than unwell. Unwell was a gross understatement. He'd been drifting in and out of consciousness for, what? Days? How long had he been in this place now? And he'd not been able to move his arms or legs since. If he didn't get some proper circulation going soon, his limbs would begin dying.

A thick fog enveloped his brain and he found himself drifting off. He shook his head to stay awake.

Pain exploded in his temples, but it had the desired effect. He needed to stay conscious, to think. Escape was paramount. The longer he remained captive, the harder it would be to keep blocking access to his mind.

"Well?" spoke the voice in the darkness.

Behnam startled, lashing out with his one good leg, but didn't connect with anything. His nerves were shot, but he mustn't crack.

Stay calm.

Silence. The thrashing had exacerbated his head. He winced and slumped back against the wall, already defeated. Feet shuffled in the darkness. There were other people here. How many? And what was their purpose?

"What do you want from me?" Behnam asked at last.

"I want to know if you felt it." It was the same rasping corpse-like voice as before.

"Felt what?" He coughed. "All I feel is pain."

"You felt it," said the voice. "You and the brotherhood all felt it."

"Felt …"

"The fluctuation. The ripple that swept through the fabric of our realm."

"I don't understand." Behnam leant his head back against the wall and took a shallow breath.

"It's the girl. She's come back. I felt it. And I know you and the brotherhood felt it too."

Behnam's head was swimming again. Jumbled visions were populating his mind's eye, coming and going in rapid succession.

"Enough!" he shouted. He forced all thought from his head. It was a struggle but somehow he managed it.

"Still fighting me?" There was a pause. "You're strong, Master Baktash, yet what little strength you have left is waning. Your time is running out. But no matter, my men will find her."

"What girl?"

"The one who almost killed me, who cut off my arm. I thought I'd destroyed her before. This time I'll do it properly, before she can fulfil her destiny. And you will help me, Master Baktash. You'll help, or those you hold dear will perish."

———

Sammy lolled from side to side, yawned, stretched and rolled over. She lay still a moment, then squirmed. Her pyjama top was damp and had stuck to her back.

She opened her eyes. Paused.

She leapt up, heart pounding, unable to breathe. The scene before her made no sense. It didn't compute.

But there it was. She pressed her hand to her chest and held her breath.

This was way wrong. She was outside and she was in a forest … a forest of glowing mushrooms. She closed her eyes and let that sink in. She opened them again. Same view.

Broad, olive-green canopies capped the top of thick, smooth trunks, while soft yellow light bloomed from the gills underneath as if the mushrooms were enormous table lamps with shallow shades. Sparkling spores filled the air like fairy dust, folding themselves around Sammy as she moved, and spiralling in her breath as she exhaled.

The largest mushrooms were tree-sized, two, maybe three storeys high, but they ranged in height down through sun canopy-sized, to café table, footstool and even regular mushroom size.

A whole forest of glowing mushrooms, as far as the eye could see, and in all directions.

Sammy turned slowly on the spot, taking in her surroundings.

Other vegetation occupied space amongst the mushrooms. Bushes covered in limp, yellow leaves sprouted from the ground, and draped over everything, like filthy bunting, were brown, stringy creepers.

Even with the light coming from the mushrooms, the place was relatively dark, which meant it was probably still night. Thankfully it was warm. Handy, for someone still dressed in their pyjamas. That was about as positive as Sammy could get about the situation. She awkwardly tried to reach an arm around to her back to brush the soil off her pyjama top.

She should be terrified, but wasn't. The environment was too surreal, too fantastical. She watched a small white bird with a narrow beak zip past. It caught an insect circling in the mushroom light, and a moment later had gone. There were other creatures, too. Sammy followed the sound of rustling to a withered yellow bush and watched as a group of small pink mammals scattered into their burrows. They looked kind-of like hedgehogs, but instead of spines on their backs they had plates like a mini Stegosaurus.

Sammy crossed the clearing to a stool-sized mushroom. It seemed strong enough to take her weight and wasn't slimy so she sat down and brushed the dirt off her feet.

What now? What resources did she have at her disposal? Awesome ninja skills that she'd learned from watching thousands of Kung Fu movies. But not much else. Her skin prickled. She rubbed her hands up and down her arms and stood up again so she could pace. Pacing felt better than sitting.

A scream split the air and Sammy's intestines launched up into her throat.

A girl. Not far away. Sammy wiped her palms on her clothes. Time to find out what she was made of. She took a step forward and a guttural barking and crunching stopped her from taking a second step. It sounded like a fight, but what sort?

Another squeak. Was that really a girl? Sammy went to move, but her legs refused.

More movement. Scuffling. Then a thud, followed by a yelp.

Sammy waited. The noises had sounded like a girl's at first, but now that she thought about it, it had been kind of muffled. She could still walk over. Check it out. Nothing was stopping her. Except there was the wild animal that had made the predator-like noises. Not investigating wasn't cowardly. The animal could be a bear. Her dad was tough, but he wouldn't fight a bear. A bear attacking a giant mushroom-eating mouse? That's probably what'd made the squeak.

Sammy considered her options and decided she was going to start walking in the opposite direction to the growling. Away from the bear. Definitely the right decision. Hopefully, if anyone came looking for her, they'd come to the same sensible conclusion and walk in the same direction.

She set off at a brisk pace. No point in hanging around.

–EIGHT–
The Village

Sammy had been walking ages. She'd seen nothing to indicate there was intelligent life on this jungle planet, so she took a break by an outcrop of rocks that loosely resembled the Sydney Opera House. As she sat down to rest her feet, a pack of crimson mice ran out from a bush in pursuit of a large, shiny beetle. They cornered it in front of a boulder and took it in turns to distract the insect while others attacked from behind.

Interesting, but Sammy left them to it and climbed the rocks. At the top, she was still well below the tallest mushroom canopies but it afforded her a better view of the area. She turned in a slow circle, throwing her arms out every so often to keep her balance.

From her vantage point, she spied another pile of rocks through a gap in the mushrooms. No, not ordinary rocks, but blocks.

Civilisation, at last. She climbed down and made her way towards the stones, pulling apart curtains of creepers as she went. She found the blocks and, with them, a house. It had been completely obscured by vegetation and she'd almost walked past it.

Sammy walked around the side and into a long clearing where she found other houses lined up on either side of a dirt track. A village, but a deserted one.

All the buildings were built from the same grey stone blocks and looked the same, with caved in roofs and no doors or windows in any of the frames. No one had lived here in a long time; unless there was someone camped out in one of the derelict houses.

Sammy wasn't about to call to find out. Drawing attention to herself might not be a good move. There could be other giant mouse-eating bears.

She walked further into the village. It was the first time she'd left the cover of the mushrooms, and it was darker out of their light. There were a few mushrooms in town; a couple in the village square and one or two had squeezed their way up by the sides of houses, but alone they didn't produce much light. Yet despite the lack of mushrooms, the village wasn't dark; it was purple.

Sammy had been unable to see the sky fully until that moment. And what a sight it was.

A churning sea of purple cloud. Not a 'red sky at night' kind of purple—the kind that shepherds say brings fair weather—but a deep, royal purple and magenta mass of frothing foam. Fast-moving currents and vortexes spiralled into each other, both beautiful and menacing at the same time. It made her dizzy just watching it. Her balance was telling her she was right side up, but her eyes were telling her she was suspended upside-down above a raging ocean. She looked away, momentarily shaken.

This place was insane, but she couldn't waste too long thinking about it. She'd found houses, houses meant people, and people meant help.

She approached the doorway of a house and peered through the empty frame. The building was comprised of three small rooms, contained no furniture and the floor was littered with tiles from the collapsed roof.

She carried on up the dirt track towards a crumbling stone well in the village centre.

She picked up a pebble and dropped it into the well. Three seconds later, there was a pathetic little plip.

Twenty-three buildings in the settlement and no one living in them. What now?

She stood, hands on hips, surveying the area. The street carried on through the town and led back out into the forest. She'd have a look around each house first, just in case she found supplies or something worth taking. Then she'd follow the trail out of town. Hopefully it would take her somewhere populated.

Sammy crossed the street and entered a house. A brief scout around revealed the same state of ruin as the first place. No door, no panes or shutters in the windows, and the floor littered with tiles. She picked up a tile and turned it over in her hands. It was smooth to the touch with two holes at the top. One of the holes still had the remains of a rusty nail sticking out. She looked up through the open ceiling where there'd once been a roof and stared into the swirling sky. It had the same effect as watching the fruit machine in her local pub, in that she'd often find herself captivated by its dancing lights while waiting for her dad to finish 'one last pint.'

She dropped the tile, moved to the window, and ran a finger along the rusty brackets that had once supported shutters. A gust of warm air swept in through the opening, carrying dust into her face. She rubbed at her eyes.

The temperature was going up. She left the house and made her way back onto the street. The heat seemed worse outside than in. It was like stepping off the aeroplane that time her parents took her on holiday to Florida.

She smiled. Their last holiday together as a family. They'd been to all the big theme parks, eaten burgers, had cinnamon-flavoured sweets, and she'd stayed up late every night in the hotel room playing cards with her mum while her dad was downstairs in the bar. Sammy shook the memory from her head.

The sky was still dark, with no sign of daylight, yet it was still getting warmer. She pulled at her pyjama top, flapping it up and down, wafting cool air inside. And stiffened.

A figure sat on the edge of the well, right where she'd been standing a few minutes ago. A large person, indistinct in the darkness and heat haze, but visible enough to see it was cloaked entirely in black.

The few small mushrooms in the village centre nearby had shrivelled and were no longer glowing.

The figure turned its head in her direction.

Sammy checked over her shoulder. She had no idea why, there was no one around to help. No big deal. It was just a man. A very tall man, but still just a man. He would help her. So, then, why was she clenching her jaw so hard it was beginning to hurt?

The figure slowly rose to its feet and approached. It was tall, twice as tall as she was, but thin, with narrow shoulders. Its entire body was hidden beneath the cloak, the hood covering its face, long sleeves covering its arms and hands.

"You look lost," it said, in a monotonous, metallic tone.

The saliva in Sammy's mouth dried up, forming a sticky paste that glued her tongue to the roof of her mouth, and she felt unable to answer.

"Well?" it asked. "Are you lost?"

"No, I ... I'm fine. Thank you," Sammy replied, doing her best not to stammer.

"I'm here to help you," said the figure calmly, "and you're *lying* to me!" It finished with sudden fury and took several steps closer. The heat intensified dramatically as it did so, as if it was the source of the heat. It took a few more paces and stopped.

Sammy held her hands together to stop them shaking. She shuffled one foot backwards. Should she run? Would that make it angrier?

"This forest is a treacherous place. Lots of unpleasant inhabitants," the figure continued, calm now. "You're alone, scared. We'd like to make your acquaintance, to help you."

We? If its buddies were anything like it was, Sammy didn't want to make their acquaintance. She should run, but couldn't bring herself to take that first step.

The creature took another step closer and lunged. That was the trigger Sammy needed. She ducked under its arm as her legs came back to life. And she ran.

A metallic scream followed her into the dark alley between two houses. The sound of a knife scraped across steel that made her teeth hurt. She clapped her hands over her ears and kept going.

She flew from the alley into the glittering light of the forest. She chanced a look over her shoulder to find the figure coming after her, floating along the forest floor as if on roller skates, moving without any outward appearance of effort. Its arms clenched at its sides and head slumped at its chest, like a man hanging from a noose. How could anything so horrific not mean her harm? And she'd made it angry, somehow.

Sammy kept pumping her legs. The running combined with the heat at her back was making her light-headed, but she couldn't stop. She wasn't getting away, but at least *it* wasn't gaining. All she could do was keep going and hope the monster tired before she did.

–NINE–

OF DINOSAURS AND MEN

Sammy doubled over, hands on knees. A stitch bit into her side and she closed her eyes while she took a moment to breathe. She wobbled and locked her arms to brace her legs.

A flutter behind sent her wheeling around.

Just a bird. No need to get spooked. She'd lost the monster, although she wasn't sure when that had happened. The heat had subsided some time ago, but she'd kept going, just in case.

The forest was still. The only sounds audible were those of birds and insects flitting and buzzing around under the mushroom hoods.

She'd been properly petrified. She couldn't deny it this time. Even her dad would've legged it from whatever that was.

She should keep moving. She straightened up and tottered on her feet. She needed water. She dropped her head forward, back between her knees, and waited until the tattoo in her skull finished drumming.

And now she was hearing things. Faint splashing and gurgling. She poked her index fingers in her ears, wiggled them. When she took them out, the noise was still there. She surged forth, dragging her leaden legs onwards, down an incline, scrambling through mushrooms, creepers and scratchy bushes, towards the sublime sloshing and burbling noise.

She staggered to a halt in view of a stream, and gulped down a sob.

The stream snaked along the bottom of a barren and shallow gulley, its circuitous course winding through large boulders on its banks.

As Sammy approached the river, the soil took on a coarser texture and the shingle transitioned into prickly pebbles that had her performing an oo-ah hotstep to the closest smooth boulder. From there, she used the other boulders as stepping stones to reach a rock in the middle of the stream. She rolled up both pyjama trouser legs, sat down and dipped her feet in the water. The first electric tingle of icy water whooshed up her legs; freezing, painful, but exquisite too. Sammy slipped her hands into the water, pausing to savour the anticipation, and left her hands submerged as the crystalline liquid flowed in and around her fingers. She pulled her cupped hands into the air and let the water rain down over her face and neck. And shivered. Bliss.

Then she drank. Water had never tasted so good. She drank heavily until her thirst had been quenched, then she took her feet from the water and sat cross-legged on the rock.

Esther had told her not to mess with the Midnight Emerald Dial by herself. But she had, and she'd been transported to another world. This place definitely wasn't the Garden of Eden Esther had spoken of, though. It had to be somewhere else. What if there were hundreds of combinations on the dial? Would Esther be able to figure out how to get her back from here? Sammy's chest constricted. She had to calm herself. Getting upset wouldn't help. Be positive, like Mum.

She really needed one of Mama's pep talks right now. Keep positive, keep smiling. Sammy choked down the emotion. Time to move on. She'd lost the creature but it would be looking for her. It might even be in the area. She was like Arnie in Predator. He hadn't given up, he'd faced the enemy, fought and triumphed, so he could 'get to the choppa'. But Sammy's adrenaline-fuelled flight had exhausted her energy leaving an all-consuming weariness in its place. She lay back on the boulder. She'd get going in a bit. She just needed to close her eyes for a minute.

She sat up with a start, bleary-eyed and groggy. Something was coming. A faint thudding, getting louder. She got up, her legs stiff. She wasn't moving quick enough and now the thuds were vibrating the rock underneath her, large ripples bouncing back and forth across the surface of the stream.

She hobbled down, sloshed through the water and stumbled up towards the forest, head reeling. She needed to hide, but she wasn't going to make mushroom cover in time.

She turned to see two towering mushrooms on the far side of the stream bend, then snap at their bases as a dinosaur-chicken with a shell on its back shouldered its way through them. The mushrooms splintered as they hit the ground, firing spongy chunks of fungus and spores into the air.

The dinosaur kept coming, blasting water from the stream as its feet slammed into the river bed.

Sammy tripped and fell. She scrambled backwards on all fours.

And the creature stopped.

Sammy collapsed on her back, her chest heaving.

A real-life dinosaur. That was the only thought in her head. One that looked nothing like the ones she'd seen in movies or killed in video games. It had no eyes, just a bulging forehead like a dolphin's and two leaf-shaped ears the size of car bonnets on either side of its head. Its skin was covered in tan, mottled scales, but on its cheeks and down the length of its flank it had white, fur-like feathers that transitioned to red and blue around its thighs. The dinosaur stood horizontal, like a T-Rex, with small, feathered arms at the front and big, muscular legs that it used to carry a golden shell, the size of a terraced house, on its back. The shell itself was egg-shaped with a pointed apex and had another, smaller, golden egg two-thirds the size of the first joined halfway up its side.

And the creature wasn't attacking her.

"Soubh be khear!" A man's voice.

Sammy followed it to the top of the second, smaller egg. Jutting out from it like a ship's prow was a long, pointed balcony, and leaning over the railing was a young guy wearing a black turban. In one hand he clutched a brass telescope and with the other he waved enthusiastically.

"Matounhm ke kumaikitan knam?" he called.

"I don't understand," Sammy shouted back, and received a sharp static shock to her left temple. It caught her by surprise and she staggered, trying to make sense of what had just happened.

"Wait there," the man said. "I'm coming down."

Sammy rubbed her head. She'd become dizzy again and knelt down until she got her balance back.

The man appeared at ground level behind the dinosaur and came over.

"Are you feeling all right?" he asked as he drew close. He was wearing a black waistcoat with a white silk shirt and trouser combo that were both so white they made him look like he'd stepped out of a washing powder commercial. He had a long nose and a pursed mouth but beautiful hazel eyes that smiled when he did. He rolled back and forth on his heels with his hands behind his back.

Sammy rubbed her neck and got to her feet, feeling surprisingly okay again.

"You've got yellow hair," the man said, "and these are interesting clothes."

"They're pyjamas," Sammy said, staring past the guy at the feathered monster waiting patiently behind him.

"Pyjamas," the man repeated. "We don't get to see the latest clothes styles on our side of the forest. I'll have to look into these 'pyjamas', as you call them. They look exotic."

"They're what I wear to bed. I don't normally leave the house like this."

The young man watched her a moment, then snapped out of it. "Where are my manners?" he said. "My name's Mehrak Omid."

Sammy opened her mouth to reply, paused. Should she tell him who she was? He could be anyone.

Mehrak smiled. "Are you going to tell me your name?"

She may as well. What difference would it make? "Samantha Ellis," she said, "but you can call me Sammy." She held out her hand.

The man didn't take it. "Your name sounds familiar. Should I know you?"

"No," Sammy said. She took her hand back. "I'm not from here."

"Well, no one is from *right* here. We're in the middle of nowhere." He paused. "How did you get here?"

"I don't know. I was messing around with the clock hands of a glowing emerald bracelet that was under my mum's bed. Then it exploded and it must've knocked me out or something because I woke up here." She looked up at the dinosaur. It had its mouth open and was angling its ears back and forth on their stalks. "Where am I?"

"You're somewhere near the centre of the Fungi Forest, a little over two days' travel from Honton Keep."

"We're not on Earth any more, are we?"

"Earth?"

"Of course we aren't." Sammy exhaled, stared down at her feet. "I've been teleported to a strange planet, in a faraway galaxy."

Mehrak put a hand on her shoulder. "I'm sure we can get you back to Earth."

"Really?" Sammy pretended to straighten up so Mehrak's hand fell away. She didn't feel comfortable with this strange person being so familiar and edged away, closer to the mushrooms.

"Sure. Tell me which towns are closest to Earth. We'll figure out how to get you there."

Sammy pulled at the hood of a waist-high mushroom. Tiny glowing spores drifted down from the disturbed gills, like dust particles caught in sunlight. It reminded her of home and the sun's rays that slanted through her bedroom window on summer mornings.

"So are you going to tell me where Earth is?" Mehrak asked.

Sammy pointed up. "Probably somewhere up there. Earth is my world."

"World?"

"Yeah. Where we have blue skies and no giant mushrooms."

"Blue skies?" Mehrak frowned, then snorted. "Where are you really from?"

"I'm not joking." Her dad wouldn't let someone disrespect him like that; although he probably wouldn't argue with a guy who had a dinosaur at his back.

"How did you get here then?" Mehrak crossed his arms.

"I told you already. The bracelet brought me here. I dialled the golden hands to midnight, and then it exploded."

Mehrak didn't say anything further, but he didn't look convinced. "Would you like a lift with us?"

"Us?" Sammy asked. "Who else is with you?"

"Louis," Mehrak said, gesturing behind him.

"I don't see him. Is he inside the shell?"

"No. He's carrying the shell. And it's not a shell, it's a cottage. Well, I call it a cottage; technically it's a caravan."

"That creature is Louis?"

The leaf-shaped ears on the dinosaur's head rotated and bent, each ear moving independently of the other and creating a series of poses.

"Yes, I know," Mehrak said to the dinosaur. He turned back to Sammy. "Louis doesn't respond favourably to 'that creature'."

"I'm sorry. I didn't realise he could ... you know, with his ears."

"He's a giant gastrosaur," Mehrak said, adopting a patronising tone. "It's what they do."

"Yeah. And, obviously, I don't know what one of those is. Because I don't come from here. You ever heard of an elephant?"

"I have, actually. I've read about them. They're extinct."

A tendril of warm air slipped out of the forest and looped around Sammy's neck. "Okay. I'll go with you," she said.

"Now you'll come?"

"Something's chasing me."

"Something?" Mehrak stiffened. "What sort of something?"

"A tall, skinny thing in a black cloak."

"Thing?"

"I couldn't see what it looked like exactly. It was person-shaped but taller."

Mehrak let out his breath and seemed to relax. "Did you see it in a ghost village?"

"Er ... yeah, I suppose. It was deserted."

"A survivor. Most people don't survive long in the Fungi Forest. But some hermits make it work. He was probably chasing you out of his territory."

"I don't think it was a person. It moved really weirdly and was really hot and burnt everything."

"Survivors are strange—you'd have to be to live out here—and the forest can get hot at times. Did he say anything?"

"*It* said it wanted to help me, kept talking about 'others', like it had friends or something. It wanted me to meet them."

"Definitely a survivor, and definitely crazy. His friends are probably a collection of funny shaped rocks."

"So you don't live here in the forest?"

"Certainly not. We're just travelling through. You're lucky Louis smelt you."

"Smelt me?"

"Relax. Louis has an amazing sense of smell; you aren't smelly. Well, to him you are, but probably in a nice way." He flushed and cleared his throat. "Anyway. What I mean is Louis smelt that you were all alone so we took a detour to come and rescue you. There's probably not another human being within six hundred stadia."

"Six hundred stadia? That sounds like a really long way."

"It's a good two days' travel for Louis and that's if he keeps a steady pace going without too many breaks. Not easy with a cottage on your back, as you can imagine."

"And you live in there?" Sammy stared up at the golden eggs shimmering in the mushroom light.

"Of course." Mehrak paused. "Come with us. I can't have you dying alone in the forest on my conscience."

"What if my mum comes after me?"

"You're sticking with that story, are you?"

Sammy folded her arms and glowered at him.

Mehrak sighed. "It's too risky to hang around here. Louis and I only passed this way because it's the quickest way to the Keep."

Sammy said nothing.

"Look. The forest's huge. Even if your mother followed you in, you'd never find each other again. Platoons of soldiers have entered the Fungi Forest and never been seen again. You're lucky to still be alive. Your best bet is to head to the closest big city and hope your mother makes it there too. Honton Keep is the nearest and biggest. And you're in luck because that's also where we're heading."

Sammy looked up at Louis and the shell caravan. What other choice did she have?

–TEN–
EGGIE

When she was younger, Sammy's mum had told her never to get into a stranger's car, so ordinarily she wouldn't have climbed into a stranger's giant egg—or pair of eggs—on top of a dinosaur, but she figured it would be much safer travelling with Mehrak than staying by herself in the mushroom forest. And odd as he was, he was nowhere near as scary as that figure in black had been.

The egg house on Louis's back did look pretty awesome too. She should at least see inside, check it out.

It was a shame her house in Sheffield wasn't on the back of a dinosaur. Everyone would notice her rocking up at school on the back of a T-Rex. The only thing missing was a couple of laser cannons on either side. If Mehrak got those installed, his house would be perfect.

"Are you hungry?" Mehrak asked. "Can I prepare you something?"

"I am hungry, I suppose." Sammy smiled, or rather tried to. Getting a lift out of the forest was probably the right thing to do, but it felt like she was abandoning her mother.

"Don't be upset," Mehrak said. "You're going to be okay now." He smiled. "I'll show you around the cottage, then rustle up some soup. It'll be nice to have some company."

Louis turned to Mehrak and his ears flapped, rotated and held three or four different poses. Then he crouched down to lie on his stomach.

"What did he say?" Sammy asked.

"That he's taking a nap. He's been walking all day and he's tired. Come on, we'll go inside."

Sammy followed Mehrak around the side of Louis and 'Golden Egg Cottage'.

"How do you know what he's saying?" Sammy asked.

"Sign language."

Mehrak stopped at the back of the main egg. There was a small, circular brass door at the bottom, like a submarine escape hatch. Sammy watched Louis's tail sweep side to side along the ground. It was as thick as a two-person canoe, and several times as long. It almost didn't look real, like one of those giant anacondas on a late night, made-for-TV, sci-fi movie.

"You really haven't heard of a giant gastrosaur before, have you?" Mehrak said.

"No. I really haven't."

"Gastrosaur voices are too high-pitched for us to hear, so they communicate with their ears. Their voices are used for navigation because they don't have eyes. Echo location, they call it. It allows them to build a mental three-dimensional image of their surroundings."

Mehrak turned the wheel on the door. There was a clunk and he pulled it open. Louis's tail curled and looped round under the opening.

"Step onto his tail," Mehrak said. "He'll hoist you up."

Sammy raised her eyebrows and gave Mehrak a pointed look.

"Come on."

Sammy maintained eye contact a moment longer, then carefully transferred her weight onto Louis's tail. She fell forward as Louis boosted her up and into the hatch. She gripped onto the stairs on the other side while simultaneously trying to hold her pyjama bottoms up. Her cheeks flushed as she imagined the view Mehrak was getting of her undignified flailing.

Sammy tucked her top into her bottoms and climbed towards the rainbow-coloured shapes swirling in the light at the end of the staircase.

She emerged into a circular, golden kitchen with a single round porthole.

The bright colours belonged to a mobile comprised of hundreds of multi-coloured paper birds. It hung from the high-pointed apex and took up the entire top third of the egg. A chunky green table sat in the centre of the room, sandwiched between two equally chunky green benches, and a copper work surface curved around one half of the wall, with cabinets above it and a plumbed-in sink at one end. A water pump above the sink fed down into a hole in the floor, and a stove and coal bucket sat against the opposite wall with various copper pots and pans dangling above.

Oil lamps fixed to the walls gave a dim but cosy glow that illuminated the birds and projected their colours onto the walls as they turned.

A second staircase followed the curve of the room to a hole halfway up the wall.

"Are they the stairs to the other egg?" Sammy asked.

Mehrak smiled. "Why don't you go up and take in the view from the top?"

Sammy sprinted up the stairs. She probably looked like a giddy child, but she didn't care. The cottage was seriously cool.

At the hole in the wall, the stairs tightened into a corkscrew as they spiralled up, emerging in the centre of the floor of the second egg. The second room was around two-thirds the size of the kitchen, but with blue walls and a wrought iron chandelier in the peak of the ceiling. Furniture-wise, everything was green and there wasn't much of it; a small four-poster bed, a wardrobe, a chair and a small set of shelves holding six books. A waist-high safety rail fenced off the top of the stairs and around it lay a red, doughnut-shaped carpet. On either side of the room were two arched doorways with red velvet curtains.

Sammy opened a gate in the safety rail and stepped into the room. "You really like green furniture, don't you?" she said to Mehrak, as he came up into the room behind her.

He shrugged. "It's not something I spend a lot of time thinking about, to be honest."

Sammy approached the doorway that she supposed led to the front balcony and pushed through the curtains. On the other side, the long, wide balcony stretched out from the tower. It reminded her of the ship's bow in the famous scene from Titanic. She walked over to stand at the end. She wasn't enough of a dork to reproduce the pose from the movie, with her arms stretched out, although for a moment she considered it.

It was dark above the mushrooms. Their hoods suppressed the glow underneath, only allowing sharp spears of light to escape the gaps, spiking upwards towards the sky, while the shifting purple cloud patterns above made muddy brown waves on their curved surfaces.

Sammy leant over the railing. Louis's head was obscured by a mushroom but she could hear him chewing on something below. He shifted then and the floor dipped. She stumbled and grabbed hold of the railing.

"You'll get used to it," Mehrak said, smiling.

Sammy let go of the railing, doing her best to downplay her moment of clumsiness. "Do you live here by yourself?" she asked.

Mehrak pulled at the hairline of his turban awkwardly and his eyes took on a vacant glassiness. "Currently, yes," he said.

She'd struck a nerve. She wished she hadn't said anything. "It's a great house," she said, "… I mean, cottage."

Mehrak stared away, across the mushroom forest, without saying anything.

"Does everyone here have a gastrosaur cottage?"

"No." Mehrak exhaled. "My wife and I were given it as a wedding present." He turned away. *Wife?* Mehrak didn't look old enough to be married. He could only have been twenty-one or twenty-two years old, max.

"I'll go downstairs and make your soup." He headed towards the tower.

"Why are you here?" Sammy asked. "In the forest, I mean?"

Mehrak stopped. "I'm on an expedition." He had his back to her and didn't turn around. "An expedition for … for a mythical artefact, a book. It's silly, really. It probably doesn't exist but …" He didn't continue.

"But you must think it does because you're out here looking for it."

Mehrak turned back towards her. "I never believed in it until my grandfather …" He stopped again. "No. It's stupid."

"Go on. Please?"

Mehrak smiled wistfully. "My grandfather was a historian. He spent most of his life travelling and we hardly ever saw him. He'd be gone for a year at a time, sometimes longer. Each time he returned, he'd tell me of all the amazing adventures he'd had, all the places he'd seen." Mehrak cast his eyes down. "But when he returned from his last trip, he had a wound across his chest. He'd tried to patch it up himself, but in the days it had taken him to get back to Dungalor it'd gone gangrenous. There was nothing anyone could do. I remember the day he died; I was only eight at the time. The doctor came to find me to pass on his final words, along with his diary. I was the only person he had a message for. There was nothing for my grandmother or mother. He passed away without saying anything to anyone, but me. Only four words, 'The book is real'."

"The diary is real?"

"Not the diary. I've read it cover to cover several times. The diary's about solving the whereabouts of the *Rule Book*."

"The *Rule Book* is the mythical book you're looking for? And it's real?"

"That's what my grandfather believed. But I can't make sense of his notes. I'm hoping my friend Bertie at the Keep will figure it out. He's a historian like my grandfather but he's also into theology and mythology. You should tell him about your exploding emerald bracelet. He might've heard of it." Mehrak paused. "Well, you know your way round Eggie …"

"Eggie?"

"Short for Golden Egg Cottage," he said. "Why don't you take a nap? You look tired."

Sammy had temporarily forgotten how tired she was. And now that Mehrak had reminded her, the weight of it hung heavy on her shoulders. She rubbed her eyes and followed him back into the bedroom.

"Get some sleep," he said, leading her to the bed. "I'll wake you when the food is ready."

————

The girl was asleep the moment her head touched the pillow. Mehrak pulled the sheets up over her and tucked them in around her slender neck. With a finger, he dragged a couple of errant strands of hair back behind her ear. Her eyes darted back and forth under her eyelids as she dreamed, yet her face was peaceful. He watched her sleep a moment, then turned and went downstairs.

Why had he told her about his grandfather and the diary? He supposed it was because she was vulnerable. And pretty. He shook his head. She was young and he shouldn't be noticing things like that; he was married. His chest tightened with guilt as he thought of Gisouie and how he missed her.

He fetched a roan shrub root from a cabinet and placed it on the work surface. With a knife, he sliced down through its orange flesh, then stopped. He'd only ever told Gisouie about the diary. Now he'd given away their secret, and it upset him. It shouldn't; it shouldn't matter in the slightest. The *Rule Book* was a myth. They'd only followed his grandfather's diary to see where it led them, for the adventure of it. They'd been forced to leave town, so why not go in search of the book? And now he felt like he'd lost a part of Gisouie by sharing their secret. Why had he even brought it up? He didn't really believe in it. He'd just met this girl and he was already telling her his secrets.

He'd been alone too long. That's all it was. He'd picked up a vulnerable young woman and he'd wanted to reassure her, tell her something about himself to make her feel at ease. But the *Rule Book*? She'd think he was a fool chasing fairy tales, like devout Zoroastrians blindly following scripture written a thousand years ago. She'd come out with an equally ridiculous story, though. The Mother World? He scoffed. But she had been so sincere; he almost wanted to believe her.

No. He was going soft in the head. Her story was a fiction. Something had happened to Sammy's parents, something traumatic. The story was her way of dealing with it. She'd convinced herself it had really happened and blocked out the real events. The poor child had probably been through hell.

When they arrived at Honton Keep, he'd drop her off … somewhere. He didn't know where yet. She'd be okay and would forget all about him and his silly quest. Then he could continue on his journey alone. Except he didn't want to carry on alone; he missed having someone around. He missed Gisouie; missed her so much his heart ached. Sammy was alone and needed someone to look after her. Gisouie wasn't here, and although he hadn't forgotten his duties as a husband, this girl needed him too.

He would take her with him, but that was all. She needed him. And for the moment, he needed her too.

–ELEVEN–
Welcome to Perseopia

Sammy woke as Mehrak kicked the stairwell gate closed behind him.

"You've slept in late," he said as he brought two steaming cups over to the bedside. "It's nearly lunchtime."

The chandelier in the ceiling swung left and right in time to slow beats that reverberated up through the cottage.

They were on the move.

Sammy rubbed her eyes with her palms.

Mehrak held out a cup. "Mushroom tea," he said.

Sammy took it. "How long have we been travelling?"

"I'm not sure exactly. We set off early this morning, so we've been going a while."

Sammy slid out of bed, cupping her tea carefully. She shuffled to the doorway leading to the front balcony, stopped for a cavernous yawn that made her hands shake and her tea slop, then she pushed forward through the curtains to find …

"It's still dark."

"It is," Mehrak said, as he followed her out. "What did you expect?"

"I thought it would be brighter." Sammy walked to the railing and leant on it. "Where's the sun? You said it was morning."

"Sun?"

"The big yellow ball that floats into the sky when it's daytime."

"I've seen paintings of that big yellow ball in museums," Mehrak said. "I've only ever read about daytime in history books, though. A bright glowing sphere in a blue sky. We used to get *the sun*, as you call it, a few hundred years ago." He stopped. "You know, you're a pretty convincing Mother Worlder."

"What's one of them?"

"That's what people from the Mother World are called. The place you say you come from—"

"Where I *do* come from. I think. And how come you've heard of where I come from? I don't know anything about this place." Sammy made a broad gesture with her cup, slopping some of its contents over the railing. "Sorry, Louis," she called down, hoping she hadn't spilt any on him. He didn't flinch so perhaps she'd got away with it.

She turned to Mehrak. "What is this place?"

"It's Perseopia," he said. "As if you didn't know."

"I don't, actually. Wait. Perseopia?" she said. "I have heard of Perseopia."

"What a surprise."

Sammy clenched her teeth and took a long breath. "The old woman that gave me the bracelet with the dial, Esther, she said something about Perseopia. So this world is Perseopia?"

"It's more of a realm than a world, but yeah, this place is Perseopia. We used to be part of your world twelve hundred years ago."

"So why doesn't anyone where I come from know about this place, except for that old woman?"

"Because Perseopia was sealed from the Mother World to keep it perfect." Mehrak made a gesture that looked like he was tracing the shape of a rainbow in the sky. "A secret paradise away from overpopulation, disease and corruption."

"This is the place that was sealed away by that shepherd."

"Yeah. His name was Yima and he sealed Perseopia with a golden ring. Information that a Mother Worlder wouldn't know."

"A Mother Worlder like me, you mean?"

"If you say so."

"Esther knew about it."

60

Mehrak shrugged. "But a Mother Worlder wouldn't."

"Says who?"

"Did she use the word 'Perseopia'?"

"Yeah."

"Because when Yima sealed the Vara, it hadn't been named. It was 'The Vara' and then it was Panoplia. It wasn't Perseopia until centuries after the realm had been closed off from the Mother World." Mehrak shook his head. "Look at me discussing this with you like you're really from there."

Sammy forced down her frustration and turned away, but it must've shown.

"I'm sorry," Mehrak said. "I just don't believe in any of it. All that stuff I told you comes straight out of scripture. I know the stories because I was forced to go to the temple with my parents as a boy. That doesn't mean I believe it all. The great Ahura Mazda, the Mother World, Yima creating the Vara, they're just stories."

"Whatever. You don't believe in the Mother World. But what's happened to this place? Esther said it became polluted by a great evil or something."

"You really don't know?"

"Pretend I'm actually telling the truth and humour me."

Mehrak exhaled. "It was a paradise for a long time, until the Assault on Aratta a hundred and fifty years ago."

"What's an Assault on Aratta?"

"The great battle of Aratta, Perseopia's first capital." Mehrak stopped.

Sammy waited for him to go on, but he didn't. She was about to say something when he spoke.

"Okay. I'll tell it," he said at last. He smiled. "It's actually a pretty good story; my nephews used to love me telling it. Just remember, though the battle and sequence of events are historically accurate, the rest of the story has been told and retold, and most likely exaggerated over the years."

"I'll bear that in mind."

Mehrak rubbed his hands together and his eyes sparkled. "When the realm was created it was called Panoplia and the first sultan was handpicked by the great Ahura Mazda himself. Or so they say."

"Ahura's your god?"

"The god of the people that believe in him, yeah. He's supposedly the uncreated creator. Anyway, Ahura picked the first sultan to rule Perseopia—or Panoplia. Then that sultan passed on the throne to his son, who passed it on to his son, and so on through the generations. Over a thousand years passed in relative peace until the last sultan, Sultan Sanjar, became ruler. He was a lazy man with little work ethic, and it wasn't long before an advisor convinced him to delegate away his duties. This advisor was Moran Razin, and he was appointed to the position of regent so that he could take care of the boring day-to-day running of the realm. And for a time the arrangement worked well. But Razin had ambition. Slowly, he began to take over. He increased taxes, seized land, built his armies. Eventually, he imprisoned the Sultan himself and took over Perseopia entirely."

"Didn't anyone try to stop him?"

"Razin was too powerful by then. He had command of the Sultan's armies. People resisted, of course. Small rebel groups formed and skirmishes broke out. Fighting raged on for years until a group began to emerge from the others, a group that grew rapidly and soon became large enough to pose a threat to Razin's men. That group was the Association of Blue Robes. They unified the other rebel groups and together they plotted to overthrow the regent. Now, one of those rebel groups was the Order of the Black Fist, run by the sorcerer Achaemen Mantis. The Order was more cult than rebel group, but Mantis possessed detailed plans of the Sultan's palace so they were enlisted. With Mantis and the Order of the Black Fist on board, the Association hatched a plan to gain access to the palace, rescue the Sultan and return power to the throne."

–TWELVE–
Paradise Ends Like This

Perseopia – 146 years ago

Dust coated Toler Ramone's face, forming a gritty paste at the sides of his mouth and stinging his eyes. He wheezed as he breathed it in, choking on the stench of twenty thousand terrified men. Stress was rising as they squeezed through claustrophobic streets. It manifested itself in twitches of the head and faster, more erratic movements. The men wanted to get to the fight, wanted the excruciating crawl to be over. The crowd jostled Toler back and forth, but always onward. Men in heavy chainmail and cloaked in midnight blue were pressing in on all sides; bodies crushing inward, then spreading out, and back in again. Metal armour plates clanked, squealed across each other. The air thick with dirt churned up from the ground.

The noise was overwhelming. Men were shouting, chanting. Some were crying. There was no dignity in war.

"Mantis!" Toler shouted to the man behind him. "Stay close!"

"I'm trying," came the reply from behind. "We're moving too slowly. We should be there already."

Only the golden dome of the palace was visible over the heads in front; their destination. The Sultan was in there somewhere. That was the only thought rattling around in Toler's head. Perhaps it was a good thing; no time to dwell on forthcoming events as the tide of men pulled him onward, relieving him of indecision. No choices to be made. Only to allow himself to be swept forward.

Aratta was a city he'd been to many times, although not so often in recent years, and never in such circumstances. He gazed up at the sky. Clouds floated carefree across the azure. The same view he'd taken in a year ago on the farm at Whitstrom. The brotherhood had sent him to Fione's farm to stand guard against the return of Razin's mercenaries. Two years earlier, they'd stolen her money and made a widow of her, and word was they were on their way back. Fione was a strong woman; she'd struggled on through the heartache of losing her husband, carried on tending the animals and the crops, and still found time to raise her daughters. Toler didn't know how she'd managed it.

He'd spent sixty days and nights at the farm waiting for Razin's thugs to arrive to collect their protection racket. And those days had been the happiest of his life. During the day, he helped Fione work the land. In the evenings, they played in the fields with the children. After supper, they'd put Sissi and Peonie to bed, then lie outside in the long grass and watch the sky turn red.

Toler made short work of Razin's men when they arrived. And, when it was over, he received his orders to move on. He wanted to stay with Fione, to be with her and become part of her family. He wanted to raise Sissi and Peonie as his own, but he didn't; he couldn't. He'd been given orders to move on and that's what he'd done. He told Fione he would return one day, when he'd made Perseopia a safe place for the children, and he often wondered if he'd be able to honour that promise. Perhaps today he would. This was the final push. They would breach the palace and restore the Sultan to the throne. When the day was done, he'd leave the brotherhood and never look back. He would return to Whitstrom, marry Fione and become the father of her children. His hand went to the bead necklace that little Peonie had made for him. Crude wooden beads, hand painted. He closed his eyes while he turned them on the string. The farm appeared in his mind's eye.

And he tripped over a body.

Clutching his staff, he steadied himself and remained upright. They'd reached the inner city. The palace loomed, frowning down on the tiny men that dared approach its walls. Not far now.

The buildings were taller in this part of the city; expensive houses owned by lords and ladies. Their height seemed to put more distance between Toler and the sky, pushing his daydream further out of reach to just a thin strip of sapphire.

A loud blast rang out, shaking the ground. Clods of earth and masonry rained from the sky, then momentary silence. Toler was transported back to his mind's eye; a place of light and clouds. Fione, Sissi and Peonie were all there. A distant ringing registered through the mists. They smiled, reaching out with their hands. He reached towards them as the sounds of battle returned, and Toler was climbing bodies. Dead Association men and palace guards; some face down, some staring up at him with glassy eyes.

Achaemen Mantis stumbled behind, clinging to the back of Toler's cloak. He was a scrawny and squinting man, with pale skin, long finger nails and shapeless black clothes that would fit a person twice his size.

Toler didn't trust him. How this man had managed to gather so many followers in such a short amount of time was frightening. And he'd convinced them all he was a sorcerer, too. Fools. Mantis had no power, he was just weird. All he had was information; information that he could've passed on to the Association instead of coming along as a hindrance.

Toler shouted back to him, "We're nearly at the gates."

"We need to go a different way!" Mantis called forward, peering over his nose with narrowed eyes, his mouth barely moving as he spoke.

The men in front parted and they found themselves facing a wall of palace guards all dressed in identical red cloaks and gold armour.

Swords clashed, people screamed. One Association man stood tall above the others, in the middle of the palace guards, cut off from his men but revelling in the carnage of battle. A bear of a man, head and shoulders taller than anyone else, baring his teeth savagely. He roared like a feral beast as he cut down the palace guards with his broadsword, swinging it singlehandedly, scything through them like grass: General Azim Azertash, known simply as the General.

Toler tried to hold Mantis back as their own men surged behind, pushing them both forward. There were too many palace guards, and no way to get through them to the General. Association men streamed past on either side and into the fray; there was nowhere else to go. He needed to buy some time. The glossy black sphere at the top of his staff ignited, releasing pure white light. He fired a burst of lightning from it, scattering the guards ahead.

A lean man with an unruly cloud of frizzy hair covering his head and chin appeared close by, firing bursts of lightning from his staff into the palace guards.

"Nasser!" Toler called out.

The man fought his way closer. "We need to get you both to the General," he shouted. "He'll get you inside."

"It's too late," Mantis said. He pointed to the palace gates as they began to close, sealing off the only route through the impenetrable outer walls.

"We'll get them open," Nasser shouted, as he fought his way into the guards. "Keep Mantis safe."

The boom of a tremendous bolt sliding home echoed across the battlefield. They'd lost their advantage, maybe even the battle. Mantis needed to be on the other side of that gate, and Toler wouldn't be able to keep him alive long enough for them to open again. Some of the Association men had made it inside, but without back-up, they were as good as dead.

"Follow me," Mantis said.

"Wait," Toler called back. "We control the protective barrier over the palace. We can remove it and destroy the gates. We just need more time."

"There's a better way. Can you get me over there?" Mantis pointed towards an alley between two houses.

Toler forced his way towards the alley, dragging Mantis behind him. They fought through the torrent of men and disappeared down the passage.

"Where now?" Toler asked as they ran. "The protective barrier strengthening the gates is controlled by the brotherhood. When more of us arrive, we can remove the enchantment."

"By that time I'd be dead," Mantis said, wiping sweat from his face with his sleeve. "My job is to lead you to the Sultan. Yours is to follow my instructions and to keep me alive."

As much as he hated to admit it, Toler had been given exactly those instructions; do what he says, keep him alive.

They left the alley, crossed a deserted street, and entered another alley. Two guards heading in the opposite direction met with cracks from Toler's staff and hit the floor. Mantis's eyes lingered on them as they passed, but he said nothing.

The clatter of battle faded as they worked their way through the maze of expensive two- and three-storey houses owned by the lords and ladies of Aratta. Women, children and cowards were locking up their homes and battening down the window shutters. They acted like supporters of Razin in public, but behind closed doors they all supported the Association. They'd give them no trouble.

Mantis stopped. "Here," he said.

A stone block structure stood detached from the other buildings. It had an octagonal footprint with a domed roof. And there was something unusual about it, something Toler couldn't place. Then he realised, no windows. The only feature in the blank façade was a wooden door braced with thick steel bars.

Mantis nodded at the bolt securing the door.

Toler blew the lock with a blast from his staff and the door swung open.

The building was a hollow shell. Toler judged it to be around three storeys to the ceiling with no internal floors, aside from the sand-covered ground floor they'd walked in on. Mantis pushed the door closed behind them. A single beam of sunlight from a hole in the roof illuminated the interior of the building.

"Now what?" Toler asked.

Mantis jogged to the centre of the space and dropped to his knees. He began sifting through the sand until he found a metal ring pull.

Realising what Mantis was doing, Toler helped clear the trapdoor and heave it open. A black void waited below. Mantis went ahead. Toler ignited his staff and set off down the curved stone staircase after him. At the bottom, a long, straight passageway, carved into the stone, sloped downward in the general direction of the palace.

"How long has this tunnel been here?" Toler asked.

"Six years. Razin built it as an escape route in the event that the brotherhood betrayed him." He scampered ahead of Toler, his shadow stretching ahead in the staff light.

"Betrayed him?" Toler said, jogging to keep up. "He betrayed his people."

"Not my words, Master Ramone," Mantis said as he ran. "Take up your argument with Razin when we find him."

"This is pointless. The protective barrier encloses the entire palace, not just the gates. It can't be tunnelled under."

Mantis kept running. "It would be pointless if a hole in the barrier hadn't been made," he called back.

Toler stopped. It wasn't possible. "No one could breach our enchantment." Yet, as soon as he said it, he began doubting himself. How else had this tunnel come to be there?

"It is possible and they have," Mantis said, pausing to catch his breath. "We've already crossed the barrier. Hurry up with the light. I can't see where I'm going."

The atmosphere had changed. When Toler closed his eyes and concentrated, he could feel it. Mantis was right; they were on the other side. "How did you know about the hole and this tunnel? Razin would have told no one."

"We don't have time for this," Mantis said, his face shining with sweat in the staff light, his eyes wide and nervous. "My plans have specific time-based deadlines. I explained this to your master!"

"You created the hole …"

"We have to keep going."

"We should stay here and wait for Razin to come to us," Toler said, panicked, his head reeling. "He knows it's only a matter of time before we remove the barrier. He'll be preparing to escape the palace through this tunnel."

"We can't take on Razin in this confined space while he has the Sultan with him, it's too risky. We need to get to the Sultan before the gates give in and Razin prepares to leave. Right now he thinks he's safe because the gates are secure. Security will be minimal. When we've rescued the Sultan, you can go back for Razin. I shouldn't have to explain myself to you. You're the muscle, not the brains. I was told I'd get your full support. Just do your job!"

Mantis turned away but Toler grabbed him by the arm and spun him back around. "You should watch your mouth. I may only be the muscle, but I know this isn't the plan you agreed with the Association. I don't know how you've tunnelled through the barrier, or why you kept this part of the plan secret, but if anything happens, I'll feed you to the General."

Mantis glared back at Toler, seething, but said nothing.

They carried on in silence, Toler's stomach clenched in a knot of rage. The situation was all wrong. He should never have taken the job of guarding Mantis. He'd been given the assignment because he always followed orders. Just like when he was told to leave Fione and the girls. He was a 'yes' man. That's what everyone thought, at least. But they were wrong. He followed orders because he believed in the cause. Once the battle was over, he'd leave the brotherhood and never return.

Toler watched Mantis scuttling along in his creepy, snivelling way. The man couldn't really be a sorcerer. No one had more power than the brotherhood. Yet, a hole had been made in their barrier; he'd felt them pass through it. The barrier had even seemed stronger than it had been when powered solely by the brotherhood. Much as he hated to admit it, Mantis did have power. It explained how he'd amassed his cult of followers and how he'd managed to gain Razin's trust. But how had a man with all that power slipped by the brotherhood undetected? In the end, Toler supposed that none of it mattered. After today he wouldn't have to worry about Mantis again.

They followed the tunnel up a gradual incline to a stone staircase. At the top, a solid wooden panel blocked their way.

"The hinge is on the left. It opens out," Mantis said, and grabbed Toler's arm. "Please try to be quiet. We're entering the Sultan's, or should I say Razin's, private quarters."

Toler shook off Mantis and pushed on the panel. It opened into an enormous, plush suite filled with beds and divans upholstered in multi-coloured fabrics and dressed in tasselled cushions. Every item seemed to be gilded, and all the surfaces were cluttered with vases or marble busts. The décor was a million stadia from the functional simplicity of Fione's farmstead and Toler wondered how anyone could need all this pointless fluff. Children were starving in the ghettos outside Aratta, and Razin still extorted taxes and hoarded wealth.

"Where now?" Toler asked.

"We head towards the command room where Razin will be running battle operations. He'll have the Sultan close in case he needs to flee, so we should check the adjacent meeting rooms."

"How do you know the Sultan won't be in the command room with him?"

"Razin won't want him with the heads of military. Many of them still believe Razin is acting on the Sultan's orders. Razin will keep the Sultan separate, but close enough in case he needs a hostage. If we're quiet, we should be able to extract the Sultan and return for Razin before he realises anything has happened."

"If the plan was always this simple, why did you need to come too? You could have told us how to find the Sultan."

"I'm the only person that can use the escape tunnel while the barrier is up. You only got through because you were with me. Razin doesn't know that's possible, so he still thinks he's safe. Why do you think the passage was unguarded?"

Toler said nothing. The plan was too simple. Mantis hadn't explained any of this to the Association. The guy was up to something. Toler couldn't decide what that was yet, but he'd remain watchful.

They prowled through the deserted corridors and staircases, working their way towards the upper floors of the palace. They kept to the shadows and ducked out of sight each time a guard patrol passed. Eventually, a tall flight of stairs took them to a vast gallery, with high leaded windows to their right.

Toler approached the glass. The golden dome bulged out above the windows. Below, the courtyard was filled with hundreds of palace guards. Some were manning the high walls, firing arrows down on the Association men on the other side. All were facing away from the palace, no doubt assuming the attack would come from the outside.

It was only at this height that Toler could appreciate the sheer volume of people invested in the battle and how small and insignificant they looked from where he stood. As Toler turned away, a terrific boom echoed up from the courtyard.

"The barrier has been breached!" Mantis yelped. "I thought we'd have more time. Razin will snatch the Sultan and head for the escape passage. Quick!"

They ran along the gallery as the palace courtyard filled below, blue robes gushing through the gates like water from a burst dam.

They took a corridor to the left, away from the windows. Two men were guarding a doorway halfway down. Toler took them out without breaking stride, two quick snaps of light from his staff and they hit the floor, wisps of steam curling off their bodies.

"This must be the room," Mantis said as he burst through the door.

Toler followed.

The Sultan was on a divan in the centre of the room, dressed in the type of silken fabrics a sultan would wear, but baggy. He was thinner than Toler had ever seen him, beaten and worn down, reduced to a puppet with hollow eyes. He still wore the ceremonial robes of a sultan, but he hadn't ruled in a long time.

There were two guards with him. And five more entered through the door behind. Razin would've sent them to fetch him when the gates blew.

Toler flew across the room, putting himself between the Sultan and the guards.

As in every fight Toler engaged in, his opponents seemed to come at him in slow motion. Each sword thrust, he calmly sidestepped, each blow carefully batted away with his staff. They all came at once and all went down the same way; a bolt to the head, each one. As he fought, the flash of a knife registered in his peripheral vision, sliding out from inside Mantis's cloak. Did the sorcerer believe he'd be of any use in the fight?

"Forgive my actions, great Ahura," Mantis cried. "Gassonda Vasso Antargarth, Le sonda Ramaask!"

Toler realised what was happening, but too late. He fired at Mantis, but he was already on top of the Sultan and they both fell together.

Toler rushed over, threw Mantis aside, and rolled the Sultan over. The blade was hilt deep in his chest, his mouth opening and closing like a landed trout. He convulsed once, twice, and his eyes rolled up into his head.

Then his stomach inflated. Slowly at first, but it kept going. As it expanded, purple smoke burst from the edges of the knife, racing out, whistling.

Toler leapt back, the smoke choking him. Viscose and cloying, it coated his nasal passages, burned his throat. He couldn't breathe, his lungs weren't inflating. He stumbled back, lightheaded, and went down.

Toler opened his eyes under a blanket of purple. His chest was in agony, but he could still breathe, just. His nostrils and throat were shredded, eyes burning. The top half of the room above him swirled and undulated. He started coughing, then retching, and couldn't stop until the contents of his stomach forced their way up and onto the floor, pooling around his hands, black as tar.

He had to get out. He wiped his face with a sleeve, spat the residue from his mouth and crawled for the door. He passed Mantis, his eyes wide and lifeless. The situation was a mess. How could he explain what had happened? He couldn't even rationalise it to himself. Perhaps he could retrieve the Sultan's body. Toler scanned the room and saw him lying on his back where the smoke was thickest, his body was inflated and his limbs floated off the floor as if he were underwater. The Sultan's swollen head turned, producing a sick, gargling noise as it did so. His eyes had popped out of their sockets and his tongue distended from his mouth like a giant pink slug.

He couldn't still be alive, could he? Toler should try to rescue him, but the smoke was too thick, and he was as good as dead with that knife in his chest.

Toler had to get out. He got to his feet and vomited again as he staggered for the door.

He met no one on his way down through the palace. When he reached the entrance hall, the palace doors burst open, splintering off their hinges.

He slumped down against a column at the foot of the stairs.

The General came striding in across the marble floor, leading a small group of Association men. "Find Razin," he shouted, as he approached the staircase. "And when you do, bring him to me."

The General stopped next to the column Toler lay propped up against and glanced down at him. "Comfortable down there, are we, Master Ramone? You relax while I clear up for you." He snorted and mounted the stairs, taking two at a time.

Toler's throat had virtually closed and he found himself unable to reply. He watched the General go. He should've tried to warn him, but it would've done no good. The General would've ignored any advice he gave. Instead, he should worry about getting himself to safety. He struggled to his feet, dragging himself across the hall and out of the doors.

Outside, the guards were fleeing and the courtyard was emptying. The battle was over.

Toler stumbled down the steps, using his staff as a crutch. At the bottom, he dropped to one knee to throw up again, puking up more tar. His body kept retching, well after he'd emptied his stomach. Behind him, a muted bang preceded an earth-shattering eruption that blew out the windows from the gallery above and spat needles of glass into the sky. The sparkling crystals hung in the air like magic dust, then fell.

Toler forced himself to move, but not fast enough. Millions of tiny knives embedded themselves into his back, and he dropped. Men that had been directly below the windows were reduced to glossy red imitations of themselves, clutching their faces, screaming and writhing on the floor.

Purple smoke billowed from the empty windows.

Most guards and Association men had gone now. Only those that had been floored by the tsunami of smoke remained. They lay where they fell, eyes bulging and fingers raking at their throats.

Toler couldn't stop coughing and couldn't get up. Then, a hand took him under the arms. Nasser was there. He had a piece of cloth tied over his face, covering his nose and mouth, but Toler recognised him by his frizzy hair. With the help of two other men in makeshift masks, they pulled Toler from the palace towards the gates, zigzagging between the bodies on the floor.

The second explosion was worse.

Nasser was at Toler's side one moment, the next, he'd gone. Toler's body skipped across the flagstones in silence, ear drums shot, bones fracturing each time they made contact with the ground. He lost track of up and down.

The pain didn't register until he rolled to a stop, and then it was all he felt; piercing and exquisite in its totality. He lay in silence, in a heap of twisted limbs, eyes clenched tight, delirious with pain. He couldn't move, couldn't control his body. Every part of him existed to cause agony.

It was some time before his hearing returned and he was able to open his eyes.

The scene before him was like nothing he could've imagined. Part of the palace dome had gone. In its place, a broad column of purple smoke rose from the hole like a gnarled and knotted rope. At the top, it curled over itself into a giant mushroom, casting a shadow over the city and bringing a premature dusk to the courtyard. Midday turned night. It was like being back at the farmstead, in the field with Fione at the end of the day. Toler imagined Fione with him now, watching the day come to an end, the fields ploughed, animals fed and the girls safe in their beds. Their troubles would be over now that Razin was dead. No one inside the palace could have survived that explosion. In some strange way, Toler felt a sense of peace. He had secured his family's safety by destroying Razin, and now they were free. Through the searing pain, he managed to get a hand to his neck, to touch the bead necklace. He turned the beads on their string, picturing his girls' faces.

He prayed that Fione would cope without him, knowing with certainty that she would. He had needed her far more than she'd needed him. A lump formed in his throat when he thought about her moving on with her life without him. If nothing else, they would be safe. He sent one final prayer to his family, then fell still.

Another explosion. A beast-like roar erupted from the palace, ferocious and jubilant, launching rubble into the sky. The debris sailed up into the mushroom cloud, turned over and then plummeted back down, crushing everything beneath.

———

"That was an awesome story."

"It's good, isn't it?" Mehrak said, as he stared out across the mushrooms.

"But not true?"

Mehrak shrugged. "The battle happened. And the skies began clouding over with smog the very same day."

"And there's been no sunlight since?"

"Well. Since the last hundred or so years. It took a while for the skies to completely cloud over."

"But hasn't anyone gone back to find out what happened?"

"Some have tried. But the smog's poisonous. You breathe it in; you hallucinate, you die. Out here in the forest, it's way above our heads so it's not an issue, but in Aratta it's still a problem. A few people have travelled into the city, but none have made it all the way to the palace where the smog's thickest. The few that went in and returned alive raved about angels, monsters and other weird stuff. None could sleep afterwards. I heard they all suffered terrible nightmares and wound up killing themselves."

"And no one knows why it happened?"

"There are theories, but nothing confirmed. Some think that Perseopia existed in a delicate balance of good and evil, and when the Sultan was murdered, it threw out that balance, bringing about the ruin of our paradise. Religious types say that after the Sultan was murdered, our god, Ahura Mazda, lost faith in humanity. And, because all sultans are descended from Yima—the divine appointment by Ahura himself—Ahura allowed demons to pollute the lands with nightmares to cause insanity and create a fifth level of hell."

Sammy shuffled uneasily. "What do you think?"

Mehrak shrugged. "Some sort of ecological disaster? An earthquake rupturing a pocket of poisonous gas? Maybe Mantis was a sorcerer dabbling in the dark arts, who knows? I admit, it's a coincidence that it all happened on the day of the Assault, but I don't believe it's anything to do with 'the Great Ahura Mazda' punishing us for killing the Sultan."

Sammy watched the mushrooms pass them by, bending slowly out of the way and squeaking against the sides of the cottage; the same noise rubber gloves make when dragged across wet crockery.

"I think you came across a waster," Mehrak said.

"Sorry?"

"The person that chased you. Wasters are members of a cult that wander the outer districts of Aratta to experience the hallucinogenic effects of the smog. They claim that it gives them powers of divination—before they die in agony."

"I don't think the creature in the cloak was a person. It was more like a tall, thin monster."

"Skinny, dressed all in black, and we're close to the old capital. I didn't think they ever left the city, but I can't think what else it would be."

"But it was really tall and had a funny voice."

Mehrak shrugged. "Maybe he was just really tall. And the smog burns your throat. Maybe it'd damaged his voice."

"Why do they go into the city if they know the smog will kill them?"

"To see the future before it happens? Because the smog is a drug and they get addicted? Take your pick."

"So eventually this whole realm is going to fill up with smog and everyone who lives here is going to hallucinate until they commit suicide?"

"When you put it like that, it sounds pretty grim. But it'll take hundreds of years for the realm to completely fill up."

"But it's dark and creepy."

"Perseopia's been dark for the best part of a century. No one's old enough to remember what it was like beforehand so no one misses daylight."

"How do you know when it's morning without daylight?"

"The purple clouds stop a lot of the light, but they get slightly brighter during the day. You'll get used to it."

Sammy watched Louis trundling along below, knocking mushrooms aside, causing them to shed thick clouds of glowing spores. Occasionally, she lost him beneath the canopies, giving the impression that the balcony was a boat cutting through an olive-green sea.

"We're okay out here, though, aren't we?" Sammy asked.

"From the smog? Yeah. But there are worse things out here than smog."

–THIRTEEN–
CRABMEN

Sammy peered into the upturned mushroom head in front of her. It was the size of a cereal bowl and inside sat a pile of ground meat, jumbled together with celery-like stalks.

"So that woman that gave you the bracelet," Mehrak said, sitting down in front of her. "She didn't say anything else about how it worked?"

"No," Sammy replied. "I think she was going to …"

"But you fiddled with it before she had the chance?"

"Yeah, something like that." Sammy poked at the food with her fork.

"You think she wanted you to come to Perseopia for a specific reason?"

"I'm not supposed to be here. It should be her instead. She told me she was some sort of chosen one. I think I might've messed things up a little."

"Oh." Mehrak frowned. "Don't play with your food."

"You sound like my mum," Sammy said. She wasn't sure if she wanted to eat the lumpy bits of meat congealing in the sagging mushroom bowl that sat before her. "What is this?"

"Baby mushrooms stuffed with creepers and rat mince."

Sammy's hand flew to her mouth. "Rat? Urgh."

Mehrak flinched. "I spent a long time preparing this while you slept. You don't have to eat my food." He made a move to take it away.

"Wait," Sammy said. "I am hungry. It's just—well—we don't eat rats in the proper world. They have diseases."

Mehrak retracted his hand. "Rats aren't easy to catch. I could have given you some chewy stegohog fillets, but no, I wanted your first meal to be special. Proper world indeed …"

Sammy scooped up a blob of rat mince and creeper stalks. The food sagged on her fork as a thin liquid ran through the prongs. She took a deep breath and shoved it into her mouth. And chewed. It was actually quite good. Mehrak raised his eyebrows, waiting for a reply. Sammy kept her expression neutral and said nothing.

"Would you like a sprinkle of salty legs?" Mehrak asked.

"Salty rat legs?"

"Insect legs. They're good." Mehrak held up a tin can with irregular holes punched in the lid.

Sammy puffed her cheeks out and the word 'gross' lingered on her lips, but she resisted the urge to say it. "Thanks, but I prefer my vermin plain," she said.

"I suppose you don't eat insects where you come from either?" Mehrak tipped the can upside down and shook little twig-shaped appendages over his lunch.

"Not on purpose."

After the meal, Mehrak explained where Sammy could find clean clothes and sent her upstairs with a bucket of water to get cleaned up. She returned to the kitchen in a turquoise wrap-around top, matching silk shoes and a pair of white baggy trousers that pinched in at the ankles.

Mehrak was at the sink, drying the last of the dishes. He turned as Sammy reached the bottom of the stairs and smiled wistfully at her.

"You look beautiful," he said.

Sammy's chest swelled. She wasn't often complimented on her appearance.

"You remind me of my wife."

And the high had gone. She didn't want to hear about Mehrak's absent wife. Then felt guilty for thinking it.

"How much longer until we get to that city?" she asked.

"Honton Keep? A day, day-and-a-half, perhaps."

"What do we do until then? What do you normally do for fun?"

"Well ... I reread my grandfather's *Rule Book* diary or one of his travel journals, and I have some other books too," Mehrak said. "I'm trying to improve my Sanskrit and to learn some Bactrian too, so I suppose I do some of that."

Sammy said nothing.

"We could sing a song?"

Sing? Sammy stared at the multi-coloured birds gliding over the table, hoping that if she didn't make eye contact, the suggestion would glide away too.

"How about we play Chaturanga?" Mehrak said at last.

"Thank God," Sammy said. "How do you play Chattychanga?"

"Chaturanga."

"Whatever."

"I'll get the board," Mehrak said, and went upstairs. He returned not long after carrying an oddly marked chessboard and small cloth bag. "I can't wait to play again. I tried playing Louis once, but he can't see where the pieces are and keeps knocking the board over when he tries to move. And explaining where the pieces are over and over gets boring, fast."

Mehrak laid the board on the table and tipped out the bag, emptying an assortment of red and blue figures and several small stones onto the table. Of the figures, there were elephants, men on horses, men without horses, boats and two noblemen who looked like kings. He arranged the pieces on the board so that the red pieces were in front of Sammy and the blue pieces in front of him, then he sat down.

"How come I have fewer pieces?" Sammy asked.

"I lost some of the originals. It's fine; I've used stones for the missing pieces. We can make the first game a practice round until you get up to speed."

A few moves into the first game, Sammy was beginning to regret the decision to play. The rules had taken ages to explain and she'd already forgotten half of them. Being cooped up in the kitchen all morning was making her jittery too, and she was dying to get outside and burn off some energy. Her attention span was suffering as a result and she stared at the board, trying to remember the rules Mehrak had taught her.

"That's not a valid move," Mehrak said as Sammy tried to move one of her pebbles three squares to the right.

"You did that move last go."

"I didn't. I moved my elephant three squares, that's your sultan."

"You said the elephant was the stone that looked like it was smiling. This one's smiling."

"That one's sad. It's upside down. See." Mehrak turned the pebble around.

Sammy sighed and slid a different stone forward two squares. Mehrak didn't react so she took her finger off and settled herself for the wait with her head in her hands.

"You okay?" Mehrak asked as he shuffled up and down the bench, trying to view the board from every possible angle.

"Fine."

"You know, it's alright to be upset over missing your parents."

"I'm fine ... really. My dad thinks I should be more independent. It's my mum I'm worried about. She doesn't cope well when I'm not around."

"I'm sure your dad likes having you around too."

"I'm sure he does. But he's got a new family and a new kid, so he has someone else to spend time with. Unless I'm playing football; then he might make time to watch me. That's if there isn't anything good on telly, and the weather's okay. If I make it back to my world in time for my club's cup match, he might come to that. And when he sees how good I am now, he'll want to spend more time with me."

"Football's a game you play in the Mother World?"

"A sport. Yeah."

"What's a telly?"

"Doesn't matter."

"Does your mum go to watch you?"

"Yeah, she never misses a game, but she isn't that interested in football. She cheers every time I touch the ball, even when I don't make a pass. Dad knows what's going on."

"But your mum's always there?"

Sammy pictured her mother shivering on the sidelines. Her expensive clothes soaked and stained, high heels squelching in the mud and mascara running down her face. Then she pictured the proud grin and the excited victory dance Mama did each time Sammy scored. She rubbed at her eyes with a sleeve.

Mehrak moved one of his pieces. "You'll have to teach me that game," he said.

Sammy looked up. "Football?"

"Yeah. I'd like to play it with you."

"I mostly play it because my dad likes it." Sammy moved one of her pebbles. "But yeah, that would be good."

"Sorry to be a stickler for the rules ..." Mehrak said.

"... but that wasn't a valid move?"

"Your last go didn't involve the cavalry."

"You made this *exact* same move and yours wasn't after moving the cavalry."

"Oh, right," Mehrak said. "I'll move this instead."

"I thought you said you could only move the boat every other go?" Sammy closed her eyes and rubbed her temples.

"I didn't mean to move the boat last time," Mehrak said. "Let's just carry on, shall we?"

Chaturanga was garbage, but at least it was something to do while they were travelling, and it took her mind off worrying about her mum. When they next stopped, Sammy would find something they could use as a ball. She may as well let Mehrak enjoy his victories in Chaturanga before she destroyed him at football.

Unsurprisingly, after a boringly long period of time, Mehrak claimed to be the winner even though Sammy had more pieces left and couldn't see how she'd lost her sultan.

"Don't feel too bad." Mehrak polished his fingernails on his waistcoat before inspecting them. "It's a hard game to master and I have many more years' experience than you do. Fancy another game?"

"Do you have any other games?"

"No."

Sammy sighed as loudly as possible. "Fine, let's have another go."

Three games later, Mehrak was smiling broadly and looked like he was about to announce a fourth victory when Eggie jolted, causing the Chaturanga pieces to topple and a few to roll off onto the floor.

"What was that?" Sammy asked.

"That," Mehrak said, "was Louis ruining my game. You'll give me that win, won't you?"

"It didn't look like you were going to win to me."

Mehrak frowned as he ran for the stairs. Sammy followed him up and onto the front balcony.

Louis was barrelling along below, faster than Sammy had seen him move before. Mushrooms were zipping by on either side, rebounding off the cottage and wobbling like bouncy castle turrets in their wake.

"You ruined our game." Mehrak called down. Louis stopped, causing Golden Egg Cottage to come to a lurching halt. Sammy was thrown towards the railing and caught the banister across her middle. She slumped to her knees and groaned. This would be what a wrestler experienced when he got clotheslined.

Mehrak picked himself up from the floor and made a big show of pulling his clothes together and tidying his turban.

"Louis! What is going ..." And he stopped, paling like someone had turned down his colour setting. Sammy was about to ask what

84

the matter was when he moved his finger to his ear, indicating that she should listen. There was a faint chattering, coming from far away, like a thousand crickets chirruping together.

The noise was unnerving. It conjured images of insects; clouds of creepy crawlies with hundreds of limbs swarming over each other. Sammy squirmed. "What is that?" she asked.

Mehrak didn't answer. Speaking to Louis instead, he asked, "What are our options?"

Louis rotated his ears back and forth, periodically pausing in different positions while Mehrak wrung his hands.

"You're right, let's go north. They'll never know we were here. Quiet, but as fast as you can."

Louis pulled forward again. Mehrak was ready and grabbed hold of the railing; Sammy wasn't and went flying towards the tower. Thankfully, there was nothing to injure herself against this time and she slid to a stop before reaching the curtains.

Louis changed direction once, but kept going at full speed.

Sammy got up. She could no longer hear the chattering over the creaking of the cottage and pounding of Louis's feet, but she couldn't shake the memory of it. "Are you going to tell me who *they* are?" She wiped her trembling palms on her trousers trying to make it look like she was brushing herself down.

"There's a group of crabmen heading this way. We're taking a detour north."

"Crab-men?"

Mehrak's nose curled. "Vile creatures," he said. "They're sort of man-shaped from the waist up—hence the name—but they've got spider legs and claws for arms."

"Seriously? Creatures like that exist here?"

Mehrak nodded.

"What would they do to us if they caught us?"

"They kidnap you, but I don't know why ..." His voice trailed off. "Louis always smells them, though," he said after a moment. "They smell like rotten fish, apparently."

Sammy said nothing.

Mehrak tried to smile. "As long as you don't wander too far from Louis, you'll have nothing to worry about."

"What if they come when Louis's asleep?"

"There's a harpoon under the bed for emergencies, but we shouldn't need it—even if Louis were asleep, they smell bad enough that they'd wake him before they got close."

Sammy watched the mushrooms race by in silence. Mehrak's gaze never left the horizon. His nose had gone blotchy and his eyes glassy. He was hurting and she should say something, but she didn't want to. She didn't want to open herself to someone else's pain. She hardly knew him. They weren't close enough to share feelings and Sammy was happy to maintain that distance.

Mehrak sniffed.

She had to say something.

"They got your wife, didn't they?" she said at last.

Mehrak nodded but said nothing more. That was good. A perfect interaction. Sammy had acknowledged his pain, he'd acknowledged her concern, now she'd go inside and give him a moment to himself.

Then he spoke. "She used to walk in the mornings before I woke up," he said. "She was a morning person, Gisouie. 'It's when the realm is most alive', she'd say. She'd go out every morning to forage for soup ingredients. It was the smell of her mushroom soup that woke me each morning," Mehrak's jaw set and his face became dark. "You wouldn't believe how hard it is for me to get up now without it. I have to make it myself. It's not as good as hers, of course, but occasionally, if I make it just right and close my eyes, it's like she's still here."

Sammy waited for him to go on, but he remained silent.

"How did the crabmen get past Louis?" she asked at last.

Mehrak shrugged and shook his head. "I don't believe they did. There was barely a whiff of them. Louis rocked me out of bed when he realised he could no longer smell Gisouie. She must have walked further than normal. We'd had an argument the night before ..." Mehrak went quiet. He stared at the sky, blinking away tears. "We searched for her, Louis and I. We tracked groups of crabmen. Tried to get close enough to smell a human over their smelly carcasses, but there was no trace of her."

"What about the crabmen coming after us?"

"Louis let them get close enough to smell for her," he said. "But she wasn't with them." He snorted and shook his head. "I risked her life chasing this stupid fairy-tale book, and now I've lost her." He squared his shoulders. "I'm going to find her, though. Someone at the Keep will know where the crabmen take their victims. And when I find out, I'm going after her."

–FOURTEEN–
ACCLIMATISATION

Most of the day had gone before Mehrak decided they were far enough from the crabmen to be safe. Only then did he allow Louis a rest.

Sammy used the opportunity to stretch her legs. She needed a break from Mehrak. He'd moped around for ages after she'd mentioned his wife. And only after they'd played some more Chaturanga did he cheer up. She needed a break from that game, too. How many games had they played now? Somewhere around the fifth match, the cottage walls seemed to be squeezing in, creating a pressure build-up behind her eyes. Mehrak's smug face feigning modesty after each win was the icing on the cake.

Mehrak held the hatch open for Sammy and helped her down.

"Don't wander too far," he said.

Sammy said nothing as she watched him skulk off in search of some disgusting creepy-crawlies. He'd kitted himself out with a fine-mesh insect net, wire traps and canvas bags. She considered following him to see how he was going to catch their dinner, but at the same time she figured she didn't want to know what slithering vermin she'd be attempting to force past her gag reflex later.

She turned and walked off in the opposite direction.

Mehrak was annoying, but she decided she liked him. He was genuinely interested in her; probably the first person other than her mum that was. While they'd been cooped up, he'd asked her all about her home, her parents. He'd even offered to play football with her. If she couldn't get back to the Mother World then would it be so bad hanging out with Mehrak in his golden cottage?

A pang of guilt plucked a heartstring. No, she wouldn't abandon her mother. She'd make sure she got home. There was no question of that, and it would be a good opportunity to prove to her dad that she was self-reliant.

She walked on through the clouds of glittering mushroom dust, running her fingers over the smooth trunks of the biggest mushrooms. When she was sure Mehrak couldn't see her, she planted a side kick into one, making a hollow thud.

She dug a stone out of the dirt at her feet. Rolling it in her palm, she observed its curve and texture, seeing the years that had elapsed as it had been shaped by erosion. She tossed it into the air, then volleyed it into the forest.

She felt alive in the Fungi Forest; far more than she had done back in Sheffield. It was like a heightened sense of clarity, as if she'd been viewing the world through a layer of Vaseline, and now, in Perseopia, smells were richer, colours more vibrant. Even sound had a weight, a kind of resonance like a crystal goblet. The stories Mehrak had told her about the smog and those crabmen didn't seem so bad out here. Like he'd said, the smog wouldn't bother them for hundreds of years. And the crabmen? How bad could they be? She wouldn't let some freaky crustaceans scare her. She ran at a short mushroom and used it to springboard herself into the air, where she pulled a flying kick and scattered a flock of white birds from a patch of brown creepers. She landed, fell into a forward roll and then leapt up with a roundhouse kick followed by a flurry of rapid punches to the trunk of a mushroom. She'd teach those crabmen a lesson.

Birds returned to the creepers, insects buzzed under the canopies and funny looking mammals dug holes in the dirt. She felt connected to them all, a part of their ecosystem. She would've been fine if Mehrak hadn't appeared. She'd managed to find water. She could have braved the forest, too.

She was glad he'd turned up when he had, though. He was annoying and a bit on the scrawny side, but he was kind and had pretty eyes. She was getting side-tracked. Find a way home to Mama. That was what she needed to focus on.

Sammy gulped down the thick lump of anxiety that rose in her throat. She pictured her mum in the police station waiting room, head in hands. Did her dad know yet? She figured he'd be pretty disappointed with her, imagining that she'd run away like a coward. Would he be expecting her to look after herself? All the classic action heroes could survive in the wilderness. Rambo defeated those deputies in the forest. Arnie took out the Predator by himself.

Then she cringed as she recalled how she'd dealt with the waster. Not her finest moment. She liked to imagine that next time she found herself in that situation she'd choose fight over flight. Perhaps a sucker punch to the solar plexus to double him over, followed by a reverse roundhouse kick to the face. Perhaps, but probably not. She knew in her heart that if it happened again, she'd probably do the same thing and run like a baby. Or not a baby, as babies couldn't run.

Sammy planted a side kick into the trunk of a parasol-sized mushroom. Her foot rebounded off the rubbery stalk at a funny angle and she fell over. She got up quickly and brushed the dirt off. A side kick shouldn't have resulted in her sprawled on the floor. She'd had eleven whole Karate lessons. Unless the training montages she'd watched in Kung Fu movies had been wildly misleading, she should virtually be a ninja by now. Perhaps she'd practise her fighting skills a bit more before she took on another waster.

Reclining in bed that evening with a full belly, she was beginning to feel better about her situation—partly due to Mehrak not divulging the contents of the casserole they'd eaten, but also because Golden Egg Cottage was beginning to feel like a second home. Mehrak was good company when they weren't playing

Chaturanga. He'd carved a ball from a lump of mushroom and they'd set up a goal between two mushroom trunks, using creepers to build a net. Then they'd played football all afternoon while Louis rested.

Mehrak was asleep on the floor at the foot of the four-poster in a makeshift bed he'd thrown together from blankets and cushions. He'd fallen asleep reading a book that was still propped on his stomach like a mouse's tent. She watched his eyes moving under their lids and his lip pouting as he dreamed. She wondered what the crabmen had done to his wife and how long he'd been travelling alone.

Soon, thoughts of Mehrak's loss turned to those of her own. Bedtime was when she missed Mama the most. It had always been that way, even when she was downstairs at her dad's house alone on the futon. She'd stopped asking to climb into bed with him for a hug years ago. Even at ten, she'd been 'too old' and he didn't see the point of hugging anyway. He'd grown up an orphan, beaten every day by his foster father. He'd never been hugged and it hadn't done him any harm. Hugging made you weak, made you reliant on others.

Mama survived on hugs. They made her stronger. Like superman recharging himself from the sun. A jagged knot formed in her chest. She pictured her mum alone in bed, crying herself to sleep. Sammy pulled the covers over her head and, for the first time since her dad had left them, she cried.

–FIFTEEN–
Perseopian Pond Life

With a battered metal bucket in each hand, Mehrak clattered his way downstairs and out of the backdoor.

Sammy followed.

Louis had found them water. Lots of it.

A black lake stretched out before them filling a vast expanse of low land, between mushroom-blanketed hills. Mushrooms teetered at the water's edge all the way around, and purple clouds spiralled on its surface, mirroring the sky above.

"Is this where we're going to wash?" Sammy asked.

"No," Mehrak said. "You should wait inside while I fill the buckets. There are unpleasant creatures lurking at the bottom of these lakes."

"Like monsters?"

"Something like that. I'll tell you about them once we've left this place."

Sammy stayed by Louis and watched Mehrak carry the buckets towards the lake. He stopped short of the water's edge and waited.

What was he doing? Sammy was about to call out when Mehrak dashed the remaining distance to the water and dipped the buckets in, making barely a ripple. When both were full, he lunged away, back towards Eggie.

"What was that about?" Sammy asked as Mehrak returned.

"What do you mean?" Mehrak was breathing hard, wild-eyed. "Everything's fine."

"It clearly isn't. Look at the state you're in."

"If you'd heard some of the stories that I have ..." Mehrak put the buckets on the floor and bent over, hands on knees. He sucked air in, blew it out, then stood up, putting his hands on the small of his back.

"That bad?"

"Bad, yeah." He took another gulp of air. "I'm also out of shape. So there's that too."

When his breathing returned to normal, he grabbed the buckets and lifted them up into the back door. "Don't get any ideas about walking down to the water," he said as he got boosted up by Louis's tail and disappeared inside.

With Mehrak gone, Sammy experienced a prickling sensation on her skin and, with it, the realisation that her surroundings had become uncommonly still. The birds had stopped chirping and the ground-dwelling animals had stopped scratching.

Now that she came to think about it, where were all the birds and animals? A single mosquito buzzed past then and, in the sound vacuum, its wings tore up the air with the ferocity of a chainsaw.

The backdoor crashed.

Sammy yelped.

"You're edgy, aren't you?" Mehrak said as he scrambled out of the doorway with the now empty buckets.

"Of course I'm edgy." Sammy balled her fists. "You just told me that the lakes here have monsters, then you sneak up behind me and slam the door."

"I wasn't sneaking. And I didn't mean to scare you."

"You didn't scare me. I just flinched ... a bit."

Mehrak rolled his eyes. "If you say so. I've got to make another trip to the lake. When I get back I'll cheer you up with a story of the time I beat the laird of Dungalor at Chaturanga."

Sammy crossed her arms. "Take your time."

She stood there, teeth clenched. Louis turned towards her and signed, *Okay?*

She didn't respond. She didn't want to talk, or communicate via sign language. Not that she'd be able to do much communicating, as 'Okay' was pretty much the only sign Louis made that she could recognise.

She had an overwhelming desire to prove to Mehrak that she wasn't scared. Maybe she'd go down to the water herself. As long as she didn't get too close she'd be fine.

She waited for Mehrak to put some distance between them, then crept after him,. She stopped about ten paces behind and watched him prepare to fill his buckets.

Then she had an idea. She could sneak up and scare him. He was already trembling. Sweet justice. She could almost taste it. She crept closer. Two more paces and she'd be right on top of him. She glanced out across the water as she savoured the anticipation. The shimmering reflection of the mushrooms on the far side of the lake took her back in time to the twinkling harbour lights of Dover when she'd crossed the channel with her parents. They'd made the trip to fill their car with cheap booze, and while her dad played the slot machines, she'd stayed up on deck with Mama watching England float away across the channel. She smiled as she stared out across the water. The surface of the lake was silky smooth, except for a slight distortion in the centre.

She paused. A distortion? She checked again. Nothing. It was probably her mind playing tricks on her, yet she waited and watched. Just in case.

A ripple. Definitely a ripple that time. Closer than before.

"Mehrak!"

She almost sent him into the stratosphere. Mehrak leapt up with such a high-pitched scream that she thought she'd caused him physical pain. He sloshed water over himself as his arms windmilled and he fell onto his bottom.

"There's something in the water," she said.

"What? Where?" Mehrak slopped his wet turban back from his face.

Ripples again. Closer. Sammy thought she saw a smooth mound break the surface, then submerge, but she couldn't be sure as it was as shiny and as black as the water itself.

Mehrak stumbled backwards, keeping his eyes on the lake. He grabbed the half-full buckets and bundled Sammy back towards Louis.

She wanted to see what the thing was, and tried to look over her shoulder as they ran, but Mehrak kept her moving. At the backdoor, Mehrak unceremoniously boosted her up into the hatch, shoving her in by her bottom.

"Go! Go! Go, Louis!" he shouted. He thrust one of the buckets into Sammy's hand then climbed up after.

Sammy stumbled on the stairs as Louis got up and lurched forward, losing some of her water behind her and onto Mehrak's head. He spat out the water, cursing as he followed.

Sammy ditched the bucket on the kitchen table, then darted for the stairs. She ran to the top and out onto the back balcony.

Louis had already carried them out of sight of the water by the time she got there, although she could still see the large gap in the mushrooms where the lake was.

Mehrak joined her at the railing as the empty patch of forest receded behind them.

A moment later came a thud and the mushrooms nearest the lake edge shook as if a colossal object had crashed into them.

A trembling bass moan accompanied by a high-pitched squeal sailed over the forest, similar to the sounds humpback whales made on natural history programmes.

Mehrak put a dripping hand on Sammy's shoulder.

"If you hadn't been there ..." He breathed out heavily.

Sammy turned to face him. His earnest hazel eyes locked on hers. He moved closer, gulped, opened his mouth to say something. Then closed it again. "Thank you," he said finally, then turned and walked away into the tower.

Sammy watched him go, her heart racing.

–SIXTEEN–
THE MAN

At dusk—which was as dark and creepy as every other part of the day—Mehrak went out to scavenge the forest floor for scuttling beasts. It appeared to Sammy that the people of Perseopia weren't as close to the top of the food chain as they were where she came from. She couldn't understand why Mehrak wasn't able to snare anything larger than rats or bugs. Weren't there any wild pigs, cows or giant mice or something?

She watched him go. He was so enthusiastic about his foraging. It was really quite sweet. If any of the boys she knew were as eager to do their school work as Mehrak was to forage, they'd be bullied mercilessly.

Sammy turned away and bounded up the soft, spongy hoods of several small mushrooms, using them as springy stepping stones to take her higher. And it didn't take long before she reached Louis's head height.

Louis waved an ear at her. She was beginning to recognise more of the signs he made using his ears. The few basic words she'd picked up already included: hungry, thirsty, tired, yes, no, and—of course—mushroom. Although mushroom wasn't always obvious as Louis seemed to have as many words for mushroom as Inuit's had for snow.

On this occasion, Sammy couldn't understand what he was signing so she called out to Mehrak.

A moment later, Mehrak appeared below, carrying a dirty, turnip-shaped vegetable.

"What is it?" he called up. He put the turnip in a bag and wiped his hands with a small cloth that hung from his belt.

Sammy nodded in the direction of Louis's rotating ears.

"It's a man," Mehrak said.

"Where?"

"Somewhere in that direction," Mehrak pointed. "Ten stadia away, sitting by a campfire."

"Ten stadia? How far is that?"

"Erm." Mehrak looked about, searching for something. His eyes stopped on Louis. "See Louis?"

"Yeah," Sammy said. "I see him." He was pretty hard to miss, being roughly the length of a train carriage.

"Imagine twenty gastrosaurs, just like him, in a row, head to tail. That's one stadion."

"The man is two hundred gastrosaurs away? Louis can smell him that far away?"

"He can. He can hear the snap of the man's camp fire too, if he angles his ears just right."

"Interesting," she said as she started making her way down the mushrooms.

"Louis warned us of the crabmen the other night. And they were twenty stadia away."

"Are we going to go over there and meet him?" she asked as she reached the ground and walked over.

"Meet him? The man?"

"Yeah."

"No." Mehrak picked up his vegetables and carried them to the backdoor. "He might be dangerous." He stepped onto Louis's tail and got lifted to the hatch.

"Why?" Sammy took the tail lift up, closing the hatch behind her. She turned the wheel to lock the door and went up the stairs after Mehrak. "Will he be a wolfman who shoots laser beams from his eyes?"

Mehrak stopped. "A wolfman?" He took a spoon and tried the soup that was bubbling on the stove. "That's hardly likely, is it?"

"Crabmen, wasters, lake monsters, wolfmen—everything that lives in Perseopia is horrible."

Mehrak pointed at himself with the spoon. "Everything?"

"Maybe he's nice like you are."

Mehrak gave the soup a stir then carried it to the table. "You can't pick up everyone you meet in the Fungi Forest. There are a lot of crazies."

"You picked me up."

Mehrak poured the soup into two bowls. "That's true, but Louis could tell you were young, scared and sort of familiar." He shrugged. "You're young and naive. This man is, er, a few years older. I'm sure he can look after himself."

"How old was your wife? She wasn't fine."

Mehrak bristled, but said nothing. He put the empty pan in the sink, sat down at the table, and concentrated on stirring his soup without make eye contact. Eventually he put the spoon down, rubbed his temples, groaned, then said, "Finish your soup first."

–SEVENTEEN–
Perfect Victory!

They waited on the front balcony as Louis took them towards the campfire. And the man.

Mehrak didn't want to meet him. No good could come of it. But Sammy was so excited about seeing someone new that he hadn't been able to say no. He wasn't very good at saying no. Not to Gisouie and now not to Sammy, either. If he'd been better at it, maybe Gisouie wouldn't have walked off. His stomach squirmed. The guy would want a lift, and that would be just his luck. It was the last thing he wanted, so it was bound to happen. Sammy complemented the atmosphere in Eggie. She breathed life into the place. Everything was new and exciting to her and he was able to see Perseopia anew through her eyes. He loved seeing the delight on her face as she spotted some new animal. Or the enthusiasm she had as she ran, climbed mushrooms and explored. It was the same feeling he'd had when he first met Gisouie and it was the happiest he'd been in a long time. He felt guilty thinking that way, but it was true. The last thing he wanted was to ruin their dynamic by picking up a stranger, but maybe they should. He liked Sammy, maybe a little too much. Perhaps if they picked up someone else it would stop him getting too close to her. He was still a married man, after all, and couldn't abandon the hope that one day he'd be reunited with his wife.

Mehrak slumped on the front balcony railing. Louis's ears danced, twirled and flicked a message up to him.

"Louis doesn't like the smell of him," Mehrak said. "He says he smells of smog."

"Like a waster?"

"Well …" This was his opportunity to put her off. Maybe they wouldn't have to pick the guy up. His heart lifted.

Louis signed back. During the sequence of words, he folded his left ear down and pointed out his right ear horizontal to the floor. Mehrak watched Sammy's expression and noticed the glimmer of recognition. He never should've taught her gastro-semaphore. A smile spread across her face.

"Louis said, 'No'," she said.

"Louis said, 'No, I don't *think* he's a waster', not, 'No, he definitely isn't a waster'. The man's got a fire going, which is something most wasters have lost the ability to do. He's probably a member of the Black Fist."

"The Black Fist from the Assault? They're still around?"

"Unfortunately."

"Are they bad?"

"I don't know. They're weird. Ramus VorMask, their current leader, is a shady character. Not a lot is known about him but I've heard rumours he has dealings with the crabmen."

"Why would the Black Fist smell of smog?"

"Because they're often seen near Aratta."

"Even though the smog will kill them?"

Mehrak shrugged. "I don't know. Some people say the Fist have an immunity. They certainly still have close ties to Aratta and what happened during the Assault. All I know is that when you come across them, they always smell of smog."

Sammy went quiet.

Mehrak hoped she was reconsidering the decision to meet the man. But she didn't ask Louis to stop, and soon a faint orange glow appeared ahead in the distance.

"Are you sure you still want to do this?" Mehrak prompted.

Sammy chewed on her lip. She said nothing but gave a nod.

———

Louis stopped and Sammy ran for the stairs. She heard the campfire snap as she rounded the back of Golden Egg Cottage and saw the amber glow through the creepers.

"Wait for me," Mehrak called from somewhere still inside Eggie.

He was trying to put her off seeing the guy. It had almost worked when he told her the man smelt of smog, but she still wanted to see him. What was the worst that could happen? She could handle herself. And if that didn't work, she had a dinosaur-chicken at her back.

She pushed through a cluster of bushes and into a tennis-court-sized space.

Sat in the middle, holding a skewered rat over a fire, was a scruffy young guy with dark, tangled hair that fell to his shoulders. He turned sharply as Sammy entered the clearing.

She stopped. His piercing, bloodshot eyes scanned her up and down as he stood. He was dressed in tatty brown clothes and a black cloak pockmarked with burn holes, yet he stood tall with shoulders back and head held high. And, although Sammy was trying not to notice, he was actually quite buff, too. At his feet lay a long white staff with a shiny black sphere, the size of a fist, wedged into a crack at the end.

He stepped forward.

"Hello," he said, and held up a hand. He was young, early twenties maybe. A similar age to Mehrak, but he had an authority about him, the sort exuded by a head teacher, and he made Sammy feel young and silly. He eyeballed her, his teeth clenched, the same way her father did when he was trying to work out whether to punish her or not.

Sammy had been looking forward to meeting someone else, but now she wasn't sure she'd made the right decision.

"Hello," she replied.

The man bowed without taking his eyes off her.

"Hami Hootan," he said. He seemed on edge, poised for something.

Mehrak bustled into the clearing behind Sammy.

"It's a pleasure to meet you both," Hami said as he scrutinised Mehrak. "Will you two join me by the fire?"

Mehrak stopped. "That's kind of you to offer," he said. "But we must be going. My friend, here, is lost and I need to help her get home. You might want to move along yourself. We ... er ... only stopped to warn you there's a patrol of crabmen to the south and they're heading this way."

Hami erupted into a coughing fit that ended with him doubled over, retching. He kept going until he vomited up black engine oil, or something that closely approximated it.

Sammy had never seen anything so disgusting.

Hami took several deep breaths and regained his composure. He stood up, face pale. His eyes remained hollow and vacant for a second before snapping back to life.

"Where do you come from?" he asked.

"Okay, time to go," Mehrak said. He reached for Sammy's hand.

"Are you alright?" Sammy asked. "Do you need a doctor or something?"

"I'm fine," Hami replied, his chest heaving. "How long have you been lost exactly? Two days? Something like that?" He raised an eyebrow and moved his right hand to hang over the staff at his feet. He held his arm motionless, fingers twitching.

"Come on, Sammy," Mehrak said. "Let's leave him to enjoy his food in peace. We're sorry to have troubled you, Hami. But we need to leave, and if you'd rather not be abducted by crabmen, I suggest you finish your meal quickly and do the same." Mehrak took Sammy by the hand and tugged her back towards Louis. "You can't trust everyone you meet in the Fungi Forest," he whispered to Sammy. "Did you see him throw up that black stuff? He's been into Aratta and is halfway to becoming a waster."

Sammy glanced back at Hami.

"You aren't from here," Hami said. "Are you?"

Sammy stopped. She pulled her hand free of Mehrak's and turned to face him.

"I thought so," he said, a roguish smile lingering on his lips. He took a step towards her. "We don't get many girls with yellow hair in Perseopia. I didn't think we'd find you so soon."

Mehrak moved in front of her and Louis took a plodding footstep forward behind them, making himself known.

"You're the guy who chased her," Mehrak said.

"What?" Hami's eyes widened. "What guy?"

Sammy shook her head. "It wasn't him."

"A guy chased you?" Hami took another step closer. "Did he say who he was? What did he look like?"

Mehrak held Sammy behind him at arm's length. Louis shifted forward again.

Hami held up his hands. "I'm here to help Sammy."

"Well, you're too late," Mehrak said. "She's already in good hands."

"Help me?" Sammy said. She shrugged off Mehrak. "How do you know what help I need?"

Louis shifted again, this time turning his head from the clearing towards the forest.

"Let's go," Mehrak said to her. "The crabmen are getting close."

Louis signed a short sentence.

"Or perhaps not," Hami said. "Your gastrosaur says the crabmen are fleeing in the opposite direction."

Mehrak rolled his eyes. "Well done, Louis."

Hami's face became grave. "Something's scared them off." He turned from Sammy and Mehrak to the forest.

"We should go," Mehrak said to Sammy.

"You're right," Hami said, still facing the forest.

"I am?" Mehrak replied. "I mean, yes. Of course I am."

"The Fungi Forest isn't safe. You should both get out of here as soon as possible. I presume you're on your way to Honton Keep?"

"That's none of your business," Mehrak replied.

"We are," Sammy said. "Is that where you're going?"

Mehrak threw up his arms and huffed audibly.

"I am," Hami said. "Maybe I could join you. As protection."

"You? Protect us?" Mehrak stabbed his finger at Hami as he spoke. "Louis and I have travelled thousands of stadia together. All over Perseopia …" Louis's ears began flapping up and down. Mehrak stopped. "Louis! What?"

"That's why I offered protection," Hami said.

The colour in Mehrak's face washed away quicker than a chalk drawing during a British summer, and he wobbled as if he were about to pass out.

"How far away is it?" Hami asked.

Sammy looked from Hami to Louis to Mehrak. "How far away is *what*?"

Louis trembled and Golden Egg Cottage creaked in its harness. Hami calmly repeated the question.

Louis signed something that Sammy didn't recognise.

"We're going to have to stand our ground," Hami said. "It's too late to run. It's almost here."

"Why didn't you warn us sooner?" Mehrak screamed at Louis.

"It's only eight stadia away," Hami said. "It's covered ten since your gastrosaur first detected it. We were never going to outrun it."

"Get back in Eggie!" Mehrak shouted. "I'll get the harpoon." He grabbed Sammy's hand and pulled at it, but she barely moved. Everything was moving too fast. Nothing felt real.

"You haven't got time to get a harpoon," Hami said. "Just stay back and let me handle this." He turned to face the forest. His foot slid beneath the staff on the floor and he flipped it up into his hand.

"Here it comes!" Mehrak cried as the staccato of thundering feet became audible.

Mushrooms and beast exploded from the forest as electricity screamed from Hami's staff.

The blast hit the creature head on, stopping it mid-leap, and dropping it to the floor, where it scrambled to its feet and began prowling, golden eyes focused on Hami.

It was a tiger the size of a shire horse, with shaggy, crimson and black-stripped fur, and sabre teeth growing upwards from its bottom jaw.

The orb at the end of Hami's staff, no longer black, shone a brilliant white, bathing the clearing in stark light.

A tremendous roar erupted from the tiger's mouth, vibrating Sammy's internal organs before subsiding with a throaty rumble, and continuing to throb like a Harley Davidson engine.

The tiger pounced again, but with the grace of a matador, Hami sidestepped and swung the ball of his staff hard into the tiger's temple. Plumes of light burst from the point of impact as the beast roared in pain. It launched a barrage of claw swipes, each of which Hami deftly batted away. Explosions of light accompanied each strike of the staff, fizzing and sparking like fireworks.

Mehrak stopped trying to drag Sammy and watched the fight play out, eyes wide and mouth agape.

The tiger was slowing, labouring against Hami's assault. It failed to block a devastating blow and, for a moment, lost its balance. It growled and stumbled backwards, punch-drunk, shaking its head. Hami twirled the staff above his head, then levelled it at the beast. The orb grew bright and, in desperation, the tiger launched itself again.

It met with a roaring column of lightning.

When the light disappeared, the body of the tiger hit the ground at Hami's feet, and his staff orb faded to black.

Hami turned from the tiger to Sammy and Mehrak. "I think it's safe to assume that this fellow caused the crabmen to turn and flee."

Sammy's entire body trembled. "That was so awesome!" she said, as she tentatively approached the tiger. "Can I get a wizard's staff?" she asked. Then to Mehrak, "How come you don't have one?"

"Because I'm not a magus."

"What's one of them?"

"A member of an ancient brotherhood of warriors."

Hami rubbed at his temples. "I'd say *Protector* is a better description."

"Semantics," Mehrak said. "It's the same thing."

"But are you a magus?" Sammy asked as she edged closer to the tiger for a better look.

"I am, yes."

Mehrak crossed his arms. "Shouldn't we get going? You know, before that tusked manticore springs back to life and eats us?"

"An important consideration," Hami said. "We should get out of here. He won't be regaining consciousness any time soon, but you should definitely put some distance between you and it."

"A tusked manticore?" Sammy said. "That's so cool. If I had one of those staffs could I shoot tusked manticores?"

A sly grin spread on Hami's face. "If we had more time together I could show you the other things it can do." And with a wave of the staff, he extinguished the camp fire.

"How did you do that? Do it again!"

"A simple trick. I'd be able to show you more … if I were offered a lift." He maintained eye contact with Mehrak, and shrugged innocently. "Or you could head off by yourselves and see how far you get." His smile waned. He staggered and then vomited again. He bent double and put his hands on his knees to support himself while he recovered, and spat out the last of the black gunk.

"We can't leave him," Sammy said to Mehrak. "Not after he saved us."

Mehrak let out a long sigh, not even bothering to hide it. "We can take you as far as Honton Keep," he said.

Hami grinned, his gums and saliva black. "We should leave for the Keep immediately, then. The manticore scared off that last patrol of crabmen but there have been a lot in the forest recently. And I don't have the strength to fight another."

"Another what?" Mehrak said. "Manticore? I'm surprised we saw this one. We're thousands of stadia from the Atrabiliar Mountains. The chances of us coming across another must be somewhere in the millions. They don't roam this far south."

"It was unusual, wasn't it?" Hami said. He smiled. "But don't worry. I'm here to protect you now."

–EIGHTEEN–
Fate of the Abductees

Eggie lurched forward and Hami slumped down at the kitchen table. Mehrak shovelled more coal into the stove, filled a pot with water from the sink and carried it to the hot plate. Sammy took the bench opposite Hami.

"What else can you do with that staff?" she asked.

"Light fires, put them out—like you saw. Some basic healing. I can use it as a torch or as a weapon. A few other things, but those are the most useful."

"Magi can also get inside people's minds and steal their thoughts," Mehrak said as he sliced a mushroom into chunks and plopped the pieces into the pot.

"Who told you that?" Hami asked.

Mehrak turned from the stove and fixed Hami with a frown. "My grandfather told me about the mindreading. He had dealings with your sort."

Sammy cringed. "Have you read my mind?" She felt violated, like when a burglar had broken into their house and emptied their drawers. Hami would discover she wasn't as tough as she made out, how she wasn't popular at school and how she'd cried the other night.

"No," Hami said. "I haven't read your mind. Magi don't do that."

Sammy relaxed a little, but not entirely.

The magus watched her, as if he were looking through the windows of her eyes into her head. She stared down at the table.

Perhaps if she didn't make eye contact he couldn't see what she was thinking.

"The magi share a brainwave network," Hami went on, "but that's between ourselves. We use it to communicate telepathically and to share each other's knowledge if we choose." Hami tapped a finger on the table to prompt Sammy to look at him. Their eyes locked. "I can't read your mind," he said.

"I heard the magi brainwashed a man once," Mehrak said. "And turned him into a slave."

Hami slammed his fist down on the table. "Why do you peasants always bring that up?"

Sammy jumped and Mehrak shrank away behind the stove. "It's just … someone told me about the Naziarabad …" he stuttered.

"The Naziarabad *terrorist*," Hami said, his eyes burning. "A terrorist! The Mephralytes were plotting to destroy the Naziarabad monument, the most holy structure in our realm. The magi accessed one terrorist mind to expose the location of their base. That's all we did. Only the Grand Master was powerful enough to do it and it took days of planting suggestions to get the terrorist to reveal the location. We wouldn't have done it if thousands of lives weren't at risk." Hami closed his eyes and put his hands over his face.

If Sammy's dad had delivered that rant, this would be the point where he'd slump back on the sofa, stare into his beer bottle and tell her that he'd try to spend more time with her after the football season.

"The magi haven't done it since," Hami said, looking up, calmer now. "And even that time we did it, we didn't read his mind, we got him to lead us to the base. Reading minds is not the way we operate. It's unethical. And most of us aren't as powerful as you think. Abilities beyond telepathy and fast reflexes are uncommon." Hami coughed and clutched at his chest. "The majority of the magi network is supported by the strength of a few top tier magi, currently Grand Master Aegis and four others. They're the powerful ones."

"What are you?" Sammy asked.

"Excuse me?" Hami replied.

"Are you a weak or a powerful magus?"

"I have enough power for my duties." He coughed again. "That's all I need."

"But enough to defeat a fully grown manticore," Mehrak said, flinching when Hami's bloodshot eyes snapped to his.

"Are there female magis?" asked Sammy.

"No," Hami said. Then he seemed to reconsider. "What I mean is, currently we don't have any. But there have been a few over the years. We don't get many, but when we do, they're usually powerful and often top-tier magi."

"Could I become one?" Sammy asked.

"It's not something you can learn. You're either born with it or you aren't."

"So I can't get a staff to blast stuff?"

"There's more to being a magus than blasting stuff."

Mehrak stirred the pot on the stove slowly. "Are the magi still trying to stop the crabmen?"

"What kind of question is that?" Hami asked. He moved his red-rimmed eyes to focus on Mehrak again.

Mehrak pinched his lips together. "The infestation seems a lot more … prolific than it was a few years ago." He didn't look up and concentrated on stirring the pan on the stove.

Hami regarded Mehrak, opened his mouth to talk, closed it again, and sighed. "You look like you've lost someone close."

"You could say that," Mehrak replied.

"Then what I tell you won't come as much consolation. We're still fighting, but we're losing. The crabmen outnumber us hundreds to one. And their numbers are increasing. There aren't enough of us. We're investigating—"

"Investigating?" The word seemed to catch in Mehrak's throat. There was a look of incredulity on his face but he continued to stir. He dipped a spoon into the liquid and raised it to his mouth.

Hami gritted his teeth but let the comment slide. "The crabmen are a formidable species. Merely *investigating* has cost many lives. There are too many to fight and there's no way to stop all the kidnappings. Ten to twenty people are taken a day."

Mehrak choked on the soup. "Ten to twenty? A day?"

"Several thousand a year, yes. And that number's rising."

Mehrak shuffled uneasily. "Why are they doing it?"

"You'd have to ask the person controlling them."

"Ramus VorMask?"

"Most likely. Either him or someone else in the Order. We have a theory that the crabmen are controlled by a hive mind, like ants or bees. The person controlling them is acting as a pseudo-queen to get them to kidnap people for slavery."

"Why does the controller need slaves when they've got a crabman army?"

"Crabmen aren't intelligent. They communicate using a simple language known only to themselves. And they don't have hands, so they can't build. Killing and kidnapping is what they've been bred for and that's all they're useful for."

"What do they need humans to build?"

"The Tower of Silence in Aratta city, for one. Other slaves are used for other things. There are three main sites they get taken to. The tower in Aratta, a snow base in the Atrabiliar Mountains, and then there's the Cataclysm. The Cataclysm gets most of the slaves."

"But, hypothetically," Mehrak said, "if someone were kidnapped in the middle of the Fungi Forest, then they'd most likely get taken to the Tower of Silence in Aratta? To the closest site?"

Mehrak glanced at Sammy.

Hami watched them. "No," he said. "They're more likely to go to the Cataclysm. Three-quarters of kidnap victims get taken there. That would be the first place I'd look if I'd lost someone close."

Mehrak nodded to himself.

"We're in the process of investigating all three locations," Hami went on. "To find out what the slaves are being used for. I was sent to the tower."

"That's why you're sick," Mehrak said. "Because you've been into the old capital?"

"That's right. I was sent to investigate the tower, but my mission was a failure and I had to leave early. Others have fared better at the Cataclysm. It's the location we know most about and the subject of discussions to be held with the Regent at Honton Keep."

"What is a cataclysm?" Sammy asked.

"*The* Cataclysm is a huge crack through the centre of Perseopia," Hami said. "It's ten stadia deep with molten magma at the bottom. The slaves that get taken there are put to work excavating rock on narrow ledges inside."

"Why?" Mehrak asked.

Hami gave a tired shrug. "We think they're looking for something, but we don't know what."

"What about the lava pterodactyls?"

Sammy sat up. "There are lava pterodactyls? As in, flying dinosaur pterodactyls?"

"Exactly that," Hami said. "They live inside the Cataclysm. The crabmen hand the slaves over to the pterodactyls at the top, then they get flown down to a ledge and put to work."

Mehrak paled. "And that happens to most slaves? Why do they keep working if they know they're going to die?"

"Fear," Hami said. "If they stop, they're either thrown to a fiery death below or ripped to bits and eaten by the pterodactyls."

The kitchen fell silent, save for the sound of Mehrak pouring tea. He didn't stop when the liquid reached the top of the cup and it overflowed onto the table. Only when the tea ran onto the floor did he seem to realise what he was doing and put down the teapot. He stared down at the liquid pooling around his feet.

Sammy grabbed a cloth from the sink and mopped up the spill. Mehrak stared at the floor a while longer then turned to Hami. "You said you were on your way to the Keep but also looking for Sammy."

"I was pursuing someone when I left Aratta. He fled into the Fungi Forest and I followed. I lost him not long after. Then the brotherhood felt Sammy enter the realm. We recognised the sensation from the last time someone arrived in Perseopia."

Mehrak stared at Sammy. "People have entered Perseopia before?"

"A long time ago."

"How did you know where she'd be?"

"I didn't," Hami said. "When I lost the fugitive I was chasing, the magi decided I should continue on to Honton Keep to inform the Regent of events at the Cataclysm. I never expected I'd run into Sammy. Or even that she'd be found so soon."

"How did you know it was me?" Sammy asked.

"You've got yellow hair, for a start. That's fairly uncommon in Perseopia. And I can feel an aura around you that's stronger than anyone else's in this realm. Something that isn't from here. An ancient resonance, but familiar." He narrowed his eyes and tapped his chin with a finger. "There was only one place that was ever familiar to Perseopia, because it was once linked to us."

Mehrak's mouth fell open and he slowly shook his head.

Sammy's stomach dropped away. Hami watched her intently, a wry smile playing on his lips. "My guess is that it's the resonance of the Mother World."

Sammy looked to Mehrak.

"You really are from the Mother World," he said.

"Now you believe me?"

"I thought so." Hami smiled weakly as he held his stomach. "Perseopia hasn't been in contact with the Mother World for twelve hundred years. That's why the resonance is weaker in us than it is in you." He wretched hard, making Sammy flinch, but nothing came out. He coughed several more times, then stopped himself. He took a deep breath. "How did you get here?"

Sammy told him about Esther, the market, the bracelet with the Midnight Emerald Dial, altering the clock hands, then waking up in the Fungi Forest.

"The Midnight Emerald Dial?" Hami said. "The magi aren't aware of such a device. I've been communicating with Grand Master Aegis since I met you both and neither of us thought you'd come here using a gem. The magi council assumed that you'd cut your way into Perseopia with a shard from Yima's poniard."

For a time they sat silently as they cupped their drinks in their hands.

"I suppose Sammy needs to find a way back to the Mother World," Mehrak said at last.

Hami's mouth drew into a line. "Did you bring the Midnight Emerald Dial with you?" he asked.

"I don't think so," Sammy said. "It wasn't with me when I woke up."

"It probably didn't make the transition, then. Portal gemstones never do." Hami stared at her gravely. He opened his mouth, then closed it. His shoulders slumped and his eyes dropped to the floor. When he looked up again and made eye contact, Sammy already knew what he was going to say.

"I think you should get used to living in Perseopia."

Sammy zoned out, experiencing a numbing dizziness. She got up, then flopped back down on the bench. Every object in the kitchen seemed distorted as if she was viewing the room through a fish tank. She wanted to cry out for her mother, but couldn't make any noise come out. Mehrak was talking, saying something. Soft, meaningless reassurances.

A singular sense, a smell, filtered into Sammy's consciousness. Food burning. Mehrak had left the food on the stove too long. Mama always put baked potatoes in the oven and then forgot about them. Sammy had to be the responsible one who cleared away the resulting charred lumps. It was the burning smell that brought her crashing back to reality with the question: Who will be there for Mama?

Sammy put her face in her hands and burst into tears.

–NINETEEN–
SLEEP

Sleep eluded Sammy. She lay in bed staring at the chandelier as it swung side to side. Mehrak had tried to comfort her, but nothing he could say made a difference. When she heard him snoring on the floor at the foot of the bed, she got up and went downstairs.

Hami was still sat at the kitchen table, staring into space.

"Hey," Sammy said.

Hami dipped his head but said nothing. He stared down at his wrists and scratched at them absentmindedly.

Sammy approached the stove and stood with her back to it, hands behind her bottom, palms out. The position she adopted at her grandmother's stove; a large, enamelled, oil-burning oven that remained hot all year round and radiated warm comfort.

"I didn't mean to upset you," Hami said eventually.

"At least you told it like it is."

"Right," Hami said. He stared at his hands. "I didn't want you to have false hope."

Sammy said nothing.

Hami coughed, got up from the table and went to lean over the sink. He threw up and remained hunched over, his chest rising and falling as he gasped for breath.

"Are you going to be alright?" Sammy asked. "Mehrak said that if you breathe in the smog …"

"Then you die?" Hami turned to face her. "I don't know."

"Can you go to hospital or something? To get better?"

A fleeting smile crossed his face, then he became despondent. "When I've had my meeting at the Keep, I'll return to my garrison

116

for treatment." He washed his face in the sink, then came over and sat on the bench opposite, but away from Sammy. He put his elbows on the table and his face in his hands.

"Can I get you anything to make you feel better?"

Hami shook his head.

Sammy laid her head on her arm and watched him. He was a good-looking guy, his face spoiled only by the grimace he wore as his permanent expression. Was it purely sickness that was troubling him? He seemed so sad. Could there be something else on his mind? He took a long, shuddering breath but remained hidden behind his hands.

Sammy closed her eyes and, despite the Katamari ball of thoughts rolling around in her head, she drifted into an uneasy sleep.

———

Behnam stumbled along the tunnel, blind, his arms ahead of him, feeling for obstacles. He tripped, fell, got up, kept going.

His pursuer scampered along behind him, giggling girlishly and childlike, but maniacal and insane at the same time. He should turn back and tackle her, whoever she was. But that laugh, it terrified him. It was unhinging his brain. He couldn't think straight, couldn't control his emotions. Fear drove him on.

He kept going, staggering, stumbling. He seemed to be in a permanent state of falling forward, yet somehow he remained upright. The laughing was getting closer, then further away, then close again. He was being toyed with.

Then light. Far away at the end of the tunnel.

Behnam forced himself on, close now. He was going to make it.

He stumbled out of the tunnel into a long cavern. Two men dressed in white stood at the far end. Each held a burning torch and each, unbelievably, had wings. Were they angels? What were they doing there?

In between them, a circular opening yawned wide.

Behnam struggled towards the winged people. "Help!" he called.

A giggle behind sent him spinning round to face the dark tunnel he'd left. His pursuer was getting close, he could hear her feet pattering on the stone. Then nothing. Quiet. Behnam leaned closer.

There was a giggle behind him and he wheeled back round towards the angels. A girl stood in the circular opening of the tunnel behind them. A slim teenage girl with yellow hair. She smiled a tight-lipped smile. Then screamed, baring pointed triangular teeth, her eyes lighting up a burning red.

Behnam fell to the ground, his heart palpitating, terror paralysing his body. The angels turned on him, teeth bared, fangs in their mouths, snarling like wild animals.

The girl giggled, high pitched, then getting deeper until it became booming and demonic. She heaved up a wide, golden disc from the floor, lifting it high, then she stared Behnam in the eye as she snapped it above her head.

Black shadows screamed from the crack, racing towards him. Crying faces unfurling in the smoke.

Behnam woke, drenched in sweat, shivering and crying. The nightmares had begun. Surely he couldn't have long left.

–TWENTY–
THE MOAT

Sammy woke at the kitchen table, head resting on its surface, face tucked into the crook of her elbow. It was cold and her neck had gone stiff. She rubbed at it as she stood up. Hami had gone, the stove was out, and the cottage was sliding from side to side over Louis's hips. They were on the move.

She found Mehrak in the bedroom putting clothes away in the wardrobe. The room was darker than it had been. A fine mist had gathered in the ceiling forming a halo around the chandelier, and a chill prickled the skin on her arms

"Is it foggy in here?" Sammy asked.

"It is. We're getting close to Honton Keep. Did you sleep okay?"

"No," Sammy replied. She had a dull headache and her eyelids were heavy and dry. She kneaded them with her fingers. "Where's Hami?"

"On the front balcony."

Sammy yawned. "It's gone really cold," she said, shuffling towards the curtains.

She pushed through and a swathe of icy fog folded itself about her, snatching her breath away and filling her lungs with a shrinking tightness.

There were no mushrooms. Only a dark grey fog that boxed in Golden Egg Cottage on all sides.

Sammy rubbed her hands together and approached Hami, who was leaning on the railing at the prow, staring ahead.

Two powerful oil-lantern headlights hung from the balcony projecting beams of light across the barren hard-packed dirt below and out into the fog.

"Where are all the mushrooms?" Sammy asked, shivering.

"We left them behind earlier this morning."

"We've left the forest?"

"Technically we're still in it. This is the Moat. It's a clearing, a hundred stadia in diameter, in the middle of the forest. The Keep is in the centre. The Moat was created so advancing armies couldn't use mushrooms as cover."

"But it's dark without the mushrooms. The armies could use that as cover. And the fog."

"They could try." Hami coughed and hacked up a lump of phlegm, which he spat over the balcony. "The Moat is patrolled by the Marzban guard riding karkadann." Sammy's expression must've conveyed confusion, as Hami followed up with, "Karkadann are a large breed of woolly rhino. They're carnivorous and come from the same mountains as that manticore I fought. In fact, they're often known to attack and eat manticore. Ferocious beasts. They've got a tremendous sense of smell, which the fog enhances. Not much gets past them."

"Will we get past them?"

Hami snorted but said nothing.

Sammy hadn't been joking. She seriously wanted to know, and was about to say as much when Mehrak came outside wearing a thick, grey-striped fur coat. He held out a flat loaf of some sort to her.

"Breakfast," he said.

Sammy's teeth started to chatter. She rubbed her hands up and down her arms before she took the bread.

"I'll get you a coat," Mehrak said, and went back into the tower.

Sammy folded her arms tightly across her chest. She was thinking about following Mehrak back inside when two distant blasts of a horn rang out.

"What was that?"

"The Marzban," Hami said. "Their karkadann have smelt us. Two blasts is a low threat. Good sense of smell, eh?"

"Not as good as Louis's," Mehrak said as he returned with a second fur coat, which he placed over Sammy's shoulders. The coat was heavy and hung to her knees. "Louis smelt them a while ago," he said. "They've only just smelt us."

Hami ignored the comment. "We're a low threat so we'll be getting a Marzban commander to meet with us to find out what we want."

"What if we were a high threat?"

"Then we'd have heard four blasts on the horn, followed by the sound of a regiment of the Regent's fiercest karkadann charging us down."

Sammy stared at the flatbread in her hands. She didn't feel so hungry all of a sudden. "How do they know we're a low threat?"

"Because we don't smell like crabmen. Crabmen are the only high threat you're likely to find out here. You don't want to be entering the moat smelling of crabmen."

"What about a manticore?"

"As unlikely as seeing another manticore would be, it would probably be a medium. Three blasts on the horn. A couple of Marzban could dispatch a rogue manticore without too much difficulty."

Below them, Louis twirled his ears in his unique style of sign language.

"Louis says they're getting close," Mehrak said. "And they aren't charging." He smiled awkwardly at Sammy, which she assumed was supposed to put her at ease.

Giant, meat-eating rhinos getting close. Sammy hoped her tingling fingers and elevated heart rate was from excitement rather than fear. That's what she told herself anyway. No big deal. She'd seen rhinos in the zoo. Sure, they'd been of a non-flesh-eating variety and they'd been in enclosures. But karkadann couldn't be *that* bad. They had people riding them so it stood to reason that they'd be tame. Maybe.

"There they are," Mehrak said.

"Where?" Sammy asked. "I can't see them." She leaned further over the railing.

Golden Egg Cottage creaked to a standstill. The mist continued past, spiralling slowly in the fog-lights.

Three faint lights appeared high in the fog, rocking side to side as they floated closer. Then the silhouettes of three beasts formed underneath. As they neared, their grey, washed-out shapes filled with colour, resolving into rhinos the size of African elephants. Each was covered in thick, rust-coloured fur and bore a single horn, the length of a man, pointing straight out of its forehead.

The three karkadann stopped in front of Golden Egg Cottage, grunting, their heads lowered. On their backs, Marzban guards sat on red and gold saddles, dressed in dark purple uniforms with flowing navy robes. Each man wore a pale pink turban with a red gem set in a golden brooch on the front. Curved swords hung from their waists and they held long, lance-like spears with lanterns hanging from the sharp ends.

"Greetings," called the Marzban in the centre. He had dark eyes, the beginnings of a black beard and a rugged manly face, spoiled only by a scar that started just below his right eye and ran diagonally across his nose and down his left cheek. He looked like a convict, yet he clearly outranked the other two men, with gold epaulettes on his shoulders and a larger, darker-furred karkadann. He came forward, raising his hand to shield his eyes from the fog-lights.

"What is your business here?" he called up.

Mehrak leant over the balcony and closed off the lamp shutters. The Marzban remained spotlighted under their lanterns, but the karkadann disappeared into shadow, giving the illusion that the men were floating on restless mounds of hair. Sammy shuffled uneasily in the dim light of the balcony.

"Hami Hootan of the magi brotherhood," Hami called down. "I've come to see the Regent."

The Marzban commander's eyes widened. "Hami Hootan?" he said. "As in Principal Hami Hootan?" The two men behind him shared furtive glances.

Hami raised his staff and the orb at the end illuminated, bathing the balcony in white light.

All three Marzban stared up, open-mouthed, then, remembering their manners, bowed their heads.

"Narok Grotta, Second Chief General of the Marzban Guard," said the main man. "Would you allow me the honour of escorting you to the Keep?"

"You may. Thank you," Hami said.

Mehrak shot Sammy a look and raised his eyebrows.

Narok and the Marzban bowed again, then turned their karkadann and led the way towards the Keep.

Louis and Golden Egg Cottage followed.

"Are you a celebrity?" Sammy asked Hami.

Hami looked down his nose at her. "A what?"

"Those guys think you're a big deal."

"They do, don't they?" Mehrak said. "What is the deal? You appear unannounced and only have to say your name to get an audience with one of the highest-ranking lords in Perseopia."

"I'm an old friend," Hami said.

"Sure," Mehrak said, and turned to Sammy. "Your lips are blue. Go downstairs and sit by the stove."

"It's gone out," she replied, suppressing a shiver. "Why did it turn so cold anyway?"

"It's the fog," Mehrak said. "The magi made it cold to deter crabmen."

"The brotherhood created the fog as a protective barrier around the Keep," Hami said. "Crabmen need a warm climate; they can't survive in the cold."

Sammy was freezing, but she wasn't going inside; not while they had three giant rhinos escorting them. It was too unreal. The best part was how important Hami had turned out to be. The Marzban had been properly star-struck. Maybe she should start hanging out with the guy, seeing as he was handsome and famous. Some of his popularity might rub off on her.

They saw no one else as they followed the guards through the barren, fog-filled terrain. After a while, a lone karkadann materialised from the fog like a spectre. It was saddled like the others, but riderless, and had its back to them, feeding frenziedly, crunching something in its jaws. Sammy leant forward as they drew parallel.

Underneath the animal's head was a lumpy grey and blue blob with long, hairy legs splayed out from it.

Something changed for Sammy in that moment. Perseopia no longer seemed like a fantasy adventure, it'd become real. Pinpricks of sweat beaded her forehead and her stomach seemed to drop away. The manticore had been terrifying, but Hami had finished the fight cleanly, like heroes in Saturday morning cartoons, or like when Pokémon battled. This was messy, gruesome, complicated reality. How would her dad react to seeing something so disgusting? Would he act tough and pretend not to feel sick? Would he genuinely not feel sick?

"I can't believe a crabman made it this far," Mehrak said, his mouth set in a grimace.

"That was a crabman?" Sammy replied. The shapeless pile of flesh and legs didn't particularly look like any kind of creature she'd seen before.

"They must be getting more foolhardy trying to get this close to the Keep."

"Or tougher," Hami said.

Sammy tightened her grip on the railing. Then felt Mehrak's hand on hers.

"It's just one crabman," he said. "We'll be safe when we're at the Keep. Nothing can happen to us there."

With a violent lurch forward, Hami suddenly retched. "Sorry," he mumbled as he wiped a trickle of black goo from his chin. The exertion had made his eyes red and watery. He blinked away the tears. Then his gaze became distant and he scratched at his wrists again.

"Are you feeling okay?" Mehrak asked. But Hami turned without answering and stumbled away through the curtains and into the bedroom.

–TWENTY-ONE–
Honton Keep

The Moat was never-ending. Fifty stadia turned out to be a lot further than Sammy had imagined. She was about to go inside and climb under the bedcovers when a horizontal line of pale yellow lights appeared high in the fog, like a row of windows on the side of a passenger plane.

"Look." She pointed them out to Mehrak. "Up there."

"Muniment Rock," Mehrak said. "And Honton Keep at the top."

"What is a keep, anyway?"

"A stronghold. Or prison. This keep was a prison."

"We're going to a prison?"

"Former prison. The last hundred years or so, it's been a city." Mehrak's eyes sparkled and a smile twitched on his lips. "You know, the Marzban have been around longer than the city. They were here when it was a maximum-security prison used to house the most evil and sadistic creatures ever to wander Perseopia. It's funny" —Mehrak smiled wistfully— "at first the Marzban were here to keep anyone from escaping, and now their job is to stop anyone getting in."

"Yeah, funny," Sammy said. So they were being led to a prison in the heart of a giant, rhino-patrolled wasteland? Nice.

"Where does everyone live if it used to be a prison? Don't tell me we're going to stay in a cell?" Liam, one of her dad's football mates, had spent the night in a cell after assaulting a police officer. Her dad told her he'd been forced to go to the toilet in a bucket.

"Will I have to poo in a bucket?" she asked.

126

"Don't be silly. Honton Keep is a massive city now. The people of Aratta needed somewhere safe to live when the skies clouded over, so they carved out the whole top layer of Muniment Rock. There are houses, streets, suburbs, even a palace up there."

"Does that make Honton Keep the capital?"

"Well, no. New Ecbatana became capital. It's much bigger and safer—kind of. Not that Honton Keep isn't safe. It's completely safe."

"What about the crabman we just passed?"

"The karkadann probably dragged it into the Moat. It couldn't have got that far in by itself. And we passed it ages ago. It was still a long way from reaching the Keep."

A Marzban on his karkadann loomed out of the mist, travelling in the opposite direction. He saluted Narok but didn't stop, and carried on past.

As they went on, other riders came and went, each one dipping their head or saluting Narok before dissolving back into the fog in their wake.

After a time, Hami returned to the balcony and took up a position at the railing. "We're almost there," he said. "You'll be safe now." He smiled at Sammy, but the gesture lacked honesty and it came across more like a constipated grimace. Who was he trying to convince with that? She found herself more worried than if he'd kept his mouth shut. Hami himself showed no relief that they were almost at the Keep. Which meant he either didn't need the luxury of being safe, or that there were worse things to worry about.

Soon a network of campfires appeared ahead in the fog. A campsite of twenty to thirty animal-skin tents sat in between those fires, and behind the campsite loomed a wall of rock. A sheer cliff face stretching as far as the eye could see; left, right and straight up. At the base were three steel platforms connected to thick cables, which ran vertically up into the fog.

The entire area bustled with Marzban. It was the most people Sammy had seen since she'd arrived in Perseopia and she found it strangely stressful being thrown into such a busy environment after the quiet of the forest and Moat. She wasn't sure why it affected her so. School was chaotic enough and she'd gotten used to that, but there, no one ever paid attention to her. High up on the balcony, she was exposed, and she was drawing attention.

A unit of female Marzban eyed her as they jogged past and a separate group of men that had been circuit training stopped to watch. Even the guards cupping mugs by the fireside fell silent as the golden caravan pulled up and stopped.

Sammy shrank behind Mehrak. The Marzban were all looking at her. She was conspicuous, on display. Not how she imagined being a rock star on stage would be. Maybe it was something you got used to. She should start small, get a few people to notice her before expanding to crowds.

"Time to go," Hami said. "Grab your things."

"I don't have any," Sammy said as Hami disappeared into the tower.

Mehrak bent over the railing and pulled up the fog-lights. "I'll pack you some stuff," he said as he extinguished the lights and the balcony went black.

The camp was a dark place. The Marzban, no longer interested in Sammy, continued with their duties, carrying lanterns to cast out the dark, forcing shadows to slink away and pool around rocks and tents.

Sammy went after Hami. If she was going out into the giant rhino-infested fog, she wanted to be in the company of a badass celebrity warrior.

Narok was at the backdoor hatch to help Sammy down when she got there. His large karkadann wasn't present, probably one of a group loitering outside camp, now barely more than silhouettes. Sammy glanced warily in their direction.

Hami stood a little way off, his back to them as he stared out into the fog. Narok cleared his throat tentatively. "Principal Hootan," he said. "It's truly an honour—"

Hami held up his hand to silence Narok as he coughed a thick, phlegmy cough. He cleared his throat, hacking up a lump of black sputum that he spat onto the ground. Then he turned to face the man.

Narok's eyes widened as he stared at the phlegm. He gulped. "We don't often get magi at the Keep," he said. "At least, not many with your reputation."

"I'm sure," Hami said, wiping his mouth on his cuff.

Narok gestured for two other Marzban to come forward. Sammy hadn't noticed them until then, but they'd clearly been waiting to be called over. The first of them was big—American wrestler big, with a puffed-up chest and cleft chin. He had arms like The Rock's and a broad chest. "Leiss Rustam," Narok said. "One of our finest fighters and the strongest man in the guard."

Leiss bowed. "An honour," he said. It came out as a nasally grunt, almost a single word, *Anonor.*

"And Borzin Vorna." Narok gestured to the other man, a young, fresh-faced lad who was probably the same age as Hami, but seemed younger. He was shorter than Leiss, but still tall and athletically built. "Borzin is one of our new recruits, but a master swordsman and a natural with the karkadann."

"Pleased to, er …" Borzin gulped. He kept shifting his weight from one foot to the other. "A real honour …" He reminded Sammy of an excited puppy. She reckoned if she threw a tennis ball over his head, he'd go running after it and return with it in his mouth.

Hami acknowledged the two men with a disinterested nod.

"I believe you know our First Chief General," Narok said, leading Hami into the campsite.

Borzin and Leiss watched him go. "I can't believe we just met Principal Hootan," Borzin said, grabbing Leiss's arm.

Leiss shook him off, but smiled. "Calm down, will you?"

Marzban were pointing and whispering as Hami moved further into the campsite. They fixed their belts, tightened their turbans and brushed themselves down. No one was interested in Sammy now, which was a relief but, simultaneously, a disappointment. She was from the frickin' Mother World, baby! But then, they probably didn't know that and maybe that was for the best.

An overweight Marzban officer covered in so much bling it would've made Mr T self-conscious came out of one of the tents to meet Hami. Sammy figured he must be the First Chief General. He put his arm around Hami's shoulder and they began to talk.

As Sammy watched, two karkadann appeared behind her, and she jumped. The animals carried on past, led by a young guard.

Thankfully, no one had seen her tough girl façade slip. Her reputation was intact. She didn't like the fog, and the way massive rhinos could suddenly appear right behind you. But more than that, she hated the way everything in Perseopia scared her. She couldn't go five minutes without something freaking her out. She tried to put it out of her mind. She wasn't the sort of person that was easily spooked, but perhaps she had life too easy back in the Mother World. She shuffled closer to Louis.

Eggie's back door crashed open and she jumped again.

Mehrak fell out of the backdoor hatch, followed by two leather cases, which landed on top of him. Sammy pinched her lips together, stifling the scream that threatened to escape. She wanted to be angry that his moment of clumsiness had rattled her, but the way Mehrak had landed was also pretty hilarious. She took a deep breath and tried not to laugh.

"You just stand there and watch me struggle," Mehrak said when he saw her.

"If you say so." Sammy grinned.

Borzin and Leiss came to the rescue. They introduced themselves, collected the luggage and led Mehrak and Sammy into camp.

Louis bounded after them.

"Whoa!" Leiss shouted. He dropped the bags and raised his arms to halt the enthusiastic gastrosaur. "Stay! Stay boy!"

Borzin joined Leiss in trying to block Louis's way.

"What's going on?" Mehrak asked. "What are you doing?"

"He's trying to follow us."

"And? He wants to come too."

"He can't. He'll crush the tents."

Louis signed something to Mehrak.

"He's scared," Mehrak said. "He doesn't want to be left alone."

"I'm afraid he doesn't have a choice. He won't fit in the lift."

"He'll be fine here," Hami said, striding over to meet them. "And well looked after."

Louis bent his head down and Mehrak smoothed the scales on his cheek. Sammy felt she should probably stroke or pat him too, but wasn't sure if she knew him well enough yet. And then the moment had gone, because Hami put his hand on her back and gave her a gentle shove towards the lifts.

"I'll come back down to camp later," Mehrak called back to Louis as he shuffled after Hami. "To check on you." He smiled at Sammy but his eyes were sad and he kept turning back to look at Louis.

Louis lowered himself to the ground and his ears drooped. Golden Egg Cottage creaked in its harness as he hit the floor and came to rest listing to one side.

"I suppose we'll need to find somewhere to stay," Mehrak said with a sigh. Sammy couldn't understand why he was so upset about leaving Louis. He never acted like Louis was his best mate or anything.

"You don't need to," Hami said. "You're going to stay with me at the palace."

"The Regent's palace?" Mehrak said. "Says who?"

"Says me."

"You might want to square that with the Regent first."

"He'll agree to it."

Mehrak raised his eyebrows at Sammy and whispered, "And if that doesn't work out, that friend of mine should be able to put us up for a couple of nights."

Narok jogged over. "Your visit hasn't been made public at city level," he said as he caught up. "So you shouldn't get bothered." He glanced casually at Sammy. "Sammy's hair is like your boy's," he said to Borzin.

"I know," Borzin said. "What are the chances?"

The lifts were rectangular, wire mesh platforms with waist-high railings, the corners of which were hooked to steel chains that ran up into the fog.

The gate creaked as Narok opened it and led everyone on.

"Hold on tight," he said, slamming the gate after them and loudly clanging the hilt of his sword on the railing five times.

The platform wobbled off the ground, groaned and pulled away from the campsite.

Louis followed them with his ears as they accelerated up the cliff face. Moments later, he'd gone. The campfire lights remained longer, then, like Louis, disappeared too.

It was an odd sensation flying up through the fog, watching the cliff face dropping away alongside. Narok and the Marzban stared out into the fog, clearly having made the journey many times before.

Mehrak slumped over the railing, staring at the spot where Louis had disappeared. Hami was clutching the handrail with one hand and pinching the top of his nose with the other. His eyes were closed and his chest pumped as he controlled his breathing. He looked dreadful and heaved like he was trying not to be sick. Sammy wondered if she should say something to one of the others.

Hami turned in her direction then, his eyes staring past her, unfocused. Sweat pouring from his forehead. He came out of the trance and noticed Sammy watching him.

132

Sammy looked away first, looked down. She could feel his eyes on her, daring her to glance up, but she didn't. She couldn't. Something was wrong with him, something that scared her.

She continued to watch the fog drop away through the mesh at her feet, until murmuring voices drifted down from above. They got louder as the lift went higher, then separated into individuals, talking, calling, laughing.

The platform emerged from the fog, pulling free from the grasping tendrils of vapour, which unfurled and drifted back into the abyss below.

They came to rest by a square opening about the diameter of a train tunnel. Identical openings on either side curved away around the rock face in both directions. The platform dangled above the fog, suspended by two steel arms drilled into the rock above. To Sammy, it gave the appearance of being in a lifeboat hanging off the side of an ocean liner while the sea-like fog lapped against the rock face below.

Through the window, a vast cavity had been excavated out of the mountain. It was crammed with crooked, grey, stone-block buildings, and oil-burning streetlights lined the smooth, carved streets.

Thick columns supported the roof above, and huddled between them were houses built from stone blocks. Other houses were carved into the columns themselves, with doorways at the bases and small windows at various levels all the way to the ceiling. Sammy counted five storeys from the base to the top.

Narok guided her off the platform and onto the window ledge. Stairs led down inside to the cave floor where men and women weaved in and out of each other, dressed in all the colours of jelly beans in a jelly bean jar. Women were dressed in long pleated skirts, cloaks, wraps and headscarves. The men, who were no less colourful, dressed in trousers with droplet-shaped legs, silk shirts, fitted waistcoats and headgear ranging from neat turbans to tall, pointed hats.

It was warm above the fog, similar in temperature to that of the Fungi Forest. Sammy was about to shed her fur coat when Hami took hold of her shoulder and clenched it. Not hurting, but tight enough that she could feel tension in his arm.

Mehrak remained on the platform, gazing down into the fog, and not paying attention to what Hami was doing. Louis could look after himself; Sammy ... could do with some assistance.

"Hurry up, Mehrak," Hami said. "You can check on him later."

Mehrak dragged himself away from the railing. He hopped off the platform and scuffed his heels down the stairs.

A few of the Honton Keep residents watched them as they descended to street level, with most of them interested in Sammy. Then she realised; there were no other blondes. Everyone in the Keep had either deep brown or black hair. Narok had said something about hair colour. Mehrak too, when they'd first met. Perhaps fair hair was uncommon in Perseopia.

"The people just want to see what you look like," Narok said as he led the group along the street. "We haven't had many travellers since the increase in crabmen. Don't worry. They won't bother you."

A group of kids giggled and pointed at Sammy as they walked, and some followed her a little way, but by the time they'd reached the end of the street, the kids had gone. Hami relaxed as they followed Narok further into the Keep and Sammy used the opportunity to slip out of his grip. She joined Mehrak at the back of the group. Hami's eyes followed her, but she ignored him and smiled at Mehrak.

"I'll go down to the camp with you later," she said. "To see Louis."

Mehrak smiled back. He still appeared sad, but he at least seemed grateful for Sammy's offer.

Narok guided them through the meandering streets of the Keep, the houses slouching by the side of the road, crooked and slumped, the walkways lined with oil-burning lamp posts.

Further in, they entered a market square, packed with stalls selling an assortment of groceries and bright clothing, and heaving with people.

The market seemed strangely familiar to Sammy, and it left her with a niggling sense of déjà vu.

Then a young turbaned boy barged past, almost knocking her flying, and the action brought her thoughts into focus. The arrangement of stalls here was similar to that of the Sheffield market.

Sammy stopped. Not just similar. The layout was *exactly* the same. She took a deep breath.

The area to her left would be the bottom of the market, so that meant—she turned to her right—beyond the closely packed stalls, in the direction she now faced, would be where Esther's stall should be.

Neither Mehrak nor Hami had noticed her fall by the wayside. She'd lost the group, but that no longer mattered. She shouldered her way through the crowds towards the dark corner, her heart beatboxing in her chest. She had no idea what she'd find, but there was no question that she had to keep going.

She stumbled through a pair of hanging carpets. And stopped.

There stood the knick-knack stall, and behind it, Esther. Sammy stood, dumbstruck, as if her brain had rebooted to protect itself from crashing. She didn't react, because the view before her made no sense.

Esther glanced up, but then carried on counting loose change.

"Can I help you?" she asked.

Sammy said nothing.

Esther repeated the question.

"What are you doing here?" Sammy asked.

"I work here."

"How did you get here?" Sammy's brain was catching up, big mental Tetris blocks falling into place. "What have you done to me?"

"I wasn't aware I'd done anything."

"You gave me that bracelet that made me come here."

Esther frowned. "I don't sell bracelets."

"You're lying. You gave me that bracelet. You were in Sheffield. Your name's Esther …"

The name hit the old woman like a shotgun blast. She dropped the coins she was holding and wavered on the spot. For a moment she looked like she was about to faint, but she snapped out of it fast.

"How do you know that name? Who are you?" She lunged across the table and grabbed Sammy by the collar. "Tell me what you know!"

Sammy clutched the woman's hand and tried to loosen the grip, but it was too tight.

"Get off me!" she shouted. "Let go!"

The old woman let go and Sammy fell to the floor.

Hami was there. And he had the woman by the throat. He calmly lifted her from the floor one-handed. In his other hand, the orb of his staff flickered.

The woman's face was becoming red and a strained gargling bubbled up out of her throat. She grabbed at his wrist, but his grip held firm.

"What were you talking to this girl about?" he asked, his voice even, calm.

"N … noth …" She lashed out, kicking Hami in the leg, but he didn't react.

"Nothing? Are you sure?" His face was passive, but his eyes were electric.

"P … please …" Esther's eyes were wide, tears rolled down her cheeks.

"This young girl happens to be a friend of mine," Hami said, through gritted teeth. "You should not be bothering her."

Narok charged in through the carpets. "What's going on?"

Mehrak followed close behind. He came to a halt as he took in the scene playing out before him.

Hami dropped the woman. She landed hard, gasping for breath, and began to cry.

Everyone stared at the woman, then at Hami.

"Just a misunderstanding," Hami said. He smiled, or as close to a smile as he could manage. "No big deal."

Hami placed a hand on Sammy's back and gave her a gentle nudge away from the stall.

Sammy checked back over her shoulder. Esther was still on the floor, weeping, as the red-purple beginnings of a bruise blossomed at her throat.

–TWENTY-TWO–
The Palace

Hami's eyes were on her now. He wasn't going to let her wander off again.

"I told you we shouldn't have picked him up," Mehrak whispered.

"He was protecting me," Sammy said, although she wasn't sure she believed that any more. The violence he'd unleashed on that poor woman sent shivers down her spine. Her dad was an aggressive man. She'd heard the stories. But now that she'd witnessed that kind of aggression in real life, it upset her to think of him inflicting the same kind of force on another human being.

"Protecting you from that defenceless old woman?" Mehrak was struggling to keep his voice low. "Did you see what he did to her neck?"

"My dad would have done the same thing if he saw someone grab me."

"From what you've told me about him, I'm sure he would. What would your mum have done?"

"What does my mum have to do with anything? She doesn't like violence."

"Good for her." They turned a corner in the road. "Anyway, who was that woman?"

Sammy stopped. Thoughts of her father vanished as her heart lifted in wonder at the sight before her.

Below them sprawled a vast plaza filled with a dense grid of shimmering lamp posts. Further off, in the centre, sat the palace, overlooking the lamp posts. It was perched on a steep cone of rock and fused with Honton Keep's ceiling at the top.

Sammy jogged down the steps into the plaza.

The lamp posts were sculpted to look like trees. Some were of the traditional vertical pole variety, a few had branches, some forked and some only had a slight bend or crooked section in the middle. Those that had multiple branches had lamps at the end of each limb. And no two were alike.

The place had a magical quality. The feeling you get when Christmas lights go up and you know the holidays are coming, filled with sweets and presents. Sammy moved through the posts, weaving her way in and out, and hanging off the metal branches. Hami's eyes remained on her and she spied him bristling the further away she got, but she didn't care.

Mehrak caught up to her. He had a big, cheesy grin on his face, and the lamplight sparkled in his eyes. He followed her to a square, hidden among the lamp posts, where a group of men were raising buckets of water from a well.

They both stopped a moment to watch.

"That's where the Keep gets its water," Mehrak said. "There's an underground river that runs below Muniment Rock." He walked on while Sammy stayed and watched the men hauling water. All she had to do in the Mother World was turn on a tap. She wondered if she'd ever use a tap again. Maybe she could introduce taps to Perseopia. Make a few quid for herself. Maybe she could 'invent' other modern gadgets that she'd had back in the Mother World. In a few years' time she'd be rich. How did you build a PlayStation or an iPhone, anyway? Thinking about it, there wasn't actually that much she knew how to build. Could she even build a tap?

"Sammy!" Mehrak called from up ahead. "Look at the palace!"

She ran to catch up. She'd figure out how a tap worked over the next few days. Once she'd gotten that sussed out, she'd move onto games consoles and tellies.

The palace loomed above the metal forest on its cone of rock. At a glance, it seemed that the building was perched on top of a hill, surrounded by a steel forest, but in reality the palace and mound probably joined the ceiling to the floor as a colossal load-bearing structure.

Hami and the Marzban caught up to Sammy and Mehrak and led them up the stairs to the palace.

At the top of the mound, two men in crimson uniforms, navy robes and red conical hats stood to attention on either side of tall, golden doors.

Narok went to talk to them. There was a brief exchange and the men parted to let him in. Everyone else waited outside.

High up by the palace, market traders could be heard echoing across the Keep. Sammy gazed up at the expansive stone ceiling bearing down on the palace. She still couldn't get over the size of the place and how all of it had been carved into the top of a mountain.

The palace alone was an impressive piece of stone work. It stood at three storeys high, with a row of gold-rimmed windows on each floor. The architecture was heavy and functional, all right angles, thick lintels and there were bars over the windows. Probably throwbacks to when the city had been a prison. An attempt had been made at some point in the past to soften the flat, blocky surfaces, but it hadn't entirely worked. The balconies, lintels and columns had been engraved with intricate carvings to give the impression they were covered in wildlife. Balustrades on the balconies were covered with twisted vines and leaves. Columns had been turned into coiled snakes with heads at the top. The walls had spiralling patterns of dragonflies and butterflies, and spider webs had been carved under window ledges. The stone masons had tried hard, and the carvings were beautiful, but it brought to mind the phrase 'putting lipstick on a pig.'

Sammy watched Hami. His eyes were bloodshot and watering. There was no honour in what he'd done to Esther. Her dad would never have acted that way. She refused to believe it.

Hami dry-retched and noticed her looking. He smiled insincerely, showing back tar in his teeth.

Strolling through the lamp post forest, Sammy had temporarily forgotten about the significance of Esther being here in Perseopia. The woman must've followed her after she'd unlocked the bracelet. But how? And why had she acted as if Sammy were a stranger?

"I can't believe we're about to enter Honton Keep Palace," Mehrak said. "Do you know how often I've dreamt of this day?"

"Seven times?" Sammy replied. She was still watching Hami and not really listening.

"Hundreds, more like. Honton Keep Palace has the largest surviving library in all Perseopia. There are hundreds of rare books in here. There's bound to be information ..."

Hami's eyes narrowed to slits.

Mehrak faltered, cleared his throat, "... information that will be useful for my studies." He rubbed his hands together. "The years I've spent scrounging around in second-rate markets for the slimmest whiff of a book. My grandfather told me there are six storeys of books in the library here."

Hami's eyes were burning holes into the back of Mehrak's skull as he wittered on about the trials of amateur book collecting, but then Narok reappeared and gestured everyone inside.

They crossed the threshold of the palace and the doors closed behind them, silencing the sounds of the Keep outside.

The lobby was large enough to fit Sammy's entire house. The floor was tiled in an extraordinary light brown marble that looked like it had swirls of smoke captured inside, and columns of the same stone lined either side of the room. Grand arches connected candlelit anterooms, and at the far end of the hall a wide staircase rose from the floor and split in half, each section curving up and

141

around to a galleried landing above. Two sentries dressed in red stood at the bottom of the staircase.

"Luggage to the south wing," Narok said to Leiss and Borzin. The men bowed and carried the bags away through an adjoining arch.

Narok led the rest of them along a narrow red and gold embroidered carpet the length of the lobby, and up the stairs. They took the left-hand fork to the gallery, then down an adjoining corridor. At the top of a second staircase, they travelled a grand corridor, passing lecterns, urns and sculptures of royal-looking people, and arriving at a thick set of gold doors at the end.

Narok pushed the doors open and let everyone inside.

They entered a plush office the size of a five-aside pitch. It was filled with brightly coloured divans and dripped with lavish ornaments that sparkled in the candlelight.

Against the back wall sat a single wide desk.

Mehrak began examining each of the ornaments in turn. He made it halfway round the room and stopped.

"Look at all this wood!" he said. "I've never seen so much in my life. It's beautiful."

On one of the long side walls hung a large piece of carved wood. It was the size of a sitting room rug and around three inches deep. The scene carved into it showed hundreds of finely sculpted soldiers fighting in a monumental battle.

"It's an impressive carving," Sammy said as she sat down on a pink divan. "But it's only a piece of wood."

"All the trees in Perseopia died over a hundred years ago when the skies clouded over," Mehrak said over his shoulder. "Then they went rotten and there was a plague of ambrosia beetles. All the bugs left behind was mush. The Fungi Forest grew from the mush and only treated wood, a few books and some paper survived. There are only a handful of museums and private collectors in possession of wooden artefacts now. I had no idea it could be so beautiful."

"Hami's staff is wood," Sammy said. "And what about all this furniture?" She gestured around the room. "The desk? The chairs?"

"How can you not know what furniture is made from?" Narok asked. "And yet you've heard of wood?"

Hami sat down next to Sammy. "The child comes from a neglected background," he said, before she could answer for herself. "She's had an unconventional upbringing."

"But …" Sammy said and stopped. Hami's arm had slipped up behind her and his hand gripped the back of her neck. He applied pressure, and while it didn't hurt, it was enough that she knew to stop talking. Neither Narok nor Mehrak could see Hami's arm behind her or his fingers concealed in her hair.

"Mushrooms," Hami said to Sammy, turning to face her, locking eyes. "Furniture is made from mushroom stalks. The stalk is the toughest part. Cut them into sections, dry them, then varnish several times to harden. You were right about my staff, though. It's wood. But that's because it's over three hundred years old and has been well-preserved."

"I wondered why you asked me if I liked having green furniture," Mehrak said, as he continued to stare at the wooden carving. "Sammy, look." He pointed at one of the figures in the scene.

Sammy shoved herself away from Hami and darted over to him.

"This big guy here with the four spikes on his helmet, that's General Azim Azertash. The General. He was the giant warrior I told you about that fought with the Association. Look at the size of him. That must mean this carving depicts the Assault on Aratta."

"That scene is of the Second," Hami said.

"The Second?" Mehrak asked. "As in the Second Battle? It can't be. The General died when the palace blew up during the assault."

"He didn't," Hami said. "He survived and joined the Order. That carving represents the Second Battle. After he'd turned."

Mehrak frowned. "Turned?"

"Look closely," Hami said. "The men he's fighting look like Marzban. They have the same cloaks and turbans because Marzban uniform is based on the Association battle robes. The General is killing Association men in that carving."

The figure of the General was a lot larger than those of the other men. He had the neck of a bull and an undulating cloak which had been expertly cut into the wood to make it look like it was flowing behind him. In each hand he gripped a spiked club, one of which had connected with the neck of an opposing soldier; a soldier who looked a lot like a Marzban guard.

A door at the far end of the room opened then and two guards in red conical hats marched in. Their right hands hovered by their sword hilts as they entered, but a quick glance around the room softened their postures and they gave the nod.

A round man, dressed in multiple layers of red, orange, yellow and gold, pranced into the room. He had small hands and narrow shoulders, and if his frame had also been slight at one time, he'd long since beaten his metabolism into submission. On the bottom of his puffy head hung a short, neat beard, and perched on top was a fussy gold and orange turban with gold chains worming in and out of the folds. Behind him scurried three timid servants dressed all in white. They moved when he did and stopped when he did, too.

"Our illustrious Regent Mustafa Shahab," Narok announced.

Mehrak bowed. Hami just nodded. Sammy wasn't sure what to do, so did nothing.

Narok dipped his head and excused himself from the room.

"Hami!" the Regent said. He shuffled over and pulled the magus into a hug. "It's been too long." Then he let go and stepped back. "Is everything alright? You look awful. The brotherhood working you too hard?"

"Nothing I can't handle," Hami said.

"But what's happened to you? It's been a year since you last visited."

"Things have been … difficult. You are well yourself, Majesty? Honton Keep remains prosperous?"

"As prosperous as it can be with the crabman population what it is. I'm excellent, though. Fighting fit. My mother has been poorly of late. Currently bedridden, but she's still her usual chipper self."

The Regent turned to Sammy and Mehrak, who'd remained over by the wooden carving. He approached them, followed closely by his scuttling entourage.

"You've neglected to introduce your companions," he said to Hami. And his face lit up. "You have beautiful hair," he said to Sammy. "I've not seen anyone with a golden yellow quite like yours in a long time." Then he bowed. "Regent Mustafa Shahab."

Sammy curtseyed. "Sammy Ellis," she said in reply.

The Regent moved on to Mehrak.

"Mehrak Omid," Mehrak stammered.

The Regent took his hand and shook it enthusiastically, flapping his arm up and down like a windsock. "A pleasure," he said, beaming. "Please be seated."

Sammy took the divan furthest from Hami.

The Regent took a seat behind his desk and rested his hands on the surface, knitting his fingers together. The servants took up their places behind him.

"So what's the adventure this time?" he said with a smile and a glint in his eye. "Much as I enjoy your visits, Hami, I know you don't often visit without good reason."

"No adventure," Hami said. "Mehrak and Sammy picked me up in the forest and gave me free passage here. If possible, I'd like to repay their kindness by replenishing their supplies and providing them lodgings at the palace."

"That's it? Nothing exciting?"

"I have news on crabman activity."

The Regent harrumphed. "We can get to that in good time. First, I insist you get fed. A feast befitting a sultan. Then you may return and educate me about the latest crabman activities."

A servant led Sammy, Mehrak and Hami back through the palace. They passed the lobby and went through one of the connecting arches and down several more corridors, before finally arriving at a pair of tall, red doors.

"Painted mushroom," Mehrak said, tapping a door with his knuckle and raising his eyebrows.

"Yeah, I get it," Sammy said in a tone that she hoped would convey disinterest.

The room on the other side of the mushroom stalk doors was stunning. Throne-like chairs surrounded a long polished table. Above it hung a grand crystal chandelier filled with candles, and painted silk hangings covered the walls.

"This will be your accommodation for the duration of your stay," the servant said, and left.

They found their bedrooms through three separate doors off the communal dining room. Sammy had a contender for the largest bed she'd ever seen: a four-poster with blue silk curtains. Through an arch was a hole-in-the-floor style toilet, gross, but making up for that, a bath that could have bathed an entire football team, including subs, coaches and manager.

Hami was still in the communal dining room when she returned. He was staring at a painting of a bald, bearded man dressed in a black cloak similar to his own.

"Aren't you going to check out your room?" Sammy asked.

"No," he said, then coughed. "I've stayed here before."

When the servant returned, he offered to serve lunch. Mehrak assured him that, "that would be fine," and the man disappeared again.

"Well, I am, even if you're not," Sammy said as she took a seat at the table.

"Excuse me?" Mehrak said as he sat next to her.

"I'm looking forward to eating," she said.

"No one said anything."

"Hami did."

Hami turned from the painting. "I didn't say anything," he said. His mouth drew into a line, but then the red double doors burst open releasing servants in all directions.

They held aloft dishes containing meats, vegetables, fruit and cheeses, and went rushing back and forth, weaving in and out of each other like dancers in an elaborate ballet. Cutlery, plates, glasses, jugs of water and carafes of wine zipped onto the table in front of them as if someone had dragged away the table cloth with everything on it, but in reverse. The overflowing platters were up in the air one moment, the next they were on the table and the servants had gone.

Hami regarded the food with disinterest, then announced he wasn't hungry, had business with the Regent to attend to, and left.

"What's his problem?" Mehrak said as he began tugging at the leg of a suckling pig. "He seems pretty tense. What do you reckon he's going to speak to the Regent about?"

Sammy hadn't considered that Hami could be worked up about his meeting with the Regent. But now that she thought about it, something about his body language had been off. She'd put it down to his sickness, but was there something else?

–TWENTY-THREE–
THE REQUEST

Mustafa sat at his desk, trying to concentrate on the draft policy in front of him. He stared at the parchment and absentmindedly doodled on a spare sheet while his mind drifted. His guards had put out the ceiling lamps when they'd left and the room was dark. Only the candles on his desk and the surrounding pedestals illuminated the room; just as he liked it. There was something comforting about being alone with only flickering candlelight to keep you company. Such a large portion of his day was spent around people that it was nice to be alone. Only Fila, his masseuse, had remained. She stood behind his chair working his shoulders. He was a creature of comfort, without a doubt. She worked a tight knot at the base of his neck and he groaned with pleasure. Being a regent wasn't all bad.

In the dark recesses across the room the door latch clicked, and Hami appeared in the shadows, just out of reach of the candlelight.

"Back already?" Mustafa asked with a smile.

"Back indeed," Hami said.

Something about him was different; his eyes were joyless and dark. Mustafa wasn't going to enjoy this conversation.

"Are you well fed and watered?" Mustafa asked hopefully.

"I'm fine."

"I must say, you don't seem yourself."

Hami let out a long breath.

Mustafa mopped his brow. He was sweating already. "Where's Behnam?"

Hami didn't answer.

Mustafa turned his head to address the woman behind him. "That will be all, Fila. Thank you."

The girl bowed and left the room. Mustafa waited until the door shut before he went on. "You seem impatient so perhaps we should get down to business," he said, pulling at his collar. "Is there anything I can—"

"I'd like a Marzban escort."

"I can facilitate that. What's it for?"

"For Sammy. To take her to the Grand Master in New Ecbatana."

"You're not going with her?"

"We're going together."

Mustafa squirmed in his chair. "You're going with her, yet you still want an escort? I would have thought you'd be ample protection."

Hami said nothing.

"Will two Marzban be enough?"

Hami maintained eye contact as he spoke. "I need thirty."

"Thirty? What can you possibly need thirty for? Five could comfortably dispatch twenty crabmen." Mustafa paused. "What are you expecting to run into on your way to the capital?"

Hami pursed his lips. "Crabmen," he said. "Lots of them." He looked like he was about to say more, but instead turned and walked to the wooden battle scene on the Regent's wall. He coughed, retched, and swallowed.

The Regent wiped the sweat from his forehead. All the tension that had been massaged out of his shoulders was corkscrewing its way back in. "I've known you since you were a boy, Hami. I can tell when something is troubling you. There's something you aren't telling me. You're different. I ask you as a friend to share your burden. If I didn't know you better, I'd think you'd joined the wasters of Aratta."

Hami snorted.

"Hami," Mustafa said. Hami turned back towards him. "Where's Behnam?"

Hami didn't answer. His face reddened, then a cough burst from his mouth and he dry-retched. He bent over at the waist while he composed himself. A trickle of black bile appeared at the corner of his mouth. He wiped it away but Mustafa had seen it and recoiled in his chair.

"You have been to the wastes!" he said. "I should've known. It's in your eyes."

"I haven't been infected, if that's what you think." Hami approached the desk. He gritted his teeth and inhaled deeply.

"That's what happened to Behnam, isn't it? You've been to Aratta. You made it out. Behnam didn't. The crabmen got him, didn't they?"

Hami gripped the edge of the desk and raised his eyes, gulping excessively.

"I don't know what happened," he said. "We went there together, but we were split up. I left before he did, and he never re-joined the network. That was a few days ago now."

"You think he's dead?"

Hami shook his head. "I don't know. He left the network for our protection. I ..." Hami trailed off.

"It's not your fault, you know," Mustafa said after a while when Hami didn't continue.

"I never said it was."

"You didn't have to. I know what you're like. You beat yourself up about things."

"That was different. That was his sister and it *was* my fault. I could've prevented ..." Hami hung his head.

"You're not infallible. I know you think you are, because you're powerful, but you're not. Did you ever tell Behnam that you and Jamileh were—?"

"Together?" Hami screwed up his face. "Hardly. How could I tell him we were together the night she died? Tell him that it was my negligence that cost her life?"

"Is that why you're taking my men? For a rescue mission? Because I can't let you take them to Aratta; it would be suicide. I know you feel guilty for losing Behnam's sister, but you can't throw my men's lives away to save his."

"I'm not a fool, Mustafa. Your men are for exactly what I've said they're for: to escort Sammy."

"But why? Why so many?"

Hami stared into his eyes. "The Order are mobilising the crabman armies. They're building up to something."

"Mobilising crabmen? The Order are little more than smog addicts. They certainly aren't organised enough to mobilise crabmen."

"You need to differentiate between members of the Order and your typical waster. They aren't the same thing. The Order are intelligent, organised. They lured Behnam and I into Aratta, split us up, and then—I'm guessing—had the crabmen capture him."

"For what purpose?"

"Because of a discrepancy. Just over two days ago we felt a ripple in the fabric of the realm."

"You think the Order kidnapped Behnam to find out what caused it? Are you sure it wasn't the crabmen? A few Order members wouldn't pose much of a threat to a magus."

"Behnam was kidnapped before the ripple occurred. The Order knew it was coming and lured us into a trap. They knew about it and we didn't. That means they know, or at least knew, more than we do now."

"Do we know what caused it?"

"Someone arriving in Perseopia. An outsider."

"An outsider arriving? What kind of ..." Mustafa went silent as the realisation dawned on him.

Hami nodded slowly.

"The girl? Sammy? Yellow hair, blue eyes … That's why you need the escort."

"It is."

"She caused the ripple?"

"She's from the Mother World."

The Regent slumped back against his chair. "If I'd been told that by anyone else, I wouldn't have believed it." he said. "How did you find her?"

"I didn't. Mehrak did. Sammy was wandering the Fungi Forest alone and he picked her up. My path crossed with theirs yesterday when they gave me a lift here. It was pure chance."

"What was Mehrak doing out in the forest? What kind of fool travels the Fungi Forest with the crabman infestation being what it is?"

"He's an amateur treasure hunter from a small town thousands of stadia to the west, near the boundary. He's been travelling in a gastrosaur caravan, so I presume he thought he'd be okay. Judging by the journal he keeps by his bedside, I'd say he and his wife were on an expedition for the *Rule Book* when she was kidnapped by crabmen."

"Chasing the *Rule Book*?" Mustafa snorted and shook his head. "A dreamer like my mother. So his gastrosaur didn't turn out to be much help alerting him to crabmen after all. Poor fellow."

"Mehrak presumably came upon Sammy while searching for his wife."

"How can you be so sure Sammy really is from the Mother World?"

"The ripple in the protective barrier around Perseopia was the same type as the one felt by our forefathers the last time someone else arrived here. And it coincides exactly with when Sammy told me she arrived in Perseopia: two days ago."

"She could just be a gifted child that experienced the sensation and is pretending to come from somewhere she doesn't. Or she could have been put up to it by a member of the Order. They say their leader Ramus VorMask is a powerful sorcerer."

"Do you think I would be so easily fooled? I can feel she's different. And few people who are sensitive enough to experience these ripples would know what the sensation meant. Only the magi have a history long enough to understand what they are."

"Assuming she is a Mother Worlder, what does the Order want with her?"

"I don't know. She's different; she has the potential to be powerful, maybe. But I don't think that's it. I think they're scared of her, like she's here for a reason. Although I can't think what that reason would be."

Hami's gaze became vacant, focusing on a distant object behind the Regent. He started gulping again and his face ran slick with sweat. Then he vomited on the floor. He was sick several more times, and remained with his head bent over as he retched.

Mustafa said nothing.

"I'm sorry," Hami said when he could compose himself enough to talk. "I thought I could control it."

"That was my favourite carpet. But I'll get over it." Mustafa smiled, but Hami didn't acknowledge the attempt at humour.

"What do you know of the Lurker at the Gate?" Hami said.

Beads of sweat prickled the Regent's forehead. "The monster of the fog?" he whispered, his heart galloping. "The vision you get after prolonged exposure to the smog? You've seen it? You've become infected with the nightmare."

The Regent slid his chair back slowly. He was scared. Scared and repulsed. The acidic stench of Hami's vomit became overpowering. He had to get out of the room, get as far from Hami as possible. Calling security would be pointless; Hami could kill everyone in the building in the blink of an eye.

Hami watched him intently. He'd be able to tell what Mustafa was thinking. "And did you ever hear the story of the priest that claimed to have seen the Lurker?"

Mustafa gulped. "The one who said he saw the monster outside the Fifth Azaran Fire Temple?" He breathed through clenched teeth. "That was thirty years ago and he was just a boy."

"He *was* just a boy, but what does that matter?"

"A boy well known for telling tall tales. Everything he said was dismissed by the magi. The only reason people even remember him is because he claimed that Grand Master Onora Bruche was killed by the Lurker. If Master Bruche hadn't disappeared at the same time, then no one would have taken him seriously."

Hami watched the Regent, his face grim.

"Hami, you're scaring me," Mustafa said. "You're not yourself and—"

Hami held up a finger to silence the Regent. "Have I claimed to have seen the Lurker at the Gate?"

"You haven't. But you've been to Aratta and you're sick with the infection."

"I *have* been to Aratta, and I *am* sick, but I'm also in full command of my faculties. I only mentioned the Lurker and the young priest because there's more to the story than you may be aware of. An interesting accompaniment that's been forgotten in the retelling over the years."

Mustafa ran a sleeve across his forehead. His ulcer had flared up and was biting into his stomach lining.

"The young priest claimed that he'd witnessed Onora and the Lurker fighting on the bridge over the Cataclysm. He also said Onora was thrown to his death into the Cataclysm below. But what you may not know was that the boy said he saw a girl with the magus. A girl with yellow hair."

"I never heard that part."

"It wasn't important to the story. Not until now. The magi recognised the sensation of Sammy arriving as being the same as the last time someone arrived in Perseopia. The same sensation that occurred a number of days before the events the boy told of."

"So now the story the boy told is true? Another girl arrived in Perseopia before Sammy? And Onora was killed by the monster?"

"The boy witnessed the fight from inside the fire temple. And the bridge across the Cataclysm is a long stretch of rock. He'll have barely been able to make out the Grand Master, a girl with yellow hair, and a mysterious figure in black. When the Grand Master was thrown to his death by the figure in black, the boy probably convinced himself it was the Lurker. It could've been Ramus VorMask or another member of the Order. It could've been someone else entirely. But seeing a girl with yellow hair after the sensation of someone arriving in Perseopia is significant."

"I still can't believe a master magus was defeated by a member of the Order."

"The Order has recruited many powerful men over the years. Sorcerers like Achaemen Mantis. Men that claimed to be Necromancers. And let's not forget General Azim Azertash—the General. He killed several magi in his time."

"But a Grand Master?" Mustafa wiped his forehead again. "Does that mean the Order got that girl? The first one, I mean?"

"I don't know. The boy said he fled when he saw Onora thrown into the fire."

"But that was thirty years ago. If a member of the Order defeated Master Bruche and captured the girl, wouldn't they have used her for something by now?"

"Unless the girl died too," Hami said. "Or escaped. Alternatively, she might not have been the one they were after."

"But what does it all mean?"

"I believe Onora Bruche was close to something and got killed for it. Unfortunately, he'd already left the magi network at that point so we don't know what he knew, or what he thought he knew."

"What's the point of having a magi network if magi disconnect from it when they learn something important?"

"There's not a lot we can do about that now, but I'm sure he had his reasons. What's important is that the Order knows there's a second visitor and has kidnapped Behnam. I'm guessing it's to find out how much the brotherhood knows. I think the Order believes this girl poses the same threat the first did—whatever that was—and they're looking to either capture or kill her. That means we need to keep hold of her until we can figure out what's going on."

The Regent pulled at his collar. He was drenched in sweat. He'd have to bathe before retiring tonight. "So we know nothing about the girl, except that she might be powerful?"

"And there was a difference in the ripple when she arrived."

"I thought you said that the ripple was the same."

"It was the same type of disturbance, but it was bigger. The ripple that occurred around the time the first girl was sighted was the same size as the ripple that occurred when Mantis killed the Sultan. When Sammy entered Perseopia, the disturbance was three times larger than either of those two occurrences."

"Three times?" Mustafa said. "No wonder the Order is taking an interest in the girl. Perhaps the first girl wasn't powerful enough for what they wanted."

"It's possible that Sammy possesses three times the power of the first visitor. Which could be why the Order is so interested in her. That's the belief of many of my brothers."

"But not yours?"

"I don't believe anyone, no matter how powerful, could create a larger ripple."

"But you believe she has power?"

"She does. I can feel it whenever I'm in her presence. There's a very real power there that's lain dormant until now. I think entering Perseopia has awoken something in her. At the moment, she's unaware of it and it could take years to develop, maybe even longer to harness. But even so, we can't allow her to be taken by the Order. Not until we know more about her. That's why she must

156

have a full, thirty-strong entourage of Marzban to take her to New Ecbatana. Once she's there, she'll be safe until we know the extent of her abilities or alternatively what kind of threat she poses. As long as she remains in Honton Keep, she's a liability. The safest option is to get her to Grand Master Aegis."

"Why don't you wait for magi back-up instead of taking my Marzban? Not that you aren't welcome to them, but the magi would give far better protection."

"The crabmen are assembling as we speak. Honton Keep is closer to Aratta and the crab hive than it is to the magi garrison or New Ecbatana. Time is of the essence. I need your men assembled and briefed tomorrow to be ready to leave the following day."

"There are no magi in the area? Your brothers are spread across the entire realm. There must be someone close."

"The Fungi Forest is teeming with crabmen. It's far too dangerous for anyone to be in there. There *was* a magus close by, about two days from here. A lower order brother called Victa Wild. He was dispatched into the forest to investigate a potential magus recruit that had connected to the network for the first time. But we lost contact with him when a unit of crabmen attacked. Even magi are putting their lives at risk by entering the forest, hence why we've vacated the area."

"The magi aren't able to help at all?"

"Twenty of our finest men, riding the swiftest greenbucks, set off from the garrison yesterday. But they're still at least four days' ride from the Keep."

Mustafa sat quietly for a moment, deep in thought. "What if Sammy and that first girl were chosen children?"

Hami frowned but said nothing.

"Just indulge me a moment," Mustafa said.

Hami shrugged. "Go on."

"If the first girl was a chosen child that would make Sammy the last one. The legend says there were two. One that brings light. And one that will open the gates of hell."

Hami coughed. "That's what the myth says."

"Which one is Sammy?"

Hami stared at the Regent with raw eyes. "I haven't the faintest idea."

"If the first girl was the good child does that mean that Perseopia's only hope for the light returning has been snuffed out already? And if Sammy is the dark one, what are you going to do with her?"

"The chosen children are a myth, Mustafa. There are no chosen children. Besides, Sammy's eventual fate is of little importance. The magi will assess the level of threat she poses to the realm, then we will deal with her accordingly."

–TWENTY-FOUR–
CRABS IN THE NIGHT

Dressed in a silk bathrobe, Sammy shuffled back to the communal room, having spent the afternoon having her back and feet massaged. She wasn't normally one for pampering but the servants insisted and Mehrak had been up for it, so she'd agreed. The masseuse had lit a fire in the hearth and had rubbed in an oil that smelled of black fruit pastilles. The foot rub part was painful, but the back rub had been divine, and the combination of warmth and berry aroma had put her to sleep in moments.

She found Mehrak at the banquet table in the communal room.

"You look shattered," he said. "You should get an early night and some sleep." He didn't look much better himself.

"I've already been asleep, but it's made me feel worse, like I need to go back to bed again."

Mehrak let out a long, shaky yawn. "Same. I don't normally sleep during the day. I figured that's why I feel so groggy."

"We're going down to the Marzban camp to see Louis later though, aren't we?"

"Sure," Mehrak said. He looked across at a device on the far wall. It had a couple of counter-balanced weights, like ball bearings, spinning back and forth on a vertical axis. A long pendulum-style needle hung underneath and below that was a scale. On the left of the scale was a circle, and on the right, a crescent. The needle was closer to the crescent than the circle.

"We've been asleep almost all day," he said. "It's already evening."

"Can we still go and see Louis?"

"Of course," Mehrak said. He groaned. "I just wish I wasn't so tired. I can't believe we've wasted most of the day. We haven't seen anything of the palace yet. What do they put in that massage oil? I feel like I've been drugged."

Back in her bedroom, Sammy towelled off the oil and put on some trousers and a fleece. She met Mehrak back in the communal room and they set off towards the palace lobby.

With the thick smell of berries gone, Sammy was beginning to feel more awake. At the large doors that led back out into the Keep, two palace guards closed off their exit.

"A thousand pardons," one of the men said, "but may we enquire where you're going?"

"Out," Mehrak said, puffing out his chest.

The man looked to his friend; both were clearly embarrassed. "I'm afraid that isn't going to be possible," he said. "We've been given strict instructions not to let you leave."

Mehrak paled. "The Regent won't let us leave?"

"Not His Majesty," the guard replied. "Principal Hootan."

Mehrak turned to Sammy. "I told you we shouldn't have picked him up. I knew there was something funny about him. Now he's keeping us prisoner."

"He wouldn't do that," Sammy said.

"Mehrak!" It was Hami. He stepped down from the staircase leading to the Regent's office and calmly walked across the lobby. When he reached them, he dismissed the guards with a nod.

"I hope you didn't mind these gentlemen stopping you," he said. "I asked to be informed when you were leaving so I could accompany you both to see Louis. That is, if neither of you mind. Obviously, you're free to go whenever you like."

"I told you," Sammy said to Mehrak. "We don't mind. Do we?"

Mehrak said nothing and turned away towards the door.

The three of them left the palace in silence. They walked down the mound and zigzagged their way through the lamp posts at the bottom.

Tiny beetles and multi-coloured moths circled the lamps, periodically bumping into the lights, ricocheting off and looping back round to crash again.

The Keep was quiet. The men who'd been raising water from the well had gone and the marketplace was empty when they got there. The stalls had been packed up and Sammy could see all the way into the dark far corner where Esther's stall had been. Like everyone else, she'd gone. Unease fluttered in her stomach. When she'd said the name 'Esther', the woman's reaction couldn't have been more severe. It wasn't the sort of reaction you could fake.

Hami placed a hand on Sammy's back and moved her onwards, away from the market.

The Keep's residential area was darker than it had been that morning. Porch lights had been extinguished and streetlights had been dimmed. At the edge of the city, the atmosphere was darker still, reaching its blackest by the large square windows that framed the gateway to the outside world and the Moat.

Hami led the way up the steps to the lift.

Next to the lift's crank, two men were throwing coloured pebbles in a game that closely resembled marbles. They got up as Hami drew close and prepared to operate the mechanism.

Sammy stepped onto the lift platform and leant over the railing. The air outside was cool but fresh. She inhaled deeply while watching the waves of rolling fog below. The drowsiness she'd experienced at the palace blew away as the air sent electricity along her synapses. She was excited, maybe even a little scared, but she felt alive. She wanted to leave the Keep, to be back in the Fungi Forest, continuing their adventure in Golden Egg Cottage. But part of her sensed something out there, waiting, a danger she could feel, but not see.

She was letting her imagination get the better of her. There was nothing out there. It was the prospect of heading down into the giant rhino-patrolled wasteland that was unnerving her. She needed to relax.

Mehrak and Hami stepped onto the lift behind. Hami gave the nod for the operators to work the mechanism and they went down. Mehrak stared down into the fog, his thumbs beating out a nervous rhythm on the metal. Periodically, he'd shift along the railing to get a better view of below. Not that there was anything to see, but that didn't stop him from trying.

"Been missing Louis?" Hami asked.

Mehrak didn't answer.

"Look," Hami said. "I asked the guards to inform me if you were leaving because I wanted to make sure you'd both be safe."

Mehrak shrugged.

The remainder of the descent was a silent one, until the campfire lights shimmered into view and Mehrak became animated. "Look!" he said, pointing at a golden blur way below.

"Eggie!" Sammy called.

Proving, without a doubt, Louis's exceptional hearing, the golden shape lurched forward and began circling around as if it were attached to a puppy chasing its tail.

Mehrak facepalmed. "I bet he's shaken all the pots and pans from the cupboards. One of the many drawbacks of having your house on the back of an animal."

When the lift touched down, Mehrak threw open the gate and sprinted away. Sammy followed. They ran past campfires, jumped guy ropes, and zipped in and out of the Marzban, making a beeline for Louis. Unlike the Keep, base camp was still busy. Marzban were training, tending to karkadann, and sharpening the pointy ends of their lances.

"Louis!" Mehrak called when he got in sight. Louis lowered his head and Mehrak threw his arms around the big beast's muzzle—or as far around as he could get them. Sammy came to a stop, remembering she didn't know Louis well enough to do the same. She stood there, awkward a moment, and then gave him a pat on the neck.

"Leiss and Borzin are on duty tonight," Hami said when he caught up. "They've invited us to join them for a drink."

The two guards stood to greet them as they approached the campfire. There were five other Marzban in their company and they introduced themselves as Eva, Kelzar, Danush, Parang and Ali.

Mehrak and Sammy took a camp chair each. Louis lowered himself to the floor nearby while Hami excused himself.

A battered billycan bubbled over the campfire, and from the smell Sammy immediately identified its contents as chocolate. Eva got up and ladled some of the steaming brown contents into small tin cups and passed them round the circle. She smiled at Sammy.

"These boys always ask me to serve up," she said, nodding towards the men sitting around the campfire. She was petite and feminine but athletic, and moved with the sort of confidence Steven Seagal had when he entered a bar full of criminals. "I think they like me to mother them."

Kelzar laughed. "No, it's because she makes it the best," he said. "Mother us? Mothers are soft and warm; Eva's tough as karkadann hide, with balls bigger than Leiss's."

"Leave it out," Leiss said. "Eva's warm."

"And you'd know, would you?" Parang said. He was a scrawny, weasel-faced man with a thin, wispy beard. "The only lady in your life is Mummy, isn't it?" He laughed.

"I didn't mean it like that," Leiss stammered as a few of the others joined in laughing.

"It's okay," Eva said to him. "I can handle these chumps." She smiled. "Thanks, though."

Leiss blushed but smiled back.

Hami slipped back into the group and took a place next to Sammy. His eyes were watering and he was gripping his waist. He dabbed at his mouth with a black-stained cloth.

Sammy took a cup from Eva and sipped at the rich, chocolaty drink inside. It was wonderful. "This doesn't taste like the chocolate I get at home," she said. "This is much darker. Where I come from, it's sweet and milky."

As she savoured the smooth, warm liquid, a thought occurred to her. She leant over towards Mehrak. "Doesn't chocolate come from trees?" she whispered.

"No," Mehrak whispered back. "Cocoa grubs." He jiggled his cup until a lumpy, white sausage broke the surface of the liquid. It looked like the marshmallow man's arm. Sammy shuddered and put her cup down on the floor. She wished she hadn't asked.

"Where is it you come from?" Parang asked, as he squinted at her down his pointy nose.

Sammy stared at her tin cup and tapped at it with her foot. "Sorry?" she asked. She wanted to see if she had chocolate maggots in her drink.

"She comes from a small village, west of the Fungi Forest," Hami said. "Isn't that right, Sammy?" His hand had come to rest on top of hers. Sammy nodded and her face flushed.

Mehrak saw Hami's hand move, gasped and promptly choked on his chocolate.

"What's the name of your village?" Parang asked, sounding intrigued. "My family is from that side of Perseopia."

Sammy glanced nervously at Hami. Hami opened his mouth to respond, but got cut short by four long horn blasts sounding out in the fog.

Borzin and Ali—the two youngest Marzban at the campfire—leapt from their seats and looked at each other in excitement. From a different direction, a second horn sounded. Four blasts again. Tin cups were lowered from mouths. Marzban who had been performing drills stopped. And the entire campsite fell silent.

A third horn sounded from another direction. Four blasts.

"They're here already," Hami said under his breath. He took his hand from Sammy's and stood up.

Who was here already? No one else picked up on Hami's comment. All eyes were on the fog, waiting for something to happen.

Then, from out of the mist, came chattering, like millions of rattlesnakes shaking their tails at once.

"There must be thousands of them!" Danush, one of the older men, said. "There's never been three alarms before."

Then came the sound of a fourth alarm. Four blasts of a horn. That was the watershed moment. The tension shattered and the campsite went wild. Marzban ran in all directions, in and out of tents, putting on boots and fetching saddles. The portly First Chief General stumbled out of his tent in a fluster.

"Man your karkadann!" he yelled.

"Wheel out the cannons!" came the cry from another officer.

Marzban grabbed lances and swords, untied and mounted their karkadann, then thundered out of camp, spiralling the fog as blackness enveloped them. Leiss ran to a group of karkadann tied to a post and unhitched one. Borzin went to follow, but Hami grabbed him back.

"Wait here with Sammy and Mehrak," he said, then ran to the First Chief General.

Borzin remained where he stood, face flushed red.

Marzban wheeled out cannons on trailers from the larger tents. They hitched them to pairs of karkadann, a driver saddled up and took the reins, while a second guard manned the gun on the back. Other karkadann carried smaller cannons lashed to their flanks.

Once prepped, the beasts were driven out into the fog, hammering past like freight trains, roaring and pounding the earth as they left. Vibrations shook the billycan from the fire, sending chocolate and grubs slipping and skidding through the dirt.

High-pitched squealing and chattering cries reached base camp through the fog. The noise was getting louder. Closer.

"That's impossible!" Kelzar shouted as he ran by. He fumbled with his lance, dropping it then picking it up again. "It sounds like they're less than ten stadia away."

"You'd better get a move on then, hadn't you?" Eva said, shoving him onwards.

"Crabmen," Mehrak said.

Sammy was getting that bad feeling in her stomach, like she'd accidentally swallowed a chocolaty maggot.

"Sammy! Mehrak!" Hami called. He slowed up as he reached them. "Get to the lift. I want you both back up in the Keep."

"What about Louis?" Mehrak asked.

"Borzin!" Hami called to the young guard. "Take these two up to the Keep and guard them all the way to the palace. When they get there, hand them over to the palace guards. Make sure you see them into the building."

Borzin's mouth opened but nothing came out.

"Now!" Hami shouted, flecks of black phlegm flying from his mouth.

Borzin moved to grab Sammy and Mehrak.

"What about Louis?" Mehrak said, louder this time. Borzin took hold of his arm.

"He'll be fine," Hami said. "The crabmen won't make it to base camp."

"I'm not going." Mehrak pulled away from Borzin. "Louis is scared. He needs me with him."

Louis lay cowed on the floor, Golden Egg Cottage trembling on his back.

"I'm not going to ask you a second time." Hami stepped into Mehrak's personal space.

Mehrak was clearly intimidated, but held Hami's gaze. "Louis is family."

"If you leave now," Hami said through gritted teeth, "I'll have Marzban assigned to him for protection. If you don't, he's on his own."

Mehrak's lip curled into a snarl. "I've already lost one person I care about to crabmen."

"So make the choice."

They held each other's gaze a moment longer, then Mehrak turned to Louis.

"I'm sorry," he said softly.

Louis lowered his head.

Mehrak placed his hand on Louis's nose. "I have to go. It'll be okay. I'll be back as soon as it's over."

An explosion shook the ground. Karkadann roars, followed by distorted squealing, echoed through the fog. Narok thundered into the campsite riding his large, dark karkadann. The animal had a feral quality that Sammy hadn't seen before, and blue ink-like liquid drooled from its mouth.

Narok pulled the beast up in front of Hami. "Thank Ahura you're here," he said. He was panting and there were flecks of blue splattered over his clothes and face. "We need your help. They're trying to force their way to the Keep." Then he noticed Borzin. "Why aren't you on your karkadann?"

"Principal Hootan asked me to take Mehrak and Sammy to the palace, sir," he said, sounding like a scolded schoolboy.

"Well, you'd better do as he says, hadn't you? When you get to city level, have all the lifts raised. Give the instruction not to lower them until the all-clear."

Borzin stared up at the general. He looked like a child who'd been told Santa would be filling his stocking with dog turds for Christmas.

"Go!" Narok shouted.

Borzin grabbed Sammy and Mehrak by their arms and forcibly moved them through the campsite.

"You'll be alright, Louis!" Mehrak called over his shoulder. "It'll be over soon and we'll be back."

As they were rushed towards the lift, Sammy turned to see Hami make a superhuman leap into the air, perform a forward somersault and land on the back of a karkadann. A horizontal motion in the air with his arm untethered the animal from its post and the leash whipped up to his hand. The karkadann reared up, roared, then charged out of camp, followed closely by Narok.

Borzin pushed Sammy and Mehrak onto the lift, slamming the gate behind them and clanging the railing.

The platform began its steady climb and the campsite soon vanished into the cloudy depths of the fog.

Mehrak had his eyes closed and the lift railing gripped with both hands.

The cries of battle remained constant. Even with her hands over her ears, Sammy couldn't escape the chatter and screaming.

They were trapped, dangling in the air, crawling up the side of the rock painfully slowly with nowhere to escape to. At any moment the crabmen would come, scaling the rock after them. She couldn't bear it. She had to get away from the noise.

Then she felt a hand take hers. Calloused and masculine, but gentle: Mehrak's. The gesture had an instant effect on her. A calm optimism eked into her. He gave her hand a squeeze.

"It'll be all right," he said.

She wanted him to throw his arms around her, to pull her into him. She wanted to bury her face in his chest. But the hand-holding was enough. It worked. And despite the excruciating lift ride, they eventually made it up to Honton Keep. Mehrak had done this for her. He could've stayed with Louis, but he'd chosen to look after her instead.

Borzin went to get the other lifts raised. Sammy and Mehrak remained where they were, still holding hands, still looking out across the fog, while behind them a quiet Honton Keep slept, unaware of the battle raging below. The noise of war had been dampened by the mattress of fog, somehow distancing them from the reality of it.

Mehrak put his arm around Sammy's shoulder as a light flashed in the distance. A second later, the cannon boom caught up, followed by inhuman screams.

"I should be defending my kingdom," Borzin said when he returned. He kicked at a pebble by his feet and wandered halfway down the stairs that led into the Keep.

"Hami and Louis are going to be okay," Sammy said. "Right?"

Mehrak didn't appear to have heard her. He continued to stare out across the slowly undulating fog. "Hami will be fine," he said at last. "He's a magus. They always look out for themselves."

"Louis will be too," Sammy said.

Mehrak didn't reply. He turned from the railing and walked away down the steps into the Keep.

–TWENTY-FIVE–
Not Out of the Woods

Mehrak said nothing on the walk back to the palace. Or when Borzin dropped them off. He said nothing in the communal room and went straight to his bedroom without so much as a 'good night'.

Sammy went to her room and sat on the bed. Why couldn't she have just left the Midnight Emerald Bracelet alone? She took off her shoes, placed them neatly together, and then climbed into bed, pulling the cover over her head.

She woke when she heard someone moving around in the communal room. She sat up, slipped out of bed, crept over to her bedroom door and opened it a crack.

Hami was at the table, arms folded, head down.

"You're alright?" she asked as she entered the room.

Hami nodded, but didn't look up. He looked worse than ever. If he hadn't moved, Sammy might have thought he was dead. His face was pale, his cheeks and eye sockets hollow and purple. His brown clothes were somehow scruffier than they had been and he had cuts on his hands and face.

"What happened?"

"A full-scale attack." He opened his eyes to reveal the whites had turned red.

Mehrak burst into the room. "What happened to Louis? He'd better be okay—"

"He's fine!" Hami snapped as he turned on him. "The crabmen didn't make base camp. And I had four Marzban assigned to him, like I promised!"

Mehrak stopped. "I ... I'm sorry. I've been so worried. I barely slept."

"I *haven't* slept," Hami said. "At all. I just got back."

"I'm sorry." Mehrak turned to leave.

"It's alright," Hami said. "You were worried. I get it. But he's fine. So let's all keep calm."

"Is it over?" Sammy asked.

"Almost." Hami picked up a small root vegetable from the bowl in front of him. "The Marzban are clearing the last of the crabmen from the area—the ones that haven't already fled or been killed." He inspected the vegetable then dropped it back into the bowl.

"How many were there?" Mehrak asked.

"The fog made it impossible to tell. A lot. They outnumbered us something like twenty to one."

"You really are alright though, aren't you?" Sammy asked.

Hami smiled. It might have been the first genuine smile she'd seen on him. It made him seem younger. He looked closer to his actual age in his early twenties, not the beaten down, middle-aged man he appeared to be at other times. He was nice-looking when he smiled.

"Yes. Thank you," he said.

"Did you kill any?" Sammy asked. "What about Narok? Did he kill some? And the other Marzban, are they okay?"

Hami's smile waned. "Slow down. Narok's fine; a lot of the others weren't so lucky. I think we lost around fifty men and women with many more casualties. Which, considering the numbers we were up against, is a miracle."

The room lapsed into silence.

"I'm going to take Sammy to visit an old friend of mine at the Keep," Mehrak said after a time. "Will you be accompanying us?"

"No," Hami said. "But thanks for the offer. I have to help plan for our departure tomorrow."

"Our departure?"

"Mine and Sammy's. Honton Keep isn't as safe as I originally thought. I need to take her to the capital and into the protection of the magi."

"Sammy's and *your* departure? When was this decided? She's staying with me. You can go to the capital if you want ..."

"Sammy is not going to wander Perseopia unprotected. She's from the Mother World. She's too important. I'm taking her to Grand Master Aegis in New Ecbatana. She'll be safe there."

"You're going to kidnap her?" Mehrak said.

"Don't be dramatic. Sammy's not yours to keep and I'm not leaving her to drift through the Fungi Forest in a ramshackle caravan."

Mehrak's face flushed.

"Sammy needs protection," Hami said. "And she's going to get it. End of discussion."

"I actually care about Sammy," Mehrak said. "She only matters to you because she's special."

"Don't I get a say in what happens to me?" Sammy asked.

Hami turned to her. "You've arrived in Perseopia with no family and nowhere to live. What are your options? Keep Mehrak company until he finds his wife? Once she's back in the picture you'll find yourself ditched in the middle of the forest again."

"I would never do that!" Mehrak blurted out. "Gisouie would understand."

"Would she? You're shacked up with a young, beautiful sixteen-year-old who's living with you and sleeping in your bed."

Beautiful? Sammy suppressed a smile. That probably wasn't the correct response in this situation, but she hadn't received that particular compliment before, other than from her mother. Not that beauty was something she necessarily wanted to define herself by, but it was pretty cool.

"It's not like that," Mehrak said. "Gisouie trusts me."

"Regardless of your good intentions, Sammy also needs protection. And you can't provide it, which you've already demonstrated by losing your wife. I can't, in good conscience, allow a visitor from the Mother World to die wandering the Fungi Forest. The crabmen attacked the Keep in force last night. We need to leave and get Sammy into the safe hands of the magi."

Mehrak scowled but didn't respond.

"I would've thought you'd welcome someone else taking responsibility for her. You'll be free to carry on looking for your wife. The Cataclysm isn't far off the route we'll be taking to the capital. That's as good a place as any to look for her. The Regent has signed off on an entourage of thirty Marzban and karkadann for us. You should take advantage of that and travel with us."

Mehrak's eyes narrowed. "Thirty Marzban? Isn't that a bit excessive?"

"Sammy's safety is our top priority."

"You really have her best interests at heart?"

"I do," Hami said, without breaking eye contact.

Mehrak said nothing.

Hami got up. "I need to make preparations for our departure tomorrow. I've asked for a couple of Marzban to accompany you around the Keep today. They've given us Leiss and Borzin."

"Does that mean we're no longer safe up here in the Keep?" Mehrak asked.

"The crabmen attacked the Keep from four separate directions last night: north, west, south-west and south-east. It took all the Marzban to hold them back."

"A four-pronged attack. I'm no soldier, but I know it makes sense to strike your target from multiple directions."

"That's true, but they could've spread out more. There was a gaping hole between the north and south-east prongs on the side of the Keep opposite base camp; a hole that we could only spare a couple of Marzban to sentry."

"You think they were creating a diversion? Did the sentries pick up anything?"

"One said the area stayed quiet all night. The other is missing."

Typical. Vafa was already at his post and looking alert.

Teymour laboured up the steps to the window at the edge of the Keep. He was getting too old for these long shifts. He'd been fighting crabmen all night and was beaten. Vafa, on the other hand, looked like he'd just leapt out of bed after a full night's sleep. The lad could fight all day and still be spritely for a sentry shift.

At the top of the steps, Teymour took a deep breath and blew it out. The cool breeze that skimmed off the top of the fog wasn't enough to perk him up, but it helped.

Vafa had propped himself against the frame of the window, arms crossed, one foot against the stone. He smirked.

"Struggling are we, grandad?"

"You wait until you get to my age," Teymour said.

"Maybe a sip of this will wake you up." Vafa reached into his cloak and pulled out a small silver flask.

"I can't believe your wife sewed a pocket into your cloak so you could drink on the job."

"It's great isn't it?"

"I think it's disgraceful."

Vafa smiled. "So you don't want any?"

"Well. It'd be a shame to let it go to waste." Teymour took the flask. "Obviously I wouldn't be doing this if we'd been given proper work to do."

"Obviously."

Teymour took a long draught and sighed contentedly as the warming liquid slipped down his throat.

"Do you think we've done something wrong?" he asked. "I mean, we've been fighting crabmen all night, then they give us an early morning sentry shift on the wall. I could understand if we'd been given base camp side. But here on the quietest section of wall with no lifts? What's that all about?"

"I know, right? Are those crabbies really going to sneak past our karkadann and scale the rock?"

Teymour handed the flask back. He put his hands on his hips and exhaled loudly. "Right. I need to take a leak," he said.

"You just got here. I suppose you're losing bladder control in your old age too?"

"Enough with the old jokes." Teymour shuffled back down the steps and entered a narrow alley between two houses. He'd just found himself a discreet corner and relaxed when Vafa called out:

"Teymour! Come and look at this!"

"I can't," Teymour called back. "I've already started."

"There's hot steam coming up from the Moat."

"Okay. Wait," Teymour said. "Just give me a moment." He pulled at his trousers, tucked himself in and rushed out of the alley.

"What—?"

Steam was rising from the Moat and coming in through the large square window.

Vafa had gone.

"Vafa?" Teymour jogged to the top of the steps, his earlier tiredness forgotten.

Vafa's silver flask was on the floor. Teymour groaned as he bent over to pick the thing up. Was this a prank? It was the sort of thing the boy would do. But something didn't feel right.

The temperature was going up and thick steam was coming up from the fog, making it hard to see. Maybe Vafa had become disorientated and fallen off the edge.

Teymour fumbled inside his uniform, pulled out his whistle and put it to his lips.

He didn't blow. They'd both been drinking. If Vafa was playing a prank and he sounded the alarm, they'd both wind up in big trouble. He'd have a quick scout around first, then, if Vafa didn't show up, he'd call it in.

First he was going to find out where the steam was coming from. Vafa might've had the same idea and fallen over the edge when he'd gone to look, so Teymour wasn't going to take any chances. He lay down on his chest and eased himself along the floor, scraping his clothes on the stone as he did so. He imagined what his commander would say if he could see him ruining his uniform in such an undignified manner. What would his wife say when she saw his scuffed buttons?

He stuck his head out into the column of steam and flinched as the hot vapour hit him. He closed his eyes and rubbed his face. He was going to have another look anyway. He covered his face with his hands and peered through his fingers.

His heart stuttered in his chest. There was someone below, clinging to the side of the rock. Just a black shape, but definitely a person.

"Vafa!" Teymour shouted.

No reply. The figure shifted, and pulled itself higher. Closer.

Teymour extended his hand. "Almost there! I got you, buddy."

A hand shot up and grabbed his wrist. It was scalding hot, burning his skin. Before he could scream, it yanked him off the edge and he was in free fall.

———

Five stadia below the Keep, Teymour's body hit the rocks. It flopped haphazardly, tumbling over itself like a ragdoll, until it came to rest at the bottom of a pile of stones, next to his friend Vafa, who lay dead beside him.

–TWENTY-SIX–
Pearls of Portal Paths

Sammy shivered and glanced over her shoulder.

Lamp post trees, and no one hiding in them. The same view as in front. Hami had made her paranoid. They'd only just left the palace and she was rattled. Something didn't seem right, though. Just like it hadn't the previous night before the crabmen attacked. Mehrak had explained that the only way up to the Keep were the lifts at base camp, and because the crabmen hadn't made it there, that meant they were safe.

Sammy wasn't convinced.

Mehrak handed his friend Bertie's address to Leiss, and the big Marzban led the way. He took them through the metal lamp posts, looping round the back of the palace and heading in the opposite direction to the lift site. Apparently Bertie lived on the north-east side, past the industrial district.

Borzin followed silently, probably disappointed to be babysitting again.

"Can we go to the market on the way home?" Sammy asked.

"No," Leiss said. "The marketplace is off limits. We've been ordered to accompany you to Bertie's house, then straight back to the palace. No detours."

"You're magi property now," Mehrak said to Sammy. And then he whispered, "Maybe we should ditch these guys."

"Great idea," Sammy whispered back. "Except you've already handed them Bertie's address so they know where we're going."

Mehrak had no response to that.

The industrial quadrant was a sprawling mass of stone block warehouses, which, according to Leiss, were mostly textile factories. They weaved their way through the dusty streets, passing blacksmiths and carpenters that had set up shop in amongst the big buildings, beating their glowing iron weapons or planing strips of mushroom.

On the way out of the industrial district, they took a dark alleyway between two tall warehouses. A filthy path, strewn with broken blocks, stained rags and food waste.

"It's sketchy here," Sammy said. She shuffled closer to Mehrak.

"You can see why we left this place out of the Honton Keep tourist guide," Borzin said.

"This is the quickest route to your friend's neighbourhood," Leiss said. "Maybe you'd have preferred to lead the way, Borzin?"

Borzin rolled his eyes and smiled at Sammy. "He's just grumpy because his mum's giving him a hard time."

"She's always given me a hard time. And thank you for sharing my personal problems with our guests."

"Tell her to move out. She's never done you any favours, and it's your house."

"She's not well. I can't just kick her out. It's not the right thing to do."

"The right thing?" Borzin shook his head. "You don't owe her anything. She singlehandedly destroyed your marriage."

"Give it a rest," Leiss replied and walked on in silence.

The passage led to a cramped and dirty residential area. The streets were arranged in a tight grid and the houses were crammed together side by side and back to back. They found the right street and Mehrak counted the house numbers until they reached a squashed terrace house surrounded by other squashed terraces. He rapped on the door and had barely finished when the door was yanked inward and replaced with a tall, skinny woman in a blue sari.

"Yes?" she asked.

Mehrak took a step back. "Dori?"

The woman's brow furrowed. She had long, grey hair plaited down her back and tied up by a delicate gold chain, and was one of those slim, attractive older women who infuriated Sammy's mother by retaining their figure well after they should've started sagging and growing bingo wings.

"It's Mehrak," Mehrak said. "Mehrak Omid. Bertie's an old friend of my father's."

Dori's face brightened. "Mehrak? Really? Bertie's told me so much about you. I didn't mean to be rude. I thought you were the kids who kick our door and run off. One of the many downsides of Bertie not holding down a proper job and forcing me to live in this ghastly area."

Mehrak gave an embarrassed smile. "Is he in?"

Dori led them inside. "Bertie's always *in*," she said. "*In* his workshop tinkering, or *in* his study with his books." She took them along a cramped hallway and into a small sitting room. "Make yourselves comfortable and I'll go fetch him."

The sitting room was dark and pokey. The carpet and furniture were threadbare, and the walls were covered in a mixture of charcoal portraits and illustrations of mechanical devices. Books, cups and general clutter sat in piles on any available surface, encouraging shadows and dark recesses. Only the fire in the hearth gave the room any kind of light and brought it back into the realms of being a home rather than a cave.

Leiss and Borzin wedged themselves onto a small sofa that didn't look at all comfortable. Sammy remained standing and worked her way through the charcoal-drawn portraits on the walls. She stopped at a sketch of a young man standing with a boy. The boy was unquestionably a young Mehrak.

"That's you," she said.

"You recognise that handsome fellow?" Mehrak asked.

"No, but you're the boy next to him, aren't you?" Sammy said with a wink.

The door at the opposite end of the room opened and a middle-aged man with a shiny, red face entered the room. On his head he had a black turban, on his chin a scruffy white beard and the rest of him was covered in greasy overalls.

"Mehrak, my boy!" he said, holding out his arms.

"Uncle Bertie!" Mehrak replied.

They shook hands, slapped backs, then Mehrak introduced Sammy. Leiss and Borzin were briefly referenced with a 'don't worry about them'.

Bertie stood hands on hips, grinning broadly, and then frowned. "Where's Gisouie?"

The smile vanished from Mehrak's face.

"No." Bertie shook his head slowly.

Mehrak nodded. "Crabmen. Over sixty days ago."

"Are you okay?" Bertie put a hand on Mehrak's shoulder and guided him to a second small sofa.

"Bearing up." Mehrak sat down. "I'm going after her, though. I came …"

"… to ask me about your Auntie Kimia?"

"Has there been any further news?"

Bertie sighed. "I can tell you what happened, but I think you know most of it already and I'm not sure it will help. There's been no news since I last wrote." He took a seat in a high-backed chair. Sammy sat next to Mehrak.

"Your letter was over a year ago. There's been nothing since?"

Bertie cast his eyes down. "We've heard nothing of Kimia since the night she was taken. The last letter from Dungalor was Mrs Gendra's, saying there'd been a magus investigating her disappearance."

Mehrak nodded but said nothing.

"My sister's wasn't a typical kidnapping, though," Bertie said. "Her papers and equipment disappeared with her and there was no sign of crabmen in the area. Previous letters she'd sent indicated that she was close to a breakthrough in her research. I think that's why she was taken."

"What was she researching?

Bertie shrugged. "I don't know. She never said. She was paranoid her letters would get intercepted so she didn't go into specifics. Mrs Gendra forwarded everything that was left; some odd bits of paperwork and some meteorological charts. I read everything but I don't understand any of it. Science isn't my thing, as you know. Kimia referred to 'weak points' in her research, but I've no idea what she was talking about."

"And it definitely wasn't crabmen?" Mehrak asked.

"Who knows anything for definite? The only other thing Mrs Gendra's letter told me was that strange men in furs had taken rooms at the inn the night Kimia disappeared. In the morning some had gone. The others claimed they didn't know anything."

Mehrak leant back on the sofa. "I heard that some kidnap victims get taken to a base in the mountains. That would explain the men in furs. Crabmen wouldn't survive the temperatures in the mountains so the Order would have sent men to do their dirty work."

"A base in the mountains?" Bertie asked. "I've not heard of it. Who told you that?"

"A magus," Mehrak said. "One we had the misfortune of meeting on our way here." Mehrak explained how they met Hami, about the crabmen activities and what Hami had told them about people being kidnapped to become slaves.

Dori reappeared through a side door, holding a tray and tea set aloft in one hand. "It's very sombre in here," she said. "This is the most miserable reunion I've ever seen."

Mehrak smiled weakly. "There was another reason I came here," he said.

"Okay," Bertie replied.

"To bring Sammy. I found her near the centre of the Fungi Forest."

"Near the centre?" Bertie turned to Sammy. "How did you manage to get all the way in there, my dear?"

Sammy glanced at Mehrak.

"Tell him," Mehrak said. "It's alright."

"I thought it was supposed to be a secret," she said. She glanced nervously towards Leiss and Borzin.

"What's supposed to be secret?" Leiss asked.

"Nothing," Mehrak said. "She thinks I'm going to tell Bertie something I shouldn't be, but I'm not." He turned his head away from Leiss and Borzin and raised his eyebrows at Sammy.

She got the message, but didn't want to betray Hami's trust. He'd saved them from the manticore, and from Esther when she'd attacked. And soon he'd be the one taking her to the capital.

"So how did you get that far into the forest?" Bertie asked. "Did you escape a kidnapping or something?"

"Nothing like that," Mehrak said. "She'd been playing with a golden device with an emerald set on the front. The emerald exploded and she got transported into the forest."

Bertie frowned. "Where from?"

Mehrak took a deep breath and rubbed his hands together. He was clearly savouring the big reveal. Sammy wished he'd get on with it before Leiss smashed his face in.

"Get on with it," Bertie said.

"Yeah, come on," Borzin echoed. He'd shuffled closer and was poised on the edge of his sofa.

"The Mother World," Mehrak said, enunciating each word with relish.

Borzin gaped. Dori frowned and looked at Bertie. Bertie remained silent.

"That's ridiculous," Leiss said at last.

"Whatever you say," Mehrak said, sitting back and smiling smugly.

Borzin looked confused. "Principal Hootan told us Sammy came from a small village west of the Fungi Forest."

"It must be true then," Mehrak said.

Borzin opened his mouth. Then shut it.

Leiss stood up. "We're going," he said. "You shouldn't be talking about this."

"You aren't taking them seriously, are you?" Borzin asked.

Leiss moved purposefully towards Mehrak.

"Wait," Mehrak said, holding up his hands. "Please. Hami hasn't told us to keep this secret. It's nothing to do with the magi. It's about Sammy. We aren't interfering with any of their plans by telling Bertie this. I promise. Please."

Leiss stopped but remained standing.

"I can keep a secret," Bertie said. "You don't have to worry about me."

"Who's he going to tell?" Dori said. "He's a hermit."

"Yes, thank you, Dori!" Bertie said. "This isn't the time. Why don't you pop over to Mildree's house so you can moan about me to her?"

"I do that every day. There are only so many ways to tell someone how useless your husband is. And do you think I'm going to miss this? This is the most interesting thing that's happened in our house since, well, since forever."

Bertie sighed and the room fell silent.

Sammy became aware that all eyes were on her. None more blatantly than Borzin's, whose face had gone slack as he stared at her. Leiss remained standing over her, wide-eyed, regarding her as if she was an extra-terrestrial, which she supposed she kind of was. She'd probably stare if she was in their shoes. She didn't like it, though. She'd spent her whole life wishing people noticed her, and now that everyone did, it wasn't all it was cracked up to be.

"It's true, isn't it?" Bertie said.

Mehrak nodded gravely, eyeing Leiss tentatively as he did so. "Yeah. The magus is convinced of it. He believes it enough to have us under constant watch. Hence these guys. And he's even keeping us at the palace."

"*Keeping* you at the palace?" Bertie got up from his chair and paced to the wall. He turned back to Mehrak. "Do you know what the magi want from her?"

"I don't know," Mehrak said as he glanced at Leiss. "But even if I did know, I wouldn't betray the magus's trust," he added quickly. "All I know is that he's taking Sammy to the Grand Master in New Ecbatana."

Leiss sat down with a grunt. "If at any point I think you're discussing something you shouldn't be, I'm going to physically remove you from this crappy little house."

"Don't rub it in," Dori said. "Some of us have to live here."

Mehrak shuffled uncomfortably and itched his hairline under his turban. "What I want to know," he said to Bertie, "is separate to whatever Hami wants." He looked to Leiss. Leiss frowned but said nothing. "Is there a way back to the Mother World from Perseopia? I figured that if anyone knew anything about it, you would."

"Did you ask the magus?" Bertie asked.

Mehrak looked at Leiss again. Leiss watched him closely. "He has his own agenda."

"You must respect the magi," Leiss said. "If they have plans for Sammy, then you honour them."

"I am," Mehrak said. "I mean we are. We're respecting the magi's orders. Aren't we, Sammy?"

Sammy nodded.

"We're going to do what Hami says. We just want to know if there's a way for Sammy to go home. She needs to know that, at some point in the future, she'll see her mother again. You understand that, don't you?"

"I understand," Borzin said gently.

Leiss stared at him.

"If you had children, Leiss, you'd understand."

Leiss rolled his eyes. "Fine. Carry on."

Bertie rubbed his hands together. "I had one thought while you were talking," he said. "Do you think Sammy's a chosen child?"

"The chosen children," Mehrak said. "I hadn't considered it. One of two from the Mother World returning to Perseopia? One to bring darkness, the other light?"

"That's them," Bertie said. "That's the most common Mother World myth. And as Sammy is a child and from the Mother World …"

"I prefer young adult," Sammy said.

"And as Sammy is a *young adult* and from the Mother World," Bertie said, "the chosen child lore is probably a good place to start." Bertie got up from his chair. "I'll be right back."

He left the room and returned shortly after with two books. He sat on the sofa next to Mehrak and dragged the coffee table over. Mehrak slid the teacups and tray to one side while Bertie placed the volumes on the surface and opened the top book.

Dori sighed loudly. "Well, this party has taken a dive," she said. "Sorry guys, but when Bertie cracks open his books, that's my cue to leave." And she collected the tray of empty cups and plates and left.

"Ignore her," Bertie said. "She's just attention-seeking." He flicked through the first half of the book. When he found the right page, he scanned down and pointed out a paragraph to Mehrak.

Sammy glanced at the book but the text was written in the same strange looping handwriting that was on the dial of the Midnight Emerald bracelet, so she sat back and waited for a verdict.

"This is the lore surrounding the chosen children," Bertie said.

Mehrak's mouth moved as he read the text. "Yes." His eyes sparkled in excitement. "This bit here. A portal pearl was created by Ahura Mazda at the genesis of the Vara as a gateway into Perseopia for the chosen children to return to their homeland. It says the stone was placed into a device that would lock its powers so that only the chosen might activate it."

Sammy sat up. "But Esther said that only the gifted could unlock the Emerald Dial."

"That's you. Gifted, chosen—same thing. You unlocked it."

"But I'm not the chosen one," Sammy said. "Esther is. She told me. And, anyway, I'm not from Perseopia so I can't be a chosen child returning here."

"Esther's not a child," Mehrak said.

"Maybe she was, but it took her a really long time to find the emerald."

Mehrak shrugged.

"There's more," Bertie said. "It's a bit smudged, but you can make out something about the portal pearl only existing in the Mother World."

"You said the bracelet didn't come with you," Mehrak said to Sammy.

"Then I'm stuck here for good," Sammy replied. "Hami was telling the truth." Unsurprisingly, that didn't make her feel any better.

"He might not have been telling the whole truth," Bertie said. "This next section references something about a route from Perseopia back to the Mother World using another portal pearl."

"Are you sure you're supposed to be talking about this?" Leiss asked.

"Let him go on," Borzin said, his eyes unblinking. "This is getting good."

Leiss kneaded his eyes with a thumb and forefinger.

Bertie went on, "It says, 'To return, a matching gem must be found.'"

"A matching gem?" Mehrak said. He tapped his chin. "How do we find a matching gem?"

A smile spread across Bertie's face. "And now we move on to book two."

He lifted the second book out from under the first. It was a navy-bound encyclopaedic volume. "When you first asked about a

186

way out of the realm, I thought of these," he said. He opened the book two thirds of the way through, leafed several pages back and forth until he found the page he wanted, then he pointed a passage out to Mehrak.

"Arda Viraf's gems?" Mehrak said.

"Arda Viraf," Bertie repeated. "A devout Zoroastrian who was said to have travelled to the Next World."

"Is that similar to the Mother World?" Sammy asked.

"No," Bertie said. "The Next World is where you go when you die. You journey three days through the demon lands until you reach the Chinvat Bridge, which spans a deep chasm teeming with monsters. On the far side lies heaven and light, and in the pits of the chasm, eternal damnation and torture. At the foot of the bridge, the demon god of judgement, Rashnu, decides your fate. He will either make the bridge wide for devout Zoroastrians or narrow for infidels."

"Yeah, I'd rather not go there," Sammy said.

"I'm sure it will be a long time before you do," Mehrak said.

Bertie continued, "Arda was taken to the Next World by the great Ahura Mazda and shown what happens to the human soul after death. As the story goes, Arda Viraf returned from the Next World in possession of an incredible treasure of gemstones that became known as Arda Viraf's gems. And—I knew I'd read this somewhere—they were often referred to as the pearls of portal paths."

"The pearls of portal paths," Mehrak said, his eyes alight with excitement. "You said the Ahura Mazda created a portal pearl in the Mother World to bring the chosen children to Perseopia!"

Bertie nodded slowly. "Now read this bit."

Mehrak leant over to read the paragraph under Bertie's thumb. "It is thought that Arda Viraf's gems are so powerful that, with careful selection, the holder can use specific pearls to be taken anywhere. They are even rumoured to hold a path to the Mother World."

–TWENTY-SEVEN–
THE BURNING

Sammy trailed Mehrak and the two Marzban along the street, her head reeling. Apparently there was a way back to the Mother World and she might be a chosen child. Although, that was unlikely, as Esther had told her categorically that she wasn't, and she didn't even come from Perseopia anyway. She might have guessed she wasn't important enough to be the 'actual' chosen child, whatever one of those was. It sounded awesome, though. No wonder Esther had been able to defeat those two policemen. Sammy wondered if she could be a substitute chosen child. She had some powers. She'd unlocked the Emerald Dial for starters.

Nothing happened when she thrust her arm out at stuff, though. No laser beams, or freeze rays, and she wasn't able to explode anything with the power of her mind. But still, she could kind of see herself as a superhero. Superheroes didn't have to be popular and a lot of them were loners: Batman, Wolverine, Rorschach, Bruce Banner.

Consumed with thoughts of forming a Justice League of Perseopia, Sammy didn't realise they were back in the industrial district until she stepped into the shadows of the dark alley they'd passed through that morning. The stench of rotting vegetables hit as dread leached into her skin. She squirmed. What was up with her? She hadn't felt this uncomfortable on the way to Bertie's.

"Did we have to come back this way?" she asked.

Mehrak looked up. "I wasn't paying attention," he said. "I was following Leiss."

"It's the quickest way back to the palace," Leiss said. "And you have two of the Keep's finest Marzban with you. I know it's unpleasant—"

"And hot," Borzin said. "It's roasting down here."

"Probably the heat from a blacksmith's furnace," Leiss said as he kept walking.

Borzin wiped his forehead. "It's getting hotter. Look back up the road. There's a heat haze coming off the street."

Sammy wrung her hands. "Something's wrong."

A scream echoed down the alley from behind, from the direction of Bertie's house.

"That sounded like a woman," Borzin said. He turned and took a couple of paces back along the street. "I'm going to take a look."

"No you aren't," Leiss said, grabbing him by the arm. "We've been ordered to stay with Sammy."

Borzin shrugged him off. "I'm not going to stand by and do nothing. What happened to 'doing the right thing'?"

Leiss levelled his gaze at Borzin and spoke evenly but through clenched teeth. "We follow orders whether we agree with them or not."

"Have it on your conscience, not mine," Borzin said. Leiss made a grab for him, but he side-stepped and ran off up the street.

"Get back here!"

Borzin kept going, his blue robe streaming out behind him.

"I don't like this," Sammy said.

"It's okay," Mehrak said. "Borzin knows what he's doing."

"No," Sammy said. "Something's really wrong. I can feel it. It's that creature from the forest. The one that burns everything. It's followed me here."

"The waster?" Mehrak said. "It can't be."

At the end of the street, Borzin paused to look both ways. In the heat haze he appeared little more than a shimmering mirage of himself. There was another scream and he sprang into action, disappearing around the side of the building.

Then silence.

Leiss paced back and forth. He looked about to run after Borzin, but didn't. "What is going on?" he grumbled at no one in particular.

Mehrak pointed back up the street. "Look."

A distant figure, dressed in blue and purple, reappeared, stumbling back into view and stopping in the middle of the street.

"Borzin!" Leiss shouted.

Borzin stood motionless a moment, then collapsed.

Leiss was the first to move. For a big man, he set off at an incredible pace. Impulsively, Sammy and Mehrak ran after him.

The heat made it difficult to breathe, but Mehrak took her hand and pulled her on. Leiss reached Borzin first and dropped to his knees. He let out such a heart-breaking cry that Sammy stopped in her tracks; Mehrak too. Leiss wailed again and slumped forward over his friend.

Sammy and Mehrak approached slowly.

Clouds of steam unfurled from Borzin's body, carrying with it the fatty odour of cooked meat.

Sammy stepped around Leiss's hunched frame and immediately wished she hadn't. Borzin's turban and most of his hair had gone; only a few matted tufts remained. His scalp was badly burned, crusted with bloodied welts, and the end of his nose was missing, along with his eyelids. His clothes were charred and the parts of his body that were visible through the burn holes were bleeding. Borzin's eyes bulged from his blackened skin, staring and vacant. Sammy couldn't look away.

Borzin turned his unblinking gaze towards her. "Help me," he mumbled. His lips were scabbed and partially stuck together. They split as he tried to talk and blood dribbled down the side of his cheek. "Please help me." He began crying.

Leiss stared at Borzin insensibly. "It'll be okay," he mumbled through his own tears. "You'll be okay."

Borzin began shaking. "Sammy?" he said. "Sammy?" He was becoming frantic.

"She's right here," Leiss said.

"I can't see," Borzin sobbed. "I can't see anything." Then his body went limp.

"Borzin?"

Borzin jerked forward, grabbing hold of Leiss's collar. "Help them!" he screamed. His voice was different; harsher and rasping. "Help Sammy!"

Leiss pulled at Borzin's wrists, trying to escape the stranglehold. "What are you doing? Get off me!"

"You don't understand," Borzin said. "The magi can't protect her. She isn't safe."

Leiss's face was becoming red.

"Don't leave her with the magi. Promise me! Find the way to the Mother World. And my boy, my boy. Take them ..." His words trailed off, like a robot deactivated mid-sentence, and he slumped. Borzin's fingers loosened from Leiss's collar and his head dropped to the floor with a wet crack.

"We've got to get help," Mehrak said. He pulled on Leiss's arm, but Leiss remained motionless, staring at Borzin. "Leiss." Mehrak yanked him, harder. "He's still breathing. We can help him if you act now."

Tears were streaming down Leiss's cheeks and he rocked gently back and forth.

"Leiss!" Mehrak shouted. "You're the strongest and fastest here. You have to go for help."

Leiss turned to Mehrak, staring blankly past him.

Borzin's swollen, unseeing eyes stared at Sammy. Both pupils locked on hers. He convulsed and choked up a mouthful of blood.

Mehrak noticed Sammy watching then. "Cover your eyes," he said.

But it was too late. Borzin's mouth began to move. He was mouthing something, hypnotising Sammy with silent words. She had to get away, but his eyes held power over her. She took a step backwards and, impossibly, his eyes followed.

"Sammy," Mehrak said, quietly this time. "Look away."

Borzin moaned. His pain pierced Sammy's heart, corkscrewing in. "Please ..." he whimpered.

Sammy ran.

"Sammy!" Mehrak screamed. "It's not safe!"

But she didn't stop. All she knew was that she had to get away. The image of Borzin's ruined body etched into her mind's eye.

Up and down identical stone streets she ran, on and on with no idea where she was going.

Then she tripped and the floor came up to meet her, knocking the air from her lungs. Her knees hurt, but she didn't get up. Sickness rose in her throat. She leaned forward, eyes closed, pressing her forehead against the cold stone beneath.

She concentrated on that sensation.

After a time, her stomach settled and she raised herself to her knees. She dragged her sleeve across her face, wiping the sweat from her brow, then took several long, juddering breaths.

She was at the end of a dark cul-de-sac of grey stone houses with only a single dim lamp post above. All the houses were dark.

And she had no idea how she'd got there or how far she'd run.

She took another deep breath and rubbed at the stitch in her side. It was hot, almost as hot as it had been in the dark alley.

And it was getting hotter. Sammy staggered to her feet, breathing fast.

She checked back up the street as a gust of warm air hit her in the face. She rubbed her eyes and squinted but couldn't see through the heat to the end of the road. No, she could see something. Someone coming around the corner; a tall, thin figure casting a long shadow.

Fighting sickness, Sammy wheeled around, looking for an escape route. All the houses had walled gardens.

No way out. Or was there? She could climb over a wall into one of those gardens, get through to a street behind. Maybe she could knock on a door. Someone might be in.

"Hello," said a young voice.

Sammy spun in the speaker's direction.

There was a boy leaning against a wall with his hands in his pockets. He was younger than she was and dressed in scruffy brown clothes that looked to be little more than rags. He had icy-blue eyes, partially hidden under a frown, and blond, scruffy hair. He smiled at Sammy, a mischievous, almost naughty, smile.

Where had he come from? He hadn't been there a moment ago.

The heat vanished and Sammy shot a look up the street. The figure had gone. When she turned back to the boy, she noticed he'd moved several paces closer. His eyes never left hers, and he took another step forward.

"Your hair is like mine," he said.

"I suppose ..." Sammy replied.

The boy didn't say anything more, but kept his icy-blue eyes fixed on hers. Sammy tried to look away to assess her next move, to work out what to do next. But every time she looked back she met his cold stare.

The boy took another step closer. His mouth stretched into a wicked grin, with teeth clenched. He extended an arm towards her.

"Sammy!"

She jumped. It was Mehrak. She turned to see him running up the road towards her.

"Am I glad to see you," he said. He came to a stop in front of her and doubled over, out of breath. "Who was that boy you were talking to?"

Sammy checked over her shoulder, but the boy had gone.

"I'm not sure," she said. "He didn't say."

"You shouldn't have run away like that. I've had to leave Leiss and Borzin to come and find you. Come on, we need to go back."

"I'm not going back," Sammy said. The sickness was returning, her heart rate increasing. "I can't …"

"We're not going back to the alley," Mehrak said. He put his arm around her. "We're going to the infirmary. A passer-by heard us and went to get help. Then I came to find you. Borzin should be on his way to the infirmary as we speak. I told Leiss I'd meet him there once I found you."

Sammy covered her face with her hands.

"You don't have to see Borzin. We can wait outside."

Sammy felt so weary she could collapse.

"Come on," Mehrak whispered. He took her by the arm and they left the cul-de-sac in silence.

Later, when the palace loomed into view above the other buildings, Mehrak turned to her.

"That boy had yellow hair," he said. "Just like yours."

–TWENTY-EIGHT–
RELATIONS

Sammy tried to keep her mind blank by not thinking of anything, but it was impossible. Trying not to think of anything typically resulted in you thinking about the thing you didn't want to think about in the first place. As she came to the conclusion that she needed to think of something else, in order to replace the something she didn't want to think about, she turned a corner and was dazzled by the galaxy of lamp post lanterns surrounding the palace.

She stopped and rubbed her puffy eyes.

"What's up?" Mehrak asked.

"This is the palace," Sammy said.

"Yeah. The infirmary's on the other side."

"Does Hami know about Borzin yet?"

"I don't know. He'll find out soon enough though, won't he?"

"But until then we're free. Unguarded."

"I suppose. But the lift site's manned, so we can't leave, which means we can't get to Louis."

"We're not going to leave or see Louis. We're going to the market."

"Why the market?"

"I need to see that old woman. The one Hami strangled."

"Why?"

"She's Esther. The old woman that gave me the Midnight Emerald bracelet."

"What? Are you serious? Why didn't you tell me?"

"Of course I'm serious. I couldn't tell you before because Hami was with us, then there was Leiss and … There just wasn't a good time, okay?"

"We could've gone to the market instead of going to Bertie's."

"We couldn't. Leiss said it was off limits. That's why Hami sent them with us. He knows about her, somehow. You should've seen the way he grabbed her. You missed most of it. He was like my dad when …" She stopped. "Actually, never mind."

Mehrak frowned. "I know you were impressed when Hami defeated that manticore, but using violence—"

"Can you save the lecture for later?"

Mehrak blew out a long breath. "Okay. We'd better get going. We won't have much time before Hami figures out where we've gone."

———

The streets near the market were crowded. People were out buying clothes, picking up groceries. And Sammy was gathering attention. The children were the most blatant. They pointed at her, then put their hands to their heads and giggled.

"You stick out too much," Mehrak said. "We aren't even going to make it to the market at this rate." He stopped. "Follow me." He pulled Sammy down a narrow alley between two crooked shops. "Stay down here while I find something to cover your head." Then he left.

Sammy waited in the shadows. It was far quieter in the alley than out on the street, like the passage near Bertie's house. She imagined the place getting hotter, the tall figure appearing at the end of the street. Her heart rate picked up.

She closed her eyes and held her breath. It wasn't getting any hotter; she was being irrational. She wasn't as brave as she thought. She slouched against the wall and considered how lame she was in real life. All those Arnie movies she'd studied, too. Maybe she wasn't a total coward—she was disobeying Hami. But did all adventurers feel this shaken during their escapades? Indiana Jones, Nathan Drake, Lara Croft. They wouldn't suffer stomach cramps and irritable bowels.

Sammy walked further up the alley and crouched in the recess of a doorway. She sat down, hugging her knees to her chest, and waited.

And waited.

Mehrak had been gone ages. What was he doing? She couldn't stay where she was forever. She peered round the doorframe.

In the street, two Marzban were talking to the children who'd seen her earlier. One of them pointed down the alley in her direction. The men turned towards her. Sammy ducked back into the doorway. Had they seen her? Probably not. The Keep was a dark place and the alleyway even darker.

They were coming though; she could hear them. No need to panic. All she had to do was move on and find somewhere else to hide.

She ducked out of the doorway and crept up the alley, hugging the wall.

Outside of the main, brightly lit thoroughfares, the Keep was a warren of dark, intertwining passages, which would help hide Sammy from the guards, although she'd probably lose Mehrak as a result.

The guards were getting closer. Sammy made a run for it, legging it down another passage at full pelt. And crashed head-first into someone coming the other way. She squawked as she hit the floor.

"It's me," Mehrak said as he hoisted her up. "The whole place is swarming with Marzban. Word's out already; they're looking for us. I think one of them saw me. Maybe we should give ourselves up and try another time."

"No." Sammy shoved Mehrak back up the alley, away from the pursuing Marzban. "There won't be another time; we're leaving tomorrow."

"Oi, you!" called one of the guards behind them. "Stop!"

"Down here." Sammy ducked down a passage to the left, dragging Mehrak with her. Sammy pushed him into an alcove and flattened herself next to him as the Marzban came around the corner carrying lanterns. Light sloshed up and down the walls as the lanterns swung in time with the men's footfalls. The light briefly touched on Sammy and Mehrak, but the guards didn't see them and clattered past.

The dark returned as the guards disappeared out of sight.

Mehrak let out a long sigh. "That was close." He took a ragged pashmina out of his pocket. "Sorry about the colour, but this was all I could find."

Sammy couldn't really see the colour in the semi-darkness. It was a bit browny, maybe. No big deal. If it meant finding Esther, Sammy could do brown. "It's great," she said. "Thank you."

Mehrak placed the scarf over her head and tied it under her chin. "I found it in a dog basket."

"What?" Sammy pulled the scarf off. "That's disgusting! It's probably got fleas. Why didn't you tell me about the dog basket part before apologising for the colour?"

"This was all I could find. Do you want to get into the market or not?"

"Of course I want to get into the market!" Sammy snatched the scarf back.

"I thought you liked animals."

"Not on my head."

Sammy looked at the scarf. The dog was bound to have been incontinent or have some skin disease. *Urgh.* She took a deep breath and put it on. The most important objective was to get back to the Mother World. She'd get some flea powder or whatever she needed when she got home.

Mehrak bent down, rubbed his hands in the dirt, stood up and rubbed them on Sammy's face. She squirmed as he smeared it on her.

"Bleurgh!" Sammy spat out the grit that had found its way into her mouth and dragged a sleeve across her face.

Mehrak stood back to admire his handy work. "A street urchin if ever I saw one," he said.

Sammy would get him back for that. But for now, she said, "Thanks," as unappreciatively as she could, and exaggerated spitting out more grit.

"You can thank me when you've found out how to get back to the Mother World," he said. "The market is that way." He pointed. "You won't have much time. Hami will have kept Esther a secret so the Marzban won't be guarding her, but they'll know you're headed for the market. Keep a lookout; they'll be patrolling the area. I'll go back to the street and create a diversion."

This was it, and Sammy couldn't move. Mehrak put his hands on her shoulders. "The worst thing that can happen is that they find you and bring you back to the palace."

Sammy stared into his hazel eyes. "No. The worst thing would be if they bring me back to the palace, we leave the Keep tomorrow and I never get the chance to speak to the only person in Perseopia that knows how to go to, and from, the Mother World."

"Just make sure you don't get caught, then," Mehrak said, then turned and ran in the opposite direction.

Sammy set off slowly, creeping through the crooked back alleys. It was an assault course of undesirable obstacles; mounds of damp fabrics and brown, mushy vegetables pulsating with maggots. She even stepped over a drunk, sleeping off a hangover in the gutter. He smelt worse than her dad after the coach dropped him off following an away defeat.

She sped up a bit. She was moving too slowly, she might not have long left. She flew round a corner and almost crashed headlong into a pair of Marzban. She stopped. They were facing the opposite direction and hadn't heard her. Quietly, she tiptoed back around the corner.

She'd seen the market though, just past the two guards. She'd have to double back and find another route, but time was running out. Stay calm.

Three shrill pips of a whistle chirruped in the distance behind her.

"That didn't take long," said one of the Marzban.

"A young girl and a villager from the boundary?" the other said. He snorted. "They were hardly going to pose a challenge, were they?"

Sammy ducked behind a pile of festering vegetables. She sat in the shadows on the floor, pinching her nose and holding her shirt over her mouth. She gagged as quietly as she could while the Marzban jogged past and disappeared round the bend.

"Not quite as easy to catch as you thought, scumbags," she whispered. Well done, Mehrak. Maybe I won't get you back too hard for the dog scarf.

Sammy kept her head down and the scarf pulled tight as she weaved her way through the crowded market. The scarf turned out to be an inoffensive browny-green colour. Why the heck did Mehrak even bring the colour up? Sammy rolled her shoulders back and exhaled her anger. Forget the scarf. Relax.

The market was hotter and sweatier than the inside of a football mascot's costume, and Sammy was shoved around as she made her way through the crowd of people. A chunky woman pushed past her and the scarf came loose. It was only down around her neck a moment, but that was enough. A tall round-bellied man with a beetroot face and small piggy eyes spotted her.

"Look at this girl's hair," he called. "It's bright yellow!"

Sammy pulled the scarf back over her head and rushed on.

"Come back, deary," a woman called. "He don't mean nothin' by it."

Sammy clutched the scarf by its corners, kept her head down and ran. Most of the market dwellers weren't interested in her, but a couple stopped to comment.

She rushed through the shoppers and stall owners, ducking under hanging meats, pushing through embroidered fabrics, making for the back of the market.

She staggered to a halt in front of Esther's stall, flustered and not at all prepared for what she wanted to say.

The old woman looked down at her, then flinched. She looked about nervously.

"Why did you come back? What do you want from me?" She had blotchy purple bruises around her throat, turning yellow at the edges.

Sammy stared into her eyes. "I want to go home."

Esther said nothing as she glanced at the market behind Sammy.

"The magus isn't with me," Sammy said. "What he did, that was nothing to do with me. I didn't mean for it to happen." The scarf was coming loose again. She pulled it tight.

The woman fixed Sammy with burning eyes. "Where's Esther?" she asked.

Sammy experienced an odd sensation of the ground slipping away beneath her. The woman's olive-green eyes met hers. Olive-green, not pale blue. It was so obvious, but her brain was taking an eternity to process the information. And then, like a Jean-Claude roundhouse kick to the face, it hit her.

The woman wasn't Esther.

"But ..." The words weren't coming to her, like someone had anesthetised her brain. "You're not Esther?"

"You thought ...?" The woman's eyes left Sammy and focused on something behind her. "Is there anything on the stall that I can interest you in?" she said.

"What?" What was she doing?

"I think this marble candle holder may be what you're looking for," the woman said, leaning forward to pick it up from the front of the table. As she did so, she whispered, "Don't turn around. You're being watched."

Sammy froze.

"Well?" the old woman went on, normal volume again. "Is this what you were looking for?"

Sammy could feel eyes burning into the back of her neck. "Er … yeah, I suppose," she said. She clutched the corners of the scarf.

"The girl went that way," came a loud voice from behind.

Sammy couldn't bear it any longer and chanced a look. It was the man who'd pointed out her yellow hair, Mr Beetroot-head. He was talking to the Marzban. She turned back to the woman, gripping the scarf.

"Keep calm. They haven't seen you yet," the woman whispered. Then she said louder, "That'll be four staters." She held out her hand. "Pretend you're giving me some money, take the candle holder and then walk slowly into the alleyway to my right." She tipped her head towards it.

"But I need to ask you—"

"You must hurry," the woman urged. She paused. "Too late." She dashed around the table, grabbed Sammy by the wrist and dragged her down the alley.

"Where are we going?"

"If you want to know more about my sister, stop talking and run!"

Sister. It was so obvious, she should've seen it.

"Come back!" came the call, followed by the echo of footsteps in the alley behind them.

Esther's sister dragged Sammy through the dark alleyways, navigating the maze of intersecting passages almost at random until Sammy thought they must be impossibly lost. Then, without warning, they barrelled through a crooked door into a small, dim living area. The door clattered against the inside wall, a woman screamed and a baby cried out. Esther's sister grabbed the door and pushed it shut behind her.

The woman looked up at them from her seat by the fireside, the whites of her eyes shining bright in her grimy face. "Zara? Is that you?" she said. A small face peered out of a bundle of rags on her lap and cried.

Esther's sister slumped against the door. "Yeah, it's me," she said. "I'm sorry, Labina, I didn't know where else to go. We're being followed."

"Oh my goodness. Are you alright?"

"I'm fine. I'll explain everything later. Can we use the bedroom?"

"Of course. Is this to do with—?"

"I'll explain, later. I don't have time right now. Can you keep Mito quiet, please? She'll give us away."

Zara led Sammy across the small room, passing bags of dirty fabrics, boxes that served as furniture, and through a door opposite. They entered a second, smaller room where Zara closed the door and dragged a tattered curtain across a single porthole window. Zara pulled up a box to use as a chair and motioned for Sammy to sit on a small, metal-framed bed against the wall.

Sammy sat. The adrenaline that had been driving her since Borzin's attack was dwindling and she was shattered. She almost didn't care about anything right then; all she wanted was to lie back and go to sleep.

As Sammy's eyes acclimatised to the dark, she realised Zara was so like Esther they could almost be twins.

Zara watched her. "What do you know about Esther?" she asked.

"How about you tell me what your sister's done to me first?" Sammy replied.

Zara pursed her lips. "I don't know what she's done. I haven't seen her since she left the Keep thirty years ago."

Sammy wasn't expecting that.

"Look. I'm sorry if Esther's tricked you or upset you in some way," Zara said. "But we don't have much time. It won't take the Marzban long to track us down. All I care about is where you saw her." She took a sharp intake of breath. Her eyes were filling with tears. "I thought she was … She hasn't written in so long …" She stopped herself and took another long breath and held it. When she let it out she asked, "When did you see her?"

Sammy looked into Zara's eyes. She was either a really good liar or she was actually telling the truth.

"I saw her about five days ago," Sammy said.

A laugh burst from Zara's mouth and she wiped the spit from her lips. Tears streamed down her cheeks but she smiled through them.

"Where?" she asked.

"In a market."

"Which one?"

"One where I come from."

"And where's that?"

Sammy's heart sank. Zara didn't know anything. "The Mother World," she said, and then waited for the reaction.

Zara didn't react as Sammy had expected. A wry smile spread across her lips.

"You have spoken to her, haven't you?" she said. "Esther would never admit that she was mistaken. I bet she's still living with the Hirbod, too proud to come home. Did she put you up to this?"

Sammy was tired and frustrated. She couldn't be bothered to convince Zara that she came from the Mother World. "Why do you think I'm being chased by the Marzban?" she said. "Look at the colour of my hair."

Zara raised an eyebrow.

"Esther went to the Mother World," Sammy said. "I don't exactly know why, but while she was there, she found a magic bracelet to bring her back here. Except it didn't work for her, it worked for me instead, and now I'm here and she's still there. I don't care if you believe me or not. All I need to know is how your sister got to the Mother World in the first place, because I want to go back." Tears were blurring her vision, but she forced herself not to cry.

Zara watched her. "She really made it?"

Sammy maintained eye contact. "Yeah. She really did."

Zara bit her lip. "Esther said she'd go places. She was my little sister, but so much more confident than me. She had aspirations above our class, wanted more out of life. I took over the family market stall. She showed signs of magi abilities. A female magus. No one could believe it. The first in a hundred years." Zara laughed and shook her head. "The magi were thrilled—of course—and she was taken to the magi garrison for training. We didn't see her for a long time. But one day she came back. She'd run away, left the brotherhood. She said it was because she didn't agree with their agenda, but I think she'd met someone, someone who was influencing her decisions. I once overheard her tell my mother she'd met a girl from the Mother World, and that she was going there. The girl had told her amazing stories of vibrant multi-coloured vegetation and blue skies. Then her friend Levellie, the Regent Mother, got her a job at the palace library. After that, we hardly ever saw her and she spent most of her time at work. But one night she came home excited, said she was leaving the Keep, going travelling."

Zara paused. "That was the last time we ever saw her. We received a single letter while she was staying with the Hirbod, then nothing."

A door crashed outside the room.

"They're here!" Zara said.

Sammy leapt up. "Did Esther say anything about how to get to the Mother World?"

The bedroom door burst open and four hefty Marzban officers bundled in.

The largest one stepped forward. "Principal Hootan said you'd be here." He grabbed Sammy by the arm. "Your presence is required at the palace." And he pulled her out of the room.

"Where did she go?" Sammy cried. "I need to know!"

"I ... I don't know ..." Zara called back, as the front door slammed and Sammy was dragged away along the alley.

–TWENTY-NINE–
THE REGENT MOTHER

Mehrak had been at the communal room table for a while when Sammy got unceremoniously plonked down opposite him by the palace guards. She made eye contact, shook her head once and placed her face in her hands. Her posture said it all. She hadn't found the answer she'd been looking for. It cut him up to see her this way. If only he could've done more. He'd tried his best, but it hadn't been enough.

Hami stood behind him, casting a shadow over both of them.

"You've been a silly girl this afternoon," Hami said to Sammy. "I've called in a lot of favours to provide the level of security we need to get you to New Ecbatana safely."

"I just wanted—"

"A man has lost his life protecting you and you run away, leaving him to burn to death? His children have been left fatherless."

Sammy looked up. "It wasn't like that."

"And you." Hami turned on Mehrak. "You made it clear from the start you have no respect for the magi, but I didn't think you'd jeopardise Sammy's life because of it. I'd have thought you'd learnt your lesson when your recklessness cost you your wife."

Mehrak felt his face flush, but he said nothing.

"As you've shown yourselves to be untrustworthy, I'm forced to have you both confined to the palace until we leave tomorrow."

Mehrak turned to Hami. "We're prisoners?"

Hami stared back. His silence said more than words could convey. Black pupils like windows into an abyss. A calm façade concealing a burning rage simmering beneath.

"Please try not to disappoint me further," he said. He hacked up a black lump of phlegm and spat it on the floor. "Have your possessions ready for our departure tomorrow morning." Then he left.

Sammy returned her head to her hands, which Mehrak was thankful for because he couldn't look her in the eye. He'd failed her again. He couldn't stand up to Hami physically, but he should've at least said something to defend her. He was a coward and hated himself for it.

Was Hami right, though? Had he been reckless? He'd brought Gisouie on his irresponsible quest. Was he risking Sammy's life in the same way? The magi might actually be doing the right thing. Hami was a violent thug, but he'd saved their lives, and he was only following orders, orders that came direct from the magi council and government.

Sammy lifted her head. "Do you think Louis is okay?" she asked. "He's probably wondering where we are."

"I called down to him," Mehrak said. "The guards that caught me were kind enough to take me to the lift site so I could shout down."

"How do you know if he heard you?"

"Do you listen to anything I tell you?"

"Great hearing. Yeah, I remember." Sammy hid her face in the fold of her arm.

And now he'd snapped at her. Add that to his list of failings, along with not sticking up for her and endangering her life. He'd messed everything up and now they were trapped. He stared at the wall and the bright, colourful landscape paintings that hung there. They must have been several hundred years old, before the Assault on Aratta. Bright scenes that were so alien to him, yet must be commonplace to Sammy, and were all she'd ever known until she arrived in Perseopia. He had to help her. Had to come up with a plan.

"We should have a look in the palace library," Mehrak whispered over the table. He tried his best to smile and look optimistic. "There might be a book in there that has information on routes to the Mother World."

Sammy lifted her head from the table. "Will they let us use the library?"

"I wondered that," he said, and then he lowered his voice further. "The guards will have orders to keep us in the palace, but I bet the servants don't know anything about what's going on. They won't be deemed important enough."

When the next servant came in, Mehrak asked if they could use the library.

"I'm afraid only His Excellency, the Regent, can grant permission to enter the royal library," he said. "Not even Principal Hootan is allowed in without the consent of a royal." Then he turned on his heel to leave.

"Well, that's that," Mehrak said. "Hami will have told the Regent to keep the library out of bounds."

Sammy perked up, eyes wide. "Zara said her sister got a job in the library, because of her friendship ... Wait!" she called to the servant.

The servant stopped at the door. "Yes?"

"Can we see the Regent Mother?"

"She's in no condition to receive guests. She has a fever."

"Could you pass on a message instead then, please?"

The servant paused by the door and considered the request. "I'm sure that would be permitted," he said.

"Great. Can you tell her that her old friend Esther made it to her destination?" She smiled smugly at Mehrak. "And that I've spoken to her recently."

———

Sammy waited with Mehrak and the servant outside the Regent Mother's bedroom door.

"And you thought your trip to the market had been wasted," Mehrak said, grinning broadly. "Now we're back on the trail!" He rubbed his hands together. At least Mehrak was optimistic, but would the Regent Mother be able to tell them anything?

The door opened from the inside and a hunched man with a bald head and puckered mouth appeared. He motioned them inside and dismissed the servant. Three feeble candles created a pocket of light in the centre of the room. It highlighted a single bed, two maids standing by the bedside and three tables covered in books. The room was pitch black outside the light and it was impossible to gauge how big it was.

A small, skeletal figure lay under the bedcovers, forming a ridge up the centre to where a head was propped up on a pillow.

The bald man led them through the tables to the bed.

The Regent Mother had flowing silver hair splayed out on the pillow, framing a serene and noble face. She opened her eyes as they approached and smiled; until she saw Mehrak.

"Goodness me!" she exclaimed. She moved like she was trying to sit up, and the servants rushed to stop her. "Is it really …? Sirtl?"

Mehrak paused. "Sirtl was my grandfather," he said. "How…?"

The Regent Mother relaxed. "I thought the fever had spread to my brain." She coughed feebly. One of the maids stepped forward again, but got waved away. "You look so alike," she said. "We were close friends, you know, your grandfather and I. He would often visit the palace. He never mentioned me?"

Mehrak looked awkward. "I'm sorry. I didn't know," he said. "He died when I was young. He didn't spend much time at home. He was always away, travelling mostly. My grandmother used to say she became a widow long before he passed away."

"I didn't realise he'd died so long ago." The Regent Mother became distant. Sammy thought she saw a tear in her eye, but then she smiled at Sammy. "You have news of Esther, young lady?" she asked.

Sammy explained how she'd met Esther, had acquired the bracelet, arrived in Perseopia, and about their journey so far. The Regent Mother listened patiently without interrupting.

"She really made it?" she said when Sammy had finished. "I spent all those hours helping her find the books she needed in the library, but I never thought she'd actually get to the Mother World. I assume she figured out how the Temple of Paths worked?"

"The Temple of Paths?" Mehrak asked.

"The temple that the pearls of portal paths are kept in."

Mehrak grabbed Sammy's hand and gripped it. "She knew where it was?"

"Oh yes."

Sammy's heart leapt, rising in her throat.

"She was a magus," the Regent Mother said. "All magi know where the temple is. She learned of the location from the magi network."

Sammy's heart flopped over and sank. Hami had lied to her. He knew there was a way back to the Mother World and he'd kept it from her.

"The magi know where it is?" Mehrak looked knowingly at Sammy.

"They do," the Regent Mother said. "But they don't know how to use it to get to the Mother World. That was the problem. They know where some of the portal pearls take you, but not all of them. Not the one that leads to the Mother World. Esther had to figure that out herself." The Regent Mother chuckled. "And I still can't believe she did it."

"She didn't tell you which pearl takes you to the Mother World?" Mehrak asked.

"No." The Regent Mother cleared her throat. "She didn't tell me where the Temple of Paths was either. Magi code and all that. Besides, her mission was confidential."

Sammy's heart plummeted into the pit of her stomach. Then she latched onto a word. "Mission?" she asked. "What mission? Her sister told me she'd already left the magi when she took the job here."

"I don't know what that was either, I'm afraid. Like I said, it was confidential. All I know is that she had to go to the Mother World to find someone important."

"She told me she'd been looking for me to help her return home," Sammy said. "She didn't mention anyone else. Esther said she was the chosen one."

"Esther never said anything about being a chosen one to me," the Regent Mother said. "Although she was a supremely powerful magus, so it wouldn't surprise me."

Mehrak scratched his head. "What was the point in her going to the Mother World in the first place if she was already the chosen one?"

"She never said," Sammy replied.

"Maybe she was going to before you used the Midnight Emerald Dial by yourself."

"Okay. Give it a rest."

The Regent Mother frowned, "I can only assume Esther found out she was the chosen one by going to the Mother World. We were best friends, she'd have told me if she'd known."

"Unless that information was confidential too," Mehrak said. "Or it might be that she needed to bring Sammy back with her, because she's also important." He turned to Sammy. "Hami said you're special. That's why you're going to New Ecbatana and why he lied to you about there being no way back to the Mother World."

"You think he needs my help?" Sammy asked. "I suppose that makes sense."

"I'd say you're *useful* to him. Don't forget he lied to you. He could be putting you in danger."

"I don't think he would. He's just putting the realm first. He wouldn't endanger me. He saved us from that manticore, and he protected Honton Keep last night. And Louis. I should at least see what I'm needed for before I leave."

"But why the lies? Couldn't he tell you the truth instead of forcing you to go with him? He's doing something underhanded."

"Your grandfather didn't care for the magi either." The Regent Mother chuckled. "Which reminds me; I have something for you."

She nodded for a maid to come close and whispered something in her ear. The girl went to one of the tables, slid out a drawer and took out a book, which she then handed to the Regent Mother. The Regent Mother passed it to Mehrak.

"Your grandfather left me this book," she said. "At one time it was his most prized possession."

Mehrak gently took the book from her. The cover was badly worn and the spine cracked. He opened it to the first page. "Stay safe at home in my heart," he read out aloud. "Did my grandfather write that to you?" he asked, his eyes wide. "Were you two …?"

"I think a previous owner wrote that," the Regent Mother said. Her eyes were sad. "If your grandfather had written that, it wouldn't have been for me." She took a deep breath. "He told me to look after the book and to give it to you when you came looking. He knew you'd come here. He wanted you to know that the *Rule Book*'s final resting place is written somewhere within those pages."

"He never told me about this book." Mehrak's hands were shaking. "Did he figure out the final resting place?"

"No," the Regent Mother said. "He spent years poring over the book, but it never revealed its secrets. He tormented himself over it. I didn't want to pass the curse of its infernal riddle on to you too, but he made me promise. After years of frustration, he left the book with me and returned to Dungalor, never to visit or read the book again."

The room fell silent. Mehrak stared down at the battered hardback.

The Regent Mother held out her hand to Mehrak. He took it and she closed her eyes and smiled. "He was a good man, your grandfather," she said. "Had such a temper, though." She chuckled again, but half-heartedly, and then seemed sad.

Sammy nudged Mehrak. He looked up, lost for a moment, then said, "I don't suppose you have the library books Esther read before she left?"

"I don't," the Regent Mother said. "But they'll be logged in the library records. Books aren't allowed out of the library, but each time one is taken from the shelf, it's recorded in the logbook. We'll have the books you need."

"We're not allowed in the library, though," Mehrak said.

"Why not?"

"Because only the Regent can grant us permission. And he hasn't given it."

"That's not entirely true," the Regent Mother said. "He isn't the *only* person that can grant you permission."

–THIRTY–
THE BLACK LIBRARY

The librarian led Sammy and Mehrak through the winding palace passages. He was a slim man, dressed in dark green, and walked in an unusual straight-legged fashion with his hands behind his back, which kind of made him look like a stork.

"How long have you been the librarian?" Mehrak asked as they entered a gallery with a high, vaulted ceiling and walls covered with paintings of posh-looking men and women in fancy clothes.

"Ten years. But the role has always been in my family," the librarian said with a nasal hiss.

"Did your family know Esther?"

"Ugh." The librarian peered at them over the half-moon spectacles that teetered on the end of his sickle-shaped nose. "My father had to share his job with her while she was here. He wasn't happy about it and was still moaning about it years after she left. She was friends with the Regent Mother, that's how she got the position. Fortunately for us, she didn't stay long and the role of head librarian returned to the family."

At the end of the corridor, the librarian pulled open a steel door braced with thick struts. On the other side, a narrow staircase dropped steeply towards a flickering light at the bottom. He led them down, single file.

They emerged into a barren stone room with burning torches on the walls. The decor couldn't have been more different to the plush gallery they'd just left, seeming closer to a medieval dungeon than a palace.

Two palace guards in red waited on either side of an ornate pair of brass doors. The doors had greened with age yet were exquisitely cast with images of trees and winged beasts on their surfaces. One of the guards reached inside his collar, retrieved a key that hung on a gold chain around his neck, and lifted it up over the top of his head. The librarian extracted a matching key from beneath his own collar, and they both placed them into adjacent locks, one on each door.

"On three," the librarian said. "One, two ..." They turned their keys.

Inside the door, mechanisms meshed, clanked and groaned, then there was a faint click and the librarian pushed the doors inward. Air whistled in through the opening making it seem like the library was inhaling.

Sammy stepped back from the black, gaping hole.

"This is it," Mehrak whispered. "I can't believe we've made it." He rubbed his hands together.

His enthusiasm was infectious. Sammy shouldn't get her hopes up, but it was hard not to with Mehrak dancing about excitedly by her side. The answers were in there somewhere, hiding in the dark, waiting to be found.

"This used to be the solitary confinement chamber," Mehrak said. "Some of the worst criminals ever to roam Perseopia were kept here."

Shame he couldn't have saved that piece of information until after they'd left.

The librarian went in first, disappearing into the darkness. He returned shortly with a brass oil lamp. He removed the glass and lit the wick from one of the torches on the wall. Then he replaced the glass casing, turned up the flame and gave Sammy and Mehrak the nod. Cautiously, they followed him into the tunnel.

The doors slammed shut behind, plunging them into a cloying blackness.

They both yelped.

"Let's get moving," the librarian said. He smiled devilishly, with the light of the oil lamp under his chin making a sinister spectre of himself.

Good one, loser. Sammy imagined the slamming door prank was one of his favourites. How many other visitors had he spooked with it? She brushed an imaginary speck of dust off her shoulder like it was no big deal.

Mehrak cleared his throat. "Let's go," he said in a contrived gruff and manly tone.

The librarian led the way along the barren stone tunnel. Mehrak and Sammy followed behind.

At the end of the passage, they entered an atrium. It had a circular floor and probably a circular ceiling as well, although it was too dark above to see further than the first few storeys. Square tunnels branched off the hall right the way around its circumference, like the rays of light a child would draw when illustrating the sun. Stacked above the ground-floor passages were further rows of tunnels, the same arrangement again, directly above, and then again, and again, right up into the dark, like being inside a giant bees' nest.

Nearby desks sat dusty and abandoned in a cluster with tarnished oil lamps on their surfaces. In the centre of the hall sat an enormous glass panelled sphere, connected to a point high above by a steel chain.

"Amazing," Mehrak said. He turned slowly, staring up at the warren of tunnels.

"This place doesn't get used often, does it?" Sammy said, running her finger through the dust on a table.

"Unfortunately not," the librarian said. "Our illustrious Regent, blessed by Ahura, isn't as interested in literature as previous generations. Only the Regent Mother still uses the library, although not often since her illness."

The librarian opened one of the glass panels on the big sphere. Then, removing a thin splint from his pocket, he lit the wick inside from the one in his lamp. He made an adjustment to an internal mechanism and the sphere ignited with an all-consuming brilliance that lit up the place.

Mehrak helped the librarian raise the light using a wheel and ratchet by the entrance tunnel. It wobbled up off the floor, and upon reaching the third floor, they secured the chain to the wall.

The librarian lit another two lamps for Sammy and Mehrak, then went to a metal cabinet by the entrance tunnel. He removed several tatty books, checked them over, took one and replaced the rest.

"This is the most recent logbook with Esther's name on the spine," he said, bringing the book to the table. He leafed through to the last page. "This is my father's handwriting. If we work backwards from here, we can find Esther's last entry."

Mehrak waited with the librarian as he checked each page in turn. Sammy left them to it and wandered the circular hall under the burning glass beacon. The light bleached the colour from everything. Not dissimilar to what it would be like being an ant under a magnifying glass, except, she supposed, without the burning to death part.

She walked around the edge of the atrium. The tunnels branching off were floor-to-ceiling bookshelves and books, plummeting into blackness only a few metres in. Not particularly inviting. Sammy imagined convicts hiding in the dark, ready to shank her if she got too close. She moved back to the centre of the hall and, for a second, lost her bearings. Where was the entrance? She spun round in a panic, saw the metal cabinet that held the logbooks, and relaxed. The entrance passage was next to it; the only passage without books. She let out a long sigh.

"We've got it," the librarian said.

Mehrak wasn't smiling.

"What?" Sammy asked as she came over.

"We've found Esther's last entry."

"And?"

"And it wasn't the last time Esther came here."

"My father added an entry after hers," the librarian explained. "It's dated six days later and reads, 'I know Esther has been here tonight, but she's not left a record of the books she's removed from the shelves. I've taken an inventory of the books she reads on a regular basis and found *The Arda Memoirs* missing. I've tried to find her and confront her with this allegation, however, she's left the palace with no indication of when she'll return.'"

"She took the book," Sammy said.

"It's a setback," Mehrak said. "But we can read through the other books on her reading list. Maybe one of them will point us in the right direction."

"Do you want me to fetch you the other books?" the librarian asked.

"Please. And also any books you have referencing the final trials of Pouyan or anything on the steppe map?"

"You're looking for information leading to the *Rule Book*," the librarian said with a raised eyebrow.

Mehrak shrugged. "I have a mild interest."

"Sure you do. The Regent Mother had that same *mild* interest. Follow me and bring your lanterns."

The librarian took them through a tunnel to their right. Like the others, it was filled with books from floor to ceiling and all the way down its length. At the end of the corridor, they came to the base of a staircase. They climbed three storeys and then doubled back along another tunnel, leading back towards the centre of the library.

Halfway along the passage, Sammy leapt back behind Mehrak. "What's that?" She pointed as she held him in front of her like a meat shield. It was a spiky, spherical object, the size of a beach ball, lying on the floor and silhouetted black against the light in the atrium.

"A cactus," the librarian said.

Mehrak walked towards it. "I've heard about these. They remove humidity from the air, don't they? They stop the books from getting damp and rotten."

"How very interesting," Sammy said, and walked past the cactus without looking at it. She was a nervous wreck. And getting scared by plants now. What was the deal with that?

Mehrak and the librarian followed her along the tunnel but stopped several sections from the end.

"Here we are," said the librarian. He began scanning the bookshelf. Mehrak helped.

Sammy gave the books a cursory glance, but all the text on the spines was of the strange, looping, squiggly variety she couldn't read, so she walked on to the end of the tunnel by herself. She stood on the edge, high above the atrium. From her vantage point, she could see the ceiling. It was almost the same view looking up as it was down, minus the desks. The library was big, but it somehow felt confined, as if the fear of a hundred imprisoned men still clung to the walls. She felt even further from home here than she had done in the forest. But at least Mehrak was with her. Thank God for Mehrak. Turning up when he had, taking her in, feeding her and giving her somewhere to sleep. He was still looking out for her now, working to find a way home.

"*Unusual Temples* by Armilla Citan," the librarian said, breaking the silence and Sammy's thoughts. He gently pulled a tattered, brown book from the shelf.

"And here's *Zoroastrian Religious Sites* by Yousef Moez," Mehrak said.

They went on reading out the names as they found the books and loaded Sammy up with them. When they'd found all the books from Esther's reading list, they headed back to the stairs, went around the outside of the library and up another flight to find Mehrak's *Rule Book* reference books.

Loaded up with as many books as they could carry, they staggered back down to the main hall and set them on a desk. The librarian fetched a fresh-looking logbook from the cabinet and noted the names of the volumes they'd taken.

"I'm sure you both know this already, but you aren't allowed to remove books from the library," he said. "You can spend as much time with them as you like, but they have to remain here. Now, I'm going to do some cataloguing, but call out if you need anything else."

Mehrak already had his head in a blue leather book. "Thanks," he mumbled.

Sammy picked up a black book and flicked through the pages. All the text was handwritten and looked like an ink-covered spider had crawled across the page. It didn't even flow left to right like normal text; it went from right to left instead. She flicked through another book—handwritten in scribbles, too.

She sighed. "What language is this?"

Mehrak looked up. "Avestan," he said, as if it were the most obvious thing in the world.

Sammy looked at the text. "I thought …" She stopped.

She'd recognised a word. She had no idea how to pronounce the letters or even what they were, but she knew the word. She looked further down the page. There were other words emerging; whole sentences coalescing on the pages.

"I can understand this," she said. "This chapter is telling of how the ancients believed the Acropolis at Mycolos was built by a demon worshipper."

"Interesting," Mehrak said. "I think I knew that. Not what we're looking for though, is it? Unless it also mentions pearls of portal paths or portal gems or something like that."

"That's not the point," Sammy said. "I can read it!"

"Impressive. Can you also spell your name and count to ten?"

"Ha ha. I mean I'm reading *this*. I can't read Avestan. I only know English."

"English?" Mehrak said. "I've not heard of that."

"Well, you're speaking it."

"I think you'll find we're speaking Avestan."

Mehrak calmly looked up from his book. "Hey, Mr Librarian!" he called out.

"Yesss?" came the librarian's nasally reply. He stuck his head out of one of the library tunnels two storeys above them.

"What language are we speaking?" Mehrak sat back in his chair, smiling expectantly at Sammy.

The librarian frowned. "Is this a trick question?"

"No!" Sammy and Mehrak chimed in together.

"Avestan, of course," he said, and disappeared back down the passage.

Sammy stared down at the text in front of her so as not to make eye contact with Mehrak. She clenched her teeth and balled her fists under the table.

"Were you speaking English when we first met?" Mehrak asked.

"What?" Sammy pretended to be engrossed in her book.

"When Louis and I found you in the forest, I asked if you were okay and you replied in a weird language I've never heard before. Was that English?"

Sammy rubbed her temples. "I don't know. I thought English was the only language I knew."

"Maybe Avestan and English are different names for the same language."

Sammy sighed. "This book's definitely not written in English," she said. "None of these squiggles are in the alphabet."

"They're in the Avestan alphabet."

Sammy concentrated on reading her book. She couldn't cope with Mehrak's nonsense. She scanned several passages. Not an interesting subject matter, but suddenly being able to read another language was pretty cool.

Five books later, Sammy was totally bored of her newfound super-reading ability. She knew she shouldn't be ungrateful after acquiring a superpower, but super-reading? It wasn't in the same league as super-strength or super-speed. What if that was her only special ability? She wasn't the proper chosen child, so did that mean she got crappy powers too? What if the real chosen children could fly or explode boulders with their minds? And her only power was to read obscure text in boring reference manuals. That would make her about as lame as Golden Age Aquaman. How was she supposed to help save Perseopia with reading skills? She'd had enough. She was just about to get up to stretch her legs, when Mehrak piped up:

"I've found something."

Sammy scooted round the table. "What?"

Mehrak slid the book to her. "The diagram."

"It's an island in a river."

"Read the inscription underneath."

"*Built by the ancients, the Temple houses a gateway of paths between Perseopia and the other realms and worlds.*"

"Sound like the right temple to you?"

"Sweet. Now we just need to find out where that island in the river is."

"I reckon so," Mehrak said. "If you get the librarian to fetch some charts, we can match the river in the diagram to the real one. I'll keep looking for information about the pearls. I think the Arda Memoirs book Esther took probably had the info we need, but I'll keep looking anyway."

Sammy looked up at the library honeycomb. Three storeys up, a light flickered in one of the book passages. Mehrak followed her gaze.

"Take the tunnel below, then head up three flights," he said. "That'll take you to the one he's in."

Sammy grabbed her lamp and made for the tunnel. The fusty smell of books seemed stronger than it had done during her first walk through the library. She could almost smell the history soaked into the fibres of the pages. Gilded titles on the spines sparkled in the lamplight like nuggets of gold in the walls of a gold mine. Each leather cover protecting secrets that had been passed down through generations. Sammy wondered how many people had been privileged enough to walk these tunnels and share this knowledge.

At the end of the passage, a cool draught blew across her. She shivered. A strange dread flip-flopped in the pit of her stomach and, with it, the disappointment that she was scared. Again. The library was creepy, could she use that as an excuse? What could possibly happen to her in here? There hadn't been convicts for years. The doors were thick metal and heavily guarded. Could evil entities still linger? Ghosts of the mass murderers rattling their chains? Being spooked while alone in the dark in a solitary confinement chamber was probably excusable.

Sammy gritted her teeth, marched the last few metres to the end of the tunnel and climbed the three flights of stairs to the passage where the librarian was.

The light in the atrium was almost on the level of the tunnel, lighting up dust particles so the air seemed like it was burning.

Sammy raised her hand to shield her eyes and pressed on. The librarian was just down this passage.

There was a movement ahead. Sammy paused. It was just the librarian. But she couldn't bring herself to continue. She was feeling more stupid by the minute. She took a deep breath, gripped her lamp tight and marched down the last half of the tunnel. To find—no librarian.

Down in the atrium, Mehrak was at his desk, lost in a book, with the librarian stooping over him like a vulture. How could that have happened? Was there another way down she didn't know about?

A slam echoed in the passage behind her. Sammy screamed and spun round.

Nothing there.

"Sammy?" Mehrak called up. "You alright up there?"

A thick black book lay on the floor a short way down the passage.

"It was just a book falling off a shelf," she shouted down.

The book had fallen on its spine and the pages were flicking back and forth as it reached equilibrium.

"Be careful with them!" the librarian called after her. "Some are over a thousand years old."

There was a gap on the fourth shelf up. The book must've fallen off as she'd walked past it. She bent to pick it up when a dozen more pages flipped over by themselves, and stopped.

She stared at the book, not quite sure if she'd imagined the extra pages turning. She knelt down and placed her lamp on the floor. She was about to pick up the book when the picture on the open page stopped her hand. It was a painted illustration of a child with shortish, blonde hair. It was basic, but it kind of looked like her.

"*The child with the golden hair,*" she whispered as she read the inscription below the picture.

With shaking hands, she turned several more pages, careful to keep the sheet with the illustration marked with a finger. There were other pictures. Pictures of battles, ancient stone temples hidden in the Fungi Forest, snow-covered mountains, and a tall, thin structure with bird-like creatures soaring around its peak.

Sammy flicked back to the page with the illustration of the child with golden hair and read the passage beneath the inscription.

The child arrives at midnight, under the cover of darkness.
Under no circumstances must it be allowed to fulfil its destiny.
It brings nothing but death, a darkest darkness.
Kill it. Kill the child.
Perseopia's future depends on it.

"Are you okay?"

Sammy opened her eyes.

She was on the floor. Mehrak was crouched next to her.

"What happened?" she asked.

"I was about to ask you the same thing," the librarian said. He was standing over her, scowling. "What were you doing on this row?"

"Calm down," Mehrak said. "She was looking for you and you never told her she couldn't come down this passage."

"The entrance of the passage is roped off. I'm sure even a child could guess the significance of that."

"What rope?" Sammy mumbled. Her head was spinning. "I didn't see a rope."

"How long have you been asleep up here?" Mehrak asked.

"I don't know." She tried to sit up, but her stomach lurched and she slumped back down again.

The librarian leant against the bookshelf. Below his elbow was the gap on the fourth row.

"A book," Sammy said. "A book fell off that shelf." She pointed at the gap. "Where is it?"

"What book?" the librarian said. His eyes narrowed.

"There was a book on the floor, just here." Sammy desperately tried to get up again, but couldn't. "A black one."

"There was nothing here when we found you," Mehrak said. "You got here first," he said to the librarian. "You didn't see a black book, did you?"

"No," the librarian said. "No book."

"What was it about?" Mehrak asked.

Sammy looked from Mehrak to the librarian. The librarian's eyes burned into hers.

"I can't remember," she said at last.

"I think it's time for you both to leave," the librarian said. "It can get stuffy in here. Some fresh air might do you good."

–THIRTY-ONE–
LEAVING

Sammy stood alone in the gallery that led to the library. It was deathly quiet and Mehrak and the librarian had gone. She crept along the hallway. She didn't know why she crept, but it felt as if she should. She had that tingling sensation that she wasn't supposed to be there. It didn't help that most of the lights were out and the portraits of former regents seemed to sneer down their snooty noses at her, like they disapproved of her being there.

She worked her way through the palace passageways until she arrived at the entrance hallway. It was deserted, so she crept behind a pillar. She didn't know why she was hiding, but again it seemed like the right thing to do. Better safe than sorry. What now? The entrance doors were open but a lone guard stood in the gap, facing out into the Keep. She crept silently towards him.

"Intruder!" The cry came from behind.

Sammy turned. A guard on the staircase was pointing at her. Other guards appeared behind him, skittering down from the floor above, converging together in a spill of bodies, racing down the stairs.

She ran. The guard blocking the entrance turned in time to see her barrelling towards him. He froze as she charged head-first into his chest. He grunted and tumbled out of her way.

She fled down the stairs, taking two at a time, into the lamp post forest. She could hear the men behind her as she weaved her way through the posts. Lights flashed by, disorientating and dazzling. Why were they chasing her? No time to analyse the situation, she had to keep running.

She left the lamp posts and plunged into the relative darkness of the market district. Ghosts of the lamp post lights smeared her vision but she ran on.

The market itself was deserted, as were the suburbs and streets all the way to the lift site.

Sammy stopped at the steps to the lift and bent double, her chest tearing itself in half, desperate for oxygen. She straightened up, sucked in air. The palace guards were closing in. They rounded the corner of the street, racing towards her. Sammy staggered up the steps and onto the platform, then realised there was no one to operate the lift. She couldn't get to the lever and back in time. She leant over the railing. Too far down to jump.

What now?

———

"Sammy!"

She sat up in her bed at the palace.

Hami was in the doorway to the communal room. "Get dressed," he said. "It's time to leave."

Four palace guards in red pointed hats accompanied them through the lamp post plaza, carrying their luggage.

Sammy rubbed her puffy eyes. She couldn't shrug off the dream. It had seemed so real until she woke up. It was the book that had done it; it had got to her. She hadn't had time to tell Mehrak about it. Should she bring it up now? Tell Hami as well? If the magi knew most things about history, then Hami probably already knew what it said. She watched him as they walked. He looked back at her, then turned away. He knew. She could feel it. He knew that she was the child with golden hair; the child that was supposed to be killed. Then a thought struck her. Was he really taking her to the capital? She didn't want to believe the things Mehrak had said about him, but she was beginning to convince herself. Did he really have her best interests at heart?

Mehrak was passing his grandfather's book back and forth between his hands, which meant something was bothering him too. At least it wasn't just her.

The streets in the market sector were empty. The traders hadn't set up their stalls for the day and the shop fronts were locked down. Sammy gave the empty marketplace one last lingering look as they passed. Then it was gone and they were on their way to the lift site.

Narok was waiting for them at base camp when they stepped off the lift. Behind him, outside the campsite, thirty karkadann were lined up, shoulder to shoulder in the fog. The Marzban, dressed in navy combat fatigues and turbans, were saddling up the karkadann, loading supplies and fetching weapons.

"I trust your men have been briefed with the information I told you?" Hami said. He placed a hand on Narok's shoulder.

"Yes, sir. Principal Hootan, I mean." Narok took a deep breath. "I need to talk to you about something ..." he began as Hami guided him from earshot.

Sammy left Hami and Narok to it, and followed Mehrak and the palace guards to meet Louis.

"... a magus and thirty Marzban?" a Marzban officer whispered to another as they hurried past Sammy. "I'm telling you, there's going to be trouble."

Sammy stopped. Mehrak had said something about the size of the entourage, too. She looked around to locate Hami and Narok. They were over by a secluded campfire, deep in conversation.

She ducked away from Mehrak and slipped into the shadow of a tent. She ran across to another, and proceeded to flank Hami and Narok's position as quietly as possible. Hami appeared to be stressing something important. Narok nodded anxiously.

The Marzban were now forming a line by their karkadann, ready to mount. Base camp fell silent.

Sammy crept closer to the two men, remaining behind Hami and keeping out of sight of Narok. When she got as close as she dared, she slipped behind a tent and listened.

Narok was speaking urgently: "But you've told the Regent that we're taking Sammy to the capital."

"I'm well aware of what I've told him," Hami said. "Our business is no longer his concern."

"Principal Hootan, I really think—"

"I really think you should listen to the magi, given your past indiscretions."

Narok flinched. He looked about nervously. "The magi told me I'd have a fresh start. I haven't wasted the opportunity." He gulped. "I've repaid my debt. I'm doing good work here. I keep Honton Keep safe."

"Are you forgetting the agreement we made when we found you the position here?"

"That was ten years ago. I've more than proven myself."

"Whether you have forgotten your obligations or not, you were a member of the Order and you owe us a debt."

Sammy staggered. She snatched at a guide rope to steady herself.

Narok's shoulders fell. "I have a family now. Children ..."

"You will lead us and your men towards New Ecbatana. Then, on the second day, you'll give orders to redirect to the new location I give you."

"And you've agreed this with the other magi?"

Hami didn't answer.

"Surely New Ecbatana is the safest place for the girl."

"The crabmen are regrouping," Hami said. "They're expecting us to go there and they'll be waiting."

"Why though? What do they want her for?"

Hami turned and Sammy ducked down.

When Hami didn't answer, Narok continued, "Principal Hootan, you have thirty of my finest guards. You're putting their lives at risk for this mission. You owe them some kind of explanation."

"I can't divulge any more than I already have, General," Hami said. "I need your loyalty for this mission. Afterwards, consider your debt repaid."

Narok's shoulders slumped. He acknowledged the magus with a dip of his head and turned to leave.

"One last thing," Hami said. Narok turned back. "Make sure your guards are prepped for battle."

–THIRTY-TWO–
Mobilising the Troops

Sammy had heard enough. She turned and sat with her back to the tent, clutching her stomach. She was glad she hadn't eaten breakfast. Footsteps approached, but she couldn't bring herself to look up until a shadow fell over her.

Hami.

"What you heard just now needs to be kept secret," he said. He was calm, no anger in his voice.

"You knew I was here?"

"Not at first, but I wouldn't have lasted long as a magus without knowing when someone was sneaking up on me."

"Are you part of the Order?"

Hami smiled. "No. Narok was once. But we captured and converted him, made him our informant. The Order found out and tried to kill him, but we saved him and enrolled him in the Marzban guard. He's never had the opportunity to prove his loyalty so he owes a debt to us. You don't have to worry about him."

"Why didn't you tell me the crabmen were after me?"

"What good would it have done to scare you? I wanted to get you to our safehouse without you ever having to know."

Sammy stared down at her hands and picked at a fingernail.

"This is our secret," Hami said. "Okay?" He held out his hand.

Sammy didn't take it, and got up by herself.

"Look. I'm sorry about … everything. A lot of people are relying on me. I'm stressed, sick … There is so much riding on this mission." His piercing blue eyes met hers. "And Mehrak's wrong. I do care about you. I hope you know that. I won't let anything happen to you." He put his hand on her shoulder and gripped it tightly. "Let's find Mehrak and get Golden Egg Cottage ready for the journey."

Louis waved his ears as Sammy and Hami approached.

Sammy said nothing.

Louis tilted his head towards her. *Okay?* he signed.

"I'm okay," she whispered. She walked up to him and patted his leg. Louis lowered his head and nudged her gently with an ear. Sammy wondered if he could tell how nervous she was from her breathing or body language, and whether he'd say anything to Mehrak. She didn't want anyone to know about the black book in the library or about her dream. Although, part of her wanted to open up to Mehrak, for him to tell her that everything would be alright, and that she'd be going home soon.

Eggie's backdoor slammed and Leiss came charging round the side of the cottage.

"Principal Hootan," he said when he saw Hami. His eyes were red and his face blotchy. "I need your help."

Hami looked at him blankly.

"You have to convince General Grotta to let me come with you. I know whatever killed Borzin had something to do with Sammy." He composed himself. "I want to be part of this escort mission."

"I don't think that would be wise, considering what you've been through. But I can speak to him about granting you leave if you wish."

"I don't want leave. Borzin asked me to take care of Sammy. He wanted her to have protection. General Grotta said he can't spare any karkadann, but I could travel in Golden Egg Cottage. Mehrak said it's okay."

"Sammy has enough protection. Use this as an opportunity to spend time with your family."

"I don't have a family; my wife's left me. She moved out when my mother moved in. I've got nothing to stay for. Borzin made me

promise to do this for him. I *have* to go. His last words were …"
Leiss trailed off. He took a deep breath and closed his eyes. He
turned away as tears rolled down his cheeks.

Sammy watched him struggle to get a grip. She didn't like
watching grown men cry. It reminded her of a time years ago when
her dad cried after Mama had walked into a door frame and broken
her jaw. He'd stormed out of the house, and Mama had to take
herself to A&E. Sammy went too so her mum didn't have to
explain herself to a babysitter.

Her dad didn't return home until the early hours of the
morning, well after they'd got back from the hospital. She heard
him stumble in, knocking stuff over and slurring his words. He
kept apologising and crying about something, but her mum had
said nothing. After that day, she never spoke of it again.

A deep wound opened in Sammy's chest. Mama was always so
cheerful. No matter how many accidents she had, she always put
on a brave face and had a smile whenever Sammy needed one.

She watched Leiss, guilty for feeling nothing for him. Fear for
herself was all her head had space for. Fear of the crabmen. Fear
of Hami taking her away. But mainly the fear that she wouldn't be
seeing her mum any time soon, maybe forever.

Leiss took several shuddering breaths and looked directly into
Hami's eyes. "Can you talk to General Grotta?" he asked. "He's
ordered me to man a post here."

"I think he's right," Hami said.

Leiss maintained eye contact. "I'm begging you."

Hami gritted his teeth. "I'll talk to him. Take Sammy inside and
help Mehrak prepare for our departure."

———

Sammy and Leiss were sat at the kitchen table watching Mehrak
pour the tea when the backdoor hatch slammed, followed by the
sound of feet on the stairs. Hami entered the kitchen and, without
stopping, continued to the tower staircase.

"You're in," he said to Leiss. "I hope you're already packed." And he carried on up the stairs to the tower.

Sammy left the table and went after him. In the bedroom, she saw him exit through the curtains to the front balcony and followed.

"Can you take us over to General Grotta please, Louis?" Hami said.

Louis pulled forward, heaving Golden Egg Cottage towards the line of thirty Marzban on their karkadann.

Sammy watched through the curtain.

"What's going on?" Mehrak said as he and Leiss nudged past Sammy and out onto the balcony.

"Not now," Hami said. "I'm about to address the troops."

Mehrak pursed his lips but said nothing. Leiss stood alert, his big chest puffed out.

Louis stopped at the line of karkadann. Sammy recognised Eva, Kelzar, Danush and Ali among the Marzban in the line-up. Eva smiled up at her and winked.

"Ladies and gentlemen!" Hami called out.

The campsite fell silent, the Marzban sat up, and all eyes moved to him.

"This is not going to be an easy mission," he said, "despite what you may think. New Ecbatana may only be a seven-day ride away, but there are forces out to stop us. And they will try to stop us at any cost." He paused. "See this girl?" He gestured for Sammy to come forward and approach the railing. "She is the reason the crabmen attacked Honton Keep two nights ago."

Mehrak and Leiss gasped. The other Marzban stared, unblinking and open mouthed, regarding her as if she were a freak.

Nope. Sammy still didn't like the attention.

Hami went on: "You are working directly for the magi now and you will take your orders from me. We will be engaging crabmen. And that means the Order."

The Marzban shared anxious glances and muttered to each other.

Mehrak sidled up next to Sammy. "I knew you were one of those chosen children," he whispered. "You're special."

Sammy thought back to the book in the library. Special was right. Not the sort of special Mehrak had in mind, though.

"The Order is coming for Sammy," Hami shouted. The guards fell silent again. "And it will stop at nothing, *nothing*, until it has her. Some of my brothers were dispatched to assist us, but they've been intercepted and won't reach us in time now. It's likely we'll run into trouble, too. I apologise for not revealing this sooner, but our mission is classified and must not be made public. Be under no illusion that the road ahead will be easy. There will be conflict and some of you may die. Just know that you're working towards a higher cause." Hami held his staff up and ignited the ball on the end. "May Ahura be with us!"

The Marzban joined in with the chant, but it was closer to a mumble and was without cheer. Narok pulled up alongside Louis. He was dressed in the navy blue combat gear of the other Marzban. His large, black karkadann had been equipped for battle with a streamlined saddle, and the base of its horn gilded.

Hami turned to him. "General," he said.

Narok turned to his guards, raised his sword, then let it drop. The Marzban pulled at their reins and led their karkadann around Golden Egg Cottage to form a hairy wall of muscle.

"Let's go, Louis," Hami said.

Louis performed a slow about-turn, then punched forward, carrying Eggie's passengers away from Honton Keep and out into the fog. And, Sammy supposed, in the general direction of New Ecbatana. But where they were really heading, she had no idea.

–THIRTY-THREE–
Bodies

Sammy watched the lights of the Keep fade into the fog and blew out the stress she'd accumulated over their stay in the city. It was cold outside, but fresh. She pulled Gisouie's fleece tightly about her.

The other guys had gone downstairs but she had wanted to stay up top. She'd been in the Keep less than two days, and that was enough. Honton Keep was an amazing place architecturally, but it seemed as though it had never quite lost the overbearing sense of confinement from its prison days. The oppressive stone ceiling, dark narrow alleys, stuffy atmosphere and the fortified library in solitary confinement. And then there had been the monster that killed Borzin, the one that had followed her from the Fungi Forest.

Sammy took a deep breath. That was behind her now. They were going somewhere safe. The relief she experienced at being back on the road was intoxicating. And if the monster did follow her, it would have to deal with her impenetrable barrier of thirty battle-ready karkadann.

After a time, Leiss came back onto the balcony, joining her at the railing. He watched his comrades riding alongside them, then pointed down, past Louis, to the ground below.

"This is the furthest they ever got," he said.

Deep grooves were scored into the earth, and littered about were charcoal-coloured shards that looked like pieces of broken crockery. Sammy wondered what he was talking about.

"Pieces of shell," Leiss said, as if in answer to her unasked question.

237

He was talking about crabmen. The pieces of shell didn't look like part of any animal Sammy was familiar with. They could have been looking at the aftermath of a Greek wedding, as far as she could tell.

They passed a lone sword lying on the ground; a portent of what lay ahead. There would be worse sights than pieces of shell; men and women had lost their lives here, too.

Louis shivered and slowed. Something up ahead was upsetting him. The karkadann around him slowed. They grunted and shook their heads. Golden Egg Cottage trembled, bringing Mehrak to the balcony.

"We're getting close to the bodies now," Leiss said.

"Bodies?"

"Nippers. Crabmen. You should go downstairs."

"Yeah, let's go downstairs," Mehrak said.

Sammy didn't budge. She wasn't going anywhere.

A lumpy mound appeared ahead in the fog, like the tangle of roots from a fallen tree.

The karkadann slowed further, bringing Louis to a crawl. Narok's karkadann approached slowly, then pitched the mound out of the way with its horn. A thick tussock of branch-length spider limbs flopped over, wobbled, then came to rest.

A crabman.

Louis side-stepped, giving it a wide berth.

In that moment, Sammy became aware of being in the presence of a creature entirely alien to her. She experienced a light-headedness, the ground pitching closer, then further away, tipping and spiralling. She clutched the railing. Another level of reality had added itself to what she'd previously assumed was reality. She'd levelled up on a video game. Level two with the addition of an advanced enemy type. The game had changed and her mind was struggling to cope with it.

The crabman's body was plated with sections of slate-grey shell, connected by pale pink joints. From the waist to the top of its head it resembled a human in shape and size, but without human features. The head had two stumpy, thumb-shaped eye stalks at the front, and at the bottom a compound mouth, like a locust's, but with larger mandibles. On its back it had a spiny shell, and at the base of the torso, where on a man you'd have expected two legs, were eight hairy spider legs.

The arms, however, were the most unusual parts. They didn't match, giving the body a weird asymmetry. The left side of the body was heavily built, with a thick arm and a claw like a construction crane's hook. The right side and arm were skinny, almost emaciated, the forearm of which was abnormally long, roughly the length of Hami's staff. It had a sharp, jagged ridge running along the bottom and a small, spiked claw at the tip.

Leiss watched Sammy, a wry smile on his lips. "The big claw can crush human heads like you could squish a berry," he said. "And the right. The long one ..." He sucked in air through his teeth. "... that's used like a sword. I've seen them sever men in half."

Mehrak gulped. "I've never seen a crabman this close before."

"Consider that a blessing. You think it looks bad dead? Wait until you see one alive. They may be called crab*men* because their chest and head are similar to a human's, but that's where the similarity ends. When you've seen one move, you don't ever forget it. They're nothing like people. All jerky and unnatural. That's why some of the guys call them the jerks. Their heads twitch as they look at you. And when you lock eyes, with those soulless dead eyes ..." Leiss shivered. "The first time that happens, your heart stops dead in your chest, and it feels like an eternity before it starts up again. I've seen men killed in the time it takes to get over the shock of seeing one for the first time."

"Oookaay," Mehrak said. "Now are we going downstairs?"

Sammy shook her head. She was hypnotised by the thing. It was so evil-looking, she couldn't look away.

Louis shuffled around the dead crabman and sped up again. Sammy watched it disappear behind them. When she turned back to face forward, there were dead crabmen everywhere; an armada of them drifting out of the mists. Some alone, some piled up. All were strewn across the wasteland in various stages of mutilation, the ground around them splashed with their blue bodily fluids, more like ink spills than blood.

Louis picked a course through the battlefield-turned-graveyard, trying to keep his distance from the body piles, which became a more difficult task the further they went.

It had been a massacre. Previously, when Hami had told her about the attack, she'd been unable to visualise it. She had nothing to compare it to, no concept of scale. Now she was able to witness the extent of the battle for herself, could comprehend the severity of the situation. And it was terrifying. Had all these crabmen really been sent for her? Fought to the death because of her? They didn't even know she wasn't the real chosen child. Or maybe they did. Maybe they knew she was the child who had to be killed.

And the spiralling dizziness was back again. Sammy slumped over the railing, arms dangling over the edge. She watched the corpses drifting by and zoned out, watching but not seeing.

Then she saw something.

"Look!" She pointed at a large heap of crabmen to the left, just outside the ring of karkadann. Protruding from the top of the pile was a human arm.

Louis and the karkadann slowed and stopped.

The man's arm was held aloft, like the Lady of the Lake's, but without Excalibur. Rigor mortis had frozen the hand mid-grasp, clawing for the sky while tendrils of fog dragged through the fingers.

What state was the rest of him in? That's what Sammy wanted to know. She couldn't deal with seeing another messed-up body like Borzin's.

Narok gave the order for two men, Sasan and Niro, to investigate. They dismounted and approached the pile. The other Marzban leant forward in their saddles.

Hami came out onto the balcony. "Go inside," he said to Sammy. He took her arm.

"No." She shrugged him off and gripped the railing. Morbid curiosity had her in its clutches. She couldn't look, but at the same time she couldn't look away. This would be a small act of courage for her. A mini personal victory.

Sasan unsheathed his sword and used it to poke at the pile of lifeless crabmen.

A leg twitched.

Marzban sword hilts were snatched at, gasps were inhaled and a long moment passed in frozen trepidation.

No other appendages moved so Sasan tentatively continued his inspection of the bodies. When he'd finished, Niro helped him pull crabmen down from the pile to expose the guard the arm belonged to. He wasn't too messed up, thank goodness. Just a gash on his neck that—judging from his blood-soaked clothes—was probably the fatal injury.

"It's Majid," said one of the saddled men.

Whispers raced around the circle of Marzban and they all dipped their heads. Narok ordered two further Marzban to dismount and help Sasan and Niro lift Majid's body from the pile. They raised him to the back of Sasan's karkadann, secured him, then Sasan climbed on and galloped back towards the Keep.

"And then there were twenty-nine," Mehrak said under his breath.

"He'll be back," Hami said. "He'll catch us up once he's returned the body."

Crabman corpses continued to show up with regularity until the pale glow of the Fungi Forest appeared and the large, green canopies floated out of the fog like a swarm of jellyfish.

The battle had extended into the forest and the mushrooms on the edge were in varying states of damage. Trunks were scored and chunks were missing from the caps. Several of the mushrooms had even been cleaved in half, with the heads lying upturned on the ground like radar dishes.

The karkadann led the way into the forest, grunting, snorting and flipping detached mushroom hoods out of their way, crushing the smaller bushes underfoot. The creepers were less than mild inconveniences and came apart like flimsy spider webs.

General Grotta's dark karkadann remained directly ahead of Louis, keeping the path clear and forcing a trail through anything that got in its way.

Mehrak made his way back towards the bedroom. He paused at the curtain and turned to Leiss.

"I don't suppose you play Chaturanga, do you?"

–THIRTY-FOUR–
UNNATURAL PRACTICES

They travelled all morning through the humid forest.

Around lunchtime, they came across a river and Hami allowed everyone a short break. The karkadann drank deeply, their sides heaving up and down under their rusty pelts. Louis collapsed to the floor and let his head fall into the stream. The water sloshed around his ears and over his head, and a mixture of air and water blasted from his nostrils as he exhaled.

Mehrak watched him. How would he coax the poor animal back onto the road? He couldn't convince himself that handing Sammy over to the magi in New Ecbatana was a good idea. How could he convince Louis?

He looked around at the congregated Marzban and karkadann. The troops were all hunched over, silent, and had been since the discovery of Majid's body. They'd only been travelling half a day and already the beasts were unfit for battle and the men were demotivated. If the crabmen attacked now, they wouldn't stand a chance. He couldn't abandon Sammy, though; she needed him. He'd figure something out. He would take her with him somehow. He couldn't leave her with Hami. The guy didn't have her best interests at heart.

They set off again after lunch.

Louis staggered to his feet and heaved Golden Egg onward without persuasion, which was a relief.

Mehrak tried to lighten the mood inside Eggie by suggesting a few friendly games of Chaturanga. And they'd begun innocently enough, until Leiss had promoted himself to the role of invigilator.

Or more like Chaturanga dictator. He dragged the game to a halt every time Mehrak made a mistake. Occasionally those mistakes were to his advantage, but who cared? Especially when Hami won every game. He wasn't even paying attention. Mehrak didn't mind losing, well, he did a little, but to be shown up? And by Hami?

Over the space of the afternoon, they'd slogged through seven games and Hami had obliterated him in every single one. All the while staring into space. Mehrak had concentrated, considered every move, taken his time, and when he was confident with his choice, he made the move. Immediately after, Hami would take his go. *Click.* The piece went down and then he'd stare off into space again. Sometimes he didn't even look at the board when he made the move.

Mehrak balled his fists under the table. There was something despicable about Hami. He was using the magi network to cheat. Mehrak couldn't prove it, but he knew. Hami was unstable and violent. It wasn't too much of a stretch to label him a cheat as well.

———

Sammy watched Mehrak argue with Leiss over the finer rules of Chaturanga. She could tell his problem was actually with Hami but she didn't care enough to step in. Hami was close to winning his eighth game in a row when they heard Narok's muffled call, from outside, informing everyone that they'd be making camp for the night. Louis came to a halt and Golden Egg Cottage dropped, then listed to the side, making the game pieces spill off the table and onto the floor.

"Draw!" Mehrak called.

"No, it isn't," Leiss said.

"The game's a draw because it ended prematurely."

"But the game was already won."

"I'm quite happy with a draw," Hami said.

"But you'd won," Leiss said. "There was no way Mehrak could've pulled it back."

"Hami said it was a draw," Mehrak said. "The two players are in agreement."

Chaturanga was garbage. Sammy left them to argue and went downstairs to see where they'd stopped. With the staircase leaning to the side, she had to push off the wall with her hands to keep upright as she fumbled her way down and out of the hatch at the bottom.

She exited the cottage and stepped out into the dark.

They were inside a deep ravine devoid of mushrooms. It was about the width of a dual carriageway, with a shallow stream running through the centre, and high walls dotted with blue lights that bathed everything in an aquamarine glow.

Sammy crossed the sandy shingle of the chasm floor to investigate the source of the blue lights.

Rooted into the slate ravine walls were fern-like plants, each possessing multiple floating tentacles with phosphorescent globules at the end.

Sammy poked one of the globules and her finger stuck to it.

The plant pulled at her.

She snatched her hand away and the plant's tentacles retracted inward. *Yuck.* Sammy inspected her finger. It was fine, but she didn't like the way the plant had latched on to her. She watched a moth fly into the light of a plant close by. It got stuck on a globule and was engulfed in a tight ball of tentacles.

There were some seriously twisted creatures in Perseopia. She was beginning to question whether this place had ever been a Garden of Eden. She wiped her finger on her top and trudged back towards the cottage.

The Marzban were lighting oil lanterns, casting out the blue glow of the plants and returning normal colour to their surroundings.

Louis was on the ground, gasping. The day had taken its toll on the poor creature. Sammy put her hand on his head. He'd put himself through a lot today. Neither he nor Mehrak would've made this journey if it wasn't for her, which made her realise how lucky she'd been that they'd found her; not just because they'd rescued her from the forest but because they'd become a second family. They were such a big part of her life in Perseopia that she didn't want to separate and carry on to Hami's hideout without them. Hami was cool and could look after her, but Mehrak and Louis loved her. She couldn't give that up.

"Are you okay?" she asked.

Alright, Louis motioned with his ears.

Sammy stroked his head. Mehrak came over from around the back of Eggie.

"You've done good, buddy," he said to Louis. And he fell on the big animal's head, hugging it tightly. "Why have we stopped down here?" he said to no one in particular. "If the crabmen find us down here, we're trapped."

"We would be," Hami said as he and Leiss joined them. "But because Golden Egg Cottage is taller than most mushrooms, we'd be too easy for their scouts to spot if we remained at ground level. This valley should conceal us and we're deep enough that our campfire light shouldn't be seen above ground."

Sammy looked up. The shimmering blue walls stretched upward on either side, almost converging at the top, with only a thin strip of yellow mushroom light showing in the middle.

"As long as the crabmen don't find the entrance to the ravine, they should walk right past us," Hami said. "Assuming they're even in the area."

Mehrak turned away. "Well, you clearly know best," he said. "I'm going to fetch Louis some water." He pushed up off his knees and trudged back to Eggie's back door.

Hami and Leiss went to help the other Marzban set up camp. Sammy sat on a rock by the stream and watched Hami and Danush raise a tent. This was the first time she'd had some space from Hami since they'd left the Keep. He'd stopped paying attention to her, probably thinking she couldn't go anywhere or do anything.

Mehrak came back outside with a bucket and used it to feed Louis water from the stream. No one else was around.

Sammy jumped down from the rock. "I have something I need to tell you," she said to Mehrak.

"What's that?"

"About Narok."

"About me?"

Sammy spun round. Narok was there, standing a little way off, holding his large, dark karkadann by the reins. They came closer, the karkadann crunching shingle under foot. It was the closest Sammy had come to a karkadann and 'mountain covered in hair' was a pretty accurate description of the creature. It was humungous. The thing seemed to fill her entire field of view.

The beast shook its head as it drew up, waving its six-foot horn from side to side as if it were cardboard. It had a low brow, which made it look like it was constantly frowning, and two mismatching eyes. One had a maroon iris surrounded by a thin red circle, while the other was cloudy white with a long scar across it. It came close enough that Sammy could smell its breath, a mixture of old trainers and dog owner's house.

It snorted and she shrieked.

"Don't be afraid," Narok said. He patted the animal's neck. "Indomit is actually a big softy."

"Big, I can see," Sammy said. "Soft, I don't. I suppose his eyes could be soft." Indomit snorted again. Sammy jumped again. "I didn't mean to call him soft." She held up her hands. She recalled the crazed look the creature had possessed when it came out of the fog, fresh from killing crabmen the night they'd attacked the Keep.

"Would you like to stroke him?" Narok asked.

Was he having a laugh? She wouldn't 'like to' but she thought it might be rude to decline, so she placed her hand on Indomit's muzzle and gently patted him. It was like patting a hay bale. You could probably thatch a roof with karkadann hair.

Narok smiled awkwardly and checked over his shoulder. "Would you take a walk with me?" he asked.

Sammy glanced at Mehrak. "Go on," Mehrak said. "We'll talk later."

When they'd walked a little way off, Narok turned to her. "I hear you're from the Mother World?"

"You know about that?"

He nodded. "I do, but my fellow guards don't." He paused. "I know you overheard the conversation I had with Principal Hootan." He took a long breath, blew it out. "I have done some questionable things in my life, but I hope the good I've done for the people of Honton Keep counts for something." He looked searchingly into Sammy's eyes. "Please keep what you've learned to yourself. Judge me for what I do for you now, not for who I used to be. I'm on your side, and I'll be doing my utmost to protect you."

He had intense brown eyes. They were eyes that had probably seen a great many terrible things; things that Sammy had no desire to see or to know about. But they seemed sincere.

Sammy nodded. "I'll keep your secret."

Narok smiled faintly and they walked on. "The magi are great men. I have no doubt Principal Hootan will succeed in his mission. I only wish he'd waited for the other magi instead of taking my guards. I'm sure they'd be better protection than we are."

Sammy felt a niggling slither of unease uncoiling in her stomach.

"We'll be okay, though," he went on. "I'm sure he knows what he's doing. I only hope the Grand Master will see it that way."

Why wouldn't the Grand Master see it that way? Surely Hami was following the Grand Master's orders.

Narok looked up. Hami was coming.

"I'd better help my men finish setting up," he said. He smiled at Sammy, turned and led Indomit away.

"What did he want?" Hami asked her. His eyes were red and his gums were stained black. He spat on the floor.

"Nothing. He was just saying hello." She couldn't look at him. She tried to rationalise what Narok had told her while keeping her head down. She was convinced Hami would be able to read her expression if she made eye contact.

"Can you come with me, please?" he asked and marched off ahead, through the newly erected campsite.

Sammy trailed behind, half-walking, half-running. All the tents were up now, the campfires prepared and Marzban were feeding their karkadann. Hami stopped at a freshly dug fire pit and dismissed the Marzban who'd been filling it with dried mushroom strips. He turned to Sammy. There was a sparkle in his eyes that she hadn't seen before.

"Would you like to learn how to light a campfire like a magus?" he said.

Sammy's hands and toes tingled. "That would be awesome!" she said. Maybe Hami was alright after all.

Hami stood at the edge of the fire pit and held his staff above it. "Stand back," he said, then stopped. He lowered his staff and looked at Sammy as if he were trying to weigh up a decision. A sly smile crept across his face.

"Remember how I said a magus can't teach his powers?"

"Because you aren't allowed?" Sammy looked around to see if anyone was watching.

"It's nothing to do with permission. You're either capable or you aren't."

"Does that mean I'm capable?"

"I think you might be."

Electricity surged up her legs and arms. "Am I a magus then?"

"It takes many years to become a magus. But there's something different about you. I can sense you have ... gifts."

Why hadn't Hami mentioned this sooner? She could've been shooting stuff with her own staff by now. But that didn't matter, he was mentioning it now. She couldn't stand still. This was so totally amazing! Forget super-reading. Maybe she'd get her own staff. Principal Sammy Ellis had a nice ring to it.

Hami smirked as he watched her. "Here," he said. He passed Sammy his staff. "Why don't you have a go?"

She took the staff. "What do I do?"

"I'll talk you through it."

Sammy stepped up to the ring of stones that had been placed around the fire pit.

"Right," Hami said. "Hold the staff out so the orb at the end hangs over the dried pieces of mushroom."

Sammy held out the staff, but the weight of the black sphere pulled it down into the fireplace.

"It's heavy," she said. "I can't keep it level."

Mehrak sidled up alongside them. "What are you doing?" he asked, narrowing his eyes.

"I'm teaching Sammy to light a fire," Hami said. There was an undertone of hostility in his voice.

Mehrak scoffed. "With a lightning staff?"

"Yes."

Mehrak frowned. "But she's not a magus."

"Mehrak." Hami raised a finger to his lips. "Could you leave us to it, please?"

Trying, unsuccessfully, to appear indifferent, Mehrak shrugged and wandered off in Louis's general direction. Sammy watched him pretend to collect water from the stream in his bucket. He kept looking over at them as he repeatedly filled and emptied the same bucket.

"Where were we?" Hami said. He turned back to Sammy.

"I can't lift your staff."

"That's okay. Keep hold of it, but leave the orb resting in the fireplace," he said. "Now, relax."

Sammy relaxed but held on to the staff.

"I'm going to teach you some of the fundamental rules of the universe."

"Rules?" Mehrak piped up. He dropped his bucket and scurried back over, his eyes wide. "As in *Rule Book* rules?"

Hami spoke through clenched teeth. "All physical and universal rules are in the *Rule Book*, but these are the most simple of fundamental laws. I'm sure you already know them."

"Can I watch anyway?"

"As long as you don't talk."

Mehrak made a motion of locking his mouth shut with a key.

"Right," Hami said, facing Sammy. "Everything in the universe is composed of matter."

"Matter. I've heard of matter."

"Good. Imagine everything is made of millions and billions of tiny spheres, or balls. You, me, Mehrak, my staff, the rocks. Tiny little balls called atoms that are so small you can't see them, the building blocks of the universe."

Sammy stared at the staff in her hand. The orb still rested in the fireplace. "I know about atoms. We learnt about them in school."

"Then you know that if you have enough of these atoms joined together, they can form objects large enough to see. And that there are hundreds of different types of atoms. The rocks here are made of heavier and more dense atoms than the pieces of mushroom and this makes the rocks heavier than mushrooms. We're made of loads of different types of atoms, arranged in hundreds of thousands of different combinations."

Sammy nodded. She'd covered most of what Hami was talking about in science class, but it wasn't easy to visualise everything as balls.

"Got it?" Hami asked.

"How many balls am I made of?"

"Millions and billions. Too many to count."

Sammy stared at the staff and wondered when something was going to happen.

"Close your eyes and picture the staff in your hand. Picture nothing else, only blackness."

Sammy closed her eyes and imagined the staff in her hand.

"Think of the staff in great detail. Imagine you're a tiny insect flying down towards the shaft. Smaller than an insect; a speck of dust. You're approaching the staff but there's a long distance to cover. You keep going, getting closer. The shaft now fills your entire view, you can see nothing else but shaft, yet there's still a long way to cover. You're still travelling closer and now you're beginning to see something. You can see that the staff is made up of atoms; balls. You can see a wall of balls before you, millions of them. All of them joined together, making up the staff. They're all jiggling slightly. Wriggling together, joined as one long pole. Have you got it?"

Sammy nodded again. It was gradually coming to her. She could see an ocean of white balls, like she was hovering over the biggest children's ball pit ever.

"Now, imagine the little balls lifting, getting lighter, as if they're losing weight. They're staying the same size, but they're getting lighter. They're floating. The staff is getting lighter." Hami stopped.

"What next?" Sammy asked when Hami didn't go on. "I can picture it! I can see it perfectly." She opened her eyes. The staff was suspended horizontally in her right hand. "Wow, that's brilliant," she said. "It feels light as a feather."

Hami's eyes were wide.

She wondered if she could light the staff, too. Following her instincts, she pictured herself flying along the length of the staff, reaching the orb at the end: a huge, planet-sized sphere. In her mind's eye, she saw all the dark atoms floating around inside. She imagined them moving faster, racing around, bumping into each other, crashing, creating friction, sparks and heat.

"It's working!" she yelled.

The orb was glowing, getting brighter. Ferocious white light burst from the staff, banishing the darkness from the ravine. All the Marzban turned to look at her, slack-jawed, the colour bleached from their faces and clothes—everything super white.

Hami lunged at the staff and snatched it from Sammy's hand.

The ravine sunk back into the dim orange glow of the campfires.

No one moved.

Hami cradled the staff in trembling hands. "I'm sorry," he said. "The lesson's over."

"Why?" Sammy asked. "I'll try harder. I promise."

"You tried hard enough. I wasn't expecting … You barely put any effort in." Hami turned to walk away.

"I'm sorry. I didn't mean to …"

Hami stopped. "You didn't do anything wrong, Sammy. It's my fault. I wanted to test you, but it was wrong of me. I should've waited until my brothers were here. To control …" He hung his head. "Forgive me," he said at last, and walked away.

Sammy watched him go, his shoulders slumped. He kept walking straight through the campsite and out into the darkness on the other side.

–THIRTY-FIVE–
THE ESCAPE

Golden Egg Cottage lurched, jolting Sammy awake.

She sat up in bed. Louis's feet were pounding below, accompanied by the rubbery squeak of mushrooms skimming Eggie's surface. They were back in the Fungi Forest, and moving fast. Her bed was shaking underneath her, the chandelier in the peak of the room swung back and forth, and one of the wardrobes had begun juddering its way across the room.

Sammy leapt from the bed and ran out onto the front balcony. Louis had his head down and giant mushrooms raced by on either side. It was like being on the bridge of the USS Enterprise navigating an asteroid field, except they'd lost their karkadann shield array.

Wait.

Where were Narok and the Marzban? Sammy stumbled back into the bedroom and down the spiral tower steps. She stopped where they met the stairs curving up from the kitchen.

"What's going on?" she shouted, so as to be heard over the creaking cottage and rattling crockery.

Mehrak and Leiss peered up from the kitchen table, each gripping a cup of sloshing mushroom tea in their hands.

"We're heading to the Cataclysm to rescue Gisouie," Mehrak said. He dabbed at a small puddle of splashed tea with a dishcloth. "And then we'll go into hiding until we work out how to return you to the Mother World."

"Where's Hami?"

"I don't know. Back at the campsite? Out in the forest looking for us? Who knows?"

"You're kidding me?"

Mehrak shook his head.

Sammy slid down the wall, into a sitting position at the top of the stairs. "Oh my God! What have you done? What's he going to say?"

"If we ever see him again, you can ask him. But I doubt you'll have to worry about that now."

"Someone will have seen us leave. It's not like Louis can tiptoe away. And … and Hami's a flippin' magus. He'll just know."

"Louis can sneak when he needs to," Mehrak said. "After your display with the staff at the campfire, Hami walked off. We waited for him to come back, but he didn't, so I told Narok we'd go a little way down the ravine to find him. We followed his trail all the way out of the other end. And when we didn't find him I realised that this was our opportunity to escape."

Sammy didn't know what to say. "What about you, Leiss? You're breaking orders."

Leiss looked her in the eye. "General Grotta was a member of the Order."

Sammy's mouth dropped open.

"Louis overheard them talking at base camp before we left," he added. "I'm no longer following orders from that man. And I've got nothing to return to Honton Keep for anyway. I left money with a neighbour to buy groceries for my mother, so she'll be fine. I'm going to honour Borzin's dying wish and return you to the Mother World. He died doing the right thing while I stood by and did nothing. Not again."

"What about what I want? I've got powers. I'm going to become a magus and fight for Perseopia."

"Come off it," Mehrak said. "Hami isn't going to make you a magus, he's just using you. He's using all of us. He doesn't care what happens to you. You're just an infantry piece in his game of Chaturanga."

"Shut the hell up about Chaturanga. And he does care about me. He'll track us down. Do you really think you can outrun the magi and the Marzban?"

Mehrak kneaded his eye sockets with a finger and thumb. "When we left the ravine last night, we doubled back towards the Keep. Then we found a stream, followed it down river several stadia, before turning back on ourselves again. Now we're heading north-east towards the Cataclysm. We left the ravine late last night, we've been travelling all night and it's almost morning." Mehrak yawned. "So yes, I think we lost them."

"No."

"It's for the best. You'll thank me in the long run."

"I'll never thank you! Maybe I wanted to stay with Hami. Did you ever think about that? No one knows I exist in the Mother World. I'm important here."

"Don't be ridiculous. You're more important there. Your mother needs you. Hami doesn't. He doesn't even care about you."

"You're just jealous," Sammy said. "You're jealous because Hami is important and powerful. And he does like me. He wants what's best for me. He'll train me to become a warrior and we're going to fight for Perseopia together."

"Jealous? Of him? You've only been in Perseopia a few days. This isn't even your realm to fight for. And there's more to life than fighting. Something you should maybe tell your father."

"Take that back!"

"Open your eyes and see who's really there for you."

"Who's really there for me? You? You only picked me up as a stand-in because you lost your wife. You're lonely and pathetic. And a coward for running away."

Mehrak's face went red. "After everything I've done for you. You crave attention from bullies and ignore those who actually care. And you call me pathetic? I'm risking my life for you. Do you know what Hami would do to me if he catches up with us?"

Sammy had heard enough. She ran upstairs, through the bedroom and onto the back balcony. She slumped against the railing and hid her face in the crook of her arm. She felt sick to the pit of her stomach. She knew Mehrak cared, but she hated him for what he'd said about Hami and her dad. He was wrong. Hami was going to train her to fight for Perseopia. Fighting was brave and honourable. She was going to be someone. An actual hero.

"So you tried to escape?"

Sammy spun around.

Hami stood between her and the bedroom. He stepped forward.

The cottage jerked to a stop as Louis heard him. Eggie's harness creaked as Louis moved about, trying to crane his head round to get at Hami, but they were too high and too far back. Sammy could hear Louis's mouth snapping, but there was nothing he could do without rocking both her and Hami off the balcony.

"How?" Sammy asked.

"Mehrak's too predictable."

"I didn't ask him to," Sammy stuttered. "I promise. Please don't hurt me."

Hami stopped. "Hurt you? Why would I hurt you?"

Leiss barrelled through the curtain. "Get away from her!" he shouted and lunged.

Hami casually flicked his wrist. Leiss slammed into an invisible barrier and bounced backwards onto the floor.

"Really, Leiss?" Hami said.

Mehrak came onto the balcony next, stepping over Leiss. "How did you …?"

"I knew you'd make a run for the Cataclysm," Hami said. "So I stowed away."

"Louis would've smelt you."

"I left my bag of clothes on board so there'd always be a smell of me here. Then I climbed the side of the ravine, and as you left I jumped aboard. I knew Louis wouldn't be able to tell the difference between me and my bag of clothes, so all I had to do was hide under the bed and wait."

Sammy shivered. He'd been under the bed while she slept.

"And, now that we're almost at the Cataclysm, I can alert my men to our location." The ball at the end of Hami's staff lit up.

"No!" Mehrak shouted. But it was too late. His objection got drowned out by a burst of lightning screaming upward from Hami's staff. The beam hit the smog and burst into a doughnut-shaped shockwave, cracking a peal of thunder that trembled Sammy's internal organs.

"What have you done?" Mehrak screamed. "The crabmen will see that!"

"Hopefully," Hami said. "And hopefully it will send a message to the Order letting them know our location. Better get moving, Louis."

-THIRTY-SIX-
Last Chance

Behnam remained on the floor with his arms suspended above his head. It seemed as if he'd been chained up for days, although he had no way of knowing.

Since he'd woken from the most recent of his reoccurring nightmares, he'd lost the use of his arms. At least he assumed that's when it had happened. He couldn't be sure of anything anymore. His dreams were merging into reality. He was constantly fearful, constantly expecting the demented giggling girl to catch up with him. But the dreams weren't his. He was certain of that.

He needed to escape, to run, to move his arms and legs, get his circulation going, but that wasn't going to happen. If he were unchained now, he doubted he'd be able to stand or even crawl. His body was gradually shutting down and there was nothing he could do about it. He'd been abandoned; left to rot without food or water.

It wouldn't be long before he died.

Only days ago he'd parted ways with Hami. Shortly afterwards he'd been attacked. It seemed like a lifetime ago now. He wondered if Hami had made it out of the city okay. If he'd caught the fugitive he'd gone after?

Behnam had dropped off the network before he'd been captured and he hadn't re-joined since. His brothers probably assumed him dead. He was desperate to make contact, tell them he was alive and beg to be rescued. But he couldn't do that. His brain had been poisoned. Communication could result in the entire magi network being exposed to an attack. He'd rather die than let that happen. Which was convenient, because that was exactly what was going to happen. There was nothing left to do but wait.

So he waited, and he listened.

He'd been abandoned, but he wasn't alone. There were footsteps nearby, which meant he was still being guarded. Why? He was being left to die, why not finish him off?

The guards changed often. They came, went, but never talked. Not a single word. Why did they remain silent and work such short shifts? They'd have been ordered to do so for a reason. And if that was the case then it meant he was still considered a threat. Blind, chained, and virtually paralysed, Behnam Baktash was a threat. Flattering, but not helpful. Or was it? What could he deduce from this? They'd been ordered to remain silent and to work short shifts so that no single guard spent any length of time in his proximity. That meant they assumed Behnam would try to identify them.

He'd already tried to investigate the guards using mental probes. None of his captors were magi or had the abilities to become one. They were all nobodies. That ruled out openly communicating via telepathy. So what use would it be if he identified them?

Pain was spreading from his temples, clouding his brain. What use was identifying a guard? And then he knew. He could force telepathic suggestions. That's what his captors were afraid of.

Years ago, the Grand Master Lectone Tinoplus had once achieved mind control over a prisoner and used him to lead the Regent's forces to a terrorist base. The Grand Master's powers were legendary, but Behnam was powerful too. Would he still have the strength to hold sway over a guard? Sending out suggestions in all directions would have no effect. He'd have to concentrate his energy and train all thought on one person. Not an easy task for a blind man. He couldn't single out a guard visually and they didn't talk, but still he listened. There had to be a giveaway.

He listened to the guards' footsteps as they arrived, when they left and when others replaced them. It seemed like days were elapsing and still he couldn't distinguish anyone. He began to despair. None of them stayed long enough to latch on to. They knew he'd try to influence them so they'd made it impossible.

Then he heard something. One of the men shuffled as another replaced him.

Had he imagined it? He couldn't be sure. Did the man walk differently to the others? Or had he stumbled? Behnam listened, but the man had gone.

Guards came and went, but the one that had shuffled didn't return. He was beginning to doubt himself. Eleven guards had changed over since the guard that shuffled. Behnam craned his head, desperately trying to listen. Where was that shuffle? Was there even a guard who limped? His heart raced. He was hyperventilating. There was no guard. He'd imagined the whole thing. He was dying and losing his sanity.

Then, a shuffle. Almost imperceptible, but there. The man was back! Silence as the guard manned his shift. At the changeover, Behnam heard him limp away again and he was gone.

The limping guard returned infrequently. Usually every seven to fifteen shifts, with no pattern to the order. They were making it difficult, but Behnam was able to latch on to him every time he returned, silently bombarding him with suggestions. As time passed, Behnam began to feel him before he heard the lazy foot, could sense the guard's approach, but were his instructions being absorbed? Was it having any effect? Behnam kept sending the suggestions anyway, but almost as soon as the guard arrived, he would leave again. The process was taking too long. He had to escape and re-join the network, had to communicate with the magi, warn them of the threat.

The guards were moving again. Movement he hadn't heard before: an uncomfortable shuffling, nervousness. Someone was coming, someone important. And Behnam knew at once who it was. Heavy footsteps, plates of armour clanking and squealing across each other.

The footsteps stopped, a key turned in a lock, and a door creaked open on rusty hinges.

"We've located the girl," rasped the deep voice.

Behnam's stomach turned over and waves of sickness washed over him. "The girl?"

"The one that severed my arm. The magus who came to this city with you, Hami. He's taking her to the Cataclysm."

"You know I have no knowledge of this."

"How could you? You haven't re-joined the network yet. That's why I'm here. To extend to you an offer, so you can save another magus from being thrown to his death in the Cataclysm."

Behnam coughed. "What do you mean?"

"My men are already ahead of them and there are crabmen closing in on their location. They're trapped and the girl will be stopped."

"Stopped from doing what?"

"Fulfilling the purpose she was brought to Perseopia to fulfil."

Behnam gulped down a mouthful of air. "To chop your other arm off?"

"To break the seal of the Ahriman."

Cold sweat beaded Behnam's forehead. "There's no such seal," he said.

The voice spoke slowly, rasping out the passage:

"Seek out the path, cross the river of light,

"Descend through the depths and when you alight,

"Take a trip through the gate, where the mountain will fall,

"And that's when the realm becomes darkest of all."

The words paralysed Behnam.

"By the expression on your face, I'd say you've heard that passage before," said the voice.

"It's an old nursery rhyme," Behnam stammered. "It doesn't mean anything."

"Don't you find it strange how the passage never fades from the collective memory of the magi and it echoes over the network when a magus connects for the first time?"

How could he know the enrolment whisper?

"It's been over one thousand years and your pathetic brotherhood still haven't figured out its meaning. Ordinarily, I'd leave it for the magi to solve themselves, but time is of the essence. I can't allow you all to continue fumbling around in the dark, putting the pieces together, while my existence is at stake." Behnam heard the footsteps get closer, could almost taste the rotten breath on his face. "That whisper happens to be one of the few widely known passages of the *Rule Book*. It was imparted to Zoroaster by an angel, shortly before he died and his life essence passed to the magi."

Behnam's head was spinning. He slumped back against the wall.

"Your friend is about to break the prime commandment that all magi are born to uphold. Except none of you knew it, until now. And unless you inform the brotherhood immediately, you'll be responsible for failing your prophet and bringing about the ruination of the realm. You must join the network now and stop your partner."

"It's not true," Behnam said.

"You're tired and confused. Tell your brothers what I've told you. Let them make the judgement. Spare Hami's life, before it's too late."

"I can't do that."

"Then you've left me no choice."

Behnam sensed something coming, but too late. A heavy object smashed into his head and he was gone.

–THIRTY-SEVEN–
The Order of the Black Fist

Mehrak had his head in his hands. "This whole time you knew my wife wouldn't be at the Cataclysm?"

Hami had his head in the sink. He spat the last of the black puke from his mouth. "I had to make sure Sammy would end up at the Cataclysm."

"You lied about the slaves, the pterodactyls, everything?"

"That's all true. I …" Hami coughed. "… I only left out a few key pieces of information so you'd think your wife would be there."

Mehrak looked up from the table. "Like what?"

"Like, it's predominantly men who are taken to the Cataclysm. Big men. Ones that can shift rock all day. So unless your wife's uncommonly muscular—"

"Where then? Where is she?" Mehrak placed his hands on the table. "Actually, don't bother, I can't trust anything you tell me." He stared at the back of Hami's head, a burning, hate-filled stare.

Golden Egg Cottage swayed back and forth. Louis was still going, but he was tired, and getting clumsy and stumbling. Sammy watched Mehrak. He looked beaten and worn out. She placed a hand on the back of his. He placed his other hand on top of hers.

Leiss stood by himself at the stove, his hands clasped in front of him, eyes cast down like a scolded schoolboy.

"If she's still alive, it's likely she'll be at the mountain base. It will have been men that took her. That's why Louis smelt no crabmen the day she disappeared."

"*If* she's still alive?" Mehrak shook his head slowly. Dark bags had blossomed under his eyes and he seemed to visibly age. "I brought you into my home, gave you food and shelter. And this whole time you've misled me while my wife's life has been at risk?" There were tears in his eyes. "How could you do that to me? I couldn't do that to my worst enemy."

Hami pinched his lips together as if Mehrak's words had caused him physical pain. "I've felt sick with it every moment of every day," he said. He dragged his hands down his face. "There's no easy way to say this, but Perseopia is more important than your wife. I know it's not what you want to hear. And I apologise for saying it." He turned to face Mehrak. "But the realm has to take precedence over her. I let you assume she'd be at the Cataclysm so that if we ever became parted, you'd make your own way there."

Mehrak narrowed his eyes. "Except none of this is about Perseopia, is it?"

Sammy watched Hami closely, but he gave nothing away. "What do you mean?" he asked.

"You've got a different agenda. That's why you didn't wait for the other magi to arrive. And it's why you ditched the Marzban."

Hami didn't answer. In the silence that followed, a faint rumbling vibrated through the walls.

Leiss was the first upstairs and onto the back balcony, Sammy close behind him. The rumbling was louder outside.

"Crabmen," Leiss said.

"I can't see them," Sammy replied.

"They're still a way off. You won't see them under the mushroom canopies until they catch and kill us." Leiss turned on Hami as he arrived. "You'd better have a plan."

"I've thought of nothing else for days," Hami said. "But it's not something you need to worry about. You guys will be safely inside the Fifth Azaran Fire Temple by the time they catch up. It's built like a fortress. And we're not far away now." He pointed past the tower, in the direction they were travelling.

Sammy ran through the bedroom and onto the front balcony. In the distance, a brilliant golden beacon lit up the horizon.

"The Fifth Azaran," Mehrak said as he joined her.

"It looks like a sunrise."

"That's the light from the Cataclysm reflected off the dome. You can see it thousands of stadia away in the Atrabiliar Mountains. Here comes the edge of the forest."

Golden Egg Cottage left the yellow glow of the mushroom forest and pitched into the dim half-light of a vast, barren plain filling the void between the forest and the golden temple. Louis's feet made hollow thuds on the hard-packed sand.

Then he stopped, throwing everyone against the railing.

"What's going on?" Mehrak groaned, hauling himself up.

"Keep going," Hami commanded. His staff lit up and he fired a beam that hit the desert near Louis's feet. Louis flinched.

"Now!"

Louis crept forward.

Sammy turned to Hami, but he stared straight ahead, jaw clenched.

Louis was shaking. He spelt something out with his ears.

"Something hands?" Sammy whispered. She turned to Mehrak. "What is he saying about hands?"

Mehrak was trembling. "Not hands. Fist. As in the Order of the Black Fist." He turned to Hami. "What are you doing?"

Hami's eyes remained locked on the horizon. "You have no idea how important this is."

"The brotherhood—"

"... have no idea where we are. I disconnected from the magi network yesterday."

Mehrak shook his head, fear in his eyes. "But Sammy—"

"They've got my friend," Hami said. "My negligence cost his sister's life. I'm not losing him, too."

"You can't let them take her," Mehrak said. "Please."

Sammy looked at Mehrak. What was he talking about? Then she realised. She was being traded.

–THIRTY-EIGHT–
THE STORY UNFOLDS

Silhouettes of men on horseback appeared against the light of the Fire Temple. They projected up from the black plain, casting long shadows towards Eggie, like slender fingers reaching out to them. Sammy stayed on the balcony. There was nowhere to run now. No escape for her.

Louis slowed as he drew close. Then stopped.

They were a grisly bunch of men. Dressed in thick leathers, they had lank hair and straggly beards, some had tattoos on their faces, some had piercings. They looked like a biker gang that had swapped their choppers for horses.

In the centre was the head honcho. At least Sammy assumed he was. He stood in a tarnished, battle-damaged chariot. A broad man with a thick neck and huge hands, he had a bald head and a long white beard stained with patches of yellow. A gold bullring dangled from his nostrils and hairy eyebrows teetered on the edge of a sloped brow that obscured his eyes. He looked like a post-apocalyptic Santa Claus. The sort of guy who might have fought Mel Gibson in the Thunderdome.

Filthy Santa's chariot was hooked up to six horses. But not horses. They looked equine, but their necks and legs were shorter and their skin shimmered silver like a fish's. In their mouths were crocodile teeth and their tails were long and whip-like.

Four chain-leashed manticores prowled forward, pulling their handlers along with them. Filthy Santa let out a whistle and the handlers let go, allowing the feline beasts to encircle Golden Egg Cottage.

"You set up the manticore attack," Mehrak said to Hami. "You tricked us into taking you with us."

"That manticore wasn't one of ours."

"They're not really the Black Fist, are they?" Sammy asked. "You're taking me to be trained as a magus. Aren't you?"

"No," Hami said. "I'm not." And he left the balcony.

"It's not over yet," Leiss whispered. "The Marzban will have seen Hami's flare. They'll come."

Hami rounded the side of Golden Egg Cottage, heading towards Filthy Santa. He coughed, causing a manticore to startle and growl at him. He coughed again and then vomited terrible black bile onto the floor. One manticore came close, sniffed at it, then recoiled and whimpered. Hami continued past it without a second glance and went straight up to the chariot. Filthy Santa climbed down and bowed, then gave a high-pitched whistle followed by three pips, and the manticores began growling continuously.

Hami and the man turned their backs on the cottage.

"VorMask is using the manticores to drown out what they're saying," Mehrak said. "So Louis can't hear them."

"You think that really is *the* Ramus VorMask?" Leiss said.

"I reckon so."

Ramus VorMask. The boss man of the Order, and the person in charge of the crabmen. Sammy couldn't take her eyes off him. He looked a bad sort. Scum, her dad would've called him, hungry for a fist sandwich. Ramus turned towards her then and scowled. Instinctively she stepped back.

Mehrak had been right about Hami the whole time. They should've left him where they'd found him. Sammy had messed everything up. Inviting him to travel with them wasn't even her first bad decision. Unlocking the Emerald Dial and blocking the real chosen child from coming back to Perseopia was the original sin, and still her most catastrophic lapse in judgement. Now she was about to get captured and she'd never get home. As a result,

Esther would never return to Perseopia, and the realm wouldn't get saved.

Esther had only needed her to open the portal. She'd had one job to do and somehow she'd brought about the ruination of the realm. And she'd barely been there a week.

Sammy fled from the balcony into the tower and fell onto the bed, burying her face in the pillow.

"Sammy?" Mehrak came in and sat by her. "We'll get through this. If they take you, they're taking me too. I won't leave you."

Sammy raised her head. "You're better off without me."

Mehrak didn't reply. Instead, he looked towards the back balcony. The sound was distant at first, but getting louder.

Stampeding feet. Sammy leapt up and ran for the curtain.

The Marzban! They'd seen Hami's flare and had come to the rescue. Mehrak and Leiss joined her. Mehrak put a hand on her shoulder.

"I told you they'd come," Leiss said. "We're saved."

"Saved?" Hami said, appearing on the balcony behind them, and startling everyone.

The Marzban pulled their karkadann up short. The manticores growled, but stayed their ground. Mehrak stepped between Sammy and Hami.

"You're too late," he said. "The Marzban won't let you give Sammy away."

Narok pulled Indomit forward. "Principal Hootan?" he called up.

Mehrak took Sammy's hand and squeezed it. It told her she was safe. That everything was going to be okay. Except Hami's face was calm. He'd expected this.

"General," Hami called. "Operation Crab Bait is in motion. Now is the time to brief your men."

Mehrak's face fell. "They're in on it?"

Sammy stared at Narok. She caught his eye, but he turned away. He couldn't look at her. And she'd trusted him. She'd kept his secret.

"What are you going to do to us?" Mehrak asked.

"Exactly what I told you," Hami said. "You're going to the Fire Temple while we hold off the crabmen until their boss gets here."

Mehrak opened his mouth, closed it again, then said, "VorMask is over there on the chariot, isn't he?"

"You thought Harz, over there, was VorMask?" Hami snorted then started coughing, and for a moment couldn't stop. He dry-retched a couple of times and that took the smile from his face. "That's Harz Skermesh. He's ex-Order, like the rest of his men. They've been working with the magi for years. I pulled them in on this mission because they know the crabmen's weaknesses and they're excellent fighters. The plan I explained to you still stands. I stretched the truth about your wife, but I didn't lie about the rest of it. I'm not turning Sammy in. You guys are going to hide out in the Fifth Azaran while we wait and see who turns up."

"But ..." Mehrak began, then stopped.

"Why would Ramus VorMask come all the way out here?" Leiss asked.

Hami looked him in the eye. "I'll explain everything, just give me a moment," he said and turned to Narok. "General, I need you to follow behind Louis, forming a barrier between us and the forest while maintaining a distance of half a stadion."

Narok dipped his head.

"Harz!" Hami called.

Filthy Santa brought his chariot round the side of the cottage.

"Fall in beside Narok and his guards. I need all of you to form a defensive line against the crabmen. We can't let them get to Sammy. You must stop them at all costs. And Louis?" Eggie shifted as Louis perked up. "You need to keep going towards the Fire Temple. We haven't got long left. Your lives depend on you getting there as fast as possible."

Louis edged forward past the ex-Order men, then sped up leaving them to drop behind with the Marzban.

Hami led everyone into the tower. Once in the bedroom, he walked to the stairway railing and perched on the edge. He nodded for Sammy and Mehrak to sit on the bed. Leiss stood by the curtain.

Sammy was getting a bad feeling about this. It was the same feeling she'd had outside the headmaster's office at St Josephine's when her mum was inside trying to explain the bounced school fee cheques. It was one of those times you knew you were about to learn something you didn't want to.

Hami was solemn. "We don't have much time before the crabmen get here, so I'll make this brief. Mehrak? I assume Sammy knows why the skies clouded over? About the Assault on Aratta?"

Mehrak nodded. "Yeah. I told her about it."

"You mentioned Ramus VorMask earlier. Yes?"

"Yeah."

"Know anything about him?"

"About as much as anyone else. That he's powerful. That he found a way to survive the smog. He took over the Order of the Black Fist and then Aratta. That he made the city their base of operations and then bred a mutant strain of crabmen that are being used to take over Perseopia. That's about it."

Hami waited patiently for Mehrak to finish, then said: "First of all, the Order of the Black Fist no longer exists. They split into the Order and separately the Black Fist well over a hundred years ago. The Order are enemies of the realm. The Black Fist are harmless and generally keep to themselves. Everyone makes that mistake. The second thing: What you told me of VorMask would make him over a hundred and fifty years old."

"You asked me to tell you what I know. I don't know how he lived so long. Ramus VorMask might be the name given to whoever's running the Order. He always wears black armour and a helmet, so no one knows what he looks like. We could be on the seventh or eighth VorMask by now. Or, seeing as he can survive the smog, maybe he doesn't age like everyone else. General Azim Azertash was said to have won everlasting life when he defeated Zurvan, the Lord of Time, in a duel. Some people think VorMask is the General."

"He's not the General," Hami said.

Mehrak shrugged. "So who is he?"

Hami took a deep breath. "Something much worse. There's more to the Assault on Aratta than people know. When the palace exploded and the smog poured out, everyone ran. Those that stayed and witnessed the aftermath were all killed. The only account we have of what happened that day comes from a magus called Toler Ramone. He was able to upload the details to the magi network just before he died." Hami began pacing. "We informed the royalty, the government and the people of Perseopia. Told them what had happened." He stopped and looked up. "But we didn't tell them everything. We cut it short. Kept the ending secret for fear of causing widespread panic. Something horrific was unleashed on Perseopia that day. Something that still lives on in the old capital."

–THIRTY-NINE–
THE LURKER ARRIVES

Toler rolled onto his back and the agony returned. Eyes, nose, throat and lungs burning. Limbs unresponsive. He was still alive, but wished he wasn't. He opened his eyes to find the palace courtyard dark. The sky had gone, replaced with a deep purple and magenta layer of smoke that continued to rush from the palace, spiralling up and blossoming out at the top. A few wisps lingered at ground level but most had risen to form a blanket over the city. The only sky visible was a cobalt ribbon, sandwiched between the palace walls at the bottom and the purple smoke above.

There were people nearby, running over. The first of them that reached him began tying a piece of fabric over his nose and mouth. He tried to move a hand to knock it away but was unable.

He blinked to clear his vision. They were magi and Association men, and they were trying to get him to his feet. They had cloth masks on too, presumably to protect them from the purple smoke.

They were saving him.

Then they stopped lifting, and for a moment Toler was suspended. One of the men said something and Toler was lowered back to the ground. What was going on? He was disorientated and sick, but his head was clearing. His job wasn't over yet. There was poison leaking into Perseopia, seeping towards Fione and his girls. They needed him. He tensed his neck muscles and, fighting the pain, raised his head.

The men around him were staring at something up near the palace. A blurry figure by the entrance, at the top of the steps. Toler willed his eyes to focus, but they wouldn't. He tried squinting, but the exertion hurt and did nothing to improve his sight.

The figure slowly descended the stairs.

Toler would have to wait until it got closer to see it properly. He laid his head back against the flagstones and rested his eyes. He gulped to clear the saliva pooling in his mouth and grimaced as his raw throat constricted.

Toler could feel an anomaly in the atmosphere around him. Something changed. He could feel the Association men's fear, too. Waves of it rolling off them.

He raised his head again and opened his eyes.

The figure had almost reached the bottom of the steps. A huge man, dressed in black. Toler blinked. No, not dressed in black. It was his skin; shiny black with a green and purple sheen like a beetle's shell. Each limb thick and muscular, his neck like a bull's. Small pockets of air rippled around him as he moved, as if he were moving through a viscose but transparent liquid.

The Association men remained rooted where they stood. None of them knew what to do. Not the General, not even the magi.

They all flinched as a second set of arms unfolded from the creature's back. These were not thick like the forearms but slender and long, joined to its back at the shoulder blades. They rose up and hung above its head like twin scorpion tails with long, skeletal fingers.

The creature stopped, finally close enough for Toler to get a good look, and to experience the paralysing fear that had overcome everyone else.

The creature's head had no muscle or cartilage and existed almost entirely as skull, covered in a thin layer of skin, pulled tight over it, with no eyes, just empty sockets. Its body was muscular and lean like a greyhound's, with a narrow waist that cut in under the ribcage, almost to the back bone, as if it had no internal organs.

"Greetings," said the creature, its voice deep and powerful.

One of the men cleared his throat. "Who are you?" he asked, his voice uneven and shaky.

The creature surveyed the palace courtyard with its empty eye sockets. "Ramaask," it said, no emotion showing on its skull face. "Which city is this?"

"Aratta." The same man.

"Aratta," Ramaask repeated. "Excellent. From this day forth, Aratta is my home. And you ..." He swept an arm over the congregated men. "You are my servants."

There was silence.

Finally a magus spoke. It was Nasser. "And if we don't wish to serve you?"

"Then you may leave."

An Association man drew his sword.

"Hostility?" Ramaask asked.

"Sheath your sword," Nasser shouted. But the man ignored him. He remained as he was, sword trembling in his hands.

Toler could do nothing but watch.

"You should listen to your master," Ramaask said. "Leave this place as I have requested."

"What happens if we decide to take our city back?" the man shouted, trembling as he did so.

"I will punish you."

The man rushed Ramaask.

Ramaask didn't move as the man flew at him. Only when the man lunged did Ramaask react. With godly speed, he caught the weapon by the blade in one hand, stopping it dead. The man panicked and pulled at his sword, but it didn't budge.

Ramaask yanked the blade up, dislocating the man's arm with a pop. The man whimpered and fell to his knees, cradling his lame arm.

Ramaask turned the sword over in his hands. "Is this what passes for a human weapon?"

The man tried to get up while still cradling his arm but, before he'd reached his feet, Ramaask swung the sword. It sliced into the man with such force that it went through his injured arm and body, taking the top half of him clean with it. The torso spiralled through the air, painting the courtyard crimson, before hitting the floor and rolling to a stop.

No one breathed.

Toler had the uncontrollable urge to run. A claustrophobic panic gripped his body. He must get to his girls. Protect them. He fought the pain, but his body rebelled. He couldn't get up and he slumped back, sweating and gasping for air.

Ramaask considered the bloodied blade. "Interesting," he said.

There was a moment of stunned silence, then the magi and Association men attacked.

Toler had no choice but to remain where he lay. Light flashed from magi staffs and Association men hacked with their swords. But even though Ramaask was surrounded, he didn't go down. He swung the sword he'd taken, hacking the men down with the ease of a farmer scything wheat. Agonised screams raked the air. Limbs sailed through the sky, trailing blood, flailing and flopping onto the flagstones with damp thuds. One of Ramaask's long, slender rear arms whipped over the top of his head and caught one of the magi by a leg. He lifted the man from the floor and swung the body into the Association men like a club. Cries went up as it smashed into them. The colliding bodies slapping and crunching as soft and hard body parts came into contact with each other.

Toler couldn't allow his comrades, his brothers, to die like this. He didn't have long left, his lungs were collapsing and he would be dead soon, but he had to do something. He needed to contact the Grand Master. It was all he could do to stay conscious as he sent the message. When he'd finished, the men were already retreating. The magi had quit attacking and were using long range staff blasts to stop Ramaask advancing long enough for them to escape. Toler was aware of General Azertash in the thick of the battle, but he was losing consciousness. He reached for his staff, but it was too far away. As he struggled against the sickness, everything spiralled and went black.

———

Toler woke, retching violently. He turned his head and vomited a thick black tar onto the floor. He could barely see. Everything was blurred. He could make out the palace and purple smoke still pouring from it, but that was all.

Silence.

"A survivor?" came the deep voice of Ramaask.

Toler started. He managed to turn his head to see two large black feet with hooked claws beside him.

"I've found there to be a certain satisfaction in killing men," Ramaask said. "It gives you a primal thrill destroying something living, and watching the life ebb from it. While you slept, I spent some time pulling the limbs from one of your comrades. He died before I got to his legs. I didn't think man would be such a fragile creature." He paused a moment, became silent. "Watching the life bleed from a human, however captivating, has in retrospect left me feeling hollow and unhappy. I can't say that I shall relish killing you, either. But your death, like those of your friends, will serve a purpose, a warning for those wishing to return to this city. Return here to aid me or perish at my feet."

Toler watched through blurry eyes as one of Ramaask's clawed feet came off the ground and hovered over his head. He'd communicated to the magi, he'd warned them of this new threat, but ultimately he'd failed his family. Fione was strong, she would carry on without him. The girls were young enough they'd forget he was ever a part of their lives, but all of them were in danger. The entire realm was in danger. He'd unleashed a creature far worse than the despot he'd overthrown.

"Don't do this," Toler begged as the callused foot came down to rest on the side of his head. He clutched his bead necklace and began to weep.

"Did you manage to contact your friends?" Ramaask asked.

"I have a family," Toler said. "They need me. Please!"

"I hope you contacted your friends. I hope you're still broadcasting what's happening now."

Then the pressure came. Slight at first, and then excruciating.

Toler cried out as splintering filled his ears, and his skull caved in.

–FORTY–
Goodbye, Hami

In the time it took for Hami to tell the story, Mehrak had grown dark patches beneath his eyes, making him look weary and defeated.

"So there really is a Lurker at the Gate?" he asked. "The men that returned from the city telling tales of monsters and demons were telling the truth?"

"In a way," Hami said. "Ramaask is what they saw."

"And the magi never went back?"

"The city was uninhabitable. There was purple smog everywhere, so there was no point in taking the city back. Anyone who tried got tormented by nightmares and killed themselves. Eventually everyone left."

"But the magi knew what'd happened. They let Ramaask take over the capital and they did nothing?"

"Look at me," Hami said. "I spent less than two days in Aratta. And now I might not live to the end of the year."

"But—"

"Magi *have* been back to the city, Mehrak. We've been back many times over the years. But you can't fight in the smog. It kills you faster; you get tired, you breathe in more. We're limited to short in-and-out missions to find out what Ramaask is doing."

"And?"

"Well, the first thing he did was clad himself in armour and cover his rear arms in a cloak so he could pass as human, albeit an exceptionally large one. Then he gave himself the name Ramus VorMask and began gathering followers, offering them immunity to the smog. Mercenaries, bounty hunters, even a few of the ex-Sultan's guards; the sort of people that would do anything for power. And from what we've seen, Ramaask has virtually unlimited power."

"What is he?" Leiss asked.

Hami shook his head. "Our best guess is that he's a visitor from another world, much like Sammy, but from somewhere much worse. Some of my brothers believe Achaemen Mantis was a demon worshipper and used the Sultan's life force to open a portal gate to let Ramaask in."

"Hence the nickname the Lurker at the Gate," Mehrak said.

"Yeah," Hami said. "But unfortunately for Mantis—and us—he underestimated the effect that murdering a divine appointment by Ahura would have."

"What about the Association?" Leiss asked. "They must've wanted to take the capital back."

"Their armies were weakened from the first assault on Aratta. It took five years to get a second army assembled to attempt the capital again."

"The Second," Mehrak said. "Also known as the Battle of No Return. The day Perseopia met Ramus VorMask."

Hami nodded. "As you know, the battle was a disaster. Twenty thousand men entered the city. Six survived. And that was only at Ramaask's mercy because he wanted them to spread his message throughout Perseopia: leave Aratta and never return."

"That was a hundred and something years ago," Mehrak said. "What's he been doing since then?"

Hami shrugged. "He isn't interested in taking over Perseopia. He keeps to Aratta to oversee the construction of his twisted black column. But now there's Sammy," he paused before going on. "He seems very interested in her. We think he only stays in Aratta to guard the gate into Perseopia, the one he entered through. Otherwise he'd have come after her himself."

"Guarding it from whom?" Leiss asked.

"Again, we don't know. He gets his men or crabmen to carry out anything he needs doing outside Aratta. In the hundred and forty-six years he's been here, he's only ever left the city two or three times and only when he has no other choice."

"Which is why you're using Sammy as bait," Mehrak said.

"It's not like that. She'll be safe inside the Fire Temple."

"It's exactly like that. But why here? How do you know coming to this temple will draw him out?"

Hami stared at the floor. "There was another girl," he said. "Thirty years before Sammy. She had yellow hair too. She was taken to the Fifth Azaran—and don't ask me why—but Ramaask didn't want her there. He didn't want it enough that he left Aratta to come after her."

"Did he get her?" Sammy asked. Time seemed to slow down as the wait for Hami's answer stretched out before her.

Hami's eyes met hers. "I can't say for sure," he said. "But she was never seen again."

Sammy flopped back onto the bed, her heart beating hard, but her nerves were pulling her up again, she couldn't keep still. She was in panic mode. She sat up, leapt from the bed and ran for the balcony, but Hami grabbed her by the arm.

"You'll be safe inside the Fire Temple."

"How do you know? How do you know he won't get me too? No one can kill him! We should turn around. I'm going to tell Louis. Maybe that will stop him. He'll go back to his city."

"It's too late. He's coming. We're the only ones that can stop him now. Narok, the Marzban, Harz, his men, and me. We're all fighters, and we're ready."

"This doesn't make any sense," Mehrak said. "How can Ramaask know Sammy's here?"

"He felt her arrive. We all did. Except he knew she was coming before we did. He knew she was coming and he's been preparing for her."

Mehrak's face paled. "Preparing how?"

"The crabmen. They didn't exist thirty years ago. He began breeding them after the first girl arrived. The original species only inhabited the bottomless lake to the west. They couldn't survive out of water and looked nothing like they do now. Something scared Ramaask into doing it. Somehow, he knew Sammy was coming and he mutated an already formidable species to produce the most powerful army ever to walk the face of Perseopia. There's an event coming that he believes will bring his reign to an end. Perhaps even lead to his death." Hami looked Sammy in the eye. "And for some reason, he believes Sammy to be the one to do it."

Before Sammy had the chance to completely freak out, four loud horn blasts sounded outside.

Hami frowned. "They can't be …" He pushed past Leiss and onto the back balcony. He returned a moment later, ashen. He'd lost his tough exterior, the hardened warrior had become a terrified schoolboy.

"Sammy? I need a word," he said. "In private."

Hami led her onto the back balcony. The forest was now a distant ribbon of yellow, horizontally splitting the magenta of the sky above with the dark plain below. The rumbling of the crabmen was louder, accompanied by a snapping noise, like chopsticks being broken.

"Louis!" Hami called. "You need to maintain your speed. You can't slow until you're inside the Fire Temple. If you do, everyone dies." Hami turned to Sammy. "Harz has informed the priests inside the temple. They know you're coming and the doors will open when you get close."

He took both her hands in his. "I have to leave. I'm sorry I had to do it this way, but you'll be okay. Trust me." He let go and turned towards the railing.

"Wait!" Sammy said. She had too many questions. Hami couldn't leave now. She needed to know more. But what exactly?

"Who's Esther?"

Hami froze.

"And why did you try to stop me seeing her sister?"

Hami looked out at the Marzban, then back to Sammy. "I don't have time for this."

"She was a magus. And she travelled to my world. Why?" Sammy grabbed his arm. "After everything you've put us through, you owe me an explanation."

Hami looked away. "I don't know. Esther left the magi a long time ago."

"You're lying! There's more you aren't telling me."

Hami stepped away from the railing. "Before Esther left, she interrogated the magi network for classified information. Information that only the top tier magi are allowed access to. Ancient lore, sensitive stuff. The way out into the Greater Mother World. She was warned to leave it alone, but she didn't. In the end, she was shut out of the network and dismissed from duty. We thought that would be the end of the matter, but we found out she'd taken a position at Honton Keep palace as a librarian. Obviously, we attempted to stop her, but by then she'd fled and gone into hiding. No one has seen her since. We know she was close to former Grand Master Bruche before he was killed. So it may have been on his orders that she travelled to the Mother World to find you. I think they were trying to accomplish the same thing I'm doing now. To draw Ramaask into the open to destroy him. Their first attempt failed—as I told you—so rather than wait for the next child with yellow hair to arrive in Perseopia, I presume she went looking for one."

"And she found me." Which meant Esther had always planned to bring her to Perseopia. She was always going to be the bait. Not only was she not the chosen one, she wasn't even the sidekick. She was the maggot dangling on the end of the hook. No wonder she only had a super-reading ability and no decent powers. But then if Esther, the chosen child, hadn't made it back with her, this mission was doomed to fail. Hami couldn't stop Ramaask; he wasn't the chosen one.

Hami turned away from her. "I'm truly sorry for what I've put you through. Everything. But I must do this, for my friend. For Jamileh. For Perseopia."

"There is a way back to the Mother World, then? You lied to me."

Hami's shoulders slumped. "If I survive this, I promise I'll help you get home."

He looked out over the desert. The Marzban and ex-Order members had formed a line, following them at a distance, churning up clouds of sand.

"The priests know you're coming. You'll be safe once you're inside." Then he turned and leapt off the balcony in a swan dive.

Sammy dashed to the railing in time to see him fall into a forward flip and land on the desert floor in a crouched position. He stood and, without turning back, shouted, "We'll buy you some time."

Louis didn't stop and Hami was left to fade into the blackness of the desert around him.

–FORTY-ONE–
Engaging the Enemy

Hami ignited his staff. The Marzban and Harz and his men slowed, lining up their karkadann, manticores, silverskins and horses on either side of him, facing the forest. The horses whinnied, the manticores growled and the karkadann stomped restlessly as they waited. Even the beasts understood what was coming.

A wave of slate-grey bodies spilled from the forest onto the dark plain and accelerated towards Hami and the Marzban. Thousands of stick-like angular bodies jumbled together like a river of brambles.

Hami raised his staff, then slammed the base hard on the ground. A ring of light expanded from the orb and out across the desert like a ripple on a pond. The crabmen faltered, stumbling when it hit. Then accelerated back to full speed.

————

Behnam floated up from the deep. He was leaving the cloying fluid that pressed in on all sides, the pressure loosening as he floated higher. His movements became freer as he neared the surface and he emerged. Still in the dark, but alive. His shirt hung damp on his chest. Blood. He could taste it in his mouth and it was crusted around his lips. His head rested against a suspended arm and that's where it would have to stay, because he could no longer move it.

He'd been knocked unconscious instead of killed, which meant he was still useful. It also meant that he needed to be silenced for a while, so he couldn't contact his brothers. Wasn't he supposed to be warning them?

"Hello?" he called out.

Nothing.

"Ramaask!"

No reply.

"Ramaask?" he tried again, quieter this time. It came out as a pathetic whimper. Yet still nothing. Behnam knew he couldn't contact his brothers. Ramaask was luring him into a trap, waiting for the connection to the network to be made so he could exploit it. Behnam wouldn't allow it, so all that was left to do was wait. There would be no escape for him now. This was the end. Everything seemed to hurt less than it did before. The pain flowing out of him. Perhaps this was what happened in the moments before death. He felt strangely at peace. He was dying, but that was okay. Finally his ordeal would be over.

As he sat on the cold floor of his cell, a thought formed in his head, flashing in and out of the fog that clouded his brain. Appearing then disappearing. There, but not there. He couldn't catch it. He thought back to what Ramaask had said. *Cross the river of light on the way to the path* … How had Ramaask known the enrolment whisper? And more importantly, did a seal of the Ahriman really exist? There was a seal at the Fire Temple, but was it that seal? How did Ramaask know of it? It was obvious that Behnam had been experiencing Ramaask's nightmares. But had he received them deliberately or had they been transmitted unconsciously?

Behnam's brain was slow and tired. The answer should've come to him by now. His thoughts returned to Hami. Was he really taking the visitor to the Fifth Azaran?

Then the cold dread of realisation saturated his flesh. Ramaask had been telling the truth about the seal. Hami knew that taking the girl to the Fifth Azaran Fire Temple would lure Ramaask out. Like Grand Master Bruche had done, Hami was drawing Ramaask out to try and kill him.

It was because of Behnam. Hami was doing it to rescue him.

For Jamileh.

Behnam had known about Hami and his sister all along. They'd kept the relationship secret, but they couldn't hide the way they'd looked at each other. The furtive smiles, the stolen glances. Their love for each other was obvious even to the most casual observer.

Jamileh's death had been Behnam's fault. *He* had inadvertently led the crabmen to her. Not Hami. Hami had tried to fight them but there were too many and his sister had been killed in the melee. To this day, Hami still believed it to be his own fault, and Behnam had let him think that. His sister's death had broken both of them, and there'd never been a good time to talk about it, but he should have said something.

Hami had shouldered the guilt ever since. Now he was trying to make amends, trying to save Behnam's life out of misguided obligation. Only Hami wasn't guilty of anything and he was going to get himself killed.

Ramaask had gone. Behnam knew that now. That's why he'd been silenced, so he couldn't warn Hami that Ramaask was on his way. Only now it wasn't just Hami's and the girl's lives on the line. If Ramaask was to be believed, then the Seal of the Ahriman was at risk of being broken too. Ramaask had been right about the visitor, but the seal? Whether the seal existed or not, Behnam couldn't take that risk. Unleashing the Ahriman into Perseopia was not an option.

Hami had to be stopped.

———

Hami and the Marzban faced the crabmen, unflinching. The karkadann were exhausted from chasing down Golden Egg Cottage and gulped down long, shuddering lungfuls of air before expelling excessive clouds of steam. The Marzban pulled at their reins, trying to keep the animals still and stop them wasting more energy.

"Eva, Kelzar," Hami called. "I want you two to stay back. Keep between us and the temple in case any crabmen get past. You can't allow them to catch Golden Egg Cottage—"

Then Hami felt Behnam back on the network. He was alive! And trying to make contact. Hami opened up the connection. Behnam began talking fast, spitting out information. Then, just as quickly, he'd gone.

Hami's stomach clenched and he almost vomited. The seal couldn't exist. It wasn't possible. That meant if Sammy ... No, she wouldn't know where to find it. Still, there was a possibility ...

"Sammy!"

And the wave of crabmen hit.

————

Sammy watched from Golden Egg Cottage's back balcony. She was convinced she'd heard her name being called from the battlefield, but it couldn't have been. There was no way she'd be able to hear anyone over the chattering, bellowing and roaring.

The crabmen had overrun Hami and the Marzban, but it was too dark and they were too far away to see much of anything.

From where she stood, the battle looked like a mass of ants swarming over a discarded chip. The only evidence that Hami was still holding his own were the fleeting bursts of light from his staff.

The flashes of light came and went, and each time they dimmed, Sammy prayed they would re-ignite again.

————

Crabmen everywhere. Hami struck, blasted and parried. A black wall of crabmen came crashing in, then a blast from his staff illuminated their cruel alien faces with mandibles open, and they were gone in the explosion. The darkness returned and they rolled in again on another wave of spiky limbs. Long razor arms stabbed and scythed. Thick club arms came down like mason block hammers. Hami's team were being overwhelmed.

289

Thousands of crabmen had been killed outside the Keep. There couldn't be this many left, it wasn't possible. Mentally Hami felt the fight slipping, but he kept going. For Sammy. For these men and women he'd led to their deaths. But most of all, for Behnam. He couldn't lose him too, he had to fix everything.

Narok charged past, hacking the crabmen down with his sword, Indomit crushing them underfoot. Manticores roared as they tore into the crabmen, pulling their limbs off and savaging them with their tusks. Harz carved a trail through them on his chariot, his six silverskins braying and lashing out. And throughout, the Marzban kept the line behind. Their karkadann goring and pounding down the crabmen as they crashed into them.

But the crabmen were too many. They were piling up on top of each other, forcing their way through, escaping through the cracks and making a run for Golden Egg Cottage.

———

Mehrak and Leiss joined Sammy on the balcony. They watched the thin line of crabmen leaking through the gaps in the Marzban ranks and streaming across the plain. They were coming for Sammy, spanning the distance between the Marzban and Golden Egg Cottage. And they were fast. Louis wasn't going to make the temple in time.

Kelzar and Eva were on their way, galloping from the battle, chasing the rogue crabmen down, striking at them with their lances. But they hadn't caught them all. Three were further ahead than the others. Eva and Kelzar hadn't noticed them. And they were closing in on Louis.

"Get inside, guys," Leiss said. "I've got these." He unsheathed his sword and approached the edge of the balcony.

The three front-running crabmen reached Louis's tail, leapt onto his hips, crawled up onto Golden Egg Cottage and up over its surface like spiders.

"Move!" Mehrak shouted, dragging Sammy towards the tower. But they didn't make it. Louis freaked, stumbled, and everyone hit the deck. One of the crabmen lost his footing, fell, and a moment later there was a crunch and the roar of a karkadann.

Sammy got to her feet in time to see Eva leave the pulverised crabman in her wake.

She'd come after them! But not soon enough. Two seven-foot crabmen stood on the railing, chattering and twitching their heads.

Sammy froze.

A heavy claw batted Mehrak across the balcony towards the bedroom curtain.

Leiss dragged Sammy behind him and threw himself at the crabmen, swinging his sword side to side to keep them back. "Get inside!" he shouted.

The crabmen descended on him.

Leiss held his own, his blade clanging against the hard ridges of their sword arms. He was returning their blows, but they were too strong and forced him back.

Sammy ran to where Mehrak lay wheezing.

"Get downstairs," he croaked.

Sammy grabbed his hand and tried to pull him into the tower. "I'm not leaving you," she said.

"Just go!" Mehrak pulled his hand away.

Leiss's sword hit the floor with a clatter, sliding over to where Sammy stood by Mehrak. She looked up just in time to see a heavy left claw catch Leiss on the side of his head. It didn't land properly, only a glancing blow, but it collapsed him like an accordion. The crabman stood over him. One stalk eye twitched toward Sammy, the other towards Leiss on the floor. Her blood ran cold in her veins.

The second crabman came at Sammy with the motion of a malfunctioning robot spider. She went for the sword and dragged it up. It was heavy, too heavy for her to swing.

The first crabman raised its big claw to deal a death blow to Leiss as a lance burst through its neck, spraying blue blood like a Super Soaker. It gave a gargled screech as it coughed up blood, then toppled backwards over the railing, disappearing from view.

"Crab kebab!" Eva whooped from below.

One seven-foot monster left. But it was too far from the balcony edge for Eva to get a shot at, and the crabman knew it. It had all the time in the world. Its shadow swept over Sammy as its sword arm jerked up above its head. Its eyes locked on hers, cold and soulless, but savouring the imminent kill.

Sammy couldn't move. The sword hung limply in her grip, trembling and useless. Any second now the razor-sharp sword arm would come slicing down, cleaving her in two.

The arm twitched. And she closed her eyes.

She could see the arm swinging down in her mind's eye. Millions of jiggling little balls, like Hami's staff, but rushing towards her throat. She could see the balls—atoms—getting slower. Slower, and then stopping.

Nothing happened.

Sammy opened her eyes. The crabman was motionless. The sword arm, centimetres from her throat, had stopped in mid-swing. It hung there, shaking.

Suddenly aware of the sword in her hands, Sammy tightened her grip. In a flash, the weapon became weightless and came up off the floor. Then she willed it forward and it launched from her hands, plunging hilt-deep into the crabman's chest and carrying the creature backwards, where it crashed into the railing and collapsed to the floor.

Sammy stared at the crabman, then at her hands, and then Mehrak.

His eyes were wide and his mouth opened and closed soundlessly. When he finally regained the ability to speak, he said simply, "You killed a crabman."

–FORTY-TWO–
THE PTERODACTYL

Eva and Kelzar mopped up the rest of the crabmen escaping the battle, allowing Louis to get a decent lead ahead of them. As long as he managed to maintain his pace, the crabmen wouldn't catch them now.

Sammy went to check on Leiss. He opened his eyes as she came over, but it was a few moments before he could stand without help.

"Just a mild concussion," he said. "I'll live."

When he was back on his feet, he helped Sammy get Mehrak into the bedroom.

"My ribs," Mehrak groaned as Leiss lay him on the bed.

Leiss pulled Mehrak's shirt open and checked him over. "You'll be fine," he said. "You might've bruised a couple of ribs."

"They feel like they're broken."

Leiss snorted. "Civilians," he said, and staggered back out through the curtains, returning a while later with his sword.

"What happened to those crabmen?" he asked.

"Eva got one. I got the other," Sammy said.

"Is that dead one still on my balcony?" Mehrak asked.

"I dumped it over the railing," Leiss said, while staring at Sammy.

"My mouth's really dry," Mehrak said. "Could you fetch me some water?"

"Forget the water," Leiss said, still staring at Sammy. "How, exactly, did you get my sword hilt-deep into the crabman's carapace? I struggled to pull it out."

"Because I'm a total badass," Sammy said. She polished her fingernails on her chest and inspected them with an expression that was meant to convey 'No big deal'.

"No. Seriously. I want to know."

"Maybe I'm the chosen one after all." Sammy gave Leiss the wink and the gun, then left the bedroom through the curtain to the front balcony.

The view wiped the smug grin from her face.

The Fire Temple loomed ahead, perched on a mountain in the middle of the Cataclysm, which zigzagged its way to the horizon on either side like a brilliant white-hot snake. The temple was a monster. Bigger and grander than St. Paul's, with a dome that rose from the top of the white marble walls like a magnificent golden rosebud, and four smaller domes adorning minarets on each corner.

Ahead, a stone bridge reached out from the desert, arching over the Cataclysm to the mountaintop where the temple stood.

Sammy shielded her eyes as they left the dim twilight of the plain into the light of the Cataclysm, and Louis's footfalls changed tone from hollow thuds to solid beats as he began crossing the bridge.

Beams of light projected from the Cataclysm into the sky on either side of them and played across the temple's surface, rippling like liquid sunlight.

"Sammy!" Mehrak called from the bedroom. "You got lucky with that crabman. Don't test your luck with a pterodactyl."

Sammy ignored him and walked to the railing. She hadn't *just* got lucky with the crabman. She'd kicked his arse. Bring on the crabmen! Bring on lava pterodactyls! That's why Hami would eventually take her to New Ecbatana. She was a magus. Esther hadn't made it back here but Sammy would step into her shoes. She struck a pose with clenched fists and spread legs, the kind Jackie Chan would adopt before he beat up a gang of triads.

She peered over the railing into the deep chasm below and tightened her grip on the railing. She was momentarily unsteady, her fingers and toes tingling. It was a *long* way to the bottom.

Where were the pterodactyls? Shouldn't she be able to see some? Or maybe slaves shovelling rocks? She leant further out, looking past Louis, past the stone bridge, and into the depths of the Cataclysm.

The light dazzled her, and when she closed her eyes, it left multi-coloured patterns on the inside of her eyelids. She opened her eyes again, trying to acclimatise to the light, and noticed a silhouette circling below. She rubbed her eyes. With them closed, she could see a slender bird shape etched into the colourful patterns.

"Sammy! Will you get back in here?" Mehrak called out.

A flash of red burst up from the light. Sammy stumbled back from the railing and got floored by the down beat of a colossal pair of wings. The creature continued up past Eggie and into the sky. Dark crimson, the size of a small business jet with long, slender wings, a pelican-like beak and a pointed crest on the back of its head.

"A pterodactyl!" Sammy screamed.

It circled above, then aimed itself at her, stooping into a dive bomb.

"Get inside!" Leiss pushed past her and lashed out with his sword.

The pterodactyl pulled up and banked to the side.

Sammy ran into the tower. She crouched by the curtain and peered through the gap. Maybe she'd leave this one to Leiss. She'd taken out the crabman. She'd proven she was tough. Leiss could take it from here.

Leiss stood on the balcony, turning slowly, tracing the pterodactyl's path with the tip of his sword. Every few revolutions, the flying lizard would cut across the stone bridge, snapping at Louis. Sammy stayed in the bedroom, watching through a crack in the curtain.

"What's going on now?" Mehrak croaked from the bed. He lay on his back, eyes closed and right arm draped across his forehead.

"Leiss is protecting Louis from the pterodactyl."

Mehrak sat up with a start. "It's attacking Louis?"

"I thought you had broken ribs?"

Mehrak squirmed. "They feel a little better now," he said.

"Go back to bed. Leiss is protecting us. And we're nearly at the temple."

The temple took up the entire width of the mountaintop, but sat back from the bridge on the far side of the summit. Its rectangular base stood three storeys high, built from sparkling white marble blocks, and had hundreds of narrow windows inlaid in blue and red decorative stone. Two huge, brass-plated doors, the size of aircraft hangar doors, sealed the entrance. They opened inwards a crack and two figures in long brown robes stepped out.

"The doors have opened!" Sammy called out.

The pterodactyl saw the movement too and turned sharply, propelling itself towards the temple with swept wings. The people backpedalled inside and the doors began to close.

The creature changed direction in an instant, banking, looping under the bridge and out the other side, soaring up into the sky again.

"Hey!" Leiss shouted. "Open the doors!" He stood at the edge of the balcony, waving his sword in the air. The doors stopped closing and two scared faces appeared in the gap.

"Open the doors!" he shouted again.

Crouching, Sammy edged out onto the balcony, shielding her head with her hands while checking for the pterodactyl. She turned 360 degrees, keeping her eyes on the sky. The churning purple cloud layer made it hard to see anything moving above, but eventually she spotted the pterodactyl weaving its way in and out of the smog tendrils.

"Get back in here!" shouted Mehrak.

"It's coming back!" Sammy yelled as it broke away and dipped into a steep dive.

Leiss grabbed her hand and pulled her to the ground as the pterodactyl skimmed past on a rollercoaster dip, its feet clipping the balcony railing, denting the banister and fluttering the tower curtains. Then it was climbing again.

Louis left the bridge, accelerating into a sprint finish as he crossed the mountaintop, the cottage creaking under the strain. The temple doors were fast approaching, and although they hadn't fully closed, they hadn't fully opened either.

Louis didn't slow. He crashed through the doors, throwing them open to smash against marble pillars on either side. Louis ploughed on into a colossal atrium under the dome. He staggered, then slumped to the ground, dropping Leiss and Sammy to the balcony floor.

Leiss was back on his feet in a flash. "Quick. Close the doors!" he yelled down to the brown-robed men and women that had congregated around Louis.

"Now!" he shouted. "There's a pterodactyl circling outside!"

Four of them ran for the doors.

They'd almost closed them when they were slammed open again, sending the priests flying. The pterodactyl came tumbling through the entrance, sliding across the polished granite floor, past Louis, and collapsing in a heap. It flailed on battered wings, screeching and snapping at the priests. Then it shook its head, launched itself from the floor and, in three big pulls of its wings, was on its way up into the dome.

The priests scattered in all directions, but not fast enough. The pterodactyl swooped down and snatched up a man in its feet, carrying him away into the air. It circled the dome twice, and made an attempt for the door.

Louis lurched back onto his feet and backed up to the entrance, blocking its escape and forcing it to wheel around at the last moment. It screamed and flew back into the dome.

"Get those doors closed!" Leiss shouted. "Or you'll lose your friend to the Cataclysm."

The priests scrambled for the doors, sliding two heavy bolts into place.

With the only escape route blocked, the pterodactyl came down, landing heavily on the polished granite in front of Louis, and knocking out the man in its feet.

Leiss ran into the tower as the pterodactyl hobbled forwards, dragging the unconscious priest along behind it, flapping its wings and screaming at Louis.

Then Leiss was back with something in his arms. He pointed it at the pterodactyl. There was a flash of steel, a thud, and the pterodactyl flew backwards. It landed awkwardly, sliding along the floor and coming to rest on its back, the tail end of a harpoon protruding from its chest.

The priests' shocked faces darted from the pterodactyl to the balcony where Leiss stood at the railing, grinning broadly, as a single wisp of smoke unfurled from the barrel of the harpoon gun he held under his arm.

–FORTY-THREE–
Inside the Fire Temple

Leiss rounded the base of Golden Egg Cottage at pace.

"Are the doors secure?" he asked as he closed in on the priests. "And where's the boss?"

Sammy raced after him with Mehrak lagging behind, hugging his chest.

The priests didn't get the chance to answer before chattering erupted outside, followed by the pounding of a thousand limbs against the temple doors.

Panic spread among the priests.

"Is there anything else we can barricade the doors with?" Leiss asked, as the bolts rattled in their hinges.

A short, spherical woman, with lifeless grey hair scraped back into a tight bun, forced her way to the front of the gathered priests. She had huge, lumpy boobs that she supported by linking her arms together underneath, like she'd been out gathering pumpkins.

She didn't look happy.

"What have you brought upon our temple?" She had the sort of yapping voice a Yorkshire terrier might have if dogs could talk.

"I thought Harz spoke to you," Mehrak said. "We were told ..."

"Harz did speak to me," the woman said. "About looking after a girl and some travellers. I don't recall the mention of a crabman army. That's the sort of thing one tends to remember."

A young female priest called down from a galleried landing above the doors. She was at one of the first-floor windows, dancing about in a panic. "There are thousands of them," she said. "They're

299

climbing over each other to get to the windows. They're going to get in!"

The round woman held up a hand to quiet the girl. "Calm down, Niloufar. Their shells are too wide. They won't fit through the frames. Keep back anyway; they can still reach you with their sword arms." She turned to Mehrak. "I hope your lives are worth it," she said, then raised her squeaky voice and addressed everyone. "Listen up! I don't *think* the crabmen can get in, but we should evacuate the atrium, just in case. Move everyone to their quarters. Ranok, Bodeff: take the gastrosaur to the stables and give him water and rest."

"Will he be safe?" Mehrak asked.

"The stables are bolted from the inside," the woman said. "He'll be as safe as we are. Now, come with me." She walked towards the opposite end of the atrium, which was the best part of a football pitch away.

"You'll be okay now, boy," Mehrak said to Louis. "I'll check on you in a bit, alright? Once you've had some water and rest."

Louis raised his head off the floor. Then he lay it down again. He looked dreadful.

"Thank you, Louis," Sammy called back to him. "You really saved us."

Louis perked up a little. He signed back the gastrosaur equivalent of the thumbs up.

An old priest approached the boss woman. "Lila-Maryam," he stammered. He scratched nervously at the stringy white beard under his chin. "Should we barricade the doors?"

"The front gates are as secure as they're going to get," Lila-Maryam said. "Those bolts have held armies at bay in the past and they'll do their job today. I still want all doors to the inner sanctum barricaded, though, as a precaution."

The man dipped his head and hurried off.

"Lila-Maryam," Mehrak said as he walked quickly to keep up with her. "I'm Mehrak Omid. I presume you're the leader?"

"I'm the custodian," she said, without looking at him. "There are no leaders within the Hirbod."

Hirbod? Sammy had heard that word somewhere.

"Yes, yes, custodian," Mehrak said. "Total equality. All races, genders, and all that. You know what I mean."

"I know what you mean. What are you getting at?"

"Well," Mehrak said. "I wondered if you agreed with what the magi are doing?"

Lila-Maryam raised an eyebrow but kept walking.

"What I mean is, are they forcing you to comply with all this, or are you doing it because you believe you're helping Perseopia?"

Lila-Maryam shook her head. "You're fishing, aren't you?" A sad fleeting smile. "You don't even know why you're here."

"We know why we're here," Leiss said. "Don't we?" He looked at Mehrak, but Mehrak looked away distractedly.

Sammy jogged after them, trying to figure out what they were talking about. She was also trying to concentrate on the elusive memory she couldn't pin down. Who had used the word Hirbod? And in what context? She could almost hear them saying it.

Lila-Maryam said nothing more as she led the way out of the atrium and into another vast and beautifully decorated hall. Gold and marble columns stood proud, holding up a vaulted ceiling above a red-and-white-chequered marble floor below.

The ceiling was covered in various intricately painted frescos, each depicting people interacting with either angels or demons. One had a priest and an angel giving to the poor. Another had demons whispering in the ears of barbarians as they ransacked and pillaged. Around the edges, the pictures became more sinister still, showing brutal battle scenes with angels and magi fighting demons and other dark creatures. There was no subtlety in any of the paintings. Each one clearly representing good versus evil, or light versus dark.

In the middle of the hall, curved pews were arranged in concentric circles around a brass oil dish with a flame dancing over it. It smelled of exotic spices, lemon and pine. The scent was subtle, but filled the hall and had a fantastic relaxing quality. It almost took Sammy's mind off the fact that thousands of crabmen were beating down the doors, while an invincible, all-powerful monster was making its way towards her.

"Is Sammy going to be safe in here?" Leiss asked.

"She'll be fine. You'll all be fine. The temple's built like a fortress. The walls are uncommonly thick and the windows are reinforced with steel bars."

"The Fifth Azaran was always one of my favourite temples," Mehrak said. "I found it fascinating that it was fortified to such an extent and I used to wonder what secrets were hidden here."

What was with all these secrets? Sammy thought. Hami had kept secrets from her, so had Esther and now so was Lila-Maryam. They all knew something she didn't, and she didn't like it.

They got led through a door at the back of the hall and into a small, windowless office, lit by candles. It had a tiny desk, some chairs and several uninspiring paintings of barren landscapes on the walls. Lila-Maryam told them to make themselves comfortable, then left the room pulling the door shut behind her.

The *something* was still nagging at the back of Sammy's mind as she took a seat alongside Mehrak and Leiss.

Mehrak leant in towards her. "At least Hami picked a good place to keep us safe while he takes on Ramaask. This place is virtually impenetrable," he said. "I wonder what's so special about this place anyway? And why are all those slaves excavating rock in the Cataclysm?"

"Unless there's something else here too," Sammy said as she stared into space.

"What are you thinking?"

"That this is it," she said under her breath.

"Excuse me?"

Sammy leapt to her feet. "This is it. The Temple of Paths!"

Mehrak's mouth opened, but he didn't say anything. Leiss only frowned.

"Remember the map in the library?" Sammy said. "This is the temple on the island. Except it wasn't an island we were looking at, it was this mountain; and it wasn't in a river, it was in the Cataclysm, a river of lava. That's what the secret is!"

Mehrak's eyes sparkled. "That would explain the fortifications," he said. "But we don't know for certain. There are millions of temples in Perseopia, and even if this is the right one, the Hirbod would never tell us where the treasure is. They might not even know about it."

"Are all priests called Hirbod? Or just the ones here?"

"I don't know. I haven't heard of any others referred to as Hirbod other than these guys."

"Then this must be the right place. Esther's sister told me the last time she heard from Esther, she was staying with the Hirbod. She must've come here because she knew this is where the Temple of Paths is."

Mehrak jumped up off his seat. "That's why Hami brought you here! Because Ramaask wouldn't want you, the girl he thinks is the chosen child, escaping Perseopia. Ramaask wants you for himself. It makes sense." Mehrak's eyes moved from side to side, he was thinking, not seeing. "That's why the old Grand Master took the other yellow-haired girl here. He was taking her to the Temple of Paths to go home. That's what brought Ramaask here the first time and that's what Hami is trying to replicate now. He knew that if the threat of you escaping Perseopia was high enough, then Ramaask would come to stop you himself."

"So Hami knows about the Temple of Paths," Sammy said. "The old magus knew, so Hami must do too, with their brain network and stuff. He's lied to me again."

"I'm sorry," Mehrak said. "Maybe he'll let you go home once the battle's over."

"But why didn't he tell me?"

"Because he doesn't have your best interests at heart. I admit, I also wanted you to stay in Perseopia, too. But that's because you're good company and—"

"Okay, we get it," Leiss said. "You care. Hami doesn't. More importantly, Ramaask will be here soon. And, if what you're saying is true, then we need to get looking for this hidden temple. Now."

"But where do we start?" Mehrak said. "The Hirbod won't let us—"

The door handle clicked, silencing Mehrak. Lila-Maryam opened the door and entered the room. She walked around the desk and sat down, motioning for Sammy and Mehrak to take their seats.

Sammy noticed a smile play across Mehrak's lips as she sat down. Did he have a plan?

Lila-Maryam leant forward across the table, palms down, and opened her mouth to talk.

Mehrak cut her off. "Lila-Maryam," he said. "Now that we're alone, away from the ears of the other priests, I'm going to be honest with you."

Lila-Maryam raised an eyebrow, but said nothing.

Mehrak went on: "There was a woman that came here around thirty years ago. Her name was Esther."

Lila-Maryam shifted her weight on the chair. "There have been many people who have visited our temple over the years," she said. "I don't recall anyone by that name, but I would've been only thirteen at the time."

"We've been given orders from the Regent Mother to locate a book Esther took from the palace library." Mehrak leant back to let this settle in.

"Book?" Lila-Maryam said. She meshed her fingers together in her lap. Her eyes darted from Mehrak to Sammy to Leiss and then back to Mehrak again.

"We've tracked her here," Mehrak said. "If you haven't heard of Esther then we'll have to speak with the other priests." Mehrak pushed his chair backward as if he was about to get up.

"Wait," Lila-Maryam said. She hoisted herself from the chair, went to the door and closed it. Then she walked back around the table and sat down. "Esther arrived here, like you said, about thirty years ago. My father was the custodian at the time. He took her in and she became one of us. But she was only here for—I don't know—twenty days or so before ..." She paused. "Before she left. I assume that whatever she brought with her left when she did."

"You said you were only thirteen at the time. She must have left quite an impression in those twenty days if you can still remember her now."

"What are you implying?" Lila-Maryam said, mustering all her indignity.

Mehrak leaned in. "Esther arrived here thirty years ago. She joined the Hirbod and settled into your routine. But one night she entered a secret part of the temple." Lila-Maryam's eyes widened and she shook her head. "A part of the temple she wasn't meant to enter or even know about. That is why you still remember her, because what she did was a big deal. She entered the secret part of the temple and she never came out again. Which means her possessions got left behind."

"That doesn't mean we kept them. And besides, that was thirty years ago. Who knows where her things are now?"

"You know where the book is."

Lila-Maryam said nothing.

"Esther's belongings would have been destroyed so there would be no evidence of her visit. Except the book. The book held secrets about your temple. It was hidden so no one would ever read it again."

Lila-Maryam's face glistened with perspiration. "If this book held all these secrets you speak of, why would we have kept it? I'm sure it would have been destroyed along with Esther's other belongings."

"The book was written by a devout Zoroastrian and the architect of this temple. You would sooner destroy a sacred text of the Avesta. The book is called *The Arda Memoirs* and you know where it is." Mehrak narrowed his eyes. "And I bet you've read it too."

"You can't have it," Lila-Maryam said. "The book belongs with us. People cannot know what information it holds."

"That book belongs to the palace," Leiss said, getting up from his chair.

Mehrak held up his hand to silence him. "I'm willing to make a deal," he said.

Lila-Maryam said nothing.

"If you let us read it, you can keep it."

"But it belongs to the palace!" Leiss said.

"You never came here to return the book, did you?" Lila-Maryam said. "You want it for yourselves."

"We only want to read it. You can keep it here and we'll tell the Regent Mother that Esther took it with her. No one else will ever know about it."

Lila-Maryam massaged her temples. "I don't have much choice, do I?"

–FORTY-FOUR–
The Intruder

Lila-Maryam returned with a ragged, leather-bound book. She placed it in front of Mehrak, walked around the desk, sat down, and folded her arms.

Sammy watched Mehrak rub his sweaty palms on his waistcoat. She could tell he was thinking the same thing she was. That everything had come down to this book. Did it have the answers they needed? If he didn't read it, they couldn't be disappointed. Right now, they had hope. And that was all they had.

"Get on with it," Leiss said. He shifted restlessly on his chair.

Sammy put a hand on Mehrak's and smiled her most reassuring smile. He smiled back, clearly nervous. Then he slid the book off the table and cradled it in his hands. He took one last breath and set off.

He flicked through the pages, scanning each one as he went, turning them over, closing off the chapters one at a time. Half the book had gone and still nothing. He kept going, delving deeper, searching out the important section that would reveal the secrets of the temple.

Sammy edged closer. Leiss too. Not many pages left now, forty or fifty perhaps and Mehrak hadn't slowed, hadn't double checked a page or reread anything. Then he was at the end.

Mehrak remained motionless.

"Well?" Leiss said.

Mehrak flicked back through the pages until he was at a section around a quarter of the way in. He read quietly for a time then turned to Sammy, his expression apologetic.

They didn't have the answer.

"I'm sorry," he said.

"It must say something," Leiss said. He took the book off Mehrak.

Mehrak pointed a passage out to him. "This is all there is."

Leiss read aloud, *"For those who seek the Mother World, look out the world of lush greens, fresh air and grass."* He stopped. "That's it? That's all it says in the whole book? There has to be more."

Mehrak shrugged, so Leiss began reading the book to himself, mumbling the words under his breath as he went. "What is grass, anyway?" he said at last.

"It doesn't matter," Sammy said. She stared at the floor.

Leiss got up. "Look at you two," he said. "You've both given up already. We've got the same information Esther had. We'll figure out what to do when we get to the temple."

"Hold on!" Lila-Maryam said. "You never said anything about going to the … to—"

"To the Temple of Paths?" Mehrak finished for her.

Lila-Maryam flushed red. "You can't."

"We have the backing of the magi," Mehrak said. "They want Sammy to go to the temple. That's what this is all about. Harz was supposed to explain this to you. Why do you think all those crabmen are here?"

"We can't allow you access to the temple. It's our most sacred place, built by our founder. I …" Her eyes darted left and right. "And, and the temple is sealed."

"Sealed?" Mehrak asked.

"After Esther broke in we had the entrance to the temple bricked up. You won't get in."

"We'll need some tools then," Leiss said. "A stone mason's hammer, pickaxe. You got anything like that?"

Lila-Maryam's objection erupted from her throat as a squawked gargle. She didn't get any further.

In the hall outside, a door crashed and there were screams. Men and women called out for help, their pleas echoing around the high ceiling, then they were drowned out by the sound of furniture smashing.

Then silence.

Lila-Maryam stared at Mehrak, her eyes wild and her lips trembling.

Then a grinding noise. The sound of stone dragged across stone.

"What in Ahura's great creation?" Lila-Maryam rushed to the door, cracked it open, then stepped out.

The hall was black. Mehrak kept Sammy behind him at arm's length as they followed Lila-Maryam out. The lights had been extinguished, including the flame in the centre dish. All that remained was an orange glow coming from a couple of pews that had caught fire. Others were in disarray and many were smashed.

A wave of heat engulfed everyone, forcing them to shield their eyes.

"No." Sammy's heart was pounding. The sick, tired dread was seeping into her bones. She wanted to lie down, close her eyes and give up. She wanted everything to be over.

"It's that creature again," she said.

"What?" Lila-Maryam asked. "What creature?"

Then they saw the bodies. Three of them, on the floor. Badly burned and smouldering, limbs twisted into unnatural positions, eyes wide, mouths frozen in silent screams. Lila-Maryam rushed towards them.

The double doors at the end of the hall burst open. Three male and two female priests ran in.

"Lila-Maryam," called one of the men as he ran to her.

Lila-Maryam came to a stop by the bodies.

The five new arrivals staggered to a halt. One of the women shrieked and covered her face. No one else spoke.

Without looking up, Lila-Maryam whispered, "What happened?"

"Something got in," said one of the men. He gulped.

"What something? How?"

"We don't know. The doors to the grand hall are still secure." The man turned to the woman that was crying. "Memi saw it, though." He placed a hand on her arm. "Tell Lila-Maryam."

Memi didn't react. She continued to stare at the bodies as tears ran down her cheeks and into the corners of her mouth.

"I didn't see much," she said at last. "Most of the lights had gone out. I only saw a silhouette. Just a tall, thin shape, really."

Sammy covered her eyes and held her breath. Too much oxygen was rushing to her head, her chest screaming for air.

"It's him," she said. "It's the creature that chased me in the mushroom forest. The one that burnt everything it touched. It's been following me this whole time. It killed Borzin. Now it's here."

Lila-Maryam turned on Mehrak and Leiss. "You brought this creature here?"

Mehrak shook his head. "No."

"But you brought death to my brothers and sisters, unleashed an army of crabmen." Lily-Maryam turned away, trembling. "You three," she pointed at three of the priests. "I want the temple searched. No less than groups of four. Spread the word. And you two!" she snarled at Mehrak and Leiss. "You're not going anywhere. I want you both in the office. Memi? Can you look after this young lady?"

"Lila-Maryam," Leiss said. "I'm sorry that—"

"Sorry won't bring back our brothers and sisters!"

"The thing that killed them killed my partner!" Leiss barked back. "It's left his boy fatherless. Imprisoning us serves no purpose."

"If you won't go of your own free will ..."

"Then what?" Leiss said, moving into Lila-Maryam's personal space. "These scrawny little priests going to make me, are they?"

She stepped back, staring up at Leiss, her face burning with fury.

Leiss's chest deflated. "Look, I'm sorry. We had no way of knowing …"

"Lila-Maryam!" called one of the priests. He'd been on his way back to the atrium, but had stopped halfway there. He gestured towards something behind a pile of smouldering pews. "There's a hole."

Leiss was the first to move. He raced towards it, side-stepping debris and leaping over pews still on fire. Sammy and Mehrak went after him.

One of the red marble tiles had been lifted out and placed to one side, leaving a square black hole in the floor.

"The entrance to the temple," Mehrak said when he and Sammy caught up. "The creature knows about it. It thinks we're already down there."

Sammy stared into the darkness below.

"Unless it's gone ahead to lie in wait." Leiss drew his sword. "If it's gone after us, it'll know we aren't down there soon enough."

"It won't," Lila-Maryam said. "The temple is in the heart of the mountain. It'll be a long time before it realises you aren't down there and comes back."

"What temple?" asked one of the priests.

Lila-Maryam closed her eyes. "I'll explain later."

"So we have time?" Leiss asked. "The temple isn't just below the floor?"

"It's a long way off. And, yes, we have plenty of time to fill the hole before the creature comes back."

"We're going down," Leiss said. "Right now. It won't come back up. It will get to the temple first, realise we aren't there and settle in to wait."

Saliva pooled in Sammy's mouth. Her stomach tried to squeeze its contents up her throat, but she held on, breathing deep. Mehrak took her by the arm and rubbed her back, but her stomach kept cramping.

"It's okay," Mehrak said. "We'll stay here. We'll barricade him in."

"We can't," Leiss said. "The Lurker's coming. Remember?"

Sammy stared up at him. "Hami might stop him," she said.

"You clearly weren't listening to the same story I was," Leiss said. "Hami doesn't stand a chance. He's going to get himself killed. Our only hope is to get to the temple and get you home. When the other creature realises it's ahead of us, it will bed down and wait for us to come to him. It knows we'd sooner face him than the Lurker. And if the temple is as far away as Lila-Maryam says, then the creature probably doesn't know that we're behind him yet. If we're quick we might even get the drop on him."

"Maybe Ramaask wants Sammy alive," Mehrak said.

"Like that crabman was going to take Sammy alive on Golden Egg balcony?"

Mehrak had no response to that.

"Exactly," Leiss said. "We're going down." He turned to Lila-Maryam. "Slide the tile back over the hole once we've gone. Then get your boys here to weigh it down with whatever you can find. After that, get ten of them to guard the entrance. At least ten. Make sure nothing gets out."

Lila-Maryam scowled at Leiss as he spoke but said nothing. Leiss picked up a long section of mushroom timber from a broken pew and lit the end from one of the still-burning pews. Then he sheathed his sword and approached the hole.

"Wait," Lila-Maryam said. She exhaled and seemed to deflate. "You're not going to make it to the temple without proper lamps. Memi, could you fetch me three oil lamps from the wall, please?"

Leiss dropped into the hole.

"Leiss!" called Mehrak. "We need to come with you."

No answer.

"Leiss?" Mehrak tried again, quieter this time.

"I'm right here," Leiss called up. "I was just looking around. It's not that deep."

Memi returned with three oil lamps and Mehrak helped light them from splints of burning pew. He passed them through the hole and then Leiss helped him down, although not gently enough to stop him complaining about his ribs.

It was Sammy's turn next. She peered into the hole. With the three oil lamps below ground, it was brighter under the floor than the hall above.

Leiss held his hands up out of the hole. "Just lower yourself down."

"Hold on," Lila-Maryam said. She reached into the opening of her cassock and removed a golden locket, pulling it out over the top of her head.

"Take this," she said, handing it to Sammy. "It will guide you through the maze."

"There's a maze down here?" Mehrak called up.

Lila-Maryam held Sammy's shoulders and stared into her eyes. "You can still get to the temple before the creature. It doesn't know where it's going. With this locket, you will."

The locket was oval and had a burning sun on the front. On the back, written in Avestan, was an inscription that read *A wish can be as good as a map.*

Lila-Maryam stepped back. "I hope you are the one the legends spoke of. May Ahura be with you." Then she broke eye contact and turned away. "That locket is the only possession I'm allowed. It was given to me by my father. Please don't lose it."

Leiss helped Sammy down into the hole. The cavity below the hall was a small one. It had a low ceiling, stone walls, and smelled of mould. Carved into the stone at one end was a primitive arch, leading to a staircase, which spiralled down and away into the rock.

Sammy placed the locket over her head and opened it. Inside was a small multi-faceted crystal set into the casing where a photo would normally sit. She held the locket up to her lamp. The crystal sparkled in the light, but did nothing else.

"Let's get going," Leiss said. He walked ahead through the arch.

Mehrak offered Sammy an optimistic smile. "Not far now," he said.

–FORTY-FIVE–
A Late Arrival

His head was filled with a thousand crabmen chattering. Spiky shelled bodies crashing in, blocking the light from the forest and Cataclysm. Razor-sharp forearms slicing down and heavy, club-like claws trying to crush him. Hami batted each one away with his staff and blasted holes in their ranks with lightning bolts.

How many more could there be?

He couldn't keep going much longer. He hadn't slept in days. His body was weary, close to collapse, and he was getting slow. He'd already had a few sloppy near misses and was fighting on borrowed time.

Then the crabmen stopped attacking, and ran.

An overwhelming lethargy gripped Hami and dragged him to the floor. He dropped to one knee and put a hand to the ground to steady himself. Had they really given up so soon? He couldn't quite believe it.

The crabmen stopped running and fanned out, forming a vast circle around the battlefield. They were over a stadion away, and in the half-light of the plain, appeared to be a solid wall right the way around Hami and his troops.

There were eleven Marzban left. Narok, Eva and Kelzar were the only faces he recognised. He wasn't familiar with the others. Harz was still on his chariot, and he'd lost all but six men and two manticores.

They'd done well, relatively speaking. The surrounding area resembled a scrap yard of crabmen body parts. The infestation had lost many times the number Hami's fighters had. Still, he could see four dead Marzban and seven of Harz's men from where he crouched. The others were out there in the dark somewhere.

Narok approached on Indomit. The side of his turban was soaked in blood, but whatever injury he'd sustained didn't seem to be distressing him overly. He nodded at Hami, then motioned at the crabmen and shrugged.

The chattering stopped. Hami hadn't realised how loud it had been until it went quiet.

Three riderless karkadann milled around in the open, poking at dead crabmen, snorting. It was the only thing Hami could hear over his own breathing. He wanted to lie down where he knelt, to drift into a dreamless sleep; oblivion. It was almost all he could think about. He dragged a sleeve across his forehead. He couldn't have lasted much longer. None of them could. He closed his eyes and waited for his heart rate to return to normal. He knew the crabmen would stay where they were. They were waiting.

As if possessing a single consciousness, the crabmen in front of the forest parted down the middle, forming a wide opening. The Marzban looked to each other nervously.

"Are they letting us go?" Narok asked.

Hami shook his head. "No." He pointed to the sky over the forest. Then slowly raised himself back to his feet using his staff as a crutch.

Far off, skimming the mushroom canopies, a winged beast was coming. All eyes tracked it as it sailed closer with barely a movement of its wings. It dropped over the edge of the forest and swept along the crabman-bordered runway. It was a lava pterodactyl, the biggest Hami had ever seen, deep blood-clot-red, with a rider standing on its back, holding on to the beast's crest. The rider was cloaked in shadow, too dark and too far off to see properly in the dim light, but Hami knew who it was.

The rider forced the pterodactyl's head down into the ground, breaking the animal's neck with a snap, and pitching himself into the air. A shiny black projectile clutching twin battle axes.

Ramaask.

Hami flipped backwards as Ramaask slammed into the ground where he'd been standing a moment before. He completed his backward somersault, landing on his feet.

Ramaask rose up from the crater he'd made, dressed head to foot in thick, black, metal armour, while a physics-defying, dark red cloak floated behind him on a non-existent breeze. His helmet had three serrated ridges running from front to back, one in the centre like a dorsal fin and another on each side.

Ramaask raised the helmet's visor up over his head. His face underneath was shiny-black and shimmering purple, the skin of which was pulled tight over his skull with no muscle or sinew underneath and no eyeballs in the sockets.

He stepped out of the crater. He towered head and shoulders above Hami, broad as a karkadann. His slender second set of arms slipped out from under his cloak. The right hung over his head like a stooped wing, the left had been reduced to a stump, with a splintered black bone protruding from the end.

The air around Ramaask rippled and contorted as he approached, as if he was walking through liquid. A pressure build-up was causing Hami's head to pound and he staggered backwards, a thick fog enveloping his brain. Ramaask stalked closer, his hollow eye sockets gazing lifelessly on.

The Marzban edged forward, Narok at the front, leading with Indomit.

"Stay back!" Hami called.

They stopped.

None of Harz's men had moved. They'd been paralysed where they stood, fear etched onto their faces.

"Good work leading us to them, Harz." Ramaask's voice was slow and calm, yet rasping like someone on the verge of death. He sucked in a rattling breath. "I had a feeling your treachery would benefit me somehow."

Harz stared at Ramaask, trembling, his skin devoid of colour. The other ex-Order men were the same. Seven soon-to-be corpses, all pallid and waxen. Hami imagined what must be going through their heads. All of them had seen what Ramaask was capable of. All had witnessed a thousand terrible deaths at his hands. A thousand possible ways they would be going to their own graves. Their eyes were pleading. For what? There would be no chance of redemption. A swift death, perhaps?

"Why are you doing this?" Ramaask asked.

Hami looked up at the nightmarish creature before him, then realised Ramaask was talking to *him*, not Harz, and Hami suddenly felt foolish with no answer to give.

Ramaask looked past Hami to the Fire Temple. "The girl is already inside?" There was an inflection of surprise in his voice.

"What girl?" Hami said.

Ramaask fixed his blank expression back on Hami. "Why are you magi so opposed to helping me? I may act in my own interests, but occasionally those interests benefit others."

"How can murdering a young woman benefit anyone? Your crabmen were never sent to capture her. You'd planned to have her killed from the beginning."

"I hadn't. But then you brought her here and, by doing so, sealed her fate. You'll never know the deed I do for Perseopia today. But that is only because you'll be dead before it happens." Then Ramaask raised an axe in the air and roared, "Kill them all!"

The crabmen rushed forward again, crashing over the Marzban.

Hami braced himself for the impact, but none came. The crabmen hit an invisible barrier and got no further. They clamoured around the wide, elliptical space that Hami found himself inside, screaming and beating on the barrier that sealed him from the outside world. They couldn't get to him, but they didn't need to. Ramaask was inside the enclosure too, watching him from the far end. He walked slowly towards Hami.

"I've not fought a top-tier magus for quite some time," he said. "I do hope you'll give me some sport before you die. At least then I won't have come all this way for nothing."

Hami let his staff drop to stomach height and released a roaring column of lightning into Ramaask's chest. Ramaask stood his ground but was slowly pushed backwards, his heels scraping through the sand as he strained against the energy. He let it continue a moment longer, then dug his claws in and thrust his chest out, firing the lightning back at Hami.

It launched him backwards, and he came down hard, close to the edge of the invisible barrier, losing his staff as he hit the plain. Ramaask bared his long, thin teeth as he approached, the invisible bubble following him, pushing the crabmen further away from Hami.

"I'd hoped a magus with your reputation would put up more of a fight," Ramaask said, and swung down a battle axe. With animal reflexes, Hami rolled to the side as the axe carved a trench into the desert. Hami snatched up his staff and gained his feet in time to catch the second axe with the staff. He collapsed to one knee.

Ramaask then began his assault in earnest.

Hami had never known anyone out-match him in a fight before, and Ramaask was doing it with ease. The power he could command was incredible. Hami was summoning all his strength and concentration just to defend himself. But even that wasn't enough, and he was forced backwards.

"You're struggling." Ramaask said.

Hami couldn't answer. It was taking all his attention to keep himself alive as the axes came down, each one a hair's breadth from ending his life.

"You think you can hold me off long enough to save the girl." Ramaask sounded smug. "Except I know something you don't; I already have someone waiting for her on the inside. She'll be dead before you are."

–FORTY-SIX–
The Stone Column Forest

Leiss went on ahead down the spiral staircase, far enough that Sammy could no longer see the glow of his lamp. He'd reasoned that if they heard him get attacked or cry out then that would give them enough of a head start back up the staircase. However, they'd been walking so long that there was no way Sammy would be able to run back up the stairs.

She'd been performing the same movement over and over, climbing down the staircase leading with her right foot and walking on her toes. Both her left hip and right calf were tight and on the verge of snapping. There was no way she'd beat anyone to the top of these stairs.

"How much longer?" she asked.

"I don't know," Mehrak replied. "Any sign of the stairs ending?" he called ahead.

"No," came Leiss's faint reply.

"Can we have a break?" Sammy asked.

Silence.

"You still there, Leiss?" Mehrak called. He crept forward, keeping Sammy behind him.

"Leiss?" he tried again.

"I'm right here," he whispered loudly. "Stop shouting. I was making sure it was safe. We're at the bottom."

He led them through a stone arch at the bottom of the staircase into a cavern of towering stone columns.

The columns were closely packed and varied in girth from tree to industrial chimney width, making it impossible to see further than ten paces in any direction.

The staircase they'd come down was inside one of the wider pillars. Leiss walked a circuit of it.

"Pillars in all directions," he said. "This must be the maze."

Sammy looked up, following the line of the column with the staircase inside. It stretched into the black abyss above, out of the lamplight. The ceiling and fire temple were up there somewhere. And judging by how shaky her legs were, it was probably a long way up.

"Clever," Mehrak said. "The pillars are like the mushrooms in the forest. All different widths, not arranged in rows, groups, or even patterns. Easy to get lost in if you don't know where you're going, but easy to remember if you've learnt the way."

"Ingenious," Leiss said. "Is that locket working yet?"

Sammy opened it and held it up to the lamplight. "No."

Leiss sighed. "What now?"

"I suppose we start walking," Mehrak said. "Pick a direction, see what the locket does."

Leiss walked another circuit of the staircase column, dragging the hilt of his sword around it, scraping a line into the stone.

"So we can find our way back if we get lost," he said. He shuffled back and forth on his feet, every part of him was tense and ready to fight. He was making Sammy nervous. She wished he'd stand still and keep his worry to himself. She closed her eyes and drew a deep breath.

"Do you want to lead the way with your locket?" Mehrak asked her.

"Why would I want to do that? The monster's probably right behind that first pillar."

"You'll be okay. We'll feel its heat before it gets close. If the temperature goes up, Leiss can take the lead or we can change direction."

"What if he can turn his heat off?"

"Fine. I'll go first," Leiss said. "Keep an eye on your locket." And he marched ahead, scoring each pillar with his hilt as he went. Mehrak gestured for Sammy to go next and he took up the rear.

Sammy kept the locket open as they walked. She checked it every few steps, but it did nothing, and after a lengthy period of time that was probably only around ten minutes, they stopped.

"That locket doing anything yet?" Leiss asked.

"No."

"We aren't going the right way," Mehrak said. "The locket would have done something by now if we were. We should head back."

"We should keep going," Leiss said. "We might be almost there."

"We aren't. The locket hasn't done anything."

"Does Lila-Maryam know if it actually works? It might just be a good luck charm."

"We've got to trust the locket," Mehrak said. "The mountain tapers out as you come down from the temple. That means this cavern could be several stadia in diameter. Our lamps won't last long enough to explore the whole place. If they burn out, we're stuck down here forever."

Tiny needles prickled Sammy's flesh like spider feet moving up and down her arms. Stuck down here forever?

"We should head back to the staircase," Mehrak said. "Then pick another direction."

"Fine," Leiss said. "But can we at least pick up the pace?" He stormed ahead, his broad frame black against the lamplight in front of him. Sammy and Mehrak jogged to keep up. Sammy was exhausted. She'd probably expended ninety per cent of her energy through nerves and sweat. Her legs were heavy, her clothes drenched. She staggered, putting her hand against a pillar to steady herself. It was cool and smooth. She stopped.

"There's no marking on this pillar," she said.

Leiss froze, but didn't turn around.

"Leiss?" Mehrak said, panic rising in his voice. "Where are the markings?"

Leiss darted from pillar to pillar. Stopped. He staggered back several steps, his chest pumping, his sword arm limp. When he finally turned to face them, his eyes were wild.

"I thought I recognised the way."

Sammy couldn't take it any longer. They were lost, buried underground, running out of light. She closed her eyes and held her breath.

"For Ahura's sake, Leiss!" Mehrak screeched, trying not to raise his voice, but failing. "What do we do now?"

"I suppose we keep going," Leiss said. But his voice was shaky, uncertain.

Sammy's head was expanding, getting lighter; she needed to escape. She backed away from Leiss and Mehrak. Fighting the urge to run, she put several columns distance between them and her. The blackness was stifling, claustrophobic. She would rather face the crabmen than get trapped down here. She wanted daylight. She wanted to be home, she wanted her mum. She walked further, and a small light flashed.

She stopped. It had come from her chest. She held up the locket that had been open at her neck. Nothing. Then there was another flash.

"I told you not to rush!" Mehrak's voice had increased in pitch to a low shriek. "I told you—"

"Mehrak!" Sammy called.

"Sammy? Where are you?"

Sammy heard Leiss and Mehrak stumbling around looking for her. "I'm here," she called.

Mehrak was frantic when they found her. "Are you okay? What's going on?"

"The locket's doing something."

"What?" Leiss said.

The locket's crystal pulsed with light.

"Pass it here," he said, and moved to take it.

Mehrak shoved Leiss's arm out of the way. "You think we'd let you take it, after—"

"No one's having the locket!" Sammy snarled.

Both Mehrak and Leiss stopped. The outburst hadn't sounded like her at all. She'd surprised herself, but determined not to lose momentum, she went on. "I've been put in charge of the locket and I'm going to keep hold of it." Asserting her authority was a novel experience, and not entirely unpleasant.

"So how did you get it to work?" Leiss asked, through gritted teeth.

"You and Mehrak were arguing so I walked over here and the crystal flashed."

"I suppose if we carry on this way," —Mehrak indicated with one arm— "then we should be heading in roughly the right direction."

Sammy walked a few steps further and checked the locket.

"We might be close to the staircase," Leiss said. "I should start scoring the walls again, in case."

"Don't bother," Mehrak said. Then to Sammy, "Look, there it goes again."

"And again," Sammy said. They were saved. Maybe they would make it to the Temple of Paths. Maybe everything would be okay. Maybe the monster didn't know where to go and had gotten lost.

"Keep going," Mehrak said. "There was less time between the flashes then. Start counting the space of time between them. I reckon the closer we get to the temple, the shorter the gap will become."

"Don't forget that creature's down here somewhere," Leiss said. "We should stay close."

Sammy led the way through the pillars, counting the periods between flashes. Occasionally the time between pulses slowed, but in general, and after some trial and error, they more-or-less figured out the right path. They moved quickly and it wasn't long before the flashes of light were pulsing in time with Sammy's heartbeat. Mehrak held up his lamp.

"I hope it's not much further," he said. "My lamp's getting light, like I don't have much oil left in it. There might not be enough to get back, Leiss. We should blow one of ours out to ration the oil."

Leiss stopped and held them back. "What was that?" he said. "Where?"

"Over to the right." He pointed. "I saw something move in the shadows."

"It's him, isn't it?" Sammy said. "It's getting warmer. I can feel it. Can you feel it?"

"I feel it," Leiss said. He'd become unusually calm. The enemy had been spotted and he'd snapped back into elite Marzban mode. If Sammy hadn't known better she might even have thought he looked happy.

"We need to keep going," Mehrak said. "Or we aren't going to make it."

"There!" Sammy said. "The tall shadow." It was moving, circling them.

"I see it," Leiss whispered. "You two keep going. I'm going to finish this …"

"Leiss, don't," Mehrak said. "We need you."

Leiss ignored him and ran into the darkness. The light from his lamp dimmed as it became obscured by the columns and he was gone.

"Leiss!" Mehrak half-shouted, half-whispered.

"We should go after him," Sammy said.

Mehrak pulled her back. "We have to keep going while we still have light. If he wants to risk his life, that's up to him." He took her hand and dragged her on as he broke into a run.

They dashed through the columns, the pulses from the locket flashing ever faster. An agonised scream echoed through the cavern, bouncing off the columns, sounding like it was coming from everywhere at once.

Sammy's heart stopped. Borzin's ruined body appeared in her mind's eye.

"Leiss!" she screamed, slowing up.

"Don't stop!" Mehrak pulled harder. "We should've stuck together."

Sammy wanted to stop, to go back for Leiss, but she kept going. She wanted to make a stand like they did in the movies, turn back for her fallen comrade. She pulled back on Mehrak, but it was half-hearted and lacklustre. She didn't really want to go back. She was scared and couldn't bear the thought of seeing Leiss burnt and dying, and so she let herself be carried on.

And on they went, zigzagging through the cavern, terror fuelling their legs. She glanced down at the locket. The flashes were blurring together like a hummingbird's wings.

"We're here!" Mehrak said.

And they stumbled out of the columns.

There was a barren track of stone running into the darkness in either direction, wide as a single carriageway.

On the opposite side was solid stone wall.

"Which way now?" Mehrak asked.

"I don't know. The locket's stopped flashing." The gaps between pulses had shortened to nothing and the crystal inside the locket radiated a pure uninterrupted light.

"Let's try this way," Mehrak said, and dragged Sammy to the right along the wall.

After a short sprint, the locket started flashing again.

"We're moving away from it," Sammy said.

Sweat was pouring off Mehrak's face, his turban was damp around his hairline and a bib-shaped sweat patch had formed around his neck. "Okay. Back again," he said.

They turned and ran back along the wall until the locket light became constant again. They stopped. Mehrak bent double with his hands on his knees. Drops of sweat dripped off his face. They hit the fine coating of stone powder on the ground and rolled themselves into tiny dirt balls.

"The locket's telling us this is the place, but there's nowhere else to go," Mehrak said. He looked at the wall. "Wait. It's uneven here. These are stone blocks. There's an opening that's been bricked up and … and the pointing is smoothed over to make it look like solid rock." Mehrak dragged his finger between two bricks, emptying the gap of finely powdered stone.

"But if it's bricked up, we're stuffed," Sammy said.

"Stuffed indeed," came a metallic reply.

Mehrak grabbed Sammy and pulled her behind him, up against the wall.

As if floating, the tall, cloaked creature slid out from behind a pillar. A wave of heat followed, consuming Sammy and Mehrak.

Sammy shielded her eyes. They'd failed. Greater than the fear was the crushing disappointment. One moment they were going to make it, the next it was all over. She'd been convinced that everything would work out. Now they were going to die.

"I'm surprised you made it this far," the creature said calmly. "So close to your precious Mother World. Just the other side of that wall."

"What have you done with Leiss?" Sammy shouted, trying to sound braver than she felt. There was nothing to lose now. She may as well die with a shred of courage.

"Silence!" screamed the creature, shaking with rage as it had done in the Fungi Forest. Then, just as strangely, calming down again. "That is nothing that should concern you now. I need you to do something for me."

"How about you do something for me instead?" Mehrak said.

The creature laughed a cold, unsympathetic laugh. "And what would that—"

Mehrak flung his lamp at the creature. It covered its face with an arm as the lamp struck its elbow. The oil spilled and the monster went up in flames.

Mehrak stepped away from the wall, turned and charged. He hit the bricks hard, shoulder first. The wall wobbled and stone powder burst from the pointing, coating him and Sammy and exposing the brickwork. Several of the top bricks fell into the gap behind the wall. Mehrak placed both hands on the wall and locked his arms.

"Help me," he yelled.

Sammy joined in and they pushed together.

The blocks budged, tipped slowly, then dropped.

Mehrak pulled Sammy back from the falling masonry, then forwards over the pile and into the tunnel beyond, stumbling as they went.

"Stop!" screamed the monster.

A fireball flew from its cloaked sleeve and over their heads, exploding into the ceiling above. Sammy stumbled and fell. She could hear the rocks shifting over her head, could feel deep vibrations though the floor. Then Mehrak was there, heaving her up and pulling her on as boulders dislodged above them. He launched her ahead of him as an avalanche of rock thundered down into the tunnel.

The heat vanished and dust filled the tunnel. Sammy could see nothing but the glowing halos of dust surrounding her lamp and locket. Everywhere else was dark.

"Mehrak?"

Nothing.

"Mehrak? Where are you?"

A cough. "I'm right here. I'm okay."

Sammy moved towards the voice.

Mehrak was on the floor. She helped him up, and he dusted himself down.

As the dust settled, they watched the last small rocks roll down the landslide that filled the tunnel. The monster wouldn't be catching them any time soon, but they'd lost their exit.

"You were right," Mehrak said, shaking the stone dust off his turban and patting himself down. "That creature was definitely not a waster."

"I told you."

Mehrak nodded, sighed.

"I didn't mean, 'I told you so'. I'm sorry."

"Don't be sorry."

"But I am. You just saved me, and now you're stuck here. Except I'm not really that sorry, because I'm glad it's you with me, instead of Hami."

Mehrak smiled. "Even though I almost got killed for you just now, I'm glad it's me here, too. I guess I owed you one for that lake creature anyway."

–FORTY-SEVEN–
Earthquakes

Sammy handed Mehrak her lamp and walked ahead, using her locket as a torch.

"How did you know we could push through those bricks?" she asked.

"I figured it out when I saw my sweat dripping into the stone dust."

"Gross."

"Yeah. But it made me realise that the Hirbod aren't builders; they're priests. What would they cement the blocks together with all the way down here in the mountain? I figured that all they'd done was block up the entrance and fill in the gaps with stone dust mixed with water to conceal it. Besides, they wouldn't want to completely block the temple. It's a sacred place."

They walked quickly, checking back over their shoulders occasionally, in case the monster was still trying to get at them. Sammy was sure it hadn't given up, but the temperature remained constant and there was no sound coming from back up the tunnel, which meant they were probably safe for the moment.

The tunnel took them to a long cave. At the far end was a circular opening with an ornate but tarnished silver frame around its circumference. Guarding it were two stone figures on short pedestals.

Mehrak set off across the cavern. "That looks like the entrance to a temple to me," he said.

The two statues looked to be angels, standing straight with their wings neatly folded behind their backs, and each carried a spear.

Sammy turned the light of her locket towards the one nearest her. Starting at the feet, she followed the line of its legs up its body.

She recoiled as she reached the head. Its face was distorted with a hideous anger, like a wild animal, with its mouth open, fangs bared and lips curled back in a snarl.

"What are they?" she asked.

"The angels that took Arda Viraf to the Next World?"

"They don't look like any angels I've ever seen."

"Maybe they're gargoyles to scare away evil spirits."

"I don't like them."

Mehrak walked on to the temple entrance. Sammy stayed back and watched from the other side of the evil angels.

The silver frame around the tunnel had a range of geometric shapes indented into its surface and tessellated together. Spanning the base of the opening was a golden disc, sunk into the ground, flush with the floor. It had been intricately detailed like the doorframe, but with organic shapes made up of interwoven vines, tentacles and snakes.

"That thing on the floor," Mehrak said. "It looks like a seal of some sort."

"There's something over here too," Sammy said. She'd angled her locket off to the right of the entrance revealing a series of scenes carved into the cavern wall. They ran horizontally like a comic strip, starting near the temple entrance and fading away into the dark to her right. Each carving had been painted in a simplistic style, using earthy ochres, oranges, browns and charcoal blacks. They reminded Sammy of the prehistoric cave paintings she'd seen in books.

"That looks like you," Mehrak said, pointing at the image closest to the temple entrance. The scene depicted a small, yellow-haired person walking over a bridge to a golden-domed temple on the other side. "You're crossing the bridge over the Cataclysm."

Sammy followed the pictures along the wall, chasing away the darkness with her locket. Mehrak remained at the first, chewing his lip. The second image was a patterned circle with a big crack down the centre. Sammy skipped past it to the third.

"What about this one?" she said. It was the same as the first but with no one on the bridge. Instead, at the bottom of the image was a man drawn in charcoal with three arms and orange flames around him.

"That must be Ramaask," Mehrak said. "Is that what's supposed to happen to him?"

Sammy was already at the fourth picture. "I hope this isn't supposed to happen." It depicted the same yellow-haired child from the first picture, but this time it was falling. There was no scenery or background to give the image context, but the child held a circle between its thumb and index finger.

"Does that mean I'm supposed to end up in the Cataclysm with Ramaask?"

"Can't be," Mehrak said. "We've already made it to the temple. That's probably the first chosen child."

Sammy wasn't convinced.

"I want to know what this is on the second picture," Mehrak said. "I think it might explain the other pictures." He went to take another look. Sammy didn't bother. She stared at the picture of the falling yellow-haired child. She wondered if it had something to do with the book she'd seen in the library. She still hadn't told Mehrak about it and wasn't sure if she should.

"The patterns on this circle are the same as on the golden disc on the floor," Mehrak said.

Sammy didn't reply. She'd moved on to the fifth carving, which turned out to be the last. And the worst. It also made her wish she'd never spotted any of them.

"Are you feeling okay?" Mehrak asked. He held his lamp up to her face. "You don't look so good." He followed her vacant stare.

The last carving had been smashed. In the middle of it, a crater had removed much of what must've originally been there, but still remaining, around the edges, were painted faces in a state of either screaming or crying.

"We shouldn't be here," Sammy said.

"We should," Mehrak said. "We're taking you home."

"Yeah, but is this the right place? It doesn't feel right. Those evil angels, these pictures. Something feels wrong. This might not be the real Temple of Paths."

"Lila-Maryam said it was."

"She didn't, though. She never actually said 'Temple of Paths'. She knows there's a temple down here, but she might not know which one it is. I guessed this was the place. But I guess a lot; at school, in exams. And I'm normally wrong."

"It all fits," Mehrak said. "Ramaask coming here for you. The monster. He said you were 'so close to the Mother World', didn't he? You're right this time."

Sammy said nothing.

Mehrak took her hand and led her towards the entrance. "Come on. We'll go in together."

As they stepped between the angels, the earth moved.

Hami felt the tremor and Ramaask's axes stopped falling. He'd frozen mid-swing, and if his face had been capable of emotion, Hami would have sworn it exhibited fear in that moment.

"Impossible!" he roared.

Seizing the window of opportunity, Hami let forth as much power as he could extract from his staff. The lightning hit Ramaask in the chest, launching him backwards with a pained gargle. He landed on both feet and dropped to one knee. Hami let another blast go. But the second was casually backhanded away as if it were a mosquito.

Ramaask was on his feet again, charging towards him. Hami leapt upward, into a forward flip, and over the top. But Ramaask didn't stop. He kept going, powering through the protective barrier that had cocooned them and into the crabmen, who scattered as he crashed through.

He was heading towards the Cataclysm.

With the barrier breached, it collapsed inwards, and Hami found himself fighting crabmen again. He fought desperately in Ramaask's direction, but he'd already disappeared from view.

———

Sammy stopped. "What was that?"

"Subterranean tremor?" Mehrak replied.

"I think it was an earthquake."

"Aren't they the same thing? Besides, the rock probably amplified the tremor." Mehrak took a deep breath and let it out again. "I'm sure it's nothing." His grip on Sammy's hand tightened and they took another step forward, resulting in a larger subterranean tremor.

———

Hami broke through the last of the crabmen. He could see Ramaask ahead, but he'd gained a massive lead and was almost at the Cataclysm.

Crabmen chased Hami from the battle. They were faster and forced him to fight as he ran. As they caught up, he batted them away with backward swings of his staff or shot them with over-the-shoulder lightning blasts.

An explosion boomed deep underground, knocking Hami from his feet. Plumes of flame leapt up over the edge of the Cataclysm as screams echoed from its depths.

The crabmen that had been chasing him turned and fled. Those ahead of him, who'd been at the doors of the temple, were streaming back across the bridge.

Ramaask reached the bridge himself and began crossing through the retreating crabmen, shoving the ones that got in his way into the chasm.

Hami got back on his feet and ran after him. There was still a huge distance to cover to get to the Cataclysm, but he had to keep going. He had to stop Ramaask before he got to Sammy.

———

Sammy stared down at the golden disc in the doorway.

"The closer I get, the worse the earthquake is getting," she said.

Mehrak stood beside her, still holding her hand. "We've got to do this," he said. "Right?"

Sammy nodded.

"On three?"

"Wait." Sammy was tired of needing her hand held. She could do this herself. It was only three steps over the disc, maybe four. What was the worst that could happen? She rolled her shoulders back, let go of Mehrak's hand and took three large strides across the golden disc and into the entrance of the temple. She let out the breath she hadn't realised she'd been holding.

"Easy," she said. She could feel a smile on her lips. One more milestone ticked off. No problemo. She turned to Mehrak, but his expression killed her mood. His face was slack, the whites of his eyes visible all the way around his irises as he stared at the floor.

He pointed at the golden disc. It was changing colour, losing its lustre. The gold was transitioning through shades of metallic yellow to grey and then losing its shine completely and becoming dull like the stone around it.

With a crunch, it snapped in half.

The rumbling began again, increasing in intensity, building up.

"Here it comes," yelled Mehrak.

And the explosion hit.

———

A vast wall of flames burst up past the ridge of the Cataclysm.

Hami hit the floor, covering his eyes as thousands of screams cried out, and were silenced.

The bridge spanning the chasm between the plain and the Fire Temple had gone. Rubble soared skywards, turning over in the air, Ramaask and the crabmen with it.

Ramaask roared as he slowed and fell back towards the Cataclysm, disappearing into the flames.

Flaming pterodactyls soared from the fire, screeching and trailing smoke, before their wings stopped and they dropped from the sky.

Hami ran to where the bridge had been. Part of it remained, jutting out from the land like a huge diving board.

He slowed.

A black arm shot up at the far edge of the rocky protrusion, scrabbling for purchase. It was followed by a second and then a third arm.

Ramaask hauled his head and chest above the ridge. Steam billowed from his body. His cloak had been incinerated and his armour had melted to his body, still glowing orange and red in places. He pulled his helmet off with his thin rear arm and threw it aside, exposing a bald, smouldering head.

"You've made a grave mistake," he said with a wheeze.

"It is you who made the mistake," Hami said, lowering his staff to point it directly at him, "when you attacked my partner."

Ramaask managed a strained chuckle. He pulled the rest of himself up and onto the end of the bridge. He remained on all fours, his broad chest rising and falling. "You can't kill me," he said.

"I can't," Hami replied. "But the Cataclysm can." And he lowered the staff to point at the ground between them.

"No!" Ramaask yelled.

Lightning slammed into the rock, disintegrating the last of the bridge and sending Ramaask careening backwards.

"You need me!" he screamed as he fell.

Hami watched him fall and catch fire. He continued watching well after he'd disappeared.

When he could no longer stare into the light, he turned from the Cataclysm to see the last of the crabmen fleeing into the forest.

Ramaask had finally gone.

–FORTY-EIGHT–
The Temple of Paths

Sammy stopped.

"What are you doing?" Mehrak asked. "We have to keep going."

"Ramaask has gone."

"What?"

"The cave paintings were right. He went into the Cataclysm."

Mehrak frowned. "When?"

"Just now. Hami was there. I felt it happen. Don't ask me how. I just did."

"Hami defeated him?"

Sammy shrugged.

"You really are a magus then. Esther was always going to bring you here, to end Ramaask's reign. He wasn't scared about you leaving Perseopia. He was scared you'd break that seal. It must have protected him in some way."

Another subterranean explosion shifted the rock under their feet and they stumbled. The earthquake was getting stronger.

"We might not have much time left," Mehrak said. He pushed Sammy down the tunnel, leaving the broken seal behind. Ancient text spiralled around the circumference of the tunnel, from floor to ceiling and round again. No time to read it. They ran on towards light at the end of the corridor.

The tunnel ended at a small dome-shaped room.

Pale yellow light emanated from a circular pit in the centre, and on the wall, a narrow shelf ran all the way around the room. On the shelf were hundreds of glowing marbles, arranged in single file in the order that the colours appear in a rainbow; or, as Sammy had learnt in science, in light wavelength size. To the left were the violets, then the blues, greens, yellows and oranges, ending with the red balls to the right of the entrance, and they rattled in small divots on the shelf each time the ground shook.

"Is this really the Temple of Paths?" Sammy shouted over the earthquake. "This tiny room?"

"Of course," Mehrak called back. "These are Arda Viraf's gems. The pearls of portal paths!"

Sammy picked up a blood red ball and peered into it. Inside were swirling shapes and small faces, crying and pressing up against the surface. She put it back, shivered and wiped her hand on her shirt.

"The fourth picture outside the entrance," Mehrak shouted. "The girl holding a ball and falling. You're supposed to pick one of these portal pearls and jump into the pit. That's what the picture shows."

Sammy peered into the pit. It was deep. Although she couldn't tell how deep due to the brightness of the light shining up from the bottom. "Jump in? Are you sure?"

"What else can it mean?"

Another underground explosion rocked the room. Mehrak teetered near the edge of the pit. Sammy grabbed the shelf with one hand and Mehrak with the other. She pulled him back from the brink and he regained his balance.

"What now?" she shouted.

Mehrak stared down into the pit, shaking. "I, er, I suppose you should start with the greens. The gemstone on your bracelet was green, wasn't it?"

Sammy raced around the pit to the section of green portal pearls and picked one up.

"This one's the same colour," she called back.

"It has to be exactly the same. If you pick the wrong one, you could end up anywhere."

Sammy looked into the pearl. Inside were small sparks flashing in swirling clouds.

Then Sammy realised.

"Esther's book!" she shouted. "It said, *'The world of lush greens, fresh air and grass.'* That's how Esther knew which pearl to pick. The Midnight Emerald that brought me here was green with swaying grass inside. The swaying must be from the fresh air. I need the pearl that matches the one that brought me here!"

Mehrak picked up a couple of portal pearls at random. "You're right. Each gem has something different going on inside. Check all the greens. Be quick, but don't rush. You don't want the wrong one."

"Do you think I should go back?" Sammy said. "Hami might need me for—"

"Forget about Hami. He used you and you weren't even the chosen one."

"Thanks for reminding me."

"What does it matter? Really? You broke the seal. Ramaask got defeated … apparently. You might not have been the one fighting him, but you were still crucial to both those things happening. Does it matter whether you were the real chosen one or not?"

"So *you* don't think I should stick around?"

Mehrak took hold of her and stared into her eyes. "You have your life in the Mother World. All the people that care about you are there."

"All of them?"

"Well, maybe not everyone that cares about you." Mehrak smiled.

But how much did he really care? It's not like she was his wife. Or Hami's chosen one. Sammy ignored the nagging doubt and turned back to the row of portal pearls.

She concentrated on checking each green gem in turn, going as fast as she dared. She even checked the greens that weren't quite the same shade. Each one had different things going on inside:

strange animals, people, clouds, trees. It was getting harder to hold them still enough to see inside. The vibrations were coming up from the ground, through her body and into her hands. She couldn't keep the pearls still.

She couldn't fail now. Not when she was so close.

Only nine green gems left before the turquoise ones began. What if she'd gone past it, dismissing it by accident? What if there were two that looked exactly the same? Or what if it wasn't here because Esther had already used it? Only five pearls left. Deep breath. Four left. Three.

And reeds. Or grass. Whatever they were, they were in there, swaying in the breeze.

"I've got it!"

"Really? It's the right one?"

Sammy smiled and stepped over to the edge of the pit.

"Mehrak?" she said. "I …"

The rumbling grew to a crescendo, climaxing with a crunch that echoed through the mountain. And everything shifted. The room was tipping.

"The mountain's falling!" Mehrak screamed as he almost went into the glowing pit again. He crashed into Sammy and they fell, sliding to the side of the room nearest the blue marbles. Red and orange gems fell from the walls. Some dropped into the pit causing red and orange flashes as they disappeared. The rest fell around them.

Sammy gripped the pearl tightly as the room stopped with a jolt. More pearls spilled off the shelf and pooled around them.

The floor came to a rest at a shallow angle, sloping up towards the red pearls. The ones that had disappeared into the pit popped back into existence above the shelf and landed back in their divots. Sammy picked up an orange pearl that she'd been sitting on and threw it into the pit. There was a flash of orange, and then *pop*, it appeared just above the shelf and landed in its hole.

"Sammy, for Ahura's sake, just jump into the pit!" Mehrak shouted.

"But I'll never see you again."

"And if you stay, you'll never see your mother again."

"Come with me," Sammy said. "Your lamp's nearly out of oil. The mountain is falling and you can't get out anyway because of the cave-in and the monster." Sammy stared into his eyes, his beautiful hazel eyes.

"I can't." Mehrak looked away. "Gisouie needs me."

Sammy couldn't hold back. She couldn't leave him, but the rumbling was building again.

"Please come," she cried.

Tears welled in Mehrak's eyes. "You were important, Sammy Ellis," he shouted over the noise. "To Hami. To Perseopia. And to me." He took her hands and stared into her eyes.

This was the only opportunity she'd get. "Look after Louis," she said, and kissed him.

He flinched, but didn't pull away. He relaxed into the kiss and the outside world dissolved around them. Mehrak's lips pressed into hers, exquisite and bittersweet. She wasn't the chosen one but in that moment she didn't care. She was as important as she needed to be.

She let go, winked, and then stepped backwards into the pit.

She gripped the pearl as she embraced the weightlessness of freefall.

Then everything exploded into green and white light.

–FORTY-NINE–
HOME

A beam of light fell across Sammy's face. She screwed her eyes tight against it, but it seeped in under her eyelashes. She rolled over, out of the light, and realised she was in bed. Opening one eye, she spied Cyclops and Wolverine peering back.

Her X-Men bed sheets. Her bed. Sammy sat up and her right hand flared with pain. It was swollen and looked like a partially inflated rubber glove.

She massaged her palm as she slid out of bed and onto her feet.

Her body was sore all over. She rubbed her lower back as she straightened up and rolled her head on her shoulders. She was still in Gisouie's clothes, but the silk shoes she'd been wearing in Perseopia had been placed neatly by her bed. Not a dream, then. Not that it could've been. Her hand was too painful to be a figment of her imagination.

Her hand flew to her neck. No locket. It must've stayed in Perseopia, like the Emerald Dial had stayed here. She hobbled downstairs to the kitchen. Her mum was leaning against the work surface, reading a glossy magazine, while a bowl turned slowly in the microwave. The lead article on the cover said *Our stylists can make even you feel good about yourself.* Sammy ran to her mum and threw her arms around her.

"I've missed you, Mum."

"That's sweet, darling, but if you'd climbed *into* bed with me instead of underneath it, you wouldn't be missing me so much this morning." She hugged Sammy back and stroked her hair. "And how did you get back from your father's house? I hope you didn't walk home alone."

"I was under your bed?"

"Halfway under. Your legs were poking out. I almost stepped on you. You were hugging that bracelet we're looking after. And you smelt odd, like mushrooms." She shrugged. "You didn't stir when I dragged you back to your own bed this morning. You must have been shattered." Mama narrowed her eyes. "What were you doing under there, anyway?"

"Aren't you worried that I've been gone for a while?" Sammy asked.

"You were only under the bed. I know I've been out a lot recently, but sometimes I need to unwind. Maybe it's still too soon after the move."

"No. Really. I've been gone for a week or something."

"Are you feeling okay? Is this what a night under my bed does to you? Or is this one of those crying out for help moments that mothers are supposed to recognise? Actually, don't answer that. That outfit you're wearing is definitely crying out for help. I get it. The bracelet incident was your way of getting attention. I should have seen the signs."

"But, Mum …"

"Maybe I don't spend enough quality time with you."

"Mum."

"Let's go out for the day. A treat. Wherever you want."

"You're not listen …" Sammy stopped.

Mama smiled and waited. Sammy had returned to the Mother World to be with her mum. And now the woman wanted to spend time with her.

"You want to take me out?"

Mama nodded.

"Because there's a comic book shop that opened a few weeks ago."

Her mum's smile cracked. Sammy could tell she was doing her best to keep the corners of her mouth turned up. Mama did light, airy, high street shops run by beautiful people with shiny white teeth. Not dingy, backstreet comic book stores where you had to squeeze past balding forty-year-olds with ponytails.

"Sure, darling." Her mum gulped. "Anything you like."

Sammy hugged her again. "But I need to do something first," she said and ran back upstairs. She darted across the landing, into her mum's bedroom and under the bed.

The bracelet had gone.

Sammy shot back to the top of the stairs.

"Where's the bracelet?"

Mama came to the bottom of the stairs. "You promised you'd take it back this week."

"I'll definitely take it back. You can trust me."

Her mum watched her. "I know I can, sweetheart. It's behind you in the airing cupboard. The jewel on the front has gone dull. Must've been fake after all."

Sammy turned and opened the door to the cupboard. The place Mama's clothes came to die. Skirts, tops, jeans, sheepskin boots, ear muffs, a knitted hat and, sitting on top, the Emerald Dial bracelet. Both dial hands were horizontal, in their original positions.

Sammy approached the bracelet. Pins and needles prickled up and down her arms, and a cool breeze blew across her skin. In the half-light of the cupboard, she could see that the emerald had indeed gone dull like Mama had said, a cloudy black-brown with nothing inside. It looked broken.

Did that mean she couldn't go back to Perseopia? That she'd never see Mehrak again? The loss tightened in her chest. He'd touched her life so profoundly in such a short period of time, and now he'd gone forever.

She should take solace that she'd been able to meet him, for him to show her that others cared and that she was important. She hadn't been 'the one,' but her actions had saved the realm, even though she'd never get rewarded or acknowledged for it.

But then, she supposed, none of that really mattered, because now she was home and back with the person who mattered most.

–EPILOGUE–

Mehrak sat in the pool of portal path pearls. Try saying that three times quickly, he thought to himself. He was at the low edge of the room, the floor sloping up from where he sat, maybe five, ten degrees. Only the light from the pit illuminated the room. His lamp had gone out shortly after the rumbling stopped.

That had been a while ago now and there'd been silence ever since. He supposed the mountain was stable; it hadn't moved since Sammy had left. Still, he wasn't going to bother going back up the tunnel. He didn't have a working lamp, and then there was the cave-in. He thought about following Sammy to the Mother World, but he didn't know which pearl she'd used. The correct one had popped back into existence on the shelf but then, because of the angle, had rolled off and got lost in amongst the others around his bottom. Perhaps he should pick a pearl at random and take his chances. Perhaps this was the start of a new adventure. Perhaps life had more in store for Mehrak Omid.

He didn't want an adventure, though. At least not one without Sammy. Or Gisouie.

Why had Sammy's name come to him first? Had he so quickly forgotten his wife? He should at least attempt to escape his current situation, to carry on the search for her. It was his duty as a husband. But he couldn't stop thinking about Sammy. He leant his head back against the wall. The thing that'd happened, it wasn't his fault. She'd kissed him. Yet he hadn't stopped her.

He would put it behind him. Sammy had gone and wouldn't be coming back. He'd continue his search for Gisouie and everything would go back to the way it had been.

First, he needed to get out of there. He couldn't get out by himself, but that was okay. Hami would help him. He'd take care of the monster and bust him out. Then Mehrak would travel to the snow base and rescue Gisouie, and they'd continue their quest for the *Rule Book* together. It was a long shot, but he had to believe he'd find her, he owed it to her. After everything he'd—

An explosion echoed up the passage, shaking the floor and the portal pearls under Mehrak's bottom. Was the mountain slipping? He should grab a pearl and escape before it fell. He paused, and the noise receded. The mountain wasn't falling. It was the rubble blocking the tunnel. Something had cleared it. Friend or foe? Hami or monster?

Mehrak sifted through the portal pearls searching for a green one with grass in it—whatever grass was. Where was it?

"Mehrak! Hello?" A woman's voice; familiar, but different.

It couldn't be …

"Hello?" he called back. "I'm in here!"

———

Free!

Behnam stumbled through the streets of Aratta in front of the guard with the shuffle. He kept the man close behind him as he had the only pair of working eyes.

Behnam had taken over the guard's consciousness and now controlled both himself and the guard. It was a peculiar sensation, using someone else's viewpoint to navigate your own body from behind, only being able to see where you were going indirectly.

Ghobad, the man's name had been. He was still in there, alive, but exiled to a far corner of his own brain. A prisoner in his own body. Unethical, and something a magus could be banished for, but Behnam had to escape, had to tell the brotherhood what he'd learned.

By using the guard's knowledge of Aratta, Behnam moved them both through the quietest streets. Zigzagging in and out of doorways, creeping along deserted alley ways.

At first, he hadn't been able to take five steps without tripping over, constantly running into objects while trying to guide himself using Ghobad's eyes. But he was beginning to get used to it.

When Behnam first entered Ghobad's head, he had him kill the other guards. Then he got him to open the cell and drag his body to a deserted location. It was two days of recovery before Behnam could stand or even walk. But during that time, Behnam had not suffered any ill effects of the smog. Ramaask had made him immune to keep him alive, like he'd done for everyone else that worked for him.

When movement had returned to his limbs, it had been agony. They still hurt now, but at least he could walk unaided.

Behnam paused in a deserted house as a group of men dressed in furs passed them, heading for the Sultan's palace. He desperately wanted to re-join the network, to tell the brotherhood what he'd learned. He'd risked connecting briefly to warn Hami not to let the girl go, but then he'd disconnected again. He couldn't allow himself to re-join, even now after he'd escaped. Ramaask had affected him too much. Behnam only hoped he hadn't done any damage to the network when he'd connected. The last thing he wanted was to infect his brothers.

But something had changed. The skies over Aratta were black. Had the thing Ramaask feared most happened? And where was he? He hadn't returned to Aratta since he'd left several days ago. And no one had come looking for him.

Nearly at the city wall now. He had to find Hami. Fast.

Book 2 in *The Vara Volumes* is out now!
Find out what happens next in:

BACK TO
THE VARA

Journey back to the vara with Sammy Ellis as she's once again thrust into the Fungi Forest to fend for herself. Discover the events that led up to her first visit and learn of the fallout she created in her wake.

SAMPLE THE
FIRST FOUR CHAPTERS

READ ON OVER THE PAGE

BACK TO
THE VARA

By
John Kerry

–ONE–
BEFORE SAMMY

Behnam didn't have to wait long for his young partner to catch up.

Hami emerged from the shadows, his skin purple under the magenta smog that hung over the city. He strode purposefully up the centre of the street, passing through the ephemeral wisps of the smog that floated at ground level, his head up, and dark hair and black cloak flowing behind him. He had the beginnings of a smile, but one damaged by pain and loss.

The men he'd been questioning would be dead.

In hindsight, Behnam should've interrogated the men himself. He stepped out of the doorway, into Hami's path. "Should you be walking up the centre of the street so brazenly?" he asked.

"Who's going to see me?"

Behnam had hoped he'd been wrong about the men. He tried to suppress the disappointment, but it must've shown.

"They'd have given us away," Hami said, his smile gone now.

"Not if you'd tied them."

"It's safer this way."

"You'd be a master by now if you could suppress that vicious streak of yours."

"If I'd developed a vicious streak sooner, your sister might still be alive."

Behnam withdrew. The memory of that night hit him with almost physical force. It came from nowhere. The blood, the crying. The surprised look on his sister's face as she breathed her last. The pain he experienced now was as raw as the night it happened. As it would be for Hami. They'd both suffered the loss of Jamileh, but Hami had perhaps taken it harder.

Behnam decided then that he was going to tell Hami the full story. The boy had a right to know the events that led up to Jamileh's death. "You couldn't have prevented it, you know. It wasn't your fault—"

"It's not a good time."

"There's never a good time, but we need to talk about it."

"After the mission," Hami said. He softened. "Please."

Reluctantly, Behnam held his tongue. He should've kept going, relieved Hami of his burden, but instead he allowed himself to be silenced again.

Hami was right. A lengthy debate and probable argument in the old capital would be irresponsible. They needed to keep their wits about them. There were other patrols of Order members roving throughout the city and Hami couldn't kill them all. They'd already left a substantial trail of bodies through the district that had once housed the rich and powerful.

Behnam had never known this place. Few living had. The entire city had been vacated generations ago when the smog came, and only members of the Order and a few wasters remained.

He led the way off the street and into an oval courtyard surrounded by grand marble arches and pillars. At the far end stood a large circular building with a shallow dome. It was a beautiful piece of architecture with a grand doorway, carved lintels and window frames. Behnam felt almost ashamed that he didn't know the name of it. He closed his eyes and accessed the magi network, scanned for Aratta maps, articles and building plans.

"What are we waiting for?" Hami asked.

Behnam opened his eyes. "This building used to be the royal opera house. We're standing in the courtyard where the sultan and his family held social events." Silence. "There's a staircase inside the doorway that will take us to the roof."

Hami gazed up through the open courtyard at the magenta clouds churning above them. They were lower here than he was used to, fine wisps floating just above the rooftops. Hami had been born in the outskirts of Aratta, but this would be the closest he'd ever been to the centre. He'd changed a lot since then. Since the wounded street urchin he'd been when Behnam found him.

"Those men didn't deserve to live," Hami said after a time. "It's better for the realm that I've killed them."

Behnam said nothing. There was no talking to Hami when he was dwelling on Jamileh. Behnam had never appreciated how badly the boy had fallen for her until she'd been killed. It had changed him. Something inside him had broken. Behnam wanted more than ever to speak to Hami then, explain how he knew it wasn't his fault, but he suppressed the urge. On the way home he'd explain the truth. But not now, not while their lives were in the balance.

They crouched behind a fallen pillar. The smog was already making Behnam woozy. Half a day more and the hallucinations would begin. They'd need to be out long before that if they wished to survive.

"Did you learn anything before you killed them?" Behnam asked.

"They gave away the location of a base up in the Atrabiliar mountains."

"A base?"

"On the northern slopes of Dev's Peak."

"That's thousands of stadia from here. Why there?"

"They didn't know. We'll need to question someone higher up for that information."

Behnam wondered how Hami had extracted what little information he had. Then realised that perhaps he didn't want to know. He led the way across the courtyard at a crouched run and in through the opera house doorway.

"The staircase is just in here," he said. "We should have a decent view from the top."

They climbed the stairs in the dark. At the top, they emerged onto a curved balcony that circled the building.

Ahead loomed the sultan's palace. Little more than a silhouette in the smog, but at six storeys high it dominated the skyline. Thick purple smoke still billowed from a ragged fissure in the vast dome and clouds hung thick about it.

"I've never seen it this close before," Hami said.

"An impressive building," Behnam agreed. "But thankfully, not somewhere we need to visit tonight."

They walked further around the balcony and stopped.

A black tower, gnarled and crooked, had grown from the earth in the centre of the piazza ahead of them, twisting its way skyward and reaching up into the smog above. At its base, a line of men and women funnelled into the entrance carrying stone blocks. Spikey grey crabmen stood either side of the slaves, twitching in the strange manner of their kind, chattering and poking people with their sword arms.

There were human slavers too, interspersed among the crabmen. Most were dressed in furs and many were scribbling notes on parchment.

"Should we fall in with the slaves?" Hami asked. "Follow them into the tower?"

"We'd have to lose our lightning staffs if we wanted to blend in," Behnam said. "It would be risky."

"I can't see how else we'll get in."

"We don't necessarily need to. Let's take a closer look. See what we can find out from outside. We'll have to leave soon, as it is. Before we contract smog sickness."

They left the opera house and made their way towards the tower. It was an easy landmark to locate, given its height, but one that wouldn't be easy to get close to. The area around the piazza had been cleared of buildings. Those closest to the tower had been reduced to their floorplans with only a few low sections of wall remaining among the heaps of rubble.

"Do you think anyone at the top can see us?" Hami asked as he looked up at the tower.

"I doubt it," Behnam said. "It's dark down here in the shadows. And even if someone does spot us, we'll be long gone by the time they can get a message to ground level."

They crawled through the foundations of one of the derelict houses that skirted the piazza. The building had been mostly destroyed, aside from the exterior wall, which at its highest point was around waist-high. Hami and Behnam arranged themselves either side of the gap that had once been the front door and sat down with their backs against the wall to catch their breath. The house they occupied was in a row parallel to the line of slaves entering the tower. They would have to crawl through adjacent houses to get closer to the entrance.

Behnam was about to get up when the atmosphere changed. An increase in air pressure accompanied by an almost metallic tang he could feel in his teeth. A wave of panic washed over him. He turned to Hami. The young magus's eyes were wide, his chest pumping. He'd make himself sick if he didn't calm his breathing and stop inhaling smog. This was bad. And could only mean one thing. Ramaask.

Some of the slaves were experiencing the atmospheric change, too. A few had stopped walking and were clutching their heads. Others were shaking or crying.

Behnam nodded to Hami and they both dropped off the magi network. They wouldn't be able to communicate for a while. Inconvenient, but nothing compared to the risk of Ramaask sensing them.

Moving slowly, Behnam turned to peer through the doorway.

Ramaask emerged from the darkness across the square. The Nightmare, some called him. Others knew him simply as the Lurker at the Gate. Impressive titles for an impressive creature. A giant dressed in thick, black plate and trailing a cloak that floated impossibly on a non-existent breeze. His face was obscured by a visor and on his helmet, three serrated ridges ran from front to back. One at the top like a fin and one on each side.

The air around him distorted and rippled as he strode across the piazza.

Following him was an equally tall figure, but this one was thin. It was cloaked all in black, its hooded head hanging limp at its chest. It kept pace with Ramaask, gliding across the square without any outward appearance of motion, as if it were floating.

The temperature was going up as the two monsters approached. The slaves parted and backed away. All of them, bar an older man that collapsed to the ground. He tried to raise himself but didn't make it up. He spasmed as the thin figure drew close, then went limp as steam began to rise from his body.

Hami pointed to his ear. Behnam concentrated his mind, amplifying sound around them.

The two monsters were talking. Behnam hadn't realised, due to Ramaask's face being obscured by his visor, and the thin figure's by his hood. Hami had known, though. In many ways, Hami's powers were exceeding his own. How fast the apprentice was becoming the master.

"Instinct," Ramaask's deep but strained voice rasped. "I can feel a change in the air. She's coming. And I want to know: why now?"

"Does it matter?" the thin figure asked in a metallic monotone. "You already know what she'll do."

"I want to know everything else. We have the opportunity to interrogate her, and if need be ..."

They fell silent as a man emerged from the shadows of the column. A trail of smoke and glowing embers followed him across the piazza, billowing out from under his black cloak as if his body were smouldering beneath his clothes. The skin on his head was charred black, cracked with glowing orange fissures, and his eyes burned yellow.

"I must return to the mountains," the burned man said when he reached them. He stood to attention before Ramaask, dwarfed by the giant creature. "I'm needed there."

"No," Ramaask replied. "You did well setting up the installation, but the General can manage the final preparations by himself."

Hami looked to Behnam and mouthed, "The General?"

"I no longer trust him," the burned man said.

"He's been loyal to me for over a century," Ramaask replied.

"He means to use the portal for himself."

What portal were they talking about? And how was it that the magi were just learning of it now?

"You should destroy it," the thin figure said. "You know what will happen if it remains."

"Enough," Ramaask said. "We can still change the outcome. And you," he said to the burned man. "You are to remain here and oversee my tower."

"But master, you don't understand ..."

Ramaask moved closer so that he was looking down on the man. "It is you who do not understand. I don't ask twice. I thought you'd have learned that by now."

"You are right, as always, my lord." The man bowed low. He shuffled backwards before turning and walking swiftly away across the piazza.

Ramaask watched him go. "We need to find the girl."

Who was this girl they were referring to? Behnam had learned more on this mission than he'd ever hoped to, yet he could tell there was more. He had a responsibility now to stay and find out what that was.

"I've sensed roughly where she'll appear," the thin figure said. "I will retrieve her while you head to the snow base."

"I'm not leaving the city until the portal is ready. You know I won't leave Aratta exposed unless necessary."

"The portal is your gateway to the Mother World. You no longer need to guard the gate in the palace."

Portal to the Mother World? The shock in Hami's eyes mirrored Behnam's reaction. Ramaask couldn't have built a portal to the Mother World. It wasn't possible.

"You would like that, wouldn't you, brother?" Ramaask said. "But I'm not leaving Aratta until I have the girl in my possession."

"You're making a mistake. Your best hope of survival is to head to the snow base now."

"Do you think me so fragile?" Ramaask spoke quietly but with a threatening undertone. "I have armies of crabmen at my disposal, men excavating in the Cataclysm. I have the portal and my tower of silence nearing completion. I can't be stopped. I will escape this realm."

"I meant no offence," the thin figure said. "Some things are said to be fate and cannot be averted. The visitor arriving to bring your downfall. Our master to follow."

"Our master?" Ramaask said. "Your loyalty is to me now. I brought you here, rescued you from the darkness."

"Rescued me to exist in this half form. Neither extinct nor truly existing."

"Would you rather go back?"

"No!" the thin figure backed away. "I am grateful, truly, brother."

Ramaask walked towards him, closing the gap. "Your existence in this half form, on multiple planes, is to our advantage. You see things that others can't. If I give you your body now, you'll lose the abilities that make you useful to me. Abilities that will allow you to find the girl before the magi do. Assuming you wish to help me."

"As always." The thin figure bowed. "And perhaps with this gesture, I will prove my loyalty and you will restore me to my rightful form."

"I will stop the girl myself if I have to."

"That won't be necessary. I will bring her to you."

"Only when that is done will I go to the mountains to oversee the final preparations for the portal."

"As you wish," said the thin figure. "I believe the girl will be arriving soon. There is already a density of energy building in the Fungi Forest. I will seek her there."

"Go then. Seek her out, and bring her to me."

The thin figure bowed again and floated away.

Behnam nodded to Hami and pointed after the thin figure.

Hami's expression turned stricken. He mouthed 'you' and pointed back at Behnam.

Behnam fixed him with a stare until the young magus got up and crept away. Hami would be devastated about leaving Behnam alone in such close proximity to Ramaask, but it made sense to send the boy after the thin figure. He was younger, fitter and would stand a better chance of keeping up. And as an added benefit, it would get him out of the smog. Behnam would remain a while longer to see if there was anything else worth learning, then he'd catch up with Hami in the forest.

Ramaask walked to the tower and entered the doorway. Behnam gave him a moment longer, then crept through the foundations, working his way through the demolished houses and towards the foot of the tower.

After a painstakingly slow crawl through the rubble, Behnam reached the remains of the house opposite the tower entrance. There were no walls, but a pile of sandbags were stacked in the area that the front room had once occupied. It would give him some concealment, but it wasn't ideal. The building one row back was better. It was still intact and the balcony on the second floor would give him a vantage point to look down on the tower entrance. He crept into the shadows behind the sandbags, paused, and was about to move on when the atmosphere changed.

Ramaask had exited the tower behind him. Behnam shrank further down behind the sandbags. He should've kept his distance, but he hadn't, and now he'd trapped himself.

What now? Hami wouldn't have travelled far yet. Both of them together might have a chance at holding the demon back long enough to escape. Alone, Behnam was a dead man. But if he connected to the network, Ramaask would sense the transmission and might even kill him before Hami returned. There was no other option but to keep telepathic silence.

Behnam's heart pounded with an intensity he was sure Ramaask could hear. He was sweating, breathing hard and inhaling poisonous smog. It was making him light-headed, yet there was nothing he could do but wait and hope Ramaask moved on. His body trembled and an all-consuming desire to run took over.

"Lord VorMask," a shaky voice said. "We've been making excellent progress. We've gained two more storeys since—"

"Wait," Ramaask said.

"I'm sorry, my lord," said the man. "I—"

"Silence!" Then Ramaask quietened. "I smell something."

Behnam closed his eyes and held his breath. He heard Ramaask inhale deeply. Then nothing. Time seemed to stretch out for an eternity as Behnam waited behind the sandbags, heart palpitating and lungs bursting.

Finally, Ramaask spoke. "I smell … magus."

–TWO–

THE HUNTER AND THE HUNTED

The thin figure floated wraith-like along the darkened street ahead, as if no physical presence existed beneath its cloak. Yet something was there, some skeletal form beneath the fabric. Hami had never seen its like before. The creature had most likely been brought to Perseopia by Ramaask from the same dark place he came from. Brother, Ramaask had called it, yet the creature was nothing like him physically. Perhaps a brother in the same way the magi were to each other.

Hami ran through the shadows along the side of the street. He'd have more chance keeping up with the thin figure if he could get to his greenbuck, Fozmot, but the animal was tied up in a barn near where he'd entered the city. The detour would mean losing this wraith and if that happened he'd never find it again. He'd have to remain on foot and hope he didn't tire.

The smog was already in his chest, weakening him, making his limbs heavy. He'd spent too long in Aratta already and now he was accelerating the effects of the poison by raising his heart rate. But it couldn't be helped. He had to find out where this creature was going and who it was after. Ramaask had said it was a girl. Would she be like the last one that arrived in Perseopia? Like the one Grand Master Onora Bruche discovered before he was killed? If Hami escaped the city without suffering smog poisoning, perhaps he'd find out.

He wondered how Behnam was getting on. This was the first time he'd left his partner in danger since Jamileh's death and he didn't like it.

Hami always made sure he carried out the riskier tasks, but on this occasion he'd conceded to his master. Behnam had overruled him and he'd been right to, Hami was the faster of the two. He'd be more capable of keeping up with this wraith. And it was just one time. Behnam would be okay and when they met up again they'd talk like he'd wanted to. Hami would apologise. He'd open up about Jamileh's death and beg for forgiveness. Not only for being responsible, but for all the times he hadn't had the courage to speak up about it.

Behnam held a special place in Hami's heart. He'd been the one that came for Hami when he'd first registered on the magi network. The one who'd rescued him from his life of loneliness.

Hami had spent most of his early years living in a squat on the outskirts of Aratta. At eight, he became the provider for the small community he grew up in. He hunted, rats mostly, while his mother and friends ventured into the city to inhale smog and get high. He was a natural hunter and would always return with enough food for everyone. In hindsight, he'd been exhibiting magi abilities well before he'd registered on the network.

It had been a deprived existence, but doing a job that none of the others could gave him a certain satisfaction. It made him feel important to be relied upon. To be needed by people.

One night his mother and friends didn't come back. And then it was just him. He didn't go into the city to look for her. She'd never shown any affection towards him and he'd seen first-hand how the smog had changed her. He was more upset that he had no one to hunt for than caring what had happened to any of them. His mother had implied that one of the men in the group had been his father, but if she knew which one, it was never made clear.

He moved on alone, walking north and finding a deserted village to live in.

He was hunting big game when Behnam found him and took him away to the magi garrison. There he was fed, clothed and taught to use his powers. It had been difficult adjusting to his new life. A rebellious streak and anti-social behaviour got him into trouble often, and the brotherhood told Behnam to halt his training. But Behnam had seen his potential. He took him on as a student when no one else would. He taught him to read, to write, and spent countless evenings tutoring him in the magi arts. And he'd done it all without asking for anything in return. Behnam was only fifteen years older but he was what Hami imagined a real father would be like.

Then Hami had seduced Behnam's sister and led the crabmen to her home.

He drew a sleeve over his eyes to wipe away the tears that blurred his vision but he only succeeded in making them sore by rubbing in smog from his saturated clothes.

This area of the city was like the one he'd grown up in all those years ago. Pre-Behnam. Pre-everything that had been good in his life. Now he was back and similarly his life had little purpose. Only tracking and hunting.

Hami followed the wraith up a long arcade. Giant forest mushrooms had grown up in the middle of a square at the end. A small orchard of them illuminating an island of dirt, hemmed in by cobbled streets. It seemed strange to see them here in the old capital, but the warm yellow glow provided welcome respite from the churning smog that stained everything else purple.

The wraith passed through the mushrooms, swirling the glowing spores that hung in the air, and disappeared.

Hami ran towards the square, paused, then skirted left around the outside, keeping out of the light as he worked his way to the far side.

The creature had gone.

Hami slipped further into the shadows of a nearby house and waited. Some of the smaller mushrooms were burnt with shrivelled edges, and their light had been extinguished, yet there was no sign of the creature in amongst them.

17

He looked away from the mushrooms until his eyes adjusted to the gloom. He was sickening, his breath becoming ragged.

The creature hadn't carried on up the street, which meant it hadn't gone all the way through the mushrooms. The area was still warm so surely it must be close.

Had it known it was being followed? Perhaps it had run into the mushrooms, then taken a left or right down an adjoining street. Perhaps it was still here waiting to see who had followed.

Hami had been careful. He'd kept to the shadows. No one could have seen him. Could they? The longer he waited, the more distance the creature might be putting between them.

Hami couldn't risk being seen, though. Even if it meant losing the wraith. If he was spotted, Ramaask would be notified and Behnam would be compromised. There might've been a time when he'd have taken that risk. But not now. Not with Behnam.

He peered through the darkness at the houses surrounding the square. No doors in the doorways, no frames or shutters in the windows. Nothing wooden remaining. All either stolen by scavengers or decimated by ambrosia beetles.

Then he saw it. A silhouette at one of the windows. If he'd taken the right-hand path around the square, he'd have walked right past the creature and it would have seen him. It'd suspected it had been followed so had waited. Suspected or known? Why would it think anyone had followed? It hadn't long left the city centre.

Then Hami realised why.

His forehead ran slick with sweat. Bile rose in his stomach. An alarm had been sent. And he could think of only one thing that would trigger an alarm. Behnam had been spotted.

Hami clutched his stomach and vomited. It came out black and acrid, burning his throat as it launched out of his mouth. He bent double, holding his middle. He would have to get out of Aratta soon before the hallucinations began.

He looked back to the window. The wraith had gone. Hami ran to the house, up the steps and in through the doorway. He had to catch it now and find out what had happened to Behnam.

The house was empty.

He ran through to the back, leaping through a window and landing in the alley behind. Nothing up or down the path.

He picked the direction that led out of the city, the direction that closest matched the one they'd been heading in, and ran.

He didn't know how long he could keep running at a sprint, but as far as he knew the creature hadn't seen him yet, so if he kept his pace going he might catch it when it stopped. In the meantime, he'd have to pray that Behnam would be okay and that he'd re-join the network soon.

———

Behnam pressed his back up against the sandbags.

"Come out, magus," Ramaask called.

He sounded more amused than angry. Did he know where Behnam hid? Behnam didn't want to risk standing up to find out.

Over to his left was a pile of rubble high enough for someone to be crouching behind. He concentrated on a stone at the back, tipping it over so it rolled down over the other stones and made the required distraction. He peered over the top of the sacks to see if everyone's attention had been drawn.

The plan had partially worked. Nearly everyone had been distracted. But not Ramaask. He stood by the tower entrance facing the pile where Behnam hid.

Dread seeped into every extremity. There was no point continuing to hide. It was all over. He'd never see Hami again. Never have the chance to apologise and give him peace.

His body rebelled against him. Limbs numb. Palms sweating. Head dizzy.

He got to his feet and turned to face Ramaask.

The air around the demon was dark. His arms were crossed over his armoured chest and even though he hadn't raised his visor, he was clearly watching Behnam.

The men around him drew their weapons and the crabmen chattered as they spread out to the sides.

Ramaask raised a hand and they stopped.

"Leave him to me," he said. "Everyone, back to work."

The men backed away, but kept their weapons raised. The crabmen scattered spiderlike, back to the shadows.

An uncomfortable silence settled between them before Ramaask spoke. "And which magus do I have the pleasure of meeting today?" he asked.

"Behnam Baktash," Behnam said, his voice cracking.

"Master Behnam Baktash?" Ramaask took several steps towards him. "Didn't I expressly forbid anyone from returning to this city? I know that was 146 years ago, but the magi are reputed to possess a reasonably long collective memory. I would've assumed you'd remembered."

"It must have slipped our minds," Behnam said. "I'll be on my way."

Ramaask laughed a terrible, choking, death rattle of a laugh. "Now that you're here, you're welcome to stay."

Ramaask wasn't going to keep talking forever. Behnam needed to do something quick. He recalled the intact building behind him with the balcony on the second floor. It had an open arch leading inside. That was his way out.

Behnam whipped his staff round and fired at the sandbags in front of him. The explosion sent the bags in all directions and launched him up and backwards into a backward somersault.

Behnam landed on the second-floor balcony.

Ramaask ripped through the bags that came at him. He paused, tipped his head back and laughed. "Let the chase begin!"

That was Behnam's cue to leave.

He flew into the house, through the empty rooms and onto a balcony at the front of the property. There was a square below and a dense neighbourhood of houses on the other side. If he could make it across to them, he might have a chance of escape.

He dodged to the side, leaping onto the balcony of an adjacent house as Ramaask came crashing through the wall behind him, destroying the building in his wake and dropping into the square below. He turned towards Behnam as the whole structure folded in on itself, expelling clouds of dust and debris.

Ramaask launched himself at Behnam again.

Behnam dropped to the floor of the balcony and rolled to the side as Ramaask ploughed through the wall above his head.

The building collapsed around Behnam. He managed a last-ditch effort to guide himself clear of the falling masonry, yet still landed badly.

Back on his feet, he ran, half-sprinting, half-limping across the square towards the road opposite. If he could get to his greenbuck, he might be able to outrun Ramaask to the Fungi Forest and lose him.

A huge chunk of masonry sailed past, narrowly missing him and kicking up stone chips as it bounced across the cobbled square.

Behnam reached the road and ducked down the first alley to the right as a second block demolished the corner of the building he'd passed. He heard Ramaask land in the square behind him with a thump.

Behnam turned down a second passage as thunderous feet echoed in the alley he'd just left.

He fired a lightning bolt from his staff at a town house as he passed, allowing the wall to collapse into the passage behind him. He ducked into a property on the right, through the open doorway and into an ancient living area. He went up a staircase, then leapt through an open window on the second floor into the window of the house opposite.

21

He kept going, running downstairs, out of the back door, sprinting along another street and down another alley. Finally, he jumped a wall and entered a house through the back door.

Behnam stopped and ducked to the side, flattening his back up against the wall between the doorway and window.

Silence. The only sound the beating of his heart. Adrenaline was making the desire to keep running unbearable, but he couldn't let this panic force him into making a wrong move. Any error could be fatal.

Behnam took in his surroundings while he caught his breath. The room had been a simple kitchen with ceramic wash basin and tiled floor. Wooden cupboards, surfaces and tables that may have once furnished the place had long since decayed. It was dark but for the dim purple light of the smog outside. The hallway lay ahead, a black void leading into the heart of the house.

Behnam edged to the window. The walled back garden was bare, the plot hemmed in by houses on either side.

No movement.

He needed to get his bearings, figure out where the greenbucks were. But perhaps he should lie low until Ramaask moved on. Find a cellar and bed down.

Behnam peered outside one last time, then crept towards the hall.

The kitchen darkened behind him.

Behnam spun around, lighting up his staff as two shovel-sized hands clamped his head on either side and lifted him from the floor. Ramaask had his visor up and he brought their heads together. His black, skeletal face shimmered purple in the staff light and his sharp black teeth parted. It was the last thing Behnam saw as Ramaask's thumbs closed over his eyes.

He fired his staff into Ramaask's chest, unleashing everything he had. But the hands held firm and the thumbs pressed in, forcing their way into his skull.

Behnam screamed as his eyes burst and his world went black.

–THREE–

The Bully Bully

Street lights intermittently flushed the interior of the car orange through the sun roof as they navigated the streets of Sheffield.

Sammy stared out of the passenger window trying to seem interested in the grey, plastic-clad housing blocks that huddled together by the side of the ring road. If she didn't make eye contact with her mum, perhaps the woman would leave her alone. A child's game. Look away and no one can see you. But she'd been treated like a child, and now she felt like acting like one.

"Do you have anything to say for yourself?" It was the first time her mum had spoken since leaving the head's office.

"Not really."

"You're turning into a bully like your father?" She'd only said it to get a reaction, but Sammy couldn't let the comment go unchallenged.

"I'm nothing like him." She made eye contact. "Don't ever compare me to him."

"You've been suspended for beating up kids in the year below you. I'd say that sounds a lot like him."

"Five big college lads in the year below me," she said, staring back out of the window. "Five seventeen-year-old boys versus me. By myself. I'd hardly call them kids. And they were attempting to bully me. Not the other way around." She tried to sound like the conversation was boring her. "Although, if you saw what they looked like after I'd finished with them, I suppose you could call that bullying."

"That's not funny." Her mother let out a long, shuddering exhalation.

Sammy wondered how long she'd been crying for and whether some of it was for effect.

"One of those boys is in hospital with a broken arm because of you," her mother said. "If he presses charges you'll wind up with a criminal record. You know you're old enough to get one, right?"

"He tripped off the curb when I came at him. He landed badly. I didn't even touch him."

Her mum's mascara had run and she looked like a sad, pouty panda. Sammy went back to staring out of the window. Her stomach was tying itself in knots. She hadn't meant to make her mum cry, but she resented being made to feel like it was always her fault. It had been five against one. How could she be to blame? It was because she'd taken Reece's spot on the football team. Because she was a girl. It was as simple as that. The only South Yorkshire team in the league with a female striker. They should be proud, they were pioneers. But was her college celebrating equality? Were they, heck. She was their best player. She'd even saved them from relegation last season. Why couldn't the less talented players cheer her on from the subs bench and be happy to be a small part of her victories?

"I don't understand what happened to you, Sammy." Her mum just wouldn't let it go. "This is the third time I've been in the head's office this term. Do you want to get expelled from Manor Rise too? You used to be such a sweet girl …"

"… before I came back from Perseopia."

"I thought we'd stopped talking about that place."

"You hoped we'd stopped talking about it."

"Why do you think these boys pick on you, when you're completely disconnected from reality?"

So this is what it was really about. "How am I disconnected from reality, mother? Is it because of the fantasy world I travelled to? Because you know you're the only person I told about that, the one person I hoped would believe me. I haven't told anyone else." Sammy sighed. "Trust me, I know how crazy it sounds."

"You're distracted all the time. Vacant. You never engage with anyone."

"The fight started because I humiliated Reece and Connor at football. Nothing to do with me being vacant. Anyway, I'm part of a team. Isn't that engaging with people?"

The remainder of the journey home was a silent one. They parked on the road outside their stunted terrace house, then her mum left her on the pavement as she walked away up the alley between their house and the neighbour's.

Sammy stayed where she was, psyching herself up for the argument that would continue inside.

One of the street lights flickered overhead. She gazed up past it at the dark sky and the three stars visible through the city's light pollution. She liked the night. Liked the lack of people and noise. The air seemed fresher somehow, full of excitement and opportunity.

She could walk away. Give her mum some breathing space. Come back later when she'd calmed down. But that wasn't going to happen this time. Better to go in and get the rest of the argument over with.

"Mum—" she said as she closed the kitchen door behind her.

"The time for talking is over. I'll leave your dinner outside your bedroom door."

This was new. She didn't even sound angry. Was she resigned to the fact her only child was a delinquent? A lost cause, maybe? Sammy wasn't about to let that lie. "The time for talking never started. Every time I try, you shut me out."

"How can I listen when you tell me stories of secret worlds filled with crabmen?"

Sammy was done. She walked away, climbed the stairs to her bedroom and closed the door. She dropped her rucksack by the bed, planted her face as deep into her pillow as she could, and screamed. When she ran low on oxygen, she lifted her head, took a breath, then shoved her face back into the pillow and screamed again.

She got up and, clutching the pillow to her chest, walked to the dresser to look at herself in the mirror. A raging she-beast with messy hair and a red face glared back from the other side of the frame. She looked a state. Her mum had turned her into this crazed person that stood before her.

Always the same argument. Her mother was the lost cause. Not her. She'd at least tried to talk it out.

"I'm not staying here," she said to herself. She punched the pillow back at the bed and got her mobile out. She scrolled through her contacts, tapped on a number and put the phone to her ear.

"Hiya," came the tinny reply.

"I need a goalie. Meet me outside my house in twenty minutes."

"I need to revise for my General Studies A-Level."

"Do you really need to revise for that?"

"My mum said—"

"You're eighteen, Wayne, technically an adult. Why don't you grow a pair? And when you've done that, be over here in twenty minutes." And she hung up.

Sammy sat down at her dresser. She occasionally wondered if Perseopia had ever happened, whether it was a figment of her imagination that she'd created to escape her mundane reality. Yet, bizarrely, her time in Perseopia was the only part of her life that had ever felt real. It was her current existence that seemed like someone else's. An infinite grey corridor of closed doors. A linear first person shooter. No alternative paths, no side quests and no opportunities. College, home, argument, bed, college, football, fight, headmaster's office, home, argument, bed.

Sammy concentrated on a pencil resting on her desk. Imagined all the molecules connected throughout the wooden structure, willing it to move. It wobbled, tilted, and the hexagonal prism tipped over onto its next flat side, then the next, and the one after. Soon the pencil was rolling along the table.

Sammy stopped it with the palm of her hand.

If she'd never been to Perseopia, then how was that possible? Unless it was all in her mind like her mother had tried to convince her, and which, during her darkest moments, she had almost believed. She'd tried to show her mum the pencil trick a couple of times, but the woman never paid attention. Whenever the 'fantasy land' was brought up, her mum stiffened and switched off.

Sammy had found it difficult to readjust to life back in Sheffield despite spending less than a week in Perseopia. There she'd been important. Enough to be pursued by both the magi and the Order. Then she'd been dumped back into the real world where she had no purpose and no one wanted her. No one except her mother, and that was only until Jerry came along. They'd lost their closeness soon after.

She should've stayed in Perseopia. Ramaask had gone into the Cataclysm, the magi would've defeated the crabmen soon after, the slaves would've been freed and eventually order would've been restored to the realm. Sammy might even have become a magus by now if she'd remained.

She stared into the mirror. The psycho stared back. She should at least make an effort for Wayne, seeing as he was coming over for her to kick footballs at. Not that he was her boyfriend, but that didn't stop him trying to fill the vacancy. She should at least throw him a bone every once in a while and make herself look presentable. Surely he wouldn't put up with being her on-call goalie forever. Although it had worked for a surprisingly long time.

Sammy got up from the desk, swapped her jeans for leggings, put on a black t-shirt and red scarf combo that she figured looked as close to cool as she'd ever manage, and scraped her blond mop back into a ponytail. She needed something else. Make-up was too good for Wayne. Even accessories were a stretch, but what the hell? She'd do it this one time. Her mum would have something she could pilfer.

On the carpet outside her bedroom door sat a cheese-spread sandwich on a paper plate.

A poor approximation of a Mariah Carey arpeggio warbled up the stairs from the sitting room, letting Sammy know that her mother had settled in to watch a TV talent show. Sammy stepped over the sandwich, crept along the landing to her mum's bedroom and went straight to the dresser. New items would be stashed there.

Her mother spent more than she could afford each month on clothes and, because she always dressed younger than she should, there was usually something worth borrowing. Sammy rummaged through the drawers to see if there was anything new or interesting. Surprisingly, there wasn't.

Sammy moved on to the jewellery boxes stacked on top of the dresser. Her mother rarely wore jewellery yet she'd still managed to accrue three boxes worth. Some were bound to be presents from Jerry, worn once then discarded and left to tarnish in their mother of pearl inlaid coffins.

Sammy never wore jewellery. She didn't really see the point. It wasn't as if it had a purpose other than to draw attention to you. Perhaps tonight she'd find something that would persuade her otherwise.

As a kid she'd spent hours rummaging around in these boxes, dressing up in all the sparkly necklaces and rings, then at some point in her formative years she'd lost interest. From that point onwards it had been comics, books and video games.

She lifted down the boxes, arranged them in a crescent on the floor, sat in the middle, then emptied each one in turn into separate piles.

There was a selection of rings, some plain, some jewelled. There were necklaces in silver, gold, and plastic. And then there were the hoop earrings. Millions of them, and all virtually identical. Sammy smiled when she recognised a plastic tiara with the silver paint flaking off. It had been her favourite thing in the world when she'd been five. She thought her dad had binned it years ago when she'd failed to eat the macaroni and cheese he'd microwaved for her. Her mum must've rescued it from the rubbish.

Guilt pierced Sammy's heart like an adamantium claw through the ribcage. She couldn't carry on being angry with her mum. She'd go downstairs and apologise. Her mum was in the wrong, but she'd hold her tongue and fix the relationship. Standard. She began packing the jewellery away, but as she dropped a bundle of knotted necklaces into one of the boxes, a delicate gold chain caught her eye. The only golden item in the box that hadn't tarnished.

Sammy took hold and pulled at it. The chain snagged, but a second tug released a golden locket into her lap.

Sammy tilted the locket in the light. There was a burning sun engraved on the front, and on the back an inscription in the unusual looping script of Avestan; a language that she'd never been taught, but one that she'd magically known how to translate and read since her visit to Perseopia.

"A wish can be as good as a map."

Sammy shakily picked up her mobile and redialled the last called number.

"Hiya," came the tinny reply again. "I'm nearly at your house …"

"Turn around, Wayne," Sammy said. "I'm not coming out tonight."

And she hung up.

29

–FOUR–
EVIDENCE

Her mother was by the fridge, wringing the last dregs of rosé out of a three litre box into a mug.

"I don't want to fight any more," she said over her shoulder when Sammy entered the kitchen. "You don't need to be in college for the next few days. Let's talk tomorrow when we've calmed down." When Sammy didn't reply, she put down the wine and turned to face her.

Sammy remained in the doorway and held out her arm with the locket dangling from her fist.

"Where did you get that?"

"The last two years I've doubted myself. Sometimes wondering if I'd imagined the whole thing. And this entire time you've kept this from me?"

Her mother's face was hard. "The locket was around your neck that day I found you under my bed. I rescued it when I dragged you back to your bedroom."

Sammy tried her best to keep her voice calm and measured, but she couldn't keep it from cracking. "Why didn't you give it back to me when I woke up the next morning?"

"Because you'd stolen it." The hard lines of her mother's face were dissolving. Her lip trembled and tears were running down her cheeks. "Like you stole that bracelet."

"Stolen?" The accusation lodged in Sammy's throat.

"When you told me that story about a land full of giant mushrooms and dinosaurs, I knew something was wrong. I tried to take the jewellery to school to see if any of the teachers or parents claimed them." She closed her eyes. "I didn't take them to the police station because I didn't want you to get into trouble."

Sammy had heard enough. She turned away and went upstairs. When she reached her bedroom she closed the door behind her and approached the bed, readying herself for the scream that didn't come.

An eerie calm settled over her. She put the locket over her head, picked up her football and ran back downstairs.

Her mother was in the same place she'd left her.

"Where are you going?"

Sammy didn't answer, she carried on through the kitchen and slammed the front door as she left.

———

The common at the bottom of the road was dark, lit faintly by the lights in the council blocks that loomed at the far end. Dark was fine. Being alone at night didn't scare Sammy like it might other young women.

She kicked the football wide of the goal. As it lifted off the ground, she concentrated on it, imagining the molecules making up the leather and stitching. She willed it back towards the goal, spinning it, pulling it round in an arc. The ball pinged off the post and into the back of the net.

Ever since she'd returned from Perseopia, she'd been able to do that. Plenty of guys in the team could curl a ball. None of them could curl it like she could. Not even close. The least bitter guys called her banana feet. The ones who'd lost places to her on the team? She'd once overheard them call her 'soccer slut', as if being good at football somehow made her promiscuous. She imagined they said worse behind her back.

Perseopia had changed her. She was able to shift small objects if she concentrated hard enough. She couldn't do much with heavy or stationary objects. The forces of gravity and friction were generally too strong for her new powers, but airborne objects she had some sway over.

She knew things, too. Could feel without seeing. Not a lot, just the merest suggestion of someone's feelings. But it was enough. She could tell when someone was approaching. Had a vague sense of their intentions before they opened their mouths. Which meant she was never afraid of going out alone after dark. And why she never lost a fight. Punches were telegraphed well before the attacker clenched their fist, and when they swung, it was as if they were moving through treacle.

How powerful would she be by now if she'd stayed in Perseopia to be trained by Hami? He'd used her as bait to draw out the evil Ramaask. Which was not cool. But ultimately the plan had worked, she'd survived, and the realm had been saved. She didn't like it, but could see why it had been a price worth paying.

But her powers weren't focused. She needed tuition, to talk with someone who knew what was happening to her. If she'd remained in Perseopia with Hami guiding her, she could've been on her way to becoming a master magus. Instead she'd returned home to Sheffield. She'd come back to be with her mum, only to have her possessions taken away, and to be labelled a thief.

And then there was Jerry. When he came into their lives, the relationship Sammy had enjoyed with her mother had drifted even further apart. In some ways that was a blessing. Sammy was left to her own devices and that meant she could do what she wanted. But what was there to do? There was nowhere to go and she had no prospects for the future.

She was smart, and when her teachers weren't shouting at her she produced some decent work, but her grades had taken a hit by getting expelled from and changing school several times. She might not even get into University on her current trajectory. Not that she could afford to go even if that avenue presented itself to her. Jerry had offered to loan her the fees, but she wasn't taking that chump's money. She should find herself a part time job, but then she'd be stuck with her mum and Jerry until she could afford to leave. Which was never.

The future was looking bleak.

Her mum wasn't around when she got home. She'd be at Jerry's. An angry note on the kitchen table confirmed as much. Sammy balled it in her fist and threw it over her shoulder, guiding it into the bin with her mind.

The microwave clock displayed 23:45.

Sammy went to the cellar door and opened it. She shivered as she descended into the dark. Despite being summer, it was always cold and damp down there.

At the bottom of the stairs, she flicked on the light and used its dim glow to pick her way through soggy cardboard boxes to a pile of her dad's old possessions in the far corner. A chipboard TV stand, a cricket bat, an old suitcase that contained the family photos he'd been in, and behind them, a mouldy golf bag with a single club inserted the wrong way, handle up. Sammy took the grip and pulled it out.

The Midnight Emerald bracelet dangled from the head.

Sammy had stashed it in the golf bag to be protected by the repellent force of her father's possessions and the eight-legged guardians that dwelled in the webs adorning the ceiling.

She'd once found it in her mother's handbag and had decided to take it back. In hindsight, she realised it had probably been in there from one of the times her mum had tried taking it to school. If she'd rummaged deeper she might've found the locket too. Why hadn't her mum come to her first? To talk to her before assuming the worst? Sammy often had lapses in judgement, but she wasn't a thief. How had their relationship come to that?

Sammy held the golden bracelet up to the single bare light bulb.

The bottle-top sized emerald—if in fact it ever had been an emerald—was dull and brown, and had been since she'd returned from Perseopia. Looping around the gem's fixing was a stanza written in the Avestan script. The same script used on the locket dangling at her throat. Esther had translated the words for her pre-Perseopia. Now she was able to read it herself.

"Raise your hands to the skies
"on the tone of midnight,
"and you will travel to the land
"of endless twilight."

The *hands*, which she'd figured out referred to the clock hands either side of the gemstone fitting, were stiff and unresponsive.

Sammy polished the gemstone on her t-shirt and peered into it.

The emerald lit up for a split second, pulsing with green light, then returned to the dull brown that had become its natural state. Sammy never flinched. The emerald had done the same thing on numerous other occasions in the last several months. She didn't know when it had started happening. Only that it had.

She'd been down in the cellar many times since, to look at the bracelet and to remember Perseopia, Mehrak, and Louis. And more recently, Hami ... wondering if he'd saved the day. Or if he'd been arrested for treason. She would often daydream about the realm returning to life, the skies clearing, people celebrating. There was no doubt in her mind that she should've stayed.

Esther, 'The Chosen One', had never returned for the bracelet. Sammy had gone to the market every Saturday for weeks afterwards, wandered the streets of Sheffield, even waited outside the gates of her old school. Yet the woman never returned. Unlocking the portal to save Perseopia clearly wasn't as important as she'd made it out to be. Unless she'd sensed that Sammy had already used the bracelet and it no longer worked. Maybe she knew, somehow, that the realm had been saved and she could chill out. In the end, the reason didn't matter. Esther had vanished, along with any chance of Sammy ever returning to Perseopia.

It had been difficult to put the adventure behind her. She'd stopped visiting the bracelet down in the cellar and was on her way to assimilating back into an ordinary existence. Until around four months ago. She'd been in the cellar looking for a tennis ball and noticed a flash of green light coming from the golf bag.

The bracelet had been out several times since then.

Sammy had tried raising the dial's hands at midnight but they wouldn't budge. The emerald never pulsed green exactly on the stroke of midnight. Only ever a little while beforehand or sometime after. Never dead on.

Sammy switched off the cellar light and climbed the stairs back up to the kitchen. She sat at the table, placed the bracelet in front of her, and slumped over it, hands on her cheeks and elbows planted either side.

She couldn't manipulate the emerald with her mental abilities. There wasn't anything inside it to manipulate.

Sammy's phone buzzed. She fished it out of her waistband, saw the message was from Wayne, so placed her phone face down on the table.

She stretched and got up. She filled the kettle at the sink, put it back on its base and flicked it on. The time on the microwave flashed to 23:58. Almost midnight. Sammy sat back down at the kitchen table.

How many times had she been down to the cellar to fetch out the bracelet? Too many. And always after an argument with her mother. She wasn't sure why she kept trying to work the mechanism. Frustration with the status quo, she assumed. Only today she wasn't frustrated, today she was calm. Nothing would change unless she took charge of her own destiny. She'd had enough of life with mum and Jerry. And her dad. What a joke that man was. She couldn't believe how long it had taken her to see him for the bullying and abusive human waste he truly was.

Sammy absentmindedly clicked open and shut the locket at her throat. She wasn't sure that going back to Perseopia was the change she needed, but something compelled her to keep trying. Two years ago her reason had been Mehrak. She'd had a pretty big crush on him then, even though he'd been married. Silly. Nothing could've happened between them. She'd still like to see him again though, hang out in Golden Egg Cottage. Really though, it was the powers she'd developed that drew her back to Perseopia and the bracelet. She needed to find out who she was. What she was. Only the magi could answer that for her. And she had nothing left in Sheffield to stick around for.

The kettle began hissing as the water warmed up. Sammy leaned in close to the emerald on the bracelet. She concentrated her mind on the gem, imagining the atoms inside moving. Imagining swaying grass.

Nothing.

She sat back. It wasn't going to happen, but she continued to watch the gem.

Then it flashed.

In that millisecond, Sammy saw a blade of grass inside the gem. And that was all she needed. She latched on to it, her mental feelers grabbing hold, keeping the blade inside the emerald going. The light remained and now it was getting brighter. More blades of grass appeared and she latched on to them too, swaying them faster.

Sammy leaned in further, placing her thumbs under the dial hands. They budged up a little, but not enough. They wouldn't move any more. Why? What time was it? Had she missed midnight? She didn't want to look away and lose sight of the grass.

The blades were moving relatively slowly. They'd moved faster last time she'd been in this situation. She gritted her teeth and pushed harder. She imagined the atoms in the grass thrown side to side. Rushing back and forth, getting faster, the light brightening.

The clock hands shifted up a little more.

The kettle began boiling, bubbling urgently behind her.

Sammy gritted her teeth, concentrating hard, swaying the blades ever faster. The light was dazzling, almost too bright to look into.

She pushed harder still. The clock hands loosened. Her head was hurting, but she wasn't about to stop.

The gem was humming. Burning ever brighter.

Sammy gave the clock hands one final push.

Both dial hands snapped to the top and green light engulfed the kitchen.

––––––

Book 2 in *The Vara Volumes* is out now!
Find out what happens next in:

BACK TO
THE VARA

For all things Perseopian or to receive updates about John Kerry's forthcoming books:

Subscribe at eateom.com
Or like and follow us on:
facebook.com/EatEoM
X @EatEoM
Instagram @VaraVolumes